# THE CATALYST

THE COMMONS, BOOK 3

MICHAEL ALAN PECK

DINUHOS ARTS, LLC

*For Evelyn Peck, who gave me the drive, and Renée, who gives the journey meaning.*

## PROLOGUE: XENOGLOSSY

The Darkness left the safety of the shadows. It crossed to the water to seek out the Tree. It had to find the Tree before the light found the Darkness—of that the Darkness was certain.

The Darkness had knowledge but enjoyed only limited access to it. The memories and details resided inside the Darkness, but the Darkness couldn't reach them. Or wasn't permitted to. The Darkness wasn't privy to what was being kept away from it, by whom, or why. Nor did the Darkness know its purpose—if it had one.

The Darkness focused on the task at hand, which was hazardous enough. All tasks outside the shadowy safe zone meant evading the sun, which wanted to kill the Darkness.

The Darkness dwelt deep in the shade in the place of peace, where the sunlight that called the place of peace home could not get to it. The sunlight didn't want the Darkness to be there. It wanted to burn the Darkness out.

Thus was the game played, and it was a simple game at that. The Darkness hurried to the water, next to where the sunlight lived. The Darkness needed the light in order to see the reflection of the Tree in the water's surface—and not just the Tree but the door in its side that allowed the Darkness to travel. Then the Darkness had to hope that the Tree would grant it admission so that it could bridge the gap to wherever it was required to be.

The Darkness never knew its destination before its arrival. It trusted the Tree to accept it and take it somewhere where it would not face instant annihilation, such as a desert in the middle of a dead-cloudless day. It had no choice but to trust the Tree—that, too, the Darkness understood.

The Darkness knew what it wasn't, not what it was.

It was friend to none.

It had no place among the living.

It was neither welcome nor loved.

The Darkness fed. The Darkness was feared. The Darkness watched.

On rare occasion, the Darkness protected.

The Darkness knew neither of its true names. It could deduce that because it was enemy to light, then it was shadow. It also reasoned it was not one of the living because of the beings whose lives it had witnessed and ended.

Bird. Rat. Insect. Human. All of those the Darkness was not. All had names the Darkness knew without understanding.

The Darkness's familiarity with the tribe of living things was akin to the reading knowledge of a foreign language. It could absorb, but it could not comprehend. Not yet.

The Darkness did not understand why it thought what it thought or why it knew what it knew. Its memories were those of others, not of the Darkness. Some were accessible. Most were not. And perception was a rarity.

There was a word for the uncanny ability to understand a

language one shouldn't be able to understand, but that word eluded the Darkness.

So the Darkness crossed to the water and searched its surface for the Tree.

The sunbeam remained focused on the nearby bench, still unaware of the Darkness's emergence. The sunbeam was at home in the place of peace.

The Darkness had not been invited. Yet the Darkness belonged.

Sometimes the sun attempted to push its way into the shadows to cleanse the place of peace of the Darkness. Then the Darkness was forced to cower deep in the crevice in order to survive.

That was when the Darkness felt what it was to be prey. At all other times, it was the hunter.

The Tree made itself known to the Darkness on the surface of the water.

The sunbeam twitched, as if disturbed by the Darkness's proximity.

The Tree insisted on payment from others but never required anything of the Darkness. The Darkness suspected that perhaps whenever it traveled, something was being taken from it without it knowing. But it had no definite answer to that question, so it was just as if there were no question at all.

The door in the side of the Tree opened.

The sunbeam twitched again, widening now. It would be but an instant before it embraced the Darkness for the first and last time.

The Darkness stretched out over the water, toward the door in the Tree, as the sunlight came for it. It would be close.

At these times, when it wasn't clear whether the Darkness would travel or perish, it focused only on the unknown of its destination. Perhaps it would roam the underground to feed on the pincered creatures and other lower dwellers.

Part of the Darkness saw the killing as tragic necessity. Part craved prey of a higher order. All of it yearned for knowledge.

That was why, in its travels, the Darkness watched the man in the robe and the man who spoke with the waste stabber—the man the Darkness had saved from a fellow shadow beast. The Darkness didn't know why it had protected the man. That was another mystery locked away inside it.

The Darkness reached the Tree, and the sunlight reached the Darkness. There was pain, but then the Darkness was in the Tree and journeying away from the place of peace before the light could do any true harm.

Traveling.

Headed for sustenance.

And learning.

The Darkness needed to know its purpose. The Darkness had a part to play.

It didn't know why it knew that, but it knew. It still couldn't remember the word for how it knew, but that was of little consequence after all.

Things were going to move fast.

And already were.

# PART I
## PALIMPSEST

# 1

## ALL FOR THEM, NONE FOR YOU

Jeremy only started checking out more of Abel's journal a good hour or so after he'd sat down to do so. The more Truitt told him everything was all right, the more he feared he was being set up.

He was supposed to believe that Truitt and Callibeau already knew what was in Abel's journal and were giving him permission to read it all, but after opening the email from Annie Brucker, he no longer bought it.

Annie Brucker's email contained nothing. No greeting, no text, no word of explanation, no anything. But it did have an attachment called "EatMe" that was an unrecognized file type. Stranger still, the icon was that of a cake. How the operating system was able to assign an icon to a file type it didn't recognize was also a mystery.

Jeremy, who knew better than to click on unknown attachments unless picking up a virus or Trojan horse was the goal, opened the file nevertheless. Or tried to. Initially, it, too, appeared to do nothing. Then he turned his speakers on.

It was a sound file of a cat meowing.

Useless.

Why would Annie Brucker bother sending such a thing just to play a cute sound? She wouldn't. But that didn't help solve the mystery.

Jeremy set his laptop down on the couch, got up, and crossed what passed for his apartment's living room to the kitchenette. He opened the refrigerator and filled his only clean glass with cold water from the filter pitcher, leaving just enough to justify not taking the trouble to refill it.

He didn't know why Annie had sent the file. That bothered him. Still, thinking about it to the exception of anything else didn't get him anywhere. So he took a step back and relistened to some of Abel's earliest journal entries.

All were typical Abel.

He alternated between hinting at some of the inner workings of Manitou and the mechanisms it used to manage Essence. None of it committed Abel to anything that might get him in real trouble, which left Jeremy wondering what he'd done to get himself disappeared—unless overall observations and rants about society counted.

Why the United States had long since given up on being a democracy and was already pretty far down the road to being an oligarchy. "It's not just me and my fellow maniacs saying that," he said. "Research shows that the real power is in the hands of the economic elites and not citizens or mass-based interest groups."

How social class correlates with lies people tell, with the rich lying to help themselves and the poor fibbing to help others.

Why it's naive to expect corporations to be nice to their workers.

How businesses create opportunities for themselves while eliminating them for everyone else. "They want full freedom without consequences on their side and zero freedom on yours," he explained. "All for them, none for you. Never forget that."

It wasn't far from the stuff Abel spouted a few pitchers into a Billy Clyde's session.

But again, why would this, the equivalent to the venting of a freshman's first exposure to socialism, cause the heavies at Manitou to come down on Abel?

And why did that cat's meow sound strangely familiar?

Jeremy opened Annie's email to click the "EatMe" file again. Now it was called "DrinkMe," and its icon was a full pitcher of beer with a foamy head atop it. He clicked that, telling himself he deserved whatever mischief doing so unleashed on his machine.

This time, the low, growly noise of the cat was definitely familiar. And this time, it was followed by the sound of liquid pouring with the sound of multiple conversations and laughter in the background. All that, plus a faint sportscaster talking excitedly.

Jeremy clicked again. The sounds repeated.

A pop-up revealed itself with an input field, the outline of which pulsed faintly.

All of the sounds were familiar. Jeremy knew what was being asked for here.

"Billy Clyde's," he typed, hitting enter. Another meow, but the text he entered had no effect.

The field remained, pulsing, as if egging him on. Or mocking him.

Jeremy chose to see it as encouragement. "Billy Clyde," he entered. A meow again. And the pulsing. "Abel" and "Abel Dowd" were no more successful. All he got was meowing.

Duh. How'd he miss that? Sometimes Jeremy wondered why anyone would pay him anything at all, given how slow on the uptake he could be.

"Porthos," he typed and hit the enter key again.

For a moment, nothing happened. Then the input box became a cat emoji—a very familiar cat, which purred and disappeared, along with the file and the email itself.

And nothing else happened.

All that effort to put such a thing together and send it to someone—and then nothing?

Apparently so. Or maybe not.

After once again deciding to distract himself from the task in front of him and see if something might happen when he wasn't watching directly, Jeremy checked Abel's journal again. It was now more than twice the size it had been.

Now fear came into play. What if Truitt, Callibeau, and the powers-that-be at Manitou only approved of him perusing the original journal? Was he now risking who-knew-what kind of punishment with this larger version? Was this a loyalty or honesty test?

One could eat up an hour worrying about such things.

And Jeremy had.

When he finally got up the guts to open the newly expanded file, it seemed as if the journal was reviewing him as much as he was reviewing it. After all, how else would it have known to open not to where he'd left off but to Abel's discussion of the very plan Truitt had just laid out in his office?

It was all there.

The Minuteman missiles with live nuclear warheads stored in a Commons-based facility run by the same hippie soldiers, now called the Dharma Rangers, who'd been the target of Ravager forces before—and who'd helped Paul Reid, Jonas Porter, the mummy, the monk, and the girl called Rain along in Paul Reid's Journey. The missiles were a catalyst for a much larger chain reaction involving stored Essence, though the particulars of how they'd be stolen out from under the hippies and exactly where this Essence was going to come from weren't explained in Truitt's summation. Abel only briefly mentioned them in an in-the-weeds fashion, as if he assumed whoever would access this already knew how it all worked.

Bad assumption, Abel.

Jeremy barely understood any of it, and he feared that letting Truitt or anyone else of importance know might cause his name to be crossed out on a list somewhere, rendering him without value. Then maybe he'd find out a lot more about where Abel had gone.

Jeremy closed the journal file. Now all that was on his screen was the file itself, all by itself in its folder.

And it had once again grown in size.

## 2

## OUR FEAR OUTLIVES US

"You see her, right—out there with the telescope?" Lars Dawkins, the Petrel known as the Artful Dodger, pedaled himself and Po out across the Demeter landscape on one of his regular patrols. They moved at a speed rivaling that of a performance sports car. Audra and most of the other Petrels weren't sure patrolling was even necessary—they believed the water separating Demeter from the rest of New York and The Margins beyond protected them from any potential incursions. But the Dodger wasn't happy when he wasn't moving.

"Yeah," said Joel of the girl they'd spotted in the middle of the vast prairie. "The boss doesn't talk much, but he's not blind. Neither am I."

"That's not why I ask." The Dodger was amused by Joel's curmudgeon routine, which was a relief to Po. Not everyone took well to being addressed in such a manner, and it made communication quite difficult at times. No matter how often he was told to give civility a try, Joel didn't have it in him to be pleasant. It was a victory when the moody little device used proper grammar. "The Essence here and its past lives are tricky. Not everybody sees the same thing. What's she doing?"

"She's looking into it. That's a telescope? It looks like some sort of photo cannon."

"It is—and a good one at that. Most likely that was how she spent her time when she was alive, too. What you're seeing is ambient collected Essence. It's located and reformed itself into a representation of whoever it once was."

"Huh?" Joel was perfectly comfortable admitting to a lack of understanding. Mostly because he thought it was the other person's fault.

"It's her—and not her." The Dodger watched the girl as she made some adjustments and peered back into the eyepiece to study the clear blue sky. "It's probably just enough Essence and just enough consciousness to project who she used to be and what she used to do."

"Hey!"

"Don't yell at her, Joel."

"You said it's not really her."

"That doesn't mean she can't be scared. Our fear outlives us."

"Sorry." Joel's remorse didn't sound sincere.

Po lifted him so that the Tamagotchi could see his disapproval.

Joel ignored it. "What's she doing out here now? There aren't any stars to see in the daytime."

"Who said she's stargazing?"

"What else would she be looking at?"

The Dodger watched the girl make another adjustment and peer through the eyepiece once more.

Her soft, happy laugh made its way across the tall prairie grass through the yellow light and fresh air of the morning.

"Only she knows," he said.

They met in a combination candy store and tea cafe called Sweets Don't Fail Me Now.

Audra arrived first, though it wasn't quite an arrival in the traditional sense. She wasn't really there, physically. The blurring of the realms and the creation of The Margins coupled with her representing The Commons allowed her to travel in mind and spirit. And the candy store was what her mind came up with because it had to reference something. It was just another way for the melding worlds to express themselves via new rules and new ways of doing things. Adjacency allowed it for now, but it might never again, especially if they succeeded in putting the old rules firmly back in place.

That was the irony of saving the universe. You lost some of the conveniences of its broken version.

Audra surveyed the offerings, which ranged from old classics to modern-day options that never actually existed. Being a devotee of chocolate, she went with a simple high-cacao bar and took a seat at one of the small marble-topped tables.

Such places worked similarly in The Commons. There may not have been anyone behind the counter to work the register, but she had to choose something she liked before her meeting could take place.

The front-door bells jingled as Porter entered.

Audra didn't bother with a greeting because he wasn't yet aware of her. It was good to see her old friend, as always. However, watching him peruse the wrapped hard-candy options, she couldn't help but notice that while he still hadn't shown any signs of aging beyond where he'd been when she first met him, his movements were those of someone weighed down by the burden of experience.

Then again, who was she to talk? She'd carried her own

weight for so long, she couldn't remember what it was like to be free of it.

Audra already knew what Porter's choice would be. Basic peppermint.

They were that much alike. They wanted the few pleasures still available to them to be simple and pure.

Of course, Porter might not have seen his selection as candy at all. And the surrounding place might not have been a candy store to him. It only needed to be something he could comprehend in order for them to meet when they weren't in the same place.

Audra tried to recall being confused by such things. She couldn't. It had been too long.

Porter dropped whatever he'd chosen into the pocket of his car coat and took a seat at Audra's table. Now that he could see her, he behaved no differently than he had when he couldn't. They were too used to communicating in bizarre and mysterious ways for either of them to bother remarking on it. And there was too much at stake.

"I've briefed Paul," said Porter.

Audra took a nibble of her chocolate. The small pleasures would see her through. They always had. "And?"

"He understands."

"Completely?"

"As much as he needs to. For the moment."

The chocolate was delightful. In another time and place, Audra might even have been able to savor it. But under the current circumstances, all she could do was maintain the hope that she might someday have the chance to enjoy things again. "Will this work, Jonas?"

Porter smiled ruefully, as much to himself as to her. "Work." He chuckled at the sound of the word—or, perhaps, at the concept and how their efforts of late had made a mockery of such a hope. "We're up against a foe whose power is more formidable than that of the last one we faced. And the last one shut down the process of life and death for generations. Our victory empowered the current threat. All of the realms we know are falling into one another through gaps of our own creation. And we're going to try to seal them all by hijacking our powerful foe's plans, all the while praying they don't know we're doing so. Honestly, I'm gobsmacked that we've made it this far."

The brutal truth of that hit Audra harder than she would have predicted.

Porter saw it and took her hand. "It has ever been thus," he said. "Look at the two of us. We didn't get this way by facing anything less. It's just that the consequences of failure are beyond our understanding."

Was that intended to make Audra feel better? She struggled to come up with a reply.

The Speaky Shrieky rescued her, its cry as unpleasant as it was loud.

Enough of conversation; things would continue to move.

"Nice dreaming of you, Jonas," Audra said.

## 3

## I'VE BEEN DEAD BEFORE

If, at the end of their labors, they succeeded in saving all of existence, with all its realms and inhabitants, and tallied up the list of heroes, Angus the dog might well top the list. The animal had uncanny instincts and timing, and Porter's only regret was that he might never be able to express his gratitude to the floppy-eared vagabond. For it was Angus who convinced Lexi to go with Jabari for shelter and safety, allowing Paul and Porter to go on their merry way and do what they needed to do.

Well, not exactly.

What happened was that Lexi insisted on staying with Paul and Porter, no matter what danger they might be headed into, and the dog simply took off as only he could.

Given the strength of the girl's bond with him, which was close to a physical cord, her reaction was instantaneous. She ran down the sidewalk after him.

"You all right to drive?" said Paul.

Jabari watched the dog disappear into the distance, Lexi trailing behind, plaintively calling after him. "Yeah." He pulled the keys to the Midnight Angels van from his pocket. "I might not make it more than a block on foot—you know, being turned to stone and all—but I'm good behind the wheel. You guys don't need a lift?"

"This is the excuse we need to make our break," Porter said.

The boy nodded his understanding.

They received Jabari's reassurances before he drove away that he would do his best to keep the pair with him. Even if he didn't, he was reasonably confident he could find a safe place for them to stay.

If anyplace was safe.

If Lexi would stay there.

If Angus would.

Halfway through the walk to their destination, Paul's phone buzzed with Jabari's text. *Got her.* A minute later, the next one. *And him.*

Walking along Foster Avenue, which in The Living World would have been carrying a reasonable amount of traffic at the current time of day but offered only hobbled cars in its Marginal form, Porter waited for Paul's inevitable questions about their planned course of action. He looked forward to them because they'd signal that the boy had regained much or all of his memory and was fully engaged in the task ahead. Otherwise, none of it would work.

Under the ever-gray skies, they passed more and more people. Porter suspected it was a result of The Margins bringing in greater numbers of Marginals but also because what would normally be more heavily trafficked streets drew them in, like smaller drainpipes feeding into a main line. Most of them were too distracted by their phones and assorted other devices—tablets and other screen-based gadgets—to pay Porter and Paul much mind.

However, as they approached a young woman wearing an

empty homemade baby sling, she turned from the vacant windows of the featureless storefront office she was studying to watch Paul and Porter draw near.

Porter couldn't help but stop. Such was the intensity of the need in the woman's eyes. It was almost painful to witness, as if they'd intruded on a moment of intimacy.

"They won't let me in," the woman said to Porter, her English heavily accented and tentative. "They put me in there when I didn't want to go, and now they keep me out."

Neither Porter nor Paul knew how to respond.

"Seven weeks ago." The woman's hands moved to the sling, as if to comfort the infant that wasn't there before remembering its emptiness for the umpteenth time. "In there. They have him."

Porter looked the storefront office over. Seen through the windows, the space looked empty. And felt it. The same empty that made up much of the crossover realm. There were no signs. There wasn't even an address plate. And it wasn't that they'd failed to transition to The Margins, as was the case with so many other things. There was a strong sense that they'd never been there to begin with. "I don't think there's anyone here," he said as gently as he could.

The woman shrugged. Then her hands moved to the sling again.

"I'm sorry," Porter said.

She shrugged again. "I'll never leave him."

More people passed, engrossed in their phones, each of them looking like they were going to collide with Porter, Paul, or the woman before adjusting their trajectory just enough to avoid that fate.

Paul looked to Porter for guidance.

Porter had nothing for him.

Before they walked away, Paul laid his hand on the woman's shoulder but got no response.

They moved on, a sense of shame hanging over them that hadn't been there just moments before.

"Will she find her baby if we pull this off?" Paul said.

"I don't know. She had her son taken in The Living World due to reasons having nothing to do with the formation of The Margins. And those who took him are more lifeless than anyone in The Commons."

They continued in silence for a distance.

"She saw us," Paul said. "She paid attention to us. She seemed used to being here." He dodged a young girl who was furiously thumbing her screen and would've planted her head in his chest had he not taken evasive action. "All these other people seem like they're not all here."

"They weren't all there in The Living World, either." Porter sidestepped another near-collision. "That's why they're here."

"But not her."

"She's been unseen and in-between for so long that she's grown accustomed to it."

"She's comfortable with it?"

"I didn't say that."

Past a long line of houses and apartments, Porter saw their destination on a nearby rooftop but didn't want to point it out to Paul until they'd talked further. He needed Paul to ask questions and volunteer answers on his own.

The windows of the corner building were lined with posters for various types of liquor and beer. One caught Paul's eye and stopped him in his tracks. A poster for Muridine Pale Ale featured a party-animal cartoon version of a beetle-rat holding a frosty mug aloft.

One look, and all of the places Porter was bitten during their subterranean train ride began to itch. It had to be his imagination. He needed it to be. He watched Paul to see if the creature was familiar.

"I remember." Paul's voice was smaller than it had been only moments before.

"Do you?"

"It's coming back." Paul started to put his hand to the window but thought better of it and held it a few inches from the grinning little monster. He hadn't put his many hurts from the encounter with the beetle-rats behind him, either. He rubbed his ribs on his right side.

"It's your experiences from The Commons rejoining your experiences in The Living World. That's a result of the crossover of The Margins. And it's why those you see wandering around seem blank to us. They have only the memories of their one world and nothing in this one."

Paul looked back the way they'd come. "Except for her."

"Except for her. As I said, she's lived in The Margins for most or all of her life. She's just never known it."

At Clark Street, they crossed to the west side before turning north so that they had a view of their destination. Above them sat the water tower, blue with a yellow cross on it —a Swedish flag to honor the roots of the Andersonville neighborhood.

"We're going to use that to steal nukes from the hippies?"

"No. We're going to use that to get us to the place where we'll steal the nukes. And we're stealing them from the people who are stealing them from the hippie soldiers. They're called the Dharma Rangers now, by the way. They undertook a branding exercise, even though they'd die before they'd call it that."

Paul shot Porter a puzzled look.

"It's much like the Grateful Dead," Porter said. "They were counterculture, but they maintained one of the mightiest brands the world has ever known. It'll be going strong when the last of them becomes true to their name."

"D.W., Liam, and Nicolette. Right?"

"Right."

"They're okay with having their missiles hijacked?"

"Nobody's asking them. Not Manitou and not us."

"Do they know?"

"Possibly. If not, they will."

Paul looked up at the bright blue and yellow of the tower. "There's no water in it, right? That's what you said?"

"The original contained water. This is an ornament, albeit a very expensive one."

"Then how does that help us?"

"The people who live here worked hard to put that up there to mark their home after the first one had to be removed. It's concentrated Essence—a battery, essentially, filled with loyalty, love, and pride. It'll be more than enough to get us where we need to go." Porter waited for two phone-obsessed seniors to get out of his way and stepped into the street, making for the museum the tower sat atop.

Paul followed. "And that Essence will be enough to seal all the gaps in the barrier between The Commons and The Living World?"

"Not even close." Porter stopped to read a sign, suction-cupped to the inside of the museum's front door, telling them it was closed. "It's enough to get us to the next step. The nukes are the catalyst for accessing the Essence we need. But that assumes all of this works the way Audra wants it to."

"Audra's the burned woman. Your friend. I thought she died."

"So did she. It's complicated."

Paul studied their reflections in the glass of the museum windows. "You can get us in there and up to the roof."

Porter said nothing.

"And even though we're going to work with nuclear devices and massive amounts of Essence, we'll survive."

Porter doubled down on the silence.

"I've been dead before," Paul said once he understood. "I mean, I'm afraid. I am. But I'll do it."

"You were prepared to die in order to get back to The Commons. Why?"

"I knew I'd done something wrong—something really bad —without meaning to. Somebody'd used me. And I wanted to do whatever it would take to fix that." Paul shook his head. "Ray-Anne. Rain. She couldn't understand. She couldn't forgive me for trying what I tried. You don't just quit, she kept saying. You don't take yourself out."

"I'm surprised that she, of all people, would say such a thing, given what she's been through. I agree that one should never quit. However, if you can't understand why someone might see no other alternative, you're low on experience, imagination, or both."

Paul chewed that over. "You want me to die, I'll die." He looked up at the roof. They were too close to the building to see the tower. "As many times as you want. And I'll take as many of them with me as I need to."

Porter didn't doubt a word.

Paul was a boy no longer.

And that belief made Porter feel even worse about what was to come.

## 4

## CUTE TRICK

"Foundry," said the pile of stones on the conference-room floor. It had a face Charlene thought of as Quarry's, but the truth was that she didn't know if he had a distinct countenance at all.

She sat with Reinhard beside her while June Medill hovered by the door, ready to fetch Beatrice should Charlene exhibit any signs of distress. Charlene was propped up in a chair at an awkward angle, bolstered by pillows and doing her best to avoid passing out. It wasn't easy. "He's an elemental? A brother of yours?"

"Not a brother, but yes. He is to metal what I am to stone."

"You call yourselves elementals, but metal's not an element," said Reinhard. His tone was as unyielding as the topic at hand.

Charlene assumed the former Vigil had one or more means to dispose of Quarry secreted on him, even though she'd expressly told him this conversation could not end in a fight. That meant nothing to him, most likely. For a Vigil, all situations could—and often did—end with one side dying at the hand of the other. Charlene wasn't convinced Reinhard would ever let that part of himself go.

"It depends on the system you adopt," Quarry explained. "He's not one of your four."

"Not like fire."

Charlene didn't like where Reinhard's questions were heading, but when she tried to catch his eye, he either didn't notice or ignored her.

"According to Wu Xing thinking, it's the fifth element." There was nothing in Quarry's voice to indicate he was intimidated by Reinhard's hostility.

Reinhard glared in response, giving Charlene her opportunity to steer the conversation away from open conflict. "We appreciate you calling in the cavalry." As if choreographed ahead of time, a *whump* they could feel through the walls announced that one of the Dharmas' tank-killer choppers had just found a straggler outside. "You didn't have to come back, and I appreciate you helping me out of the storage room. Just tell us what happened."

"I went to the Dharmas, as promised. What I didn't know is that Foundry went with me."

"How?" Charlene adjusted herself in her chair. She was unable to find a comfortable angle at which to look down on the animated stones.

"Adjacency. His connection to me. He and I travel in a similar fashion through the ground, but I typically have an easier time of it. When all else fails, I can surface and use roads to get where I need to go. He's limited to metals. He can make use of power and phone lines, but that can confine him to settled and wired routes."

"You didn't know you had a hitchhiker?" Reinhard said.

"He wasn't hitchhiking, exactly. All he had to do was stay

close behind me and let his relationship to me carry him along. After my fighting here and the length of the trip, I was tired. I didn't pick up on his presence. Plus he's gotten much better at stealth."

Charlene wanted to believe Quarry because she needed to.

Reinhard looked tempted to pull whatever weapon he had on him.

June Medill was uncharacteristically silent.

"How did he gain control of the missiles?"

Charlene hadn't heard Nicolette enter. But that was part of the Dharma take-only-pictures-leave-only-footprints training —the hippie soldiers could be frightfully quiet. Which was probably why the woman looked so put out that someone had snuck up and stolen the Dharmas' world-destroying ordnance right out from under them. While leaving it in place.

"Metal," Quarry said. "Foundry can manipulate the arming mechanisms like you people blink your eyes."

"Why does he want ICBMs?" Nicolette was now farther into the room, though Charlene hadn't noticed her moving.

"He doesn't," said Quarry. "He only wants the warheads."

"Why?" Charlene grunted as she moved in her chair again. She ignored the concerned glances of the others.

"I don't know."

Reinhard shot Charlene a look and held it for a second.

She was careful not to respond in a way Quarry might catch.

"The gaps in your knowledge seem a little convenient, Rocky." Reinhard believed nicknames gave one power over another. Charlene never argued the point with him since most people who went up against Reinhard weren't in a hurry to do so a second time, assuming they had a choice. "You didn't know your fire brother was going to commit a mass killing within our walls. You had no clue your metal brother was along for the ride. Now you can't tell us the purpose of any of it."

Charlene shifted in her seat again. "Quarry, do you mind if we put you up on the table so that I don't have to look down at you? I'm not sure how much longer I can keep this up otherwise."

The pile of rocks mulled the question over. "Sure."

June Medill stepped forward with an empty plastic mail bin, put it on the floor, and moved the pile of rocks into it, piece by piece. With impressive efficiency, the head was reduced to a jaw and then obliterated altogether. When she was finished, Reinhard got up to help her lift the box and place it in the center of the conference table.

It took a moment for the rocks to reassemble themselves into the head again. "Cute trick," he said. "This has a wooden core. It's like suspending me in the air, so I can't go anywhere. This is how you show your gratitude for my help?"

"Because of you, our side has lost its hold on enough nuclear yield to put a real hurting on the universe as we know it," Reinhard said. "I need no forgiveness from you. Nor will I ask for any."

Quarry said nothing.

"I'm sorry," Charlene said. "Big things are in motion. On our side as well as yours. We can't risk having you work against us."

"I understand." Quarry's tone indicated nothing of the sort.

"Well, that just fills me with warm goo." Reinhard ignored Charlene's glare. "But I don't give a damn what you understand." The ex-Vigil stood up and pulled what appeared to be a modified TV remote from his pocket. He pressed a button on it until its power light dimmed and went out. "What I do care about? You're not going anywhere, so I don't need this right now."

Quarry said nothing.

Reinhard pocketed his device and left the room.

## 5

## EVERYTHING BREAKS

It was obvious something was off about Truitt's office before Jeremy made it through the door. The faraway smell of a lit cigar and a woman's muffled giggle—also faint, as if she were concealed behind heavy drapes—telegraphed it.

Truitt didn't smoke.

Nobody would dare fire up around him.

And hardly anyone laughed like that in his presence.

Jeremy stepped in and closed the door behind him. The door was gone as soon as he let go of the handle.

He wasn't in Truitt's office. He was in a large living room in near-darkness illuminated only by the glow of a vintage black-and-white TV. It was a small screen in a large cabinet.

The room was huge. As Jeremy's eyes adjusted, he saw that the color scheme matched that of the grayscale TV screen. The '50s-era furniture and carpeting were all either gray or white. There was no telling what color the heavy floor-to-ceiling curtains were because they were drawn across the numerous windows, allowing only a crack of light to penetrate through a gap in one pair. The gap looked to be no accident. It was at the eye level of a small child, as if one had been peering through it.

Truitt sat on a couch, staring at the TV, slouching uncharacteristically. At the end of the expansive coffee table, in front of another chair, sat an ashtray with the stub of a stogie sitting in it. That was the source of the tobacco stink, and its end was still shiny from being in someone's mouth.

On the screen, a young boy in a suit sat at the end of a formally set table. The dining room around him was much too large for the dinner party, which consisted of him and a couple who looked to be his mother and father. The boy glanced first at the man, then at the woman. The two adults studiously ignored the others at the table. The only sound was the clink of the boy's fork as he pushed his food around his plate.

Jeremy didn't announce himself.

The light of the on-screen table's candelabras flickered in a way that was amplified by the TV, causing the picture of the stiff dinner to alternate abruptly between lights and darks. With each shift back to brightness, Truitt squinted, as if pained.

The on-screen boy looked again at his parents, both of whom continued to focus only on their own meals. He plowed as much dinner as his fork could handle toward the edge of his plate but got no reaction from them. Then he shoveled the food over the edge and onto the tablecloth.

Still nothing.

Finally, he stood and left the table, the shot staying on him as he shrank into the distance and left via a door on the far wall.

His mother and father did nothing to mark his departure.

"Do you know what movie this is, Mr. Johns?" Truitt

squinted again as the parents patted their mouths, sat back, and waited for someone to remove their plates.

"I'm afraid I don't, sir."

Truitt watched the couple at the table, their posture perfect, neither saying a word. "It doesn't matter, does it?"

Jeremy gambled on silence being the correct response.

Truitt didn't follow up.

Maybe Jeremy had chosen correctly. Maybe it didn't matter.

The smell of the cigar remained, pungent and bellicose.

"How go the preparations, Mr. Johns?" Truitt didn't look Jeremy's way; instead, he watched a silent butler clear the plates from in front of the couple, who each thanked him too quietly to be heard.

"District Two is finished, sir." Jeremy had been warned against using the locations' real names and was careful not to do so now. "District One has presented a few challenges because it's larger and less clearly defined. But we should have the preparatory steps completed well ahead of zero hour."

Preparatory steps completed. When had he started talking like Truitt? Did he only do it with him? What if he was talking to everyone that way and hadn't realized it?

"You do know that our point of connection's reliability is limited to what he will do but not when?"

The TV's focus changed. Now it was a slow-floating shot of a playroom floor littered with broken toys. A racing car was flattened into the tile, wheels splayed, as if stomped in fury. A headless ventriloquist dummy lay upon the floor, limbs akimbo, like it had launched into a suicide swan dive from the ceiling and been decapitated on the way down. Here was a gutted teddy bear, there a cracked and drained fishbowl. Nothing had survived. And a flicker of the light revealed that the floor of the living room Truitt, Jeremy, and the TV occupied was now littered with similarly murdered playthings.

The man and woman who'd been talking and laughing before Jeremy entered were silent. He wasn't sure how long that had been the case.

"I understand, sir. We'll be ready for engagement long before we need to be."

Truitt stood and stretched, surveying his surroundings as if seeing them for the first time. He crossed to another door that may or may not have been there when Jeremy entered and left the room.

Jeremy didn't know what was expected of him, so he stayed put and tried to appear confident in his decision.

A Western was now on the TV screen, with a lone good guy confronting a table full of baddies who'd obviously been menacing a gorgeous-yet-virtuous barmaid. There was no audio; it was a silent offering without captions.

The conversation escalated until it blew up into fisticuffs. The good guy got the worst of it, which was far bloodier than any old Western Jeremy had ever seen. The bad guys put the boots to the good guy after they'd dropped him, and they kept at him with heels and pointed toes until the red was everywhere. The barmaid, safe now that the men who'd been bothering her were distracted by the destruction of another human being, calmly collected a shawl and bonnet from coat hooks on the wall and left. The carnage continued.

Truitt returned with two cocktails, handed one to Jeremy, and seated himself in a cushiony recliner at the other end of the coffee table. He rotated away from the screen to face Jeremy. "Our connections must be maintained and called upon without error, or we risk our situation developing into something far worse than it is now."

"I understand, sir."

Truitt took a sip of his cocktail and waited for Jeremy to do the same. "A Pimm's cup. I understand they've come back into style."

Jeremy had seen the drink on the menu of a craft-cocktail place he was talked into going to once, but he'd never tried one. It was delicious, but he wasn't sure he should say so.

"My father drank only these if he could help it." Truitt took another sip and surveyed the field of destroyed toys, which now covered a good percentage of the living-room floor. He considered them in silence for a while. "Nothing endured. Not anything subjected to such anger."

He wasn't just talking about toys.

On screen, the men finished with the hero. He hadn't endured, either. They looked around—only then noticing that the barmaid had gotten while the getting was good—and filed out the door in a hurry.

Jeremy hoped she'd make it.

From another room in an unidentifiable direction came the clear sounds of a man and woman having sex. Jeremy was mortified to hear it so clearly, especially being there with Truitt.

It didn't sound like there was anything loving about it. It was a violence of its own.

Truitt drank.

On screen, the camera lingered on the empty barroom. The hero was just out of frame.

He hadn't made a move to get up off the floor.

He never would.

"She never cared that I could hear. I thought they were playing, so I played, too. Then I thought they were fighting, so I did that as well." Truitt looked the shattered toys over again. "She felt guilty in her own way, I suppose." He took a sip, savored it, swallowed, and shook his head. "Everything breaks."

The sun set on the on-screen saloon, which darkened until there was no way to tell if the TV was still on.

Truitt said nothing more.

Once Jeremy's eyes adjusted to the blackness, he let himself out of the room. Before he closed the door behind him, light once again filled the space, creating a shadow Jeremy on the opposite wall of the Manitou hallway.

Jeremy knew without looking that Truitt's office was behind him once again.

## 6

## WHEELS ON FIRE

"How long?"

They were in one of the largest conference rooms, down the hall from the Octagon proper, which could be called a conference room only because Audra intended it to be one eventually. At the moment, the space contained two chairs.

None of the Petrels had been inclined to help change that. They feared that having a proper meeting spot would mean more meetings, which might chain them to a static location rather than allow them to be where they wanted—on their bikes, zipping around the city.

"Two days, ma'am."

Ma'am. Whizbang tacked that onto a response only when he suspected he or a fellow Petrel he liked needed the small boost from a show of extra respect.

"Two days." Audra tried to keep her temper from hitting the red zone. Now was not the time for discipline or repercussions, especially since their arrangement was a loose confederation, and she needed their best from them. "A lot can happen in two days. Walk me through it again."

"Yes, ma'am." A long pause. For all of Whizbang's toughness—he was built like a boxer and was known for being able to endure far longer runs than anyone except for the Dodger himself—he knew when he was wrong and understood when he was due for a dressing-down.

Audra, for her part, appreciated that it was no small thing for him to display such humility in front of his fellow Petrels. It was an additional show of respect. "You're not required to call me that. I appreciate the sentiment, but let's forget about the rules and which ones might have been broken. Just tell me again."

"Biscuit was last seen on the west side, in the forties."

"By?"

"Me."

"Okay." She responded quickly so he wouldn't be tempted to "ma'am" her again. "What did he say to you?"

"He made a joke about taking a run at the tunnel."

"The Lincoln?"

"Yes."

"Not the Holland. He wasn't talking about going downtown."

"No. I mean, he didn't say the Lincoln. But we were close enough to it that we both knew what he meant."

"And did either of you acknowledge that nobody knows where those tunnels come out due to the unstable state of The Margins? Or that the other side could be part of The L.W., The Commons, or both, so he'd have no idea what he was getting into?"

"No. But we knew."

"You knew."

"Yes."

"And he knew."

"Yes."

"What makes you think he knew?"

"We talked about it before."

"You talked about it with Biscuit."

"I think so, yes. Ma'am."

He thought so. Audra concentrated on remaining calm. Lives were at stake. Her people's lives. No one would be helped if she blew a gasket. "Then what?"

"He didn't come back. We waited. He didn't."

That wasn't all that rare, actually—particularly for scouts. Time was a soft thing in Demeter and, certainly, in The Margins. Clocks and watches didn't agree with each other. Or they might stop and start. Or stop and not start. Often, it stayed light for what felt like days. At other times, it got dark after what seemed like only a few hours. "How long did you wait?"

"A day, by my watch. Much less, by Lottie's. Roadkill's doesn't work anymore."

"Then?"

"Lottie and Roadkill went looking."

"A day ago."

"Yes, ma'am. As far as we could tell."

"And where did they say they were going?"

"The Lincoln."

To look for Biscuit where he'd last been seen, which was both sensible and beyond foolish. Officially, no one dared plumb the depths of any Manhattan tunnel. The Lincoln was powerless and pitch dark just a few scant yards past the entrance. They didn't know what it connected to. They didn't even know if it was a tunnel. If it was fueled by or connected to The Commons, it could be anything from a giant syringe to a digestive tract. But if anyone would take on a foolhardy expedition without approval, it'd be Lottie and Roadkill.

"Did any of you tell Lars?" Audra already knew that

answer. They all sought to impress the Dodger with their independence. So three people had gone Bermuda Triangle without a word to leadership. That had been enough of a problem with experienced Envoys such as Jonas. But the Petrels were mostly kids or just a few years past. The Dodger was a good decade older than the rest of them.

Whizbang glanced past her and then down again. She didn't need to be told Lars's location in the room. Whizbang had met his eye and been shamed into looking away.

The Dodger couldn't have been any happier than she was about three of their people going missing. Three. On top of the many Envoys and Journeymen said to have been lost at Envoy HQ.

Well, they didn't have to accept these losses. Audra leaned on her knees and rocked in the chair, thinking it over. Then she turned to the others in the room.

The Dodger, Lars, was exactly where she'd thought he'd be. Po stood with him. And there were a lot more Petrels in the room than there had been when she'd begun this conversation.

Word traveled quickly. No surprise there. A good many of these people had been hardcore weekend racers and bike messengers in their time. Their whole life was speed and communication. "Let's talk—fast," Audra told the Dodger.

The room cleared in silence, leaving only Lars and Whizbang, who looked to be weighing another apology.

Now was not the time, as he knew. He, too, exited.

Audra almost considered forgiving him.

Almost.

∼

Po found the Dodger inspecting and tuning Melange, his favorite ride, which was hanging on one of the maintenance racks. The Petrels all wanted to go looking for their lost teammates, so Audra had told Lars to rig up a random number generator on one of the old Windows machines and hold a drawing.

His name came up as the first to take a turn. Most of the Petrels said they believed the results were honest.

"Shouldn't you be prepping the cargo bike?" Joel didn't wait for Po to sign. Yet again, he was right about what Po would've asked.

Lars finished inflating his rear tire and detached the pump with a hiss. "Why? I need speed."

Po let Joel continue on his own. "Sure. But you need muscle, too. You have no idea what you'll be up against."

The Dodger hooked the pump hose up to the front tire's valve. "That's why I need wheels on fire. I plan to run, not fight. Then I'll come back with help."

"And they'll just let you do that."

The Dodger pumped with a little more fervor than necessary.

Joel pressed him. "You saw what happened last time. Even with you and the boss together, you almost didn't make it."

Lars finished pumping. It probably hadn't been needed to begin with. It wasn't like him to let his tires go low-pressure. With another hiss, he pulled the nozzle off. "Nobody's coming with me. Not even you. You saw the numbers I pulled. You guys weren't even in the running."

"We didn't have to be. It was assumed we'd go no matter what."

"Says who?"

"Audra."

Lars spun both wheels, checking to ensure they were true. He didn't believe them.

He shouldn't have. Joel was lying.

"Dude," said Joel. "Dude."

Nothing. The lead Petrel wiped his chain down. Then he removed one of the bike's cranks, inserted a wrench into a part Po didn't know the name of and slowly rotated it while gazing into the air at nothing, working by feel.

Po signed.

Joel hesitated before speaking. "You cheated."

The Petrel's answer was just slow enough in coming to tell Po he was right. "At what?"

"You think I'm just a kid's toy because I look like one? You rigged the lottery. The spreadsheet software told me. And even if it hadn't, the hard drive was just dying to give you up."

The Dodger said nothing. But he began prepping the two-man cargo bike.

## 7

## THE PLATYPUS PROOF

The door was the easiest part of getting into the Swedish American Museum. Porter jumped the lock cylinder to his hand, letting them in, and then jumped it back.

Everything after that was hard.

Paul was once again trapped in the pattern of the optimist born yesterday: they faced an obstacle; they figured out a way around it; Paul assumed it was the worst they'd come up against; they immediately faced something even tougher. It got so he could count on it.

In The Commons, much of what Paul, Porter, and the others had struggled through could at least be understood in discrete areas. The Commons was ever-shifting, but it tended to refashion itself in zones during Paul's Journey.

Thus, the next batch of miles would probably look like the previous batch: farmland led to more farmland, desert led to still more desert, and truck stops and suburban horror led to more of the same. Here in The Margins, however, transitions were abrupt when they could be called transitions in any sense of the word, which Porter ascribed to the invasive nature of The Living World and The Commons intersecting.

The museum interior was like the Winchester Mystery House, drawn by Escher. Both had played a prominent role during Paul's earliest days at New Beginnings, back when he'd refused to talk to anyone, and—he later found out—Pop Mike worried Paul might eventually do something to get himself booted out.

He never did, and that was partly thanks to the library, where he was able to lose himself for hours. Two obsessions that helped him disappear were the Winchester House and Escher's work, though he didn't know why at the time. He related very strongly to the rules of reality expressed by them—or the lack thereof. They were worlds he understood, with their warped logic and their sense-bending layouts. That was his world, too.

The museum's interior spaces were far more expansive than an outside view of the building would lead one to believe. A massive rotunda looked like it had been borrowed from a much larger structure. It shouldn't have fit at all. There was a reception desk behind two other reception desks and doors that opened on other doors, all of them locked—and for good reason, Porter said without elaborating.

A spiral staircase took them up at least fifteen flights until it ended at a ceiling. Porter became more unsettled and nervous than Paul had ever seen him, and they hurried back down.

"These steps were not meant for us," the gray man said as they pounded down them.

"Who were they meant for?"

"To tell you while we're on them would be pure folly."

Even at the bottom, Porter wouldn't explain his fear. After Paul pestered him for a while, the Envoy revealed little. While such stairways could be invaluable, he said, they were safe only for those who were intended to make use of them. Even then, there were no guarantees for a traveler who chose the wrong moment to try them. "The steps know stories," Porter said. "But they won't tell them if we don't ask. And that's for the best."

Finally, Porter led them to a narrow back hallway that dead-ended in shadows. He looked up at a painted-wood hatch in the ceiling and grunted. Raising his staff, he tapped around the border of it, the resulting thumps echoing down the hall with a resonance that was nothing like wood. It sounded more like something that was annoyed.

"This is the part of the movie where I say this has been too easy," said Paul.

Porter looked genuinely shocked. "Easy? Do you know how close we came to complete disaster back there?"

"On the stairway?"

"No. Well, yes, but before that. When we passed through the kitchen and stepped into the walk-in refrigerator rather than the exit just before it? My knowing to do that was the result of previous Journeys through here that ended horribly for other Envoys and their Journeymen. I know of at least two others who were faced with this interior in The Commons, assuming that this is the genuine article and not a replica. The first returned without his Journeyman. He wouldn't reveal what happened. Even when they drummed him out of the Corps, he wouldn't speak of it."

"What about the other guy?"

"Unknown. She and the little girl she was guiding were never seen again." With that, Porter concentrated on using his staff to catch a steel ring hanging from a length of twine attached to the hatch. After a number of tries, he was able to push the ring sideways across the length of the hatch. A click was followed by the grind of what sounded like heavy stone.

When the hatch dropped abruptly, Paul pulled Porter out of the way. The Envoy narrowly missed getting brained by the wooden staircase that came down with it.

"Thank you," said the gray man. "Even at your age, I wouldn't have been quick enough to dodge that."

They climbed up into the darkness, Porter insisting that Paul lead the way. It was no display of cowardice. Paul suspected he feared they were being followed, possibly by whatever they'd run from on the staircase to nowhere.

When the climb in the blackness took much, much longer than it should have, given the modest number of steps they'd seen from below, Paul wasn't surprised. The Living World had its rules, but now they were warped by those of The Commons.

"This isn't the first time this has happened." Porter didn't sound as winded as a man his age should have. Then again, Paul didn't really know how old he was. "The realms have overlapped in times past, and the evidence remains if you know what to look for. That's the Platypus Proof."

"The Platypus Proof?" Paul nearly tripped, but Porter steadied him with a hand against the small of his back.

"The platypus. An absurd creature. They glow when you shine black light on them. And the males can deliver a painful sting, to boot. So you've basically got a venomous light-up beaver with the face of a duck. No one in The Living World would design such an animal on purpose. That came from The Commons and was left behind. Some say, anyway. And if you're ever bored, search for pictures of the pink fairy armadillo or the bobbit worm. Look up the tarantula hawk, and read about what its larvae do to its prey after they hatch.

The Living World is more than capable of producing its own horrors, but it's had help from other realms."

After what seemed like another hour of climbing, Porter pulled Paul to a stop and moved up ahead of him. In the darkness, he thumped on something above them with his staff. Then came the sound of another ring sliding across another hatch, followed by another click.

This time, once the grinding of stone began, Porter pulled Paul back down for about a dozen steps or so.

The sky came crashing down. At least, that's how it seemed as Paul was forced to squint up into a wash of sunlight and blue, fighting to gaze up the ladder's length as the painful brightness of the day assaulted their dilated pupils until their eyes adjusted.

Something small whirred down from the blue above and landed on the ladder ahead of them. A grasshopper. After a moment of sizing Paul and Porter up, it foolishly jumped off into the darkness. Or maybe that was where it wanted to go. Who could say if it was even a grasshopper?

They began their climb, Porter leading the way after signaling Paul to remain silent.

Up top, they found themselves in a cornfield, two dense rows on either side of them. Paul recalled glowing eyes peering out at him from corn like this as they passed it in their van in The Commons. He fervently hoped this wasn't the same corn.

Porter stayed quiet, so Paul continued to do so, too. And he was only too happy to let Porter continue leading the way once they were on the move again.

## 8

## HIS ARCHNEMESIS, SOBRIETY

Billy Clyde's. No other place was fit for the mental cud-chewing Jeremy needed to do.

He'd intended to dive into a session to see if his old pals hops and alcohol might shake a conclusion loose after his archnemesis, sobriety, had failed. Yet here was, alone in his booth, with just one mug poured from his pitcher—a mug nearly full after more than an hour. He was unable to muster even a token attempt at a good stupor, and token was putting it kindly.

Jeremy could've passed a roadside sobriety test.

That hurt.

When he'd returned to his desk after the Truitt meeting—if it had qualified as a meeting—there was an encrypted email waiting. The email itself was just an event invite telling him a time and date to be at a certain location, which he couldn't recall at the moment.

He looked at the email several times. Every time he read it, he saw where he was supposed to go, then forgot it as soon as he closed the message. Accepting it and adding it to his calendar was no better. He looked at it on his phone, read where to go, and had it tumble out of his head as soon as he shut the app down.

It was the way of things with Manitou and Truitt. He'd remember where to go when it was time to go there. Until then, it was best for the organization if that knowledge wasn't resident in his brain, there to be stolen by—well, he didn't know.

But Truitt did.

And that was probably the way Jeremy would have wanted it if he'd known enough to have an informed opinion.

The bar was more crowded than usual. The vibe was strange, too. It felt emptier, somehow, though every booth and stool was occupied.

Nobody talked.

Even the TV, showing an infomercial for do-it-yourself rhinoplasty, had its volume turned down.

At the bar, they ignored the screen.

Jeremy couldn't blame them.

Most of the lost souls flattening the pleather-clad foam tops of the Billy Clyde's barstools used the screen like a futon for the eyes. It was a nap spot for their attention span that could be discarded if anything more interesting occurred.

Which never happened.

Another rarity for the night was that Porthos deigned to splay himself across Jeremy's table without being fed.

Not rare.

Unheard of.

Hell, even the offering of free food was only enough to get the old street fighter to pay a tiny bit of attention. To have him hang out as if Jeremy counted for something in his feline consciousness?

Never.

Yet here he was, like an old pard.

The pieces of the plan Truitt laid out for Jeremy in previous discussions were still free-floating. They weren't intended to coalesce until it was time. That time was drawing nearer, but it hadn't arrived yet. So he was left to witness the elements rotating in and out of focus, a restless kaleidoscope of detail.

Manitou was going to take control of an untold number of ballistic missiles. Jeremy didn't know where they were or how that would occur. But it was a hell of a lot of nuclear potential.

Their angle in commandeering them was all about adjacency—an intimate relationship with the ICBMs—though that adjacency had to be kept under wraps until it was ready to be used. Hiding it was of utmost importance, and it looked like Truitt, if he was ever pleased about anything, was relatively happy with how that piece was working out.

The fissile capability of the ICBMs would kick off a process that would seal all of the unwanted gaps in the barrier between The Commons and The Living World, thus arresting the growing formation of The Margins and handing control of traffic between the realms to Callibeau, Truitt, and Manitou.

Again, how that was to occur wasn't for Jeremy to know. But from his reading of Abel's journal, he had some guesses.

Oh, did he.

At the bar, a woman with her head in her hands sat up at Jeremy's thought, as if hearing it spoken aloud. She slapped both hands on the bar, bracing herself to stand. But she remained seated. Instead, she turned herself around on the stool. It looked like it took all of her strength.

It was Mallory Chiklis, the woman who'd nearly destroyed a server room with her attempted exorcism. She faced Jeremy and watched him.

Apparently, that was all she had in mind. Watching.

On the table, Porthos sat up to check her out with that

squint-as-a-blink thing cats do. Then he looked around the bar.

So did Jeremy.

Everyone in the booths, including those who'd been sleeping—and who slept in those exact spots every time Jeremy stopped in—regarded him the same way as Mallory. Porthos looked at Jeremy as if seeking amusement in the human's reaction to being the center of attention. Then he, too, fell into out-and-out staring.

Jeremy got it.

Mallory Chiklis had disappeared. She'd been Marginal. Now she was back.

Same with everyone else in the bar. And they all knew more about what his plans were—or what the plans for him were—than he did.

Even the damned cat.

On the way out, Jeremy nearly collided with the Rubbish Gladiator, who stopped his trash spearing and watched Jeremy's passing along with everybody on both sides of the street.

For once, the man had nothing to say.

## 9

## CHOO-CHOO CHARLIE

"Are you all right?" Choo-Choo Charlie asked Rain. Zach didn't really like thinking of the train man, whose real name was Emmett, by that silly-sounding name. The train man seemed decent and strong, and the name was a better fit for someone who shouldn't be taken seriously. But Zach needed a safe substitute, and Rain handed him one when she referred to what the train men had done as their Choo-Choo Charlie routine.

Zach didn't understand. Maybe it was someone who ate too much. Which also didn't fit the train man.

They sat in a field on some boxes the train men had offloaded to perform their repairs. Nearby, the train loomed over the landscape, like a living giant that knew it needed help and thus allowed the little men to weld and hammer and perform the other fixes to give the machine a head start on healing itself.

The flickering of the sparks thrown by the work played across Rain's face like lightning. She still hadn't answered Choo-Choo Charlie. *Was* she all right? "Yeah," she said. "Yeah."

"You sure?"

"Yeah." Rain watched the men work. The light of the repair work flared from damaged guns atop cars as well as from underneath, where wheels needed fixing. "How long will it take?"

"A couple hours, if all goes well. She's pretty banged up, but if we give her enough of a boost to be rail-worthy, she'll finish the job on her own. We just need to keep moving."

"Not the work," Rain said, though she continued to watch it.

Charlie glanced over at Zach to see if he was listening.

Zach gave him nothing on that front. He was always listening in his own way, and even though he liked the train man, he didn't feel the need to help him figure out what Zach was or wasn't thinking.

"You can talk in front of him." A particularly large flare lit up Rain's face, as if to emphasize the truth of that.

They could talk in front of Zach. He knew more than they did about what was going on, in fact.

"When it happens, you'll know," Charlie said. "It'll happen twice. An out and then the in. And you'll know both times." He looked a little bit sick when he said that, and Zach didn't blame him.

"What's the out again?" The light of another arc flared across Rain's eyes—red this time.

Charlie looked at Zach once more. Never mind Rain's reassurances; he really didn't want to talk in front of him. "They have to draw a sample to use for the rider. It's going to hurt. Then they have to put that sample plus the rider back in." He continued to watch Zach for a response, but Zach offered no indication that he'd heard or understood. "That's going to hurt more."

Rain gave a nod of resignation, not approval. The light

played across her face in yellow, orange, red, and a whole lot of blue. Some white, here and there, but mostly blue.

Zach knew Rain was beautiful. To him, her beauty was truth and nothing more. He had no strong feeling about it, though some of the younger train men certainly did. But nearly all of them were also afraid of Rain, and he thought he understood why—or would when he got to know her better.

He also knew he didn't fear her.

"What's keeping them off us?"

"The Ravs? I don't know. I'm not sure I want to." Charlie thought that over. "Whatever it was had enough heat to fry our girl to the point where she almost gave in herself. It's going to take a while before she comes back online entirely, even after we get her on the rails and moving again." He chewed that over, too. "Honestly, most of us think there aren't any Ravagers within striking distance. Whatever saved our asses saw to that. But more are on the way."

Rain nodded. She was thinking about something else.

When the scream came, muffled by the walls of the car where they were working on Zach's mother, Rain winced. She reacted for Zach, too. His mother's pain was awful and real—old pain, from a terrible injury of the past.

Rain and Charlie didn't know any of that. They couldn't understand what Zach understood or grasp how much of it there was.

They would.

The work continued.

Metal on metal pinging and banging. The screech of a saw blade on steel somewhere. The flashing arcs across Rain's eyes.

The second scream was longer.

Zach reached for Rain's hand before he could stop himself.

Without looking at him, she took his hand in hers and held on tight.

Choo-Choo Charlie saw it but said nothing, and Zach liked him for that.

The flashing arcs of the work continued. Orange, yellow, blue, red, and white.

All across Rain's eyes, across her face. Like the light and the screams were hers, too.

It made Zach sad to think that he would no longer be able to carry the burden for everyone else. Sometimes heat and pain were necessary for healing to begin.

Everyone was about to find that out.

## 10

## THE DISTANCE IN THE DARK

"Is it me, or is this place even bigger than it was before?" said Joel as the Dodger pedaled them over a landscape that had gone from forest to prairie to the rolling golden hills they wove between on a road following the valley floor. "These gumdrops were definitely not here before. Are you going a different way?"

"Same as before," the Dodger replied, and Po was struck once again by how he was able to rival an automobile for speed without breathing hard. "That's how much Essence is flowing in. It's growing at an exponential rate."

The terrain rolled away under the Dodger's wheels and passed on either side of them—lengthy expanses of it. It was one thing to be told how fast it was increasing and quite another to witness it.

"Where's all this Essence coming from?" said Joel. "It can't all be from you guys. No way."

"It's not," the Dodger replied. "I only have guesses about the source, though—and not particularly educated ones at that. We cyclists are a superstitious and impressionable lot, given to entertaining strange notions and theories. If you want any sane or sensible answers, you'll have to ask the boss lady." He pedaled on. "But it's big, isn't it? It is that."

The hills gave way to desert rock striped by layers of varying tones. With the viewing angles changing as the Dodger sped them past, the shapes the hills suggested morphed with the miles.

Po didn't ask Joel or the Dodger if they saw the same things he did. It was more appropriate that the visions given to him by the rocks remained his and his alone, just as Joel's and the Dodger's would have been theirs, assuming they cared enough to look and see.

Thus, a horse head became a man walking, and a woman cradling a child gave way to a man or woman with their face buried in their hands. The rocks had stories—both their own and those witnessed.

Po was honored that they shared them with him, true or not. All stories were true to their tellers one way or the other, even if it was only the tales themselves that understood that to be the case.

After much landscape passed, they came around a painted butte that seemed to have sprouted up in the way of the road just to force it to concede and circumvent it. On the other side was a two-lane covered bridge over a rushing creek.

The Dodger accelerated as he headed for the bridge's dark mouth. "You have to show your commitment." He stood on the pedals until their speed had increased significantly. "Otherwise, you end up where you came from. Or, if you've managed to piss it off, a place much worse than wherever you wanted to go to."

"Piss what off?" said Joel.

Po signed his answer into the growing darkness as they swiftly entered the unlit expanse.

"The bridge?" The Tamagotchi's tone dripped with disdain for Po's theory.

"The bridge," said the Dodger. "Roads, paths, and bridges have a purpose and power of their own in any world. It's just more pronounced here, where we're crossing over from one to the other. You need to show them you're serious about where you're going. And that you're doing it with respect."

Gloating over being right was not in Po's nature, though he'd heard Joel do it innumerable times. He pretended not to notice his victory. Often, he found, that was the best hope for Joel to learn a lesson about manners. He awaited the day when that hope might be realized.

They sped through the dark of the bridge for a long time. The water they were crossing wasn't as wide as the distance in the dark would indicate. Or was it?

"The bridge," Joel repeated, still doubtful.

"The bridge." The Dodger's defensiveness indicated Po wasn't the only one to hear skepticism in Joel's tone. "Crossing over can be a dangerous undertaking. Two words—Ichabod Crane."

The lack of a snappy retort from the Tamagotchi probably meant he was tapping into his reservoir of historical data. He assumed the name was that of a real person. The continued silence was most likely a sign that he wasn't able to find anything.

On they rode, the distance covered enough to cross many multiples of the water they'd seen from the road before entering. The blackness around them was complete. Even the rush of air had ceased, as had the sound of their wheels passing over the wooden floorboards. They were moving, but it didn't feel like it. Nor did there seem to be any oncoming traffic.

Po didn't mourn that absence. He would've worried too much about how the Dodger would avoid a head-on collision.

"Aren't you going a little fast, considering the visibility?" Joel said.

If the Dodger slowed at all in response, Po wasn't able to feel it.

Finally, the blackness began to give way to a pinprick of bluish-white light far ahead. Only then did Po realize they were not alone in their crossing.

Cyclists streamed past them on either side, outpacing the Dodger despite his remarkable strength. The bicycles and their riders were barely there when viewed directly. But from the corner of the eye, they acquired a degree of substance.

There was no way of knowing how long they'd been passing them. They, too, made no noise. And because the Dodger said nothing about them, Po did the same. Even Joel knew enough to maintain his silence. There was something about the pale riders that demanded an appropriate level of deference.

There was no point in trying to count them. There were enough that it wasn't always possible to distinguish between individuals. Riders continued to stream past while the Dodger ferried them into the light of the approaching bridge exit. As they did so, the wraith-like bicycles blossomed with diaphanous kites sprouting from the rear of their frames—spirit hitchhikers billowing up and out as they gorged themselves in the rush.

When the cyclists passed into the daylight of the territory beyond the bridge itself, they disappeared entirely.

The Dodger pedaled them out into the daylight of upper Manhattan at highway speed. As was the case when Po had last been here, the streets were not the clogged channels of normal New York. Instead, they were devoid of traffic but peopled with slow-moving pedestrians who looked to be wondering how, exactly, they'd come to be in their current location.

The distances were all wrong. At the speed they were traveling, passing building after building and block after block, they should have hit the opposite river in no time. But the avenues they crossed bore no street signs, and the street they rode on was endless.

"Ghost riders," the Dodger said.

"How's that?" said Joel.

The motion of something overhead caught Po's eye. He looked up and back. The same kind of gossamer kites and floating art that the spirit cyclists had spawned now trailed upward from the Dodger's bike, too, though these were brightly colored where the wraiths' had hardly been visible.

"The cyclists in the tunnel. You saw them, right?"

"Yeah." Joel didn't sound entirely comfortable with what he'd seen.

"They help us gather ambient Essence."

"Why can't we see them in the light? They're real ghosts?"

"Ever see the old bikes left at the sites where cyclists have been killed in the city? The ones that are spray-painted white? That's them."

"They work for you?"

"Nobody knows. We've never been able to ask them. The best guesses say that their time in The L.W. was cut short before they were able to do anything meaningful with their lives. So they gather Essence and add to our stores to make up for that."

Joel pondered that for another block or two. "That's sad," he said. And he must have thought so, for it was rare for the hard-bitten Tamagotchi to display anything other than bitterness, sarcasm, or concern for his own safety.

"You only see them in dark places, for the most part," the

Dodger said. "Whenever I'm near them, I get the sense they're ashamed of something. I don't know what. Maybe they think they're being judged for checking out so early. I guess it's a mercy they're able to do this. Essence steeped in pain is the sweetest kind for Manitou. They'd be targets for sure if they weren't able to exist in this form."

Joel didn't reply. He'd said all he had to say on the matter. Or maybe he was just rationing his expressions of empathy.

The blocks were equal parts clarity and blur as the Dodger blazed them along. They headed west on Seventy-Second Street, but Po had no idea if what was represented here was part of the Manhattan of The Living World or something from the in-between dream states Demeter and The Margins inhabited. What he did know was that distances were elastic —overly long, as he'd seen over the course of this trip, and then abruptly curtailed once they found themselves moving along the same street for a few seconds more before crossing Fifth Avenue and entering Central Park when he hadn't seen the trees approaching.

Po was no newcomer to odd environments and physical laws. His entire life had been spent in The Commons when it was broken and unpredictable. But even he found the sudden shift in physical surroundings jarring.

The sigh from Joel, who no doubt believed it was too soft for anyone to detect, told Po the Tamagotchi felt the same way.

Once in the park, Po became confused within a few turns. Po wasn't familiar with the park in The Living World, but here it was expansive and elaborate in its layout.

The Dodger sped past an artificial pond. Idled model boats bobbed listlessly within its concrete confines. The only person in sight was a thin teenaged boy who sat on the edge of the wall, his back to the boats. He didn't notice the Dodger and Po as they passed. He was completely engrossed in whatever he was doing with his smartphone. His thumbs danced as he stared deeply into the small screen, unblinking.

On the far side of the pond, they pulled up to a paved clearing with shallow steps leading up to a large statue. The Dodger hopped off the bike, opened one of his panniers, and began digging in it while Po dismounted. He intended to steer clear of the diaphanous kites, but they got out of his way of their own volition.

The statue featured a young girl sitting on a large mushroom flanked by a small man in a large top hat, a rabbit, and other figures. One of the various inscriptions on the work identified it as a memorial to a man's wife who'd loved all children. Po kept his distance in order to give the dead their due, but he was close enough to study its details.

Alice was the girl on the mushroom. The man in the hat reminded Po of someone he'd crossed paths with in The Commons, but he couldn't quite say who. Po did not get a good feeling from the man in the hat.

*They told me you had been to her, and mentioned me to him*, read one of the inscriptions on the ground around the statue. *She gave me a good character, but said I could not swim.*

"I don't get it," said Joel.

Po didn't, either, but he assumed this was yet another place with a foot in each world, which meant it commanded respect. To dishonor it would be disgraceful even without repercussions, and those were known to happen.

The Dodger removed what at first looked like a flat, shiny bag from his pannier. It was attached to a ribbon insubstantial as a spider's web. He waved it around, and the bag expanded into a balloon that strained its near-nothing thread as it tried to flee skyward. The balloon and its anchor line flashed in the daylight, and Po thought he saw an eye on its surface look right at him. But with another tug on its line from the Dodger, it was just a plain silvery balloon again, shifting colors and hues as it bobbed to-and-fro despite the lack of a breeze.

"It's a lookout." The Dodger gently grasped one of the Alice statue's fingers as if it were that of a real child and attached the unseen thread to it. The balloon shot upward until it reached the end of its tether, which allowed it to gain an impressive degree of altitude. "This statue attracts a lot of Marginals who might go into charge state around it. If that happens, we want to know so we can grab them and take them to a place of safety."

"What happens if you don't get to them first?" Joel asked.

Po had been wondering the same thing.

"Manitou." The Dodger's tone was flat. He was in no mood to elaborate.

They watched the balloon float for a while. When the Dodger seemed satisfied it wouldn't break away, they got on the bike again.

They made a loop around the southern end of the park, stopping to leave lookout balloons at various sites deemed to be attractions for Marginals pulled from The Living World who were in danger of going into charge state. They passed several people, most of them young, all of them absorbed in their phones.

Po wanted to ask the Dodger for his thoughts on the phone people but worried that they, too, weren't a suitable topic for discussion. He also wanted to check in on the anxious leopard Guardian at the castle to see if he was doing all right. However, he didn't want to pressure the Dodger into varying his route or leaving some duty unfinished because of a whim of Po's.

At Bethesda Terrace, the Dodger was even more deferential to the angel statue in the fountain than he had been to Alice. Po understood. Statues had a power of their own, and this one in particular commanded reverence. The Dodger gave the angel a slight bow. Then he attached the balloon thread to one of the large posts by the lake on the fountain's far side.

They continued their tour of the lower park, attaching lookout balloons to many of the statues and monuments, including Beethoven, Shakespeare, and a dog named Balto. Along the way, Po noticed, the Essence catchers attached to the back of the Dodger's bike grew more substantial and easier to see, and the panniers on either side of the bike grew fatter, bulging with the ambient Essence gathered.

It was a relaxing tour of the park, overall. Even Joel stayed quiet, enjoying the scenery as much as he was able to enjoy anything.

The only thing that threatened to spoil the feel of the day were the many people who did nothing but stare at their phones as the Dodger pedaled past.

"Dombies," the Dodger said.

"Come again?" said Joel.

"Digital zombies. One of Manitou's tactics. People become lost in their little screens. Once the devices have them, they're like batteries for Callibeau and Company. They're still alive, but their Essence can be tapped and diverted whenever it's needed, which means Manitou doesn't have to bother running around trying to collect ambient Essence the way we do. It's there when they want it."

Po watched a young girl on a bench. She looked fixedly into her phone, her thumbs motionless, not interacting in any way. The phone and Manitou had her now.

"Brutal," said Joel.

"Yup," the Dodger agreed. "And we can't do much for them unless they go into charge state. Before then, we're not allowed to grab them because they might still snap out of it on their own. That's the thinking, anyway. In reality, they never do."

The entranced girl shrank in the distance as the Dodger pedaled away. The idea that they couldn't do anything for her until things got worse, until she was much more vulnerable, was simply painful.

There'd been nothing to do to save Mira, the little Dharma girl, either. But Po had come upon her when it was already too late. Here were people who looked like they could be pulled back from the edge. Only they couldn't be helped.

"I know," the Dodger said, as if picking up on Po's thoughts.

"Don't hate me for asking, but has anyone ever considered hijacking those gadgets and putting those people under the good guys' control?" said Joel.

Po signed.

"Of course it doesn't," Joel told Po. "But in extreme cases?"

"Sorry, I missed that," said the Dodger. "I don't understand sign."

"He told me the end never justifies the means. And I know he's right. But."

"If it makes you feel any better, that idea gets brought up a lot," said the Dodger. "And Audra's with you. She drums it into us—when your standards drop, you're losing."

Po wasn't sure Joel was convinced, but the Tamagotchi let the matter drop.

They left the park briefly to attach a lookout balloon to the statue of General Sherman, made their way back in, and headed north. Po decided to enjoy the ride as much as he could despite spotting more dombies along the way. The weather had improved, and the day was gorgeous. Birdsong helped propel them on their way.

It was a skill Ken had taught Po amid the ever-shifting

mood and landscape of The Commons: most days were a shades-of-gray affair, so the trick was to focus on the shades that carried with them the most comfort and the least despair. It wasn't a high standard to set, but it was a standard all the same.

Po's mood lasted until they'd crossed into the zoo area and stopped to leave a lookout at the Delacorte Clock, which had animal figures sure to draw Marginals, according to the Dodger. He was enjoying the moment when the clock struck the hour and began to play "Three Blind Mice."

Immediately something in the air around them changed.

Threat.

Mockery.

It blew into their immediate surroundings with the song.

As the Dodger finished waving the balloon, and it began to float on its own, he caught Po's eye.

Three blind mice.

A trio of them on the bike.

It wasn't subtle.

When the clock finished, the birds' songs took on more urgency, as if they were delivering a warning. Po wasn't one to let imagination carry him away; the singing sounded like true foreboding.

"Boss," said Joel.

He needn't have. Po spotted the same thing the Tamagotchi had.

Through the arch of the area underneath the clock, a flattened black glove and empty black sleeve were visible, as if someone had laid out an empty uniform to suggest a prone figure had been spirited away. It was the perfect spot for an ambush, and someone wanted it to look like one had been laid here. Or maybe more than just look like.

"Familiar, isn't it?" the Dodger said. He'd noticed it, too.

Po nodded his agreement. He signaled the Dodger to keep talking and then leapt into the space, crossing the threshold too quickly for anyone waiting behind one of the other pillars to waylay him.

Empty uniforms covered the stone floor, as if their inhabitants had been waiting and sucked out of their clothes without warning. Dropped rifles and holstered pistols were scattered amongst them, pointing at odd angles where they'd fallen. If there'd been a fight here, it had been a decidedly one-sided one.

"Do you get the feeling the ambushers were ambushed?" Joel said.

Po did.

The Dodger joined Po underneath the arches. The way he regarded the guns, empty uniforms, and boots, it appeared the idea was valid to him, too. "You don't think they were waiting for us, do you? I try to vary my route, but when the lookouts expire, I do have to come back to the same statues and put new ones up. If somebody's patient, they'll catch me here at some point. And the Ravagers don't have much else to do."

Po didn't answer, mulling that over in the silence.

The silence.

The birds had stopped singing.

A high-pitched whine, approaching quickly, grew in volume as it dropped in pitch.

"Incoming," said Joel.

Po turned toward the sound, then reached out and grabbed a handful of the Dodger's jacket, pulling the cyclist to the right just in time for a fast-moving black ball to find only air where the base of his skull had been a moment before. The flying object executed a tight loop and came back at them as Po stepped into its path.

Joel started to warn Po of the foolishness of what he was

about to do, even though he'd seen him pull it off before. The whining ball, which had picked up speed, closed the gap between itself and Po in a fraction of a second.

Po waited until it was close enough for him to make out the barbed point on the front of it. Just when it was about to pierce his forehead, he dropped backward into a bicycle kick and smacked it upward.

The deadly little ball's whine hit a higher note, as if voicing its annoyance, and the projectile was redirected up into the stone of the clock's archway. Steel hit rock, and it dropped onto the pavement right behind them as Po rocked forward off his elbow and jumped to his feet again, turning to face it.

The damaged ball buzzed angrily and whirred in a circle on the ground.

The Dodger stomped it under his heel several times until it was silent and still. "Mosquito," he said. "We're leaving. Now."

He ran to the bike, and Po followed, hopping onto the seat behind the cyclist and flipping Joel around to hang on his back so that the Tamagotchi could keep an eye out to the rear. The Dodger stood on the pedals, and they were off just as fast as he could get them going, which was nothing short of inspiring. "Those aren't solitary devices," the Dodger said as he got them up to speed. "They travel in packs." With that, he put all of his effort into pedaling rather than talking, his expression grim.

The Dodger went full out—far faster than when he'd taken them into Manhattan or made his rounds. There was a warrior's resolve to his effort, the focus on survival rather than victory. It was clarifying, a distillation of one's strength into one objective: live through this.

The stone-tiled path was a blur as they wove between the

dombies—mostly young men or women who didn't bother to look up from their phones or tablets, even as they were buzzed close enough for the edge of Po's robe to brush them. When they cut particularly close to one woman, she half-heartedly raised her hand as if to fend off an attack, then let the hand drop again. She couldn't be bothered to defend herself.

The Dodger made a right down a footpath, headed for Fifth Avenue. He was forced to slow to make the turn, and with that drop in speed came the approaching whine of another attack.

"Incoming, boss," said Joel. "Over your left shoulder, high to low. Fast."

As the pitch of the approaching mosquito dropped, a dombie stepped into the path in front of the Dodger—a middle-aged man holding his screen only inches from his face. The Dodger accelerated. Disaster was only a second away for the cyclist, his passengers, and the dombie pedestrian.

The Dodger didn't slow.

## 11

## THE MANHATTAN PROJECT

Paul believed they weren't lost. He believed in Porter. Because he needed to. There was something about the routine they established—pausing at an intersection in the corn and waiting while Porter closed his eyes and concentrated long enough to choose a direction—that weighed Paul down with memories to the point where it was a supreme challenge to lift his feet and walk on.

Maybe it was the corn maze that did it. Maybe not.

Snapshots of experience came back to Paul in a random fashion, with large blocks of his memories of The Commons making their way back into his consciousness like prodigal sons. Some fit neatly with those that had already taken hold. Others were free-floating until they found their place in the chronology of what had happened to Paul and his Journey cohort.

Rain's shotgun echoing off the tile of a rest-stop bathroom.
The van blossoming into fire.
Paul and Rain walking in silence, joined in the dark.
Betrayal.

The difficulty of forgiveness.

Was Rain going through the same somewhere? Where was she, and was she all right?

Each step brought with it another visual, sound, or feeling from a past locked away during his time back in The Living World. And each moment's return made the next step more difficult, burdened by the threat of something terrible that was yet to be revealed.

Yet Paul walked on.

He'd defeated Brill.

He'd done these things.

They were his, and he would shoulder them one by one as they returned.

At another juncture, Porter reached out to grasp Paul's shoulder.

At first, Paul thought he was doing so to indicate their next move.

Porter hadn't uttered a sound since they'd entered the maze, and he was tense.

There was something on the other side of the walls. Or something ahead. Or behind. Or keeping pace with them on a parallel path.

When Porter didn't let go, Paul understood that the Envoy was leaning on him for support while he held his staff out to sample the space ahead. It was the first time he'd shown any sign of tiring.

Paul pretended not to notice. If Porter needed help, he'd say so.

Maybe.

They followed another path that looked just like every other path they'd walked. For all Paul knew, they were going over the same ground. He couldn't tell how long they'd been out here, but what had begun as the bright, new blue of morning now angled in as the just-beginning-to-wane rays of late afternoon.

Assuming time meant anything.

Porter removed his hand from Paul's shoulder, planted his staff on the turf in front of them and leaned on it. He closed his eyes once more, frowned, opened them again, and headed rapidly down the path to the left.

Paul followed, surprised at Porter's newfound energy.

A long corridor of corn lay before them. With a door at its distant end.

As Paul caught up to him, Porter made no attempt to conceal his relief. "One down. A significant one."

"Was there something waiting for us in that maze?"

"Not in it. It."

Paul walked along for a moment or two, his pride insisting he try to figure out what the gray man meant without asking. But if his experiences and the returning flow of memories taught him anything, it was that pride was meant to be overruled. "It?"

"The maze itself is the threat. One of the keys to making it through to the other side is understanding that the danger comes from the entity that encompasses it, not from anything inside it. It's not the only key to passing through, but it's important."

"What were you doing when you closed your eyes that wore you out so much?"

"An old trick I haven't been foolish enough to try for a long time." He slowed to examine the corn they passed now, pulling back the husk from an ear with silk protruding from it that was blood red rather than the pale yellow of the plants they'd been passing the entire time.

It felt like a bad omen to Paul.

*The Catalyst*

"When I was young and dumb, I experimented with jumping enough of my own consciousness around corners to get an idea of what was ahead." Porter began walking again. "I learned enough to know how risky a proposition it was."

Paul followed. "So why do it now?"

"Because you don't get a second chance when you walk the rows. The wrong choice gives you over to the maze. So I took a chance. That's the beauty of experience: if you've been paying attention, you know when the dumb option is smarter than the alternative."

"What if it had gone wrong?"

Porter's reply was unsettling in its nonchalance. "I wouldn't have made it back to my own head. I'd have been separated from myself, and you would have been left trying to revive an empty husk—pun intended."

When Paul continued in silence, Porter clapped him on the back with genuine affection. "You would've thought of something."

They neared the end of the long corn corridor. Set into a solid wall of corn blocking the way was a plain wooden door adorned only by a small window of frosted glass and a tarnished knob.

The grasshopper that had greeted them at the ladder leading up to the maze had friends here. Dozens. They hop-flew across the path at eye level, often heading straight for Paul's and Porter's faces before veering off.

Porter didn't bother to fend the bugs off, so Paul didn't, either. Mostly because he worried that Porter didn't see them, and he didn't want the Envoy thinking he was swatting at empty air.

They reached the door.

Porter put a hand out to stop Paul from getting close to it. "Are you familiar with Edward Teller?"

"The magician?"

Porter narrowed his eyes at the door, as if trying to see through it. "The physicist. A member of the Manhattan Project. He helped develop the first nuclear weapon." He glanced at Paul to see if he was following, and Paul was grateful that the Envoy didn't admonish him for not knowing the details of a history he'd only been exposed to sporadically, thanks to a childhood spent bouncing from school to school. "When he was working on the atomic bomb with Oppenheimer, Teller raised the possibility that a nuclear reaction, once started, would kick off an uncontrollable chain of subsequent reactions." He took a step closer to the door, leaning in a little to take a better look at it, careful not to get too close. "That wasn't a danger, as it turned out, but it was no crazy notion, either—particularly when we're talking Essence instead of standard matter and atoms."

The Envoy motioned for Paul to back up a few steps. Then he slowly reached for the knob, withdrew before touching it, and tapped it with his staff instead. He jumped back as he did so.

The doorknob burst wetly in a spray of blood, skin, and hair. Paul thought he saw human teeth fall to the ground, but there wasn't much time to confirm. With a bestial cry of pain, the door melted into a large flow of ichor and tissue that soaked into the ground and disappeared with a hissing splat, leaving only the wall of corn. Then an identical door appeared in the corn wall to their right.

Paul's stomach somersaulted, then cartwheeled.

Porter offered a satisfied grin.

"Are we worried that Essence might never stop exploding once it starts?" Paul needed to say something, and asking about what would have happened had Porter touched the horrific living door might've sent his gut into full-on evacuation.

"Not at all." The gray man gripped the knob on the new door and pulled it open as if everything had been normal all along. "In fact, I'm counting on it."

## 12

## A PASSING FAMILIARITY

They told Annie the truth about the pain. That only made it hurt more.

They explained she'd been tricked into accepting a life with Bobby again, which she never would've considered on her own, because of the injections into her knee port. That what they needed to do would hurt like hell. That the pain would most likely accelerate the process of returning memories, which started when she stopped taking the shots Bobby and Manitou insisted on.

Annie was as grateful to them for being square with her as she was ashamed of the sad truth her returning memories told her: she'd been taken in by the pinkies back in The Commons. Then she'd been taken in by Bobby's injections.

The withdrawal from those shots caused a fail-safe effect that nearly made her betray her own son to the Ravagers at the Wine Bunker. They told her that only her love for Zach allowed her to resist. Annie didn't see it that way. She blamed herself for putting him in danger—and for what she'd thought about him while doing so. But at least that was a source of torment she understood.

What she hadn't been prepared for was what they needed to do to fix her knee. They wouldn't tell her what was in there. They said she'd just have to trust them.

She did, but only because Zach seemed to know Rain, the girl with the shotgun. Annie thought she was, at most, familiar in the same way someone looks like someone you sort of recall from long before.

What constituted a good guy wasn't clear under the current circumstances. Hell, was it ever? But the girl seemed like something close, and she and the train crew had pulled Annie and Zach out of a real jam. They claimed to know her and her son. So Annie threw her lot in with them.

Had Zach not approved of them, she wouldn't have. And had she known what was coming, she might've had second thoughts anyway.

Nevertheless, she accepted their version of things—that they wouldn't tell her what was in her knee because she might not believe them, that they needed to draw part of it out, add something of theirs to it, and put it back in.

That it was going to hurt.

A lot.

And she needed to be awake for it, though they wouldn't tell her why.

When she started screaming, she thought she was back on the table, next to Charlene.

When it went on and on and on, she prayed they'd succeeded in getting Zach out of earshot because she didn't want him to feel responsible for what was happening to her.

By the time it ended, those thoughts were long gone. There was only room for the hurting.

After that, they gave Annie a shot.

Someone was always giving her shots.

∽

"It's a bocanna." The young man who called himself Aidan sat with Zach, across from Annie, in a train-station market cafe he wouldn't tell her the name of. They each had a drink in front of them, though she had no memory of ordering anything. She assumed he just didn't want her to know the cafe's name, though he claimed it didn't have one. Annie didn't know why she couldn't believe him on that point when she accepted that he knew what was in her knee and believed him when he said he wasn't her friend but was on her side.

Did that make any less sense than her trusting the strangers who'd put her through a world of pain before she woke up here at a table with Zach and a bespectacled, skinny twenty-something who most definitely was not what he pretended to be?

"What's a bocanna?"

"You don't want to know."

Behind Aidan, patrons browsed a nearby produce stand. One young man concentrated to an almost comical degree on a tomato he'd picked up, as if he knew that what he had in his hand was only pretending to be fresh produce.

"Sure, I do."

"No. You do not." Aidan wasn't accustomed to being questioned. He had a disarming way of looking deeply into her without blinking until, it seemed, he remembered that he was supposed to because the person he was pretending to be would have. But the blink was like checking a box. Annie couldn't help but question whether his eyes were even real. The flashing blue light on his earpiece wasn't any more convincing. It, too, appeared to be something he regarded as part of the costume. Nevertheless, he was definitely someone to be reckoned with.

"Can you tell me what it does?"

"Yes." He passed several long moments without saying anything more. He'd answered her question. Annie was about to ask him to elaborate when he caught on. "It's a spy of sorts, but worse. It also regulates memory, thought, and action."

"Thought and action?"

"It controls what you think and do."

Behind Aidan, a young woman set her day's shopping down to enter a phone booth and put the receiver to her ear. She was about to drop a coin into the slot but stopped, listening with a look of surprise on her face. Her brow furrowed, echoing Annie's own current feeling. Someone was already on the line. Someone was already talking to the woman.

"Did it make me come here?" Annie glanced at Zach, who directed his own unwavering stare at her. It was what he did when, she suspected, he was afraid that he had to take as much of her in as he could because he might never lay eyes on her again.

"No. If you'd continued with your injections as directed, it would've prevented that."

Bobby.

Directed by Bobby and Manitou. To stay put.

The pain had been worth it.

The expression of the woman listening to whoever was on the other end of the line slowly went from perplexed, to shocked, to horrified. She abruptly hung up and wiped her hand on her coat, as if that might rid her of the undesirable. She started to leave, remembered her shopping bags, picked them up, and hurried away.

Why were Zach and Aidan on the other side of the table? Why wasn't her son on her side?

"What did they do to me?"

"They told you the truth." Aidan understood that Annie meant the people on the train, not Bobby or Manitou. "They had to withdraw part of the bocanna in order to insert something of their own into it. That was the only way they could then put the resulting combination back into your knee without the bocanna or those to whom it answers understanding what they'd done. That was why it was necessary to make you experience the pain without dulling it at all."

"Painkillers would've made someone suspicious."

Aidan nodded.

"Can I trust them?"

He nodded again. "That trust is not to be questioned."

"Whose trust should be questioned?"

"Yours."

A paunchy older man stopped to look at the phone booth. He then thought better of crossing the threshold into it and walked away briskly.

"Mine? I can't be trusted?"

"If you agree to what I ask of you? No."

Annie sat back and looked the young man over again. She wasn't sure she wanted to know what he would ask of her. Had he already asked it of Zach?

It became clear to her why Zach was on Aidan's side of the table—but not why her mug was filled with a dark brown liquid of some sort when Aidan's and Zach's were empty.

"You don't have to drink yours." Aidan's gaze was unwavering. "In fact, you shouldn't."

## 13

## ROOFTOP LIGHTS WHIRLING BLUE

Po waited until the whine of the attacking mosquito was just behind his ear and ducked sideways. It shrieked past, missed the Dodger by a hair, and struck the dombie in their path in the eye, knocking him out of their way as it disappeared into his skull.

The Dodger picked up speed when they passed through an opening in the park wall, crossed the sidewalk, and went low-level airborne off the curb and onto the avenue.

Po looked back over his shoulder. The wall obscured any view of the downed dombie.

"You didn't do it on purpose," Joel said as the Dodger juked and took them east on Sixty-Sixth Street. "He planted himself there and didn't pay attention."

A block passed under their wheels before the Dodger allowed himself to divert enough energy to speak. "If I'd hit him, it would've been the same result for the dombie, and we would've been added to the list of casualties in short order. It hurts. It's bad. But I'd rather have to report one soul down than have another Petrel report all of us lost. That's the truth of it, hard as it is."

With that, the Dodger picked up speed again. His demeanor and behavior said what he didn't need to say aloud. They'd made it out of the park by the luck of the angle, and they were a far cry from escaping back to their island.

Proof of that appeared as they raced across Park Avenue and under a dead traffic light. Coming up the avenue from the south at full tilt were three black SUVs.

The Dodger continued at speed, and Po turned around to look. The trucks all fishtailed in order to make the hard right and pursue them.

Even worse were the multiple specks in the distance behind them. More mosquitos.

"Oh, joy," said Joel.

The Essence gatherers bobbed in the air as they trailed behind and above the bike, frivolous dancers in the face of the oncoming pursuit.

"You think we should pull those things in?" Joel said. "We don't need any drag right now. Am I right?"

The Dodger didn't answer. But as the three mosquitos approached, eating up the distance with worrying ease, the gatherers ceased their bouncing and arrayed themselves in a wide protective pattern.

When the pursuing mosquitos were nearly upon them, a growing hiss issued from the trailing gatherers, followed by a mini-sonic boom of an eruption. The air warped and blurred behind them, and the mosquitos ran headlong into the wave, dropping to the street dead or paralyzed.

Only then did the gatherers reel themselves in to disappear into the panniers. The bike picked up a bit of speed.

"We're not without our defenses," the Dodger said. "That one is affectionately known as the crop duster. Primitive, but effective."

"Great," said Joel. "Got any more?"

Po looked back over his shoulder. The three SUVs were in hot pursuit—sirens blaring, rooftop lights whirling blue. And with The Margins version of New York's emptiness, there were no parked cars on the street. So the SUVs had room to come two abreast, with the third one close behind.

"I'm guessing these cops aren't exactly on the side of the law," said Joel.

"Whose law?" Given how hard and fast he'd been pedaling, it was remarkable that the Dodger still had breath to speak.

Po, admittedly, was not easy to impress when it came to strength and endurance. He'd known and fought some of the best in that regard.

"How's that?" said Joel.

"It's the way with villains everywhere. Callibeau makes his own law. The Manitou law. And then he follows it. As far as he's concerned, that puts him in the right. Bad guys never think they're bad."

Bad or good, the Ravagers—for that was what Po knew they were, despite their driving police rather than military or militia-type vehicles—were gaining on them.

"Po, could you check the top of either pannier and feel around for a hose nozzle?" said the Dodger. "You won't see it. Find it by touch, deploy it, and get ready to use it, please."

Po turned until he was facing backwards and brought Joel around to his chest so that the Tamagotchi could see what was happening. Then he probed the bulging bag of Essence with his fingers and grabbed a metal cylinder. He pulled the nozzle, and the hose came with it. As was the case with so many things Essence-based, especially in the Margins, he could hardly see it when he looked directly at it. But when he looked up at another dead traffic light passing overhead as they crossed Lexington, he could make out the antique brass from the corner of his eye.

"You're going to turn the nozzle two clicks clockwise. It's going to want to extend. Don't let it until I say so."

The Dodger veered as the SUVs closed in, the one roaring down the north side of the street pulling ahead to the point where its front wheel was even with the other leading SUV's front bumper.

Both were eating up the gap.

Quickly.

Within moments, the two leading SUVs were close enough for Po to have read the make of the vehicles—had the SUVs been made by the hands or factories of humans.

"Sit tight. You're gonna let the nozzle extend. It's going to get hot, so try not to burn yourself. Ready?"

The SUVs pulled within three feet of them as Po turned the nozzle and worked to aim it without losing his seat or throwing the balance of the bike off. The last thing they needed was for his shifting weight to send them into a curb.

Closer.

"Again, it's gonna get hot," said the Dodger. "And don't let it pull you off the bike."

"Any other requirements?" said Joel. "I mean, this sounds like child's play so far." The Tamagotchi's sarcasm was at its strongest when he got nervous—which was almost a steady state for Joel.

"Not yet."

The lead SUV pulled closer.

Closer still.

Po was glad for the SUVs' heavily tinted windshields. In situations such as this, if he'd been able to see his opponents, his temper might have gotten the best of him, and he would've been on the lead vehicle's hood already, looking to smash his way in.

"Not yet."

The lead SUV was nearly upon them.

"Look—" Joel began.

"Now."

Po shifted his grip to just behind the hose's nozzle and let it do what it wanted. The nozzle thunked forward, lengthening itself against the hose. Another mini-sonic boom—a louder one this time—blew in the grill of the approaching lead SUV and spiderwebbed its windshield.

Both of the SUV's front tires ruptured, and the truck went sideways, smacking into the other SUV just beside and a little behind it. The two vehicles snarled and melded into a V-shaped wreck that screeched, steel on steel on pavement, as the lead SUV rolled with the weight of the second.

Now came the squeal of brakes as the following vehicle tried to slow in time. It plowed into its unfortunate brethren, sending the runner-up over the sidewalk and into the windows of an apartment building in a cascade of bricks and glass.

The first two went up onto the north sidewalk at the corner of Third Avenue.

Two more dombies narrowly missed being flattened into cloth and meat as the sirens continued in a painful moan, their chariots upended. Neither dombie bothered to so much as look up.

"Yes!" Joel exulted.

His celebration was short-lived.

They continued east, and another black SUV, lights glaring and siren in full-throated outrage, made a hard cutoff of Third to take up the pursuit before two motorcycles—a black-clad, helmeted Ravager on each—overtook it on either side.

Now they had three more pursuing vehicles.

As they crossed Second, two fast-moving mosquitos headed their way, too.

It was a flat-out race for survival now, and theirs depended on the Dodger's strength. That strength was pushed to its limits trying to beat the internal-combustion engine of a Ravager SUV and whatever powered the mosquitos.

The little drones were coming up on them fast, one just ahead of the other.

Po had yet to see what kind of weaponry they boasted, and he didn't want to.

The Essence hose was not very accurate. It threw the Dodger's balance off when Po cut loose with it and was less and less effective as the mosquitos learned to evade its blasts.

The hose and the Dodger's speed were all they had. And that would have to do if they were going to make it to the tunnel entrance before they were overtaken.

"Lars," said Joel.

"No." The Dodger meant it. He was a pro, and he knew the stakes. Talking would only cost him. All he could do was his best.

And would that be enough?

That was anyone's guess.

## 14

## CRITICAL AND FUZZY AS HELL

"I ask for your trust," said the View-Master for the umpteenth time. "Given wisely, there is nothing stronger. Those who work against us don't possess it. They cannot. Handed over foolishly, it's our deepest flaw. I ask you to grant me your strength."

"Again," said Charlene.

"I ask for your trust."

"Again."

"I ask for your trust. Given wisely—"

"Stop." Charlene studied the View-Master as if Audra resided within it and wasn't just using the device to relay her message. Charlene almost wished for a tiny version of the veteran Envoy, long thought to be dead, so that there could be no doubt as to the request's provenance.

"That you keep repeating it is all the answer you need," said D.W. "We don't know that it's real. Nothing else is getting in here. So how did that?" He simmered just beneath the surface when he spoke. His ICBMs had been hijacked. He was able to focus on nothing else.

Nicolette was no happier.

There was a bright side to having some mysterious force preventing any communication from leaving the building. The Dharmas weren't able to let Liam or anyone back at Ranger HQ know that their missiles had been taken from them. So there wouldn't be any off-the-cuff, angry plots hatched to try and take them back. That was a relief; there were already enough variables in play.

"These devices operate on different principles than normal networks," Charlene told D.W.

"That doesn't mean it's from Audra," Reinhard said.

True. But Charlene didn't want to admit that aloud.

"It's from your colleague," Quarry confirmed from his box prison on the table.

"Nobody asked you, Rocky," said Reinhard.

"Why do you say that, Quarry?" Charlene had to maintain some level of civility. She feared that if she allowed the tide to turn, the former Vigil and the Dharmas might band together for a good old-fashioned mutiny and use whatever Reinhard had in his pocket to destroy the head of inhabited stone. She had no doubt Reinhard was capable of it, and Quarry was trapped in the box and couldn't escape.

"The connections are distant—nonexistent, almost—but they're enough for me to confirm," Quarry said.

There was silence as everyone in the room digested that. And for now, silence was a friend.

"Isn't she dead?" said Nicolette.

"We're all dead," D.W. snapped.

"You know what I mean."

"Let's review," said June Medill after it was clear that no one else had anything to add.

Charlene didn't want to antagonize them by playing Audra's message again. And she was pleasantly surprised that the Dharmas and Reinhard allowed June to remain in the room without complaint, given her former service to Brill in The Commons. It might mean that Charlene's command of the group wasn't in jeopardy. It also might mean they all understood Brill had conscripted June against her will.

Charlene had no way of knowing at the moment. For the time being, so long as her orders were obeyed, the reasons for the respect and obedience didn't matter so much. There was probably no better sign of how much the situation had become both critical and fuzzy as hell.

June left her station by the door. She never took a seat at the meeting table, preferring to hover and absorb every detail of what was discussed. She pulled a small stack of index cards from a folder and laid them across the table in front of her, taking care not to get too close to Quarry in his box.

Charlene understood. Having been forced into believing the office job under Brill was her normal existence was traumatic enough; June had endured that plus being sewn up into one of Brill's warehouse cocoons. That she was even functional was a tribute to the woman's constitution.

"My assessment of the situation—" June's voice was much softer than usual. She looked around at the others in the room: Reinhard, Nicolette, D.W., Charlene, and the sentient pile of rocks that served as Quarry. She checked her cards again, though Charlene suspected she knew very well what was on them. She was gathering herself to speak with authority. And considering that the last time this level of conflict existed, June was working for the opposing side, her trepidation over facing this group was understandable.

"June." Charlene waited for June to meet her eye. "It's all right."

And it was. Charlene, too, had toiled for Brill without knowing who she was working for. She'd made that point to June many a time.

June nodded—as much to herself as to Charlene. "We were attacked by an expeditionary force of Ravager armor representing forces unknown, and HQ defenses sealed us off externally. All communications with the outside, save for Charlene's device, and all digital observation capabilities were severed. To date, some of our observation capabilities have been restored." Her tone was more confident and grew more so as she warmed up. "At the same time, we were also assailed by a small force of mythicals who breached the building's defenses via means unknown, causing facility defenses to activate, sealing us off internally within the building. Subsequent reconnaissance revealed . . ." She stopped for a moment, emotion seeping into her voice.

"We know what happened, June." Reinhard's tone was uncharacteristically gentle. "You can skip this part if you need to."

June nodded again. "Subsequent reconnaissance revealed what we suspect to be deep staff and future Journeymen casualties due to aforementioned mythical attacks and, potentially, other acts still unknown. After a communication foray by one of the mythicals, the stone elemental Quarry, external Dharma Ranger forces arrived and neutralized the Ravager armor. At the same time, all of the attacking mythicals have themselves exited or are otherwise unaccounted for, save for the fire elemental known as Flameout and the aforementioned Quarry, who has returned from his successful mission to seek help. Our sole communication from Envoy Command is someone who claims to be Audra Farrelly. She reports that there is a plan being carried out by a hostile entity who has not been named and that a corresponding Envoy countermeasure has been developed, the details of which cannot be revealed for security purposes."

"And why they don't trust us is mystifying, to say the least," said D.W. "We're just here to mop up, I suppose. We don't need to know anything."

Charlene let that slide. The Dharmas' frustration was justified.

"The unknown plan is assumed to be focused on the intercontinental ballistic missiles in the silos of the base overseen by the Dharma Rangers. Control of the weapons appears to have been usurped by an outside entity, also unknown, but we assume it to be Ravagers, Ravager-related, or whoever is commanding the Ravagers and the attacking mythicals. What's been shared with us as far as the details of our involvement—or desired involvement—is to remain in place, and don't interfere. Nothing is to be done apart from defending ourselves. Nothing." The final words rang with a frustration that left no doubt as to how June felt about being sidelined. She gathered her cards, tapped the stack on the table to square them up, and looked around the room.

"Thank you, June," Charlene said before anyone could respond with skepticism or sarcasm. "So where does that leave us?"

No one answered, but Charlene knew what they were thinking.

The Dharmas wanted to leave a holding force behind and return to their own facility to see about liberating their ICBMs. Sitting around wasn't their style.

Nor was it Reinhard's. But at least he could occupy his time by getting his own personal arsenal together for whatever was coming. He was only too happy to return to Vigil mode, which was his true comfort zone, when necessary.

But as the silence stretched on, with no one looking anyone else in the eye, it started to get on Charlene's nerves. Assuming the communication was from Audra, and assuming all of it was authentic, Charlene and the Envoys were officially benched.

She needed to hear someone's scheme to sidestep the requirements or bend the rules to the breaking point. She needed to know the people in the room still had that in them.

"They weren't all killed."

"Who do you mean, Quarry?" said Charlene.

"Those waiting to go on their Journeys. Your fellow Envoys and staff. Those who've disappeared from here. They weren't all killed by Flameout."

"And you know that how, Rocky?" said Reinhard.

"Because I know what happened to them. The realms have crossed over. They've gone Marginal."

Reinhard hissed in disbelief. "Now why would we listen to one word you have to say about that? I still don't believe you've jumped over to our side."

"Because that's where my fellow mythicals have gone, too. And not all of them survived the transition to The Margins. Those responsible for our orders knew that would happen." Quarry went silent for a moment, and despite the stone head's inability to form an expression, Charlene thought she saw hesitation cross the stony countenance. "They intended for that to happen to me as well. And I don't take kindly to betrayal."

"Well, we don't take kindly to being attacked," Reinhard said.

"And we don't take kindly to having our missiles stolen out from under us," D.W. added.

Charlene let all of that settle. "Why did you wait to tell us, Quarry?"

"Would you have believed me if I'd told you sooner? Trust is at a premium here, and I'm at a disadvantage. You'd have said I was lying to save myself."

Reinhard huffed. "We're saying that now."

Charlene ignored the former Vigil; the stone head had a point. "What do you propose, Quarry?" She felt more than saw Reinhard's surprise directed her way. "You're the only one who's been out and back again. I want to hear your take."

"I propose you take a risk," the rock man said. "I propose you free me to go out and scout. I assume those who sent me don't know I haven't gone Marginal along with my former teammates. I may be able to exploit that in order to discover more about their plans."

Charlene had to give the rest of her group credit. Though none of them trusted the elemental, they didn't give voice to their doubts. They merely looked to her for their cue.

She stood and went over to the box housing Quarry's assembled head, placed her hands on the top of the box and leaned in close. "Convince me. Why shouldn't I assume this is a trick after we tricked you?"

"You shouldn't. You've no reason to. But you should free me anyway."

"What do you intend to do?"

"I won't know until I get back out there. I want to see what kind of hold Foundry has on the ICBMs. I want to get an idea of what your colleagues may be planning so that we can prepare as best we can."

"And so that you can tell your buddies," D.W. said.

"You don't know that I won't," Quarry acknowledged.

Charlene looked down at the rock face, trying to draw out any sign that she should take Quarry at his word—or that she shouldn't.

No one else in the room said anything. They didn't have to. She knew they all hated the idea except for June, who would go with whatever Charlene decided. They assumed Quarry would betray them as soon as he was given the chance.

Gripping the back corners of the box, Charlene tipped it over, spilling the rocks to the floor below.

The stone reformed into a small version of Quarry—his whole body this time, not just a head. He looked around briefly, made a decision of his own, and collapsed into a small mound of rubble as the elemental fled into the floor.

Charlene looked around the room.

Reinhard and June, practiced pros, were ciphers, hiding their emotions entirely.

D.W. and Nicolette were somewhere between surprise and anger.

"I ask for your trust," Charlene said, regretting only that she couldn't give it the same gravitas as Audra Farrelly had. Then she began picking up the rocks and putting them back into the box.

Come what may, it never hurt to be tidy.

## 15

## KATY, BAR THE DOOR

Stacey Galena had an office.

Stacey Galena was at home in the Manitou corporate culture without trying.

Stacey Galena had the air of someone who'd rocket up through the ranks, leaving the likes of Jeremy behind, though they were currently at the same grade.

She'd gone to a much better school. There was nothing in her office to indicate that, but Jeremy had gone a little stalky in his desire to figure out who he'd be working with. He'd done enough online snooping to see that she'd gone to a place most people would brag about.

Jeremy wanted to hate Stacey Galena. She had everything going for her but didn't act like it, and that often made the blessed person even more worthy of a grudge. But she was actually nice. And smart. And generous in conversation.

She talked about herself but seemed more interested in hearing about him, which was rare in life and rarer still at Manitou. She wasn't digging for something to use against him, either. It was genuine interest.

Or seemed like it.

Jeremy held out the small possibility that Stacey could be a master villain with a talent for endearing herself to her intended victims, but he had a hard time believing it. Mostly because he didn't want to.

"It's called Katy, Bar the Door." Stacey was at her desk, reviewing the project notes she'd printed out. Jeremy was an all-digital guy who never put anything on paper and didn't understand those who did, but he let Stacey slide on that, too. Whatever helped you remember was fair. And she was the one pushing to go through the details when he would've been content with just being on time.

Which was probably part of why she had an office, albeit one so small that standing up from the guest chair to stretch meant he was looming over her.

"The project's called that?"

"Yes."

"Why?"

Stacey shrugged, reading on. Jeremy appreciated that she didn't feel the need to come up with an answer—any answer—when she didn't know something. Anyone else in the office would've pulled the fire alarm before they'd display such weakness. And she didn't consider it a big enough deal to express with words, which was yet another reason he couldn't hate her.

"We're just supposed to show up, correct?"

"Sorry?" She shuffled through her pages.

"To the site. We're just supposed to show up. That's all we know for now, right?"

"That's all they've told us."

"Right."

"So what I just said is not the same thing as what you just said, Johns."

Jeremy liked the fact that Stacey called him by his last

name, having moved right past the first and never even considering the hated Triple J. But that didn't mean he understood what she was getting at.

"They've told us virtually nothing," Stacey said. "So I did some searching based on contracts held by companies Manitou's invested in, client investments, and some of the side-ventures we've funded. Put that together with what we know about what we're being asked to do—that it has something to do with safeguarding gateways."

"It does?"

"It's called Katy, Bar the Door." Mercifully, she managed to repeat it without implying that Jeremy was an idiot.

Jeremy, counting himself among the craven who didn't want to admit ignorance, said nothing.

"I'm making some leaps here." Stacey chewed the safe end of a ballpoint that had already endured plenty of that treatment. She hadn't handwritten anything on her notes, so Jeremy assumed the pen was only there for gnawing purposes. Which he sometimes did himself, though he was willing to bet she never absentmindedly chomped on the business end like somebody he knew. Yet another point in her favor. "If you'll allow me to entertain some dart-throwing, I'll risk telling you that I have a couple good guesses as to where they're sending us."

"Ranked."

"Sorry?"

"You have a first and second choice or just a list?"

Stacey chewed her pen and looked her notes over.

Jeremy began to suspect she wasn't reading anything; she was deciding how much she could trust him.

"What makes you think we're both going to the same place?" she said.

The possibility that they wouldn't hadn't occurred to him. "I just assumed."

Stacey chewed and read some more. "Do you drink?"

～

ON THEIR WAY into Billy Clyde's, the Rubbish Gladiator passed them without so much as a glance.

Inside, Mallory Chiklis and the other patrons, both Marginal and regular—was there a difference anymore?—did the same. Even Porthos pretended they were nothing special until Stacey made the right noises. Then the little prince plopped himself down on the table in front of her and permitted her to scratch his belly.

Nobody got near that cat's stomach. Not unless you wanted to see if your detergent was as good with bloodstains as its ads claimed. Yet the razor-clawed bruiser opened himself up and handed his alley-scrapper cred right over.

It shouldn't have been the major reason Jeremy decided right then and there that she was definitely one of the good guys. But it was. That and the fact that she took to Billy Clyde's like a regular.

"How did I not know about this place?" Her fingers were up to the second knuckle in tummy fur.

The big cat opened one eye and peered at Jeremy, as if to say: *you will not do this to me. Ever.*

"It's that kind of bar," Jeremy said, nursing his beer. "You pass it over and over but don't go in until someone gives you a reason to. Then you're upset about all the time you wasted."

Stacey nodded and drank in modest proportions. She wasn't going heavy and trying to prove anything, and he agreed with that approach. This promising partnership was progressing faster than either of them probably would've liked, so it would be explored with relative sobriety. Her question about his drinking was meant to assess whether he did or not and, if so, what type of bar he liked.

He assumed he'd passed the test.

Porthos bared his throat completely as she scratched under his chin.

Jeremy wanted to be embarrassed for him but couldn't make it work. He'd have done the same thing in the big guy's position, though he wasn't supposed to think that way—and sincerely didn't want to.

He'd only allowed himself to notice that Stacey was pretty in a way that fit her—completely natural to the point where he genuinely couldn't say whether or not she knew it. But he put that aside. It wasn't part of a working relationship and wasn't fair to her.

Jeremy really didn't want to screw this partnership up. The most he dared to hope for was a work friend, which he needed.

"So, gateways," Stacey said. "Does that make you think of anything?"

"The tunnels. The Holland, the Lincoln. The bridges, too."

"I thought of that." Stacey worked behind Porthos's ears.

The tamed killer kicked one paw in rhythm, dog-like. Jeremy made a mental note to figure out how to mock him for that in a way the cat would understand.

"But the pieces don't add up in terms of the investments and clients I talked about before. No vendor or management contracts. Nothing like that." She scratched harder. "I kind of wanted it to be the Brooklyn. I thought there'd be some poetry to that. But no."

"Then what? The Verrazano? Manhattan? Tappan Zee?"

Stacey shook her head, took a sip, and held it in her mouth as if evaluating the beer on a professional level. One didn't want to start thinking about the quality of a Billy Clyde's pour. You'd never be back. She swallowed and delivered no verdict.

"The Midtown Tunnel?" Now Jeremy was just guessing.

"Shift context. A little less literal and a little more historical." When Jeremy offered nothing, she poured the last of the pitcher into their mugs, splitting the tiny amount. Then she drained hers and held the empty pitcher out to him, having bought the first. "Give me, your tired, your pour."

At the bar, Jeremy pretended Mallory wasn't there while she did the same for him.

He knew what Stacey was hinting at with her strained reference. Liberty Island wasn't a gateway. But it was close.

"Ellis Island," Jeremy said as he clunked the full pitcher down on the heavy wood of the table.

Porthos, too entranced with round two of the belly rubbing, didn't even flinch.

"Good. Now what's the other option?"

Jeremy didn't have another guess.

"Don't you know your New York history, Johns?"

Jeremy didn't. So he topped off both of their mugs.

"Castle Clinton. That was the entry point before Ellis."

Jeremy met her eye as she sat back to measure his response. He knew she was right. He didn't know how he knew, but she was. And for some reason, her sharing that information with him and his gut feeling about its accuracy meant something.

He didn't know what. But he wanted to find out all about his new partner. "How'd you get this job?" Funny, he'd thought he was going to ask her how she figured the two locations out.

Stacey tilted her head at him, questioning. She'd assumed he knew, which meant there was a story to be told.

"The old-fashioned way." She laughed when his face

betrayed the fear that she meant the *old-fashioned* old-fashioned way. "I'm connected."

Stacey didn't elaborate, and Jeremy didn't ask. If they made it through all this, maybe he would when they came out the other side.

## 16

## THE TINY FLAME TO DROP

The smell of gasoline kicked everything off. Audra would never be able to tolerate it again. Not since the morning the Ravagers and a handful of backup mythicals had confirmed the warning she'd been passed—they'd be coming for her.

Oh, did they.

But they didn't know she was waiting for them.

She'd liked that smell as a kid, actually enjoying the fumes whenever her father let her shadow him as he topped off his old tractor. Often, he himself wore the stink when he'd been working on the ancient International Harvester.

Fuel meant Dad. The land. Food they raised themselves.

It meant a trap Audra set when her old Zenith farm radio, the precursor to the Speaky Shrieky, let her know that the process working its way through the Envoy ranks had finally come around to her.

She'd been named and targeted. She'd also been warned to prepare herself for visitors, though she never discovered who sent that warning.

At the farm she called home, the place The Commons had

modeled almost exactly after where she'd grown up in Vermont—with some notable, weird variations—she'd formulated her plan. A greeting for her oppressors, a settling of accounts in the name of those they'd destroyed or spirited away.

It took days to haul jerry can after jerry can of fuel from the old gravity tank to the barn, where she soaked every hay bale in the loft and down below—enough to make her head threaten to float away afterward, when she sat and waited. She recalled small things from the day. A mockingbird doing a pitch-perfect imitation of a truck's back-up warning, over and over. The grind of the Ravager engines as the initial teams and their follow-ups invaded her property and, in short order, worked out where she was but wouldn't come inside. The moving shadows as they got into position. The silence of the Ravagers, who were incapable of speech. The grunted and clipped conversation of the mythicals they'd brought with them, though Audra never found out who they were. The cannon-report crack of the heavy length of wood used to bar the big barn door as it gave way beneath the assault.

Audra perched on a milking stool, of all things. There weren't cows or any other animals on the property, but that one stool had always been there, ready to support her as she bided her time before Ragnarök began.

She never saw them. She didn't need to. After they broke the door open, they weren't in a hurry, not knowing what might await them.

Anywhere was too close, but by then it was too late.

When the first crack of daylight appeared through the opening door, Audra focused on it, gathering her will.

She burned them all down.

There was something fitting about using a common wooden kitchen match pulled along the trusty striker strip of its cardboard box. Such a tiny flame to drop. Then the pent-up destruction of the gas-soaked hay was released as the world ignited around her, and she drove it out to greet them.

Audra's home was death—an open-air bomb set to devour those sent to claim her. The barn was the ignition, its horrific flame and heat at her disposal. She'd never before tried to command such a force.

In the end, she didn't need to.

Audra asked for a firestorm. Audra got one.

The Ravagers and mythicals who came for her had asked for it, too, though they hadn't known that.

The first blast of flame pushing out like a living force meant the barn was no more, that Audra was no more. She'd always been able to withstand the heat she generated and worked with, but she didn't even try once that door began to open. She was able to endure the burning far better than her attackers could, but she accepted that eventually it would spell her doom as well.

All Audra knew of the day was that she started what she'd meant to start, and after that it was all heat and conflagration, with details coming to her in the screams of the mythicals and, perhaps, those Ravagers who found their voices only as they were taken.

As she pushed further out across her property and into the woods surrounding the land The Commons had modeled after her family property, the trees added fuel, as did the gas from the Ravager trucks and the fuel and ammunition of the choppers they'd brought. It all went up.

The last thing about the day Audra could remember was the rush of air and an angry hiss as she took it all with her. She recalled wondering whose hoarse cries filled the space around her as everything became dreamlike. The cries turned to laughter when the answer came to her.

Now she awoke in the darkness of her bed to the sound of the Speaky Shrieky's alert.

More information. Or a question.

She knew what it would be about, though she didn't know who was sending it. It was the same nameless entity The Commons had sent to guide her because of the reliable pain of the burns. They'd healed after her battle in the barn, and they'd returned soon after the entity made first contact.

It started with the invitation to tea, which she accepted. No date or directions were provided. But she dreamt of sitting at a table in some sort of market in an old urban train station, one she couldn't identify, one with an old East Coast flavor to it. Just as she'd never seen the first person through the barn door, she never saw whoever it was who'd invited her. Their arrival at the market must have been what caused her old burns to revive, bringing the pain with them.

Audra awoke to find herself crying out anew, her old suffering returned.

There was nothing more for weeks after that. Then she received an apology via the Speaky Shrieky. That it was delivered by the messaging platform of the Envoy Corps meant it was legit. Or that it was from a power to be reckoned with—one sanctioned by The Commons and at least part of the Corps.

"My apologies," it began, and with those first two words came the ache of her newly active burns once again. The sender hadn't realized that their shared fire nature could inadvertently revive her old pain. It said nothing of its power. It didn't have to.

It hurt even to read, but read she had. And the information and planning the mysterious voice of the Corps brought her delivered Audra and those around her to where they were now.

Everything came true. If it said something was going to happen, it did.

So Audra listened. But receiving the messages hurt like hell. Getting out of bed to see what the Shrieky had to tell her was a matter of will.

Moving hurt. Walking hurt. Everything hurt.

She moved and walked for the greater good, as always. For she had to see the latest on the unfolding plan. When that was done, she also had to know of any word from the Dodger and Po.

Her people needed her.

So did The Commons, The Margins, The Living World.

Things were moving fast.

Just as the smaller boom of the barn doors blowing outward became the larger one that took Audra, her attackers, and her home, the tiny flame to drop would bring a greater storm with it.

It might destroy Audra again.

But this time, they were going to get it right.

## 17

## A NUMBER OF YOUS

"If you don't look away, you're lost."

Paul showed no sign of having heard. He stared at his reflection in the smeared, curved mirror, which initially distorted his proportions to display a stretched jawbone and crumpled legs but adjusted itself to a realistic image once Paul looked at it long enough, thus giving it permission to show him to himself.

Porter and Paul stood in what manifested itself as a classic hall of funhouse mirrors but was actually an old play-for-keeps challenge known to many an Envoy. Just as perilous as the threat posed by the corn maze, this one relied solely on the self-perception of the Journeyman being tested and their ability to select the reflection that best matched their true Essence. A correct choice meant you were joined with yourself and could safely pass through. A wrong one added you to the hall as yet another resident trying to trick the next Journeyman into dooming themselves.

What made the situation particularly tough was that Porter couldn't act as an advising Envoy with no skin in the game. He was being challenged, too. He and Paul both had to win.

And Porter hated to admit that he wasn't sure he was up to it. What was his measure of himself? How well did he know the man staring back at him from the scratched glass? He feared he knew the answer to that, and he was just as afraid of making a choice.

"Hey," he said.

Paul continued staring, vacant-faced, lips moving slowly as if sounding out a word he couldn't quite make sense of. In the mirror, he was smiling broadly. It was happy Paul.

Porter had never really seen that Paul, and he suspected Paul hadn't, either. Hence the fascination. "Paul. You succeeded in defeating a threat who was in power for many, many lifetimes after no one else was able to. Are you going to falter here, against something not nearly so formidable?"

Paul blinked, processing that. His eyes widened. He blinked again, looking away from the mirror to give Porter a small, embarrassed grin. "Thanks." He rubbed his eyes. "This is harder than it looks."

"Every false choice is powered by those who've failed and been kept here. It's an additional way to hurt the ones who never made it—using their energy to harm others. It makes for a potent mix. You've nothing to be ashamed of."

Paul leaned over, resting his hands on his knees like a sprinter after a race, and concentrated on the floor. "This is a holdover from The Commons, too." It wasn't a question, but rather something concrete for him to say—a confirmation that he remained able to grasp and state truth.

"Yes. It's easy for such challenges to translate to The Margins or, if it comes to it, to The Living World. They have much in common with the decisions we make every day, the consequences of which can alter a life as easily as choosing the wrong reflection. But in The L.W., the result of what seems like a small choice might not be revealed for years—if ever."

They continued down the hall, the chipped black corners of the dirty linoleum tiles on the floor serving as safe resting spots for the eyes. Each mirror remained blank until Porter or Paul looked into it, at which point their distorted reflection appeared, becoming increasingly clear as they studied it. With that clarity came an adopted demeanor or expression as the reflection sought to influence the all-important choice.

Thus, the game became one of devoting just enough attention to a given mirror to determine whether or not the reflection was worth considering. Even if it wasn't, it would do its best to hold and capture, so survival meant not only knowing which reflections to reject, but also deciding quickly enough to avoid being trapped. Stare too long, and the choice would be made for you.

"Tell me how this works one more time." Paul kept his gaze on the floor as they passed several more mirrors.

Porter paused long enough to glance at one or two options before rejecting them. "The mirrors?"

"No. The whole game, here. Why we're trying to get to the roof to begin with."

Porter stopped to consider a younger version of himself that returned his glance with a wry smile. At first, it seemed the knowing look on his doppelgänger's face was an expression of congratulations for choosing wisely. But he very quickly realized it was a premature celebration for having fooled him. He forced his attention back down to the floor. "I can't get into the details until we've made it to where we're going. There are far too many eyes and ears here who'd be happy to pass along what we say to those who shouldn't hear it."

"So they don't just want to fool us into being trapped for eternity—they're also little spies?"

"Correct."

"It's pretty evil to trick someone into trapping themselves." Paul shot a nasty look at the mirror he was passing, but just as quickly looked away before it could mount a threat. "I always look like crap in this light." He shot another hostile look at the uncovered fluorescent tubes dangling from the dirty ceiling above.

"Wait until you're my age."

They walked on, the distance covered stretching out past the reasonable physical limit of any real funhouse.

"So while we're putting all this effort into not looking into the wrong mirror, what if we pass up the right one?" Paul said.

"Precisely."

"I hate when you do that."

"Confirm that your question is its own answer?"

"Yes. That."

Porter was about to come up with a flip reply when his attention was drawn to the next mirror, which presented an undistorted version of him before he'd even had a chance to look at it. The glass was just as curved as that of the other mirrors, yet the Porter within stood in accurate proportion, looking back out at him with a studious expression. It was a Porter thinking his way toward a conclusion about the real one peering at him from the hallway proper. Porter had to admit it was how he wanted to see himself—reasoning, evaluating. He looked away for a moment while he still could, however, not wanting to commit just yet.

Paul, for his part, was just as distracted by a mirror a few feet further down the hall, on the opposite side.

When Porter glanced back at his own reflection, he was able to see Paul's mirror in his own and watch how the boy interacted with his twin in the glass. It was the first time that had happened since they started this challenge.

The Paul in the mirror was bloodied from a recent fight, a line of scarlet running from a nasty cut on his forehead down into his right eye. Or perhaps it was his left. Porter always had trouble transposing reflections. A swollen, split lip completed the impression that the boy had suffered for something he'd said—something he believed. "What do you think?" Porter said.

"This is it."

"You're sure?"

Paul nodded, still facing his mirror twin, then looked back to Porter to see if he, too, was ready.

"Let's go," Porter said. "I'll see you on the other side." He waited until the boy began to step into his chosen mirror before leaning into his own.

As soon as he did, he knew something was wrong. He thought maybe he'd picked the wrong reflection and that the jig was up due to his poor choice. But as he was swarmed by all of the mirror images of himself from everywhere in the hall, his chest was squeezed, his breath suddenly denied. A small notion became large, and Porter understood he had indeed made a big mistake—but not the obvious one.

This challenge, which had made its way over from The Commons to The Margins, was truer to its roots then he'd realized. It forbade Porter or any Envoy from trying to make it through an obstacle meant only for Journeymen.

Porter had chosen correctly. He knew that, just as he knew the weight on his chest wanted to punish him for his perceived infraction by robbing him of his life and consciousness and keeping him as part of the hall.

He was losing. He felt no connection to his ability. Even if he had, it would've been impossible to concentrate enough to will himself out of his predicament and jump himself even a few feet back into the hall.

The pressure grew. He needed air, and he wasn't going to get it. The part that frightened him most was just after the discomfort peaked. Within an instant, it went away. All he craved now was to drift down into sleep after a hard day's work. He'd found the place he'd been looking for his whole existence. He was meant to stay here among his many selves and welcome anyone he might convince to join him in this particular glass. It all fit so well—once he decided to see it that way.

A disturbance in the hands and bodies pressing upon him. Something had been wrong before and then became right.

Now something was wrong again.

Something new.

Different.

An interruption of the proper course.

Something fought through the other Porters. Someone. An enemy who'd decided Porter didn't deserve this long-desired peace after all.

The struggle became more desperate as those who'd welcomed Porter tried to protect him from this interloper. It was a violent disruption as the new, good structure that had built itself up and around him was sundered.

Hands upon his shoulders.

New hands that didn't belong.

And a different weight propelled by a different motive.

This was power, and his protectors knew it.

They redoubled their efforts, and for a moment, his attacker was rebuffed. But only for a moment, as if whoever was coming for him had to teach themselves how to fight while fighting.

The strength of the usurper won out.

With a shove that was as much pure energy as it was two hands with a body behind them, Porter was propelled out of the clutches of those trying to defend him.

Clutches.

Why did he suddenly see it like that? It was an embrace.

No. Clutches.

As Porter was ripped free of them, he understood once again what he'd known initially—the multitudes around him were not his protectors, not his friends.

Porter fell through a few feet of space that felt like a few floors' worth. What remnants there were of the desire to stay with his new—and now former—friends were knocked out of him as he landed on his back with the weight of at least one other person on top of him. Whatever air he'd managed to keep in his lungs during the ordeal in the mirror was expelled.

Mirrors.

They could be useful. But mostly they were a thing to beware.

Whoever was on top of him rolled off to lie beside him. Porter reached out to test the ground they were on and felt grit next to him. They were on a hard surface. The person lying next to him was sucking wind.

Porter, too, was gulping air in appreciation of how wonderful it can be after breathing privileges have been revoked and restored. He decided not to see, hear, or think anything for a while. These beautiful breaths demanded all of his attention.

When Porter came to later, Paul was lying next to him, blinking his own way into consciousness and waiting for the world to welcome him again. That's how it felt to Porter. He'd never put much stock in the concept of rebirth, but after what they'd just gone through, he'd reconsider the notion. "Thank you. What the hell happened?"

"My choice was right," Paul said. "But when I stepped into the glass to be with myself, I had this really strong feeling that wherever I was going, it would be without you. It felt wrong. So I turned around to come back out of the glass and see if I could go into yours, and there was nothing behind me. It was like opening my eyes underwater. So I pushed toward you. Pushed and pushed. And when I tried hard enough, I found you. I found a number of yous."

Porter looked up at the sky looming over them. They were no longer in the mirrored hall. They were on a roof, at the foot of something big and blue with a yellow stripe on it. "How'd you know which me was the right one?"

"I tore out all the ones who weren't."

The roof. The water tower. Blue with a yellow cross on it—a Swedish flag. They'd made it. They were on top of the museum. Maybe they'd just lie there a little longer, until one of them was able to stand and help the other.

"The mirrors didn't get us," Paul said. "We can still save the world."

Porter's laughter came out as a coughing fit. "We persist because we exist," he said once he was able to speak. He made his way to his feet and helped Paul up, proving to himself that the old could still rescue the young when they put their mind to it. "The world needs heroes, but it has only us. So we'll have to make the best of it—and so will the world."

## 18

## NEMATODE

The chill air was too cold for the uncovered but perfect for those with adequate layers, and the clouds looked pillowy enough to jump into. Annie was pretty sure the slow-moving train, which took its time because continued healing was its priority, would stop her if she tried going over the side. Nevertheless, the idea had its appeal.

She snuggled into the cargo blanket. It was wrapped around her for warmth—and to help dissuade the small part of her that wanted to see if she'd bounce off the clouds like a toddler on a bed when the parents weren't around.

On the opposite bench seat, Rain had her own cargo blanket draped loosely around her shoulders. Annie suspected she had no need of it but didn't want to be rude by making her superior strength obvious.

Stronger. How could she not be? Rain was probably one of the most beautiful women Annie'd ever seen in person. It was her features, but it was also her bearing—a perfect posture that was just how she held herself, not an obsession with remaining ramrod straight. Even now, there was a potency about her. And while Rain's carriage would've been in marked contrast to Annie's at any time, the fact that Annie now felt the familiar knee ache made her feel like she was more slumped than usual.

Defeated. Fooled again.

The Railwaymen told Annie the train had modified the open-air car for the express purpose of giving passengers a tranquil place to recharge, somehow maintaining an atmosphere and breathable air. Annie certainly needed the quiet time and was grateful for the car whatever the reason for its existence.

She struggled to disconnect herself from having been duped for a second time. By Bobby, an ex who'd already hurt her plenty on their first go-round. By Manitou, an organization that seemed an awful lot like Brill's, with its illusion addiction.

Emmett and some of the other Railwaymen said she was a hero for playing a key part in taking Brill down. But heroes weren't as broken and gullible as Annie. How would the good guys ever win otherwise? She pulled the blanket around herself as tightly as she could and tried to pretend it was armor.

"Are you all right?"

Annie stared at the shotgun Rain casually cradled in her lap. It was out of the holster she wore across her back so the blanket wouldn't get hung up on it. That's what she said, but Annie suspected the girl didn't want anything blocking her access to the gun should it become necessary to use it.

"I suppose," she told Rain. A qualified answer, but it was the best she could offer, given her pain and what Rain hadn't noticed yet. "You don't see him—do you?"

"See who?" Rain asked the question as if Annie's answer would confirm something she already knew.

He stood by the far wall of the car, eyeing Annie, expressionless. A small, roly-poly man with a fat-swaddled jaw balanced on his too-tight collar and bow tie. His dark suit was unflattering enough to cement the cruel nickname he'd been saddled with in the human-capital department at one of Annie's longest-running college temp jobs.

"Nematode."

Rain didn't turn to look. "A worm?"

"A guy. That was his nickname. I don't remember his real name. At this job years ago, he was the one responsible for keeping our pay as low as possible."

"That's the bocanna. The rider. Your mind's aware of the spy in your knee, and the little addition we made to it has upped your awareness of an external presence in you. So now you see it as someone watching and listening. They said that might happen."

"So we shouldn't talk in front of him."

"We can. That's what the addition does. It whispers in his ear without him knowing it, changing what we say before he processes it. So he's sending boring made-up stuff back to Manitou, and they think their little spy is still operative."

"Is that what he is?" Annie rubbed her knee. The idea of the presence inside her, betraying her, was a concept she needed to wrestle down so she didn't lose her head over it. "A spy?"

Rain started to turn to look at Nematode but stopped herself. "I can't let him know I'm aware of him. If he recognizes that he's been compromised, he's of no use to us."

Annie stared the little man down. He monitored her without exposing any thought or feeling, like a bored-but-attentive guard focusing on one particular screen in a whole bank of them. "You'll have to help me here." She kept her eye on Nematode while speaking. "I've just finished recovering my memories, so I'm trying to adjust to a past that wasn't what I thought it was. Maybe if I were used to it, I'd feel a lot braver than I do right now. But I'm having a tough time believing it was me who went through all that with Zach, even though I know it was. And I'm having an even tougher time with the present."

Rain shifted her gun a bit. She somehow managed a pose that made her look both relaxed and ready to blow someone's head off as soon as it came to that.

Maybe Nematode's, Annie hoped before her guilt over thinking such a thing slapped the notion down. It wasn't even the real man from her past, but still she couldn't easily wish that on him.

"Me, too," said Rain.

"What?"

"I was living a fake narrative, too." She shifted her gun again. Or maybe it shifted itself. She and it were as one. "And Paul. Though I'm not sure he's aware of that yet. I don't know where he is."

The crack in Rain's invincibility went right to Annie's heart. "I'm sorry," Annie said. "Here I've only been thinking about me—me and Zach. I'm not usually like that."

"Don't worry about it." Rain sat up, letting the blanket fall partly away. She really didn't need it. "You should be thinking about you and Zach. We're still in a relatively safe zone cleared by whatever that was that helped us. But once the train finishes healing, we'll get back up to speed. Things will get hot again. They always do."

"Where are we going?"

Rain sat back against the bench and left the gun on one knee, where it hung motionless, perfectly balanced. It really was part of her. "I don't know. I don't think any of us do yet. That way, we can't tell the wrong person."

"But you know why I'm here. And what they put in me."

"I only know that we needed to get you and Zach clear of your husband and Manitou so that they couldn't build any more adjacency with you. They already built plenty while you were working the VR rig and diving into their data, which is why they had you doing it."

Annie nodded. The thought made her unable to look Rain in the eye.

Defeated. Fooled.

She'd done what they wanted, and now they had the connection to her. Her knee. Always her knee. It would never be better. She looked at Nematode and swore the little worm man was smirking at her. "When do I get rid of him?"

"When it's all right for Manitou to know we're aware of him and can do something about it. We have to be careful."

Nematode. It was the perfect name for him. The real one always delighted in telling people about the inadequate or nonexistent raises they'd be getting. Almost as much as he enjoyed telling them they were being let go.

"Careful how?"

Rain hesitated, then shook her head. "I thought they were kidding when they said they hadn't told you."

"Told me what?"

Rain shifted the gun back into her lap, sat up even straighter, and looked Annie in the eye. "About neutralizing him as quickly as possible."

Yes, Nematode was definitely smirking.

"Why?"

"Because," said Rain, "as soon as Manitou knows what we're planning, he's going to do everything he can to hurt you."

## 19

## THE CONSIDERABLE CHANCE OF ENDING THEM BOTH

The streets and buildings of Marginal New York passed in a gray, gritty blur. It seemed to Po that they crossed more avenues going out than they had coming in. But The Margins made its own reality and didn't care if it was valid to whoever wandered into it.

On they sped, the SUVs slowly gaining and the mosquitos rapidly closing the gap. The Dodger was forced to avoid dombies who, lost in their oblivion, stepped off curbs into his path or simply stood in the middle of the street, absorbed utterly in whatever it was they saw on their screens. Periodically, a stream of curses made its way back to Po as the cyclist navigated the mindless obstacles.

The nearer mosquito closed in, twin cylinders emerging from its sides. Po recalled what similar weaponry on its larger brethren did to the van he, Porter, Ken, and Rain traveled in, and he couldn't afford to wait and see what these were capable of. So he leveled the Essence hose as best he could and cut loose.

Perhaps the little machine was less responsive with its weapons engaged, but it didn't move in time, and the concussive force caught it full on. It plummeted to the pavement and cartwheeled itself into shards as they crossed another avenue. What was left was crushed under the wheels of one of the pursuing SUVs.

The second mosquito drew nearer and deployed its weapons.

Once again, Po took aim with the Essence hose.

"Don't lean on that too much," said the Dodger. "I'm not sure how much we have left."

The cyclist's warning was all too prophetic. With the next attempt, a modest *bang* issued forth from the nozzle.

The mosquito dipped, evading the feeble attempt. The two cylinders on its sides began to spin, building up speed to the point of blurring. Gatling guns.

Joel shouted, but the Tamagotchi's voice was lost in the rush of air as the Dodger maintained his breakneck speed.

The mosquito's guns buzzed just as the bike veered to the side and then back again.

A grunt by Po's ear.

A dombie, this one a woman of indeterminate age, fell facedown into the asphalt.

The Dodger cursed.

Another lost soul. Had the Ravagers not been chasing them, that unnamed woman would have been free to roam the streets, engrossed in her pixels, until another fate— perhaps a better one—found her.

The mosquito came on again, catching up to them and steadying itself in the air. It would fire again within moments.

Po tensed, his anger at his pursuers growing along with the hopelessness of their situation. He'd mastered his temper through long practice, but now he felt it getting the best of him.

Injustice was injustice. And Po and the Dodger had done

nothing to prompt this aggression from the Ravagers, whoever they worked for now.

He prepared himself to leap from the bike and sweep the drone from the air. That way, the Dodger would escape, and Po would take his chances with those in the trucks.

Joel spoke again, and once more his words were lost to the speed of the chase.

Po didn't need to hear. The Tamagotchi was trying to talk him out of what he had in mind because it carried with it the considerable chance of ending them both. It mattered little to Po once his ire was up. He would happily go down fighting rather than let himself be passively picked off the back of the bike. He measured the distance.

He and the mosquito never saw their showdown.

Just as Po was about to jump, a mass from above stopped him. Winged, meaty, and solid, it dropped from the sky, taking the mosquito out before hitting Po full on and wrapping itself around him.

The bike heeled sideways. The Dodger cursed with renewed heat as he fought to keep them upright.

Po's inadvertent savior kept him in a grip too tight to shake. Any serious effort to dislodge the thing would take him and it off the bike and probably claim the Dodger, too.

So Po hung on, and gradually he recognized that whatever it was that had landed on him was doing the same and nothing more. His sense of it—a scaly hide, feathers—painted more of a picture for him as its familiar voice struggled to say his name.

The serpentine grip that held him without squeezing too tight. The gentleness. The familiarity.

Effie.

The demon had saved him by dropping quite literally from thin air. She was exhausted, injured, or both.

"What the hell?" The Dodger brought the bike under control but had to have noticed the extra weight of the demon, which was not inconsiderable. "What hit us?"

Effie.

Po tried to help the demon maintain her grip. He cradled her head as best he could. She was bleeding from a wound on her face, whether from her impact with the mosquito or from something suffered during the long trip to find him.

"Hang on," said the Dodger as the SUVs ate up the gap more quickly due to Effie's added weight. "Almost there."

Holding Effie close, Po turned and faced forward again. Up ahead was the entrance to the covered bridge.

Ahead, but not near. Certainly not near enough to make it before the SUVs caught them.

The engine of the closest SUV growled as the Ravager driver, unseen behind the tinted windshield, punched the accelerator. The black truck leapt forward and closed to within inches. All the SUV had to do was nudge them, and they'd disappear under its wheels.

Miraculously, the Dodger found new strength and pushed harder. They managed to stay just a little ahead of the truck. But their fate was sealed. Even he wouldn't be able to get them to the tunnel in time.

So tantalizingly close.

And not close enough.

The noise of the engine grew nearer still.

Po didn't have to look to know that the SUV was almost upon them. He held Effie tight. He had no idea what had led her to come after him. But he wanted her last moments to be spent knowing she'd reached him, that he was aware of that, and that he was grateful. Even if he'd never know why she'd done this to herself.

Nearer still.

Po concentrated on the black mouth of the tunnel as it grew closer—but not close enough.

It would be but moments before the grill of the SUV took them down.

The blackness of the tunnel mouth shifted, something within emerging to meet them.

A party of ghost riders, solid in the twilight that was aided by the building shadows, shot out from the tunnel—a good dozen of them.

The Dodger let out a rebel yell and somehow found it within himself to go faster yet. Such a feat seemed impossible, but there it was in the startling moments of the desperate chase, with Effie the demon appearing out of nowhere and the ghost bikers joining her in the surprise.

Before Po could wonder what the ghost cyclists planned to do to help them, they made it clear. They went straight at the Dodger's bike, head-on, parting to either side to let him through.

The deathly sound of multiple impacts from right behind Po, one after the other, told him what happened next.

The ghost cyclists rode full on into the pursuing SUVs.

Po didn't chance a look back.

The sounds of flesh on windshield glass, of tires passing over metal and the riders themselves, of squealing rubber and of a truck hitting a curb and then a building told the grim tale.

The ghost bikers had sacrificed themselves to save them.

The Dodger cheered no more. He pedaled on as fast as he could.

The darkness of the bridge swallowed them.

Then all Po knew was the hum of the bike wheels, the warmth and weight of Effie, and the time or two she managed to get his name out before she joined the blackness in its native silence.

## 20

## ENOLA GAY

Charlene was staring at the View-Master, as if sheer need might force it to cough up another message from Audra, when someone knocked on the door. "It's open," she said without much enthusiasm. Unless June or whoever was looking to talk had some new information for her—and if they did, it wasn't likely to be anything good—she wanted nothing more but to concentrate on the View-Master until Audra let her know what to do next.

The door didn't open. Instead, whoever wanted in rapped harder, and this time Charlene realized it didn't sound quite right. It was too sharp to be knuckles, like someone bouncing a marble off the wood. And it was too close to the floor.

She got up and opened the door to find no one there. Something bounced off the toe of her boot—one of the Quarry rocks from the conference room lay on the floor at her feet. It spun in place, building up momentum, then launched itself at her boot again. Bouncing off, it rolled a few feet down the hall and stopped to wait like a TV dog trying to lead the dumb human to where its boy had fallen down the well.

"June!" Charlene scooped up the rock as she headed down

the hall to the conference room. How long had Quarry been trying to let her know he was back?

June Medill poked her head out of the ladies' room, drying her hands.

Charlene told her to go get Nicolette and D.W. Then she hurried to the conference room and dumped the box of rocks onto the floor.

~

"Two minutes and counting on the prelim." Liam's faint voice was relayed to Nicolette and D.W. via Quarry's stone head. "Then the launch countdown begins."

Nicolette and D.W. conferred in low voices, trying to come up with a plan.

"Can you give me the ten-second rundown?" Reinhard asked Charlene, his voice low as well so that he wouldn't interfere with whatever decision-making process the two Dharma leaders had going.

"Quarry got to Dharma HQ just in time to find out that all of the ICBMs are armed and counting down to detonation." Charlene watched D.W. and Nicolette to see if either of them might suddenly volunteer an answer to the very big problem.

"Can't they stop it?"

"No. They tried."

"Why not?"

Charlene hardly understood it herself. "It's based on *Final Countdown*, an '80s-era postapocalyptic computer game. Specifically, the scenario leading up to when the game starts, bad animation and all. They communicate with the missiles by playing it. The setup is that a virus starts the countdown for the missiles in the game. All of them at once. Base command has to decide whether to launch, even though they don't know the targeting and have no idea where the birds will hit. But if they don't launch, they'll detonate in their silos and take out the entire base."

Reinhard chewed on that for a moment. "And that's—"

"Exactly what's happening now."

"One and change," said Quarry in Liam's voice. He was barely audible, given the distance. Quarry had traveled a long way there and back, the return trip done in a big hurry, and he was keeping a connection open over terrain that was not solid stone. It was a wonder he could do it at all. "If we're going to make a call, we need to do it real soon."

"Dee?" said Nicolette.

"Target, Liam?" D.W. responded.

"Same as ever. Unknown."

D.W. nodded to nobody in particular. The nervous tap of his foot—or someone's foot—became audible and got faster and louder. He'd reached a decision. "Nic."

Nicolette nodded. They were aligned.

"Unknown?" Reinhard softened his tone further.

"Unknown," said Charlene. "The player has to decide whether to launch at all. If they don't, the missiles blow up the base, and the game goes one way. If they do, the base is saved for the time being, and they follow a different story branch."

"Minute even," said Liam.

"Can you hear me, Liam?"

"Yes, Nicolette."

"Do it. Go."

Quarry's head collapsed into a mini-pile of rubble yet again. He'd said it would, given the import of the message he was to deliver. He couldn't relay the command in Nicolette's voice. He had to return to Dharma HQ and deliver the command in person for the game to listen.

In the moments after the stones flattened, nobody in the room said a thing.

"Do we have any guesses on the destination?" Reinhard looked around the room, but nobody had an answer. "So for all we know, they could be coming down on our heads. I mean, this unknown foe is calling the shots, correct?"

D.W. looked Reinhard in the eye. He wasn't second-guessing himself. "I don't know. But I wasn't going to sacrifice our people to find out."

Reinhard let that sink in. He understood.

"Enola Gay," Nicolette volunteered.

"What?" said D.W.

"The co-pilot of the Enola Gay. Remember what he said after they dropped the bomb on Hiroshima?"

No one had an answer.

"He wrote it in the log," said June Medill from the doorway. " 'My God. What have we done?' "

## 21

## FOR FRIENDS ON THE EDGE

"G-man thought it was you coming back. They shot him." Effie was coiled up on a bed in one of the Octagon's old resident bedrooms. It said something about the state of Demeter and, possibly, The Margins beyond that the bed looked as if someone had just made it up fresh that morning.

The Dodger and Joel had argued about how to position the demon most comfortably until Audra hushed them both, and in the end it hadn't mattered. As soon as Po put her down, Effie wrapped herself in her wings. Then she slept for what seemed like days.

Po didn't leave her side. He wasn't going to let another good light go out if there was anything he might do about it. Not that he'd come up with anything yet.

"We weren't ready for them." Effie gathered her strength to continue. "We were bugging out, like Daddy told you we were going to. We should've stayed put. The Pines fire entity wasn't what we should've been afraid of. They were waiting for us to open up and make ourselves vulnerable. A move was the perfect time."

She paused. Po leaned forward to see if she'd fallen asleep again.

Effie was merely saving her energy, making use of the moments Po prayed she had plenty more of. "They were ready for us. Daddy said they had special ammo for dealing with demons. We fought our way out after we pushed the initial wave back and lost a lot of good folks on our side. We grabbed G-man to take him with us. At that point, we weren't even sure he was alive. Whatever they were shooting us with, it worked."

Audra entered. She took a few steps in, knowing she'd be heard, and waited to see if it was all right for her to be there. When Po continued to watch Effie, signaling tacit approval, she came to his side to listen.

"You might think we'd gone soft in those offices, sitting at computers for so long, but we stayed true to form. Daddy always said we would. The Ravagers had their hands full. Problem was, so did we. We had a whole escape plan ready for something like this, and they weren't expecting that, so some of us would have gotten out. But not enough. I made a decision."

Indeed she had. Effie had already been over the basics of this part. She seemed to need to keep talking once she'd started. With a serious force of Ravagers on hand to wipe them out, the demons would have been lucky to get away with even a fraction of their numbers. So she'd created a diversion to give them a better chance and maybe reach Po so that the Envoys and the powers-that-be would be aware of hostile Ravagers about. She had no way of knowing Brill's former forces had already made their presence known on several fronts.

She'd gone looking for Po. She had tracking abilities she'd never told him about. Miraculously she managed to evade the deadlier shots from her Ravager pursuers until she located Porter's gateway, which wasn't supposed to still be there.

The jump through it nearly killed her in her already taxed state. And when she got to the other side, there was a small host of Ravagers waiting. No telling how they'd pulled that off. Most likely, it was just dumb luck. They'd been going for the Dodger and Po and just happened to spot Effie on her way in.

"Daddy was yelling. Yelling and yelling. I'm sure they had to hold him back. I've never pushed that hard in my life."

Po waited while she rested more. It seemed as if every word cost her. "Effie," he signed, "do you know why the Ravagers came for you?"

"No, but we had our guesses. Daddy thought it was because they knew we'd been close to the fire entity and wanted to find out what we knew. He thought maybe they have something planned and didn't want us to mess it up. But that was just a guess, even though we're really good at tracing things through adjacency. That's how we cheat."

That wasn't something J.R. would've wanted his daughter revealing, certainly. But Effie had never been one to help the old demon break the rules.

Her breathing changed. She struggled for air.

Po reached out to comfort her.

She draped a wing over his arm, her breathing more labored still. "I don't think they cared about what we knew or didn't know." Her voice was much weaker now. "They were going to kill us just to play it safe. They wanted to make sure the fire entity hadn't told us anything."

Po stroked her skin. It wasn't any comfort to her, most likely. But he hoped it might be.

"You were surprised I knew how to sign, weren't you?"

He gave her a sad smile and a nod.

Her eyes gleamed weakly in return. "I knew about you

before I ever met you. I wanted to be able to talk to you, so I taught myself. Is that silly? I guess it is."

Po signed that he didn't think it was silly at all.

"It was important to me to understand what you might say." Effie's voice was hardly audible. "I hoped that one day we'd have a chance to talk. I wanted to be sure I could hear you."

Audra made her way out.

Po sat with Effie for an indeterminate time after that.

She didn't speak again. She didn't wake up.

Sometime later, Po understood she was not going to. Yet still he sat to see the young demon off, wondering if there'd ever be anything to do for friends on the edge besides honor their point of departure after they'd gone.

He decided then and there to discover or create whatever that thing might be.

Then maybe they wouldn't have to leave.

Maybe they'd have more time to enjoy.

And maybe he wouldn't have to be so alone.

## 22

# THE ONLY PART OF THE NIGHT THAT MADE SENSE

Jeremy stuck to the Ellis Island Immigration Museum because it was the farthest he could get from the contagious-disease wards and the former hospital and morgue. Those creeped him out to no end.

Truitt said he could count on being there for at least a number of hours, if not overnight. So when he was dropped on the island, he wandered to get his bearings.

Initially, he thought his unease at nearing the structures was just the heebie-jeebies of being on the island by himself. But after real darkness set in, and every survival instinct he had began screaming at him to get out, he listened.

It wasn't just a fear of the dark. The lighting came on after the sun set, holding the night at bay. His self-preservation instincts didn't care. They provided a light of their own and would not be calmed.

Ellis Island was a gap under Manitou control, he was told in the briefing on why he was being sent here, and he understood what wasn't said aloud. A gap between worlds meant a gateway, and many of the things that came through that gateway to help carry out Manitou's wishes were not what a living being should mess with. Not if he wanted to continue among the living. And there were no promises that death would come easy or fast.

So Jeremy gave the wards plenty of space. He also kept the island's watery center between him and those buildings, though he suspected that made no real difference.

Jeremy didn't know what his mission was. The email he received right before leaving said he'd be taken by boat to Ellis Island to oversee—okay, nobody told him what he'd oversee. He'd been granted access to a network directory and told he'd have plenty of time on the island to review it. Reviewing it would be the only thing he'd have to do. He was grateful for that duty because otherwise all he'd have to contemplate was the slow passage of time and the likelihood that something stepping through an interdimensional doorway into one of the wards would arrive craving a snack.

At least Stacey had been spared. She was stationed at Castle Clinton, which was the other Manitou-controlled gap between worlds. As Jeremy understood it, that location was a backup. Nothing came through there because the Ellis gap was more than able to handle the transfer volume while also ensuring that anything entering accidentally would be stuck without Manitou to transport it to the mainland. Thus, any dangerous undesirable couldn't go tearing into New York proper, running up a body count.

Assuming it couldn't swim or fly.

Jeremy needed to stifle such thoughts so he didn't flip out. But he also needed to be on the lookout. Why had he taken this assignment again?

Oh, yeah. No choice. Orders straight from Truitt.

Though the museum was closed, Jeremy could peer in through the glass at a bit of the signage for the exhibit closest to the front. "Journeys: The Peopling of America 1550–1890," said the only sign with enough light hitting it to be legible. Something about the word *Journeys* jumped out at him for no reason he could name.

Anyway, time to work. While looking for something to use as a table, it occurred to him that he might have crossed over from New York to New Jersey, but he wasn't sure where the state line was.

No matter. He chose a bench with a view of the water, woke his laptop up, and dove into the file. It filled in many of the holes in the body of information he'd first begun collecting via Abel's journal.

And it wasn't good.

If this stuff was to be believed—and because Truitt had sent him here with this, and Callibeau's signature was on the release forms, Jeremy was a believer—he was sitting on a piece of territory critical to Manitou and Callibeau himself.

Many gaps had been punched through the barrier between The Commons and The Living World. Too many. The idea was to have enough throughput for Manitou to harness the Essence-control abilities of The Commons here in The Living World, thus allowing them to exploit or store charges and Essence however they wished. What they'd ended up with was a Swiss-cheese barrier.

Paul Reid had been too strong.

Or Brill.

Both, maybe.

Theories abounded.

What mattered was that the worlds were collapsing into one another, creating the overlap known as The Margins. And if it were allowed to continue, that would pull in a place called The Pines, which was like opening a tunnel from Arkham Asylum into your living room and inviting the Joker and Killer Croc to hang out on your couch and drink all your beer.

Worse, nobody was quite sure what would happen after that. A theory that carried weight with those in the know held that the barriers between the worlds would continue to sag and everything would collapse in on itself like a bouncy castle murdered by a pair of stiletto heels.

That wasn't something Jeremy had made up. One of the experts who'd consulted on the report actually used that analogy.

So Callibeau ordered Truitt to do something big. And fast. If all went right, Truitt's plan would result in every gap being sealed except for one under Manitou control.

The problem was that nobody could say for sure which of the ones they controlled—and Jeremy only knew of Castle Clinton and Ellis Island—would be preserved. Anybody stationed at the wrong one was more likely than not to get fried by the ridiculous amount of Essence required to seal it.

Stacey.

She and Jeremy were sacrificial lambs. They probably weren't alone.

But why? Why would Truitt put their people there to be killed?

Jeremy pulled his phone out, fully expecting to have no signal, given what was about to go down and the kind of force that would be unleashed. But he had bars.

*Stace*, he thumbed. His nerves made him more fumble-fingered than usual, and he accidentally hit "send" after entering only most of her name.

*I know*, she replied before he was able to try again. *Sit tight.*

Sit tight? They were about to die.

Jeremy didn't worry about that for long. The sound of an approaching motor reached him from across the water. The echoes in the open air made it tricky to identify the direction.

Then he spotted the lights of a boat heading toward the dock in front of the museum.

It looked like the same Boston Whaler that had dropped him off. This time, a familiar face was there to grab the mooring ring and secure the boat amid the squeaking of bumpers as the pilot who'd motored Jeremy over expertly eased them alongside.

As the motor died, Stacey was already on the dock and headed for him. "Grab your stuff," she said before he could ask what she was doing. "We're getting you out of here."

"What do you mean? How'd you swing a ride here? And why?"

The pilot sat and settled in, a professional used to making himself a statue as conversations happened around him. But Jeremy knew he'd fire the boat right back up and have them on their way as soon as he was told to.

"I got an inside word about which gap's going to stay open. It's Castle Clinton. If you stay here, you're toast. All of the buildings and anything that's not living at a higher level will be fine when the gap's sealed, but anything with a mind will lose it if they try to stay and ride it out."

"When?"

"Any time, so hustle up. Let's get the hell out of here. We're headed back to the castle." She gestured toward the boat and the pilot. "Logan's our ride."

"No."

Stacey took a step back. "No? If we stay here, we're dusted."

"I mean no, let's not go back to the castle."

Her expression tightened. "If we don't go back to the castle, Truitt will have our asses. I'm already going to have to explain why I took you off the island. But the fact that I'm saving your life should carry some weight, don't you think?"

"No." Jeremy went back to the table to grab his computer. "We have to go back to the office."

"The office? Why?"

"Think about it. How many people do you suppose they've stationed at the other gaps Manitou's aware of? I don't know why, but maybe it has something to do with directing the Essence to the right place. We have to find out who's where and let them know to get out before they're microwaved."

Stacey chewed that over. "We'll fight on the boat. Logan, how fast can you get us out of here?"

The pilot didn't move. He hadn't since shutting the motor down.

"Logan." Stacey began to walk toward him.

Logan turned his head their way, his eyes unseen behind his aviator shades. It was only then that Jeremy thought to wonder why he was wearing them at night.

"He's finished fulfilling his orders for now," an all-too familiar voice said from behind them as they heard the museum door open. "You were misinformed."

Truitt walked toward them with his usual easy confidence. "But in defying me to save Mr. Johns, you've proven that you are admirably altruistic, Miss Galena. And in wanting to make sure the others are safe, Mr. Johns has done the same." He stopped in front of them and gave Logan a nod.

Logan got up, undid the line from the mooring ring, and pushed the boat away from the dock. Then he started the engine and began to ease out into the water.

"Everyone stationed at the other gaps has been called in. No one is in danger. Ellis Island will be spared, and I have the pleasure of watching this all play out in the company of two people who, despite working for me, have just proven they may yet have a shot at moral redemption. That matters to some, I suppose—though I don't usually spend my time with that sort." Truitt tipped his head back toward the museum. "There's a bar inside. Shall we toast your pure spirits with some spirits while we save countless worlds and witness our ascent to the heights of power unimagined?"

Jeremy waited for Stacey to say something.

She waited for him.

"Come now," Truitt said. "We've work to do. We're not going to be gods, but we'll be the closest humans can get. Are you really going to make such a transition sober?"

Jeremy thought about it. It was the only part of the night that made sense thus far.

When Truitt began walking to the door, he followed.

After waiting long enough to maintain her aura of independence, Stacey joined him.

## 23

## I DON'T FEEL LIKE A HERO

They stood, arms around each other's shoulders, foreheads and free hands pressed against the water tower. They'd been doing it long enough for Paul's shoulder and back to ache. "I don't feel like a hero," he said.

Porter didn't react.

Paul might've suspected the gray man had fallen asleep with his head resting on the vertical stripe of the tower's Swedish flag, but the idea was absurd on its face, given the discomfort of their current stance. It would've made more sense if he'd died, but that wasn't a possibility to even contemplate. "Porter. I really don't."

"I need to concentrate. And so do you." Porter was silent again for a long stretch. "Okay, explain that."

"I don't remember feeling good about what I did to Brill." The weight and truth of that made Paul's stiffness and cramping fade to the background. He hadn't given it much thought before, but his restored memory now allowed him to reach new heights of self-doubt and second-guessing. "I don't think I had the time to before I came back, and then I forgot everything."

Porter shifted his stance but never pulled head or hand away from the tower's surface.

"Everything is screwed up because of me. Because of what I did. If I'm to believe you—and I do—Brill and I made the barriers between the worlds practically useless with our fight."

"Technically speaking, you launched the process. Then the holes made themselves. It's complicated."

"It was still my fault."

"No, it was Brill's fault. He alone was responsible for arresting the critical process of The Commons and leaving untold amounts of Essence and consciousness to curdle and go mad."

Now it was Paul's turn to move. He did so carefully, lest he separate himself from the tower. He didn't want another screwup on his record. "What do you mean? The Essence in The Commons went crazy?"

"Again, technically speaking? No. But it was as if it did. I once had a Journeyman whose family kept their dog penned up for years when she was growing up. The poor thing was never once allowed to see the world outside the fence. One morning, the dog dug under a rotten fence post. Ran right into the street in front of a garbage truck. End of the line. It never had a chance because freedom was a drug it had never experienced."

Paul pondered the meaning of that. "So I'm a crazy dog that got squished?"

"I didn't say that." Porter shifted again. "Well, I suppose I did. Let me concentrate. This is going to happen without much warning, and you'll have to tune your response to mine. Can you talk and do that at the same time, having just remembered your abilities after having them go unused for years?"

Paul shifted position again, hoping it might take the sting of Porter's words away.

It didn't. They were true.

"I apologize." Porter sounded like he meant it. "I'm sorry you feel ashamed, as if you were duped. You're being too hard on yourself. You allowed a process to restart that no one had been able to fix—myself and everyone else who was with you included. For that, you are owed a debt of gratitude. A substantial one."

Paul tried to let that soothe him. It should have. But the anger and shame ran too deep. "The bad guys were waiting for Brill to get knocked off. They knew what it would take to do that, and they knew it would open up the gaps they needed. I did that for them. How would you feel?"

Porter would feel the same. Paul knew it.

So did Porter.

"Look, if it helps—and if it means you'll let me focus—I'll violate my principles and throw a self-help business term at you from one of the books the suits made me read after they took over the Corps," Porter said. "Resulting."

"Resulting.?"

"It's what you're doing." Porter shifted slightly. "You're judging our actions by how they turned out, not by the legitimacy of our cause or our motivations. There were unknown factors. They weren't our fault—or yours. We did the right thing. It turned out wrong because of players we weren't aware of."

"So?"

"So stop beating yourself up. Fix it."

Paul considered that. "You read a business book?"

"I may have skimmed."

Beneath Paul's head and hand, the tower jumped as if something living had woken up inside. One of his many foster mothers once let him feel the kick of her baby during the last months of her pregnancy. It was like that. And it was another source of shame. Paul wasn't around for the birth. By the time the child came along, he'd hitched his way across four states. He never even knew the baby's name or whether it was a son or daughter. "What kind of water's in this thing?" He hoped Porter wouldn't catch the change in his voice.

"Quiet." Porter moved again as another pulse made its way to the tower's surface. "You already know." His voice was barely a whisper now. "Essence."

"Whose?"

Another pulse.

"It's the love of a symbol. This tower isn't the original. The first one was taken down after winter weather damaged its wood. This is fiberglass. And it was empty when it was put up. But it's long been the icon of this neighborhood, and people went to great trouble to put it back up for that reason. That's what's filled it now. It's like a giant battery."

"That's what I'm feeling when it jumps?"

Porter shook his head while keeping it against the tower, and Paul was proud of himself for stifling a giggle. "It's connected to something larger. Much, much larger. You'll see."

"When?"

"Quiet. I mean it."

Paul shut up.

Porter's breathing changed.

Several more tremors worked their way out to the tower surface. Whatever was inside was restless, to put it mildly.

"Paul?"

"Yes?"

"You are a hero."

Paul wanted to thank him but said nothing.

A hard jolt nearly knocked the two of them away from the tower. The image of a radiation symbol and then that of an atom flashed across Paul's vision—black and white and grainy, as if lifted from an old duck-and-cover film. That was replaced by a glimpse of something greater and more majestic, yet humble at the same time—a tree with an open door in its trunk.

Paul recognized the tree, and he knew it required an offering. Something of value.

"It's covered," said Porter.

"What are we giving up?"

Porter continued to concentrate. "Trust."

"In who?"

"Us."

Despite everything happening to them and around them, Paul struggled to make sense of that answer. But he wasn't given the time.

Porter's grip on Paul's shoulder tightened, the gray man's arm stiffening. "Now." He lifted his staff and brought its heel down upon the tar of the roof three times. Then Paul heard him give it a turn. "This might feel a bit—"

Paul knew what the next word would be. And just as he remembered why he knew, the world ended in a flash that started on the backs of his eyelids and finished when his very existence blinked out.

And it was odd indeed.

## 24

## THE MEASURE OF YOUR FRIENDSHIP

"Her family will know she's gone," Audra told Po. She'd coaxed him away from Effie's bedside and taken him for a ride out into the expanses of Demeter.

Po appreciated the gesture. It got him away from the well-meaning attention of the Petrels, who wanted to be in his presence to let him know he wasn't alone but didn't understand that space and solitude were what he needed.

Audra understood that he wanted to be alone. But she needed to talk to him because Effie's sad sacrifice would probably be but one among many—and that number would only grow if they weren't prepared for what was coming.

Now they sat on a turnabout by a field that winked with fireflies. Thousands of them, floating above high prairie grass that stretched toward pink clouds in an azure sky as if nobody'd told it of the futility of its task. To life such as the grass, touching the heavens was but a matter of will.

"Will the demons send someone for her? You know them better than anyone."

Po nodded. Whatever had become of the demons after the

Ravager attack, J.P. would send someone to collect his daughter, assuming he wasn't able to do it himself.

"If we could find them or get to them, I'd have one of the Petrels go and tell them to sit tight," Audra said. "Anyone who meets their fate here in Demeter usually becomes part of it. We're subject to the few rules applying to The Margins that way. Effie may well be gone by the time we get back."

Perhaps Audra expected Po to react strongly to that. But Effie was gone already.

"I'm sorry," Audra said after they'd watched the light show for a while. "I don't have the measure of your friendship, but if she came all that way and put herself at risk for you, it certainly says something about how she saw it."

Po could only nod again.

"Pretty," Joel said of the fireflies' display after another long silence. "The lightning bugs."

Audra laughed. "Careful what personal data you reveal, Joel. One can start to pinpoint your region when you call them that. "Tell me what you call a hero, and you'll make it even easier."

"I call a hero a jerk living on borrowed time," the Tamagotchi countered, and Audra's laughter tailed off. She'd meant the sandwich. But Joel knew that.

Sometimes Po felt sorry for those who didn't realize just how jaded Joel was until they'd sampled his darkness firsthand. Po was no longer shocked. Sadly, he'd come to understand it.

"Lightning," Audra said after letting Joel's bitterness dissipate a bit. "That applies to what you're looking at in more ways than one, you know. All of this landscape is Essence expressing itself, which some refer to as living lightning. Not a bad model, but not always an accurate one. Sometimes it's as unpredictable as a bolt from above or a ball of electricity floating through your house, yes. But at other times, you can see the outcome was easy to predict. The problem is that it's often only clear in hindsight."

"So what model would you use?" said Joel.

"It depends on which realm we're talking about. In The Living World, Essence is not sentient because it's wedded to those who are alive. That's why those we're up against are based there. The Essence can't rebel against them as it did against Brill. In The Commons, Essence has its own will under the right circumstances, when it's not under the control of its environment. That's also why they thought their plan would work if they stayed in The L.W. and pulled in the ability of The Commons to tell Essence what to do so that they'd literally have the best of both worlds. Their mistake, of course, is that with the crossover of The Margins and their miscalculation, their control will never be what they think it is, and that's for the good and ill of all of us. Good fences make good neighbors, and good barriers make stable realms. For the most part."

"That still doesn't tell me what your model is."

Audra made only a paltry attempt to hide her amusement at his insolence. One really couldn't be insolent to Audra. It would require her to be haughty in the first place. She carried herself more like someone's strong-spirited grandmother. One who naturally prompted the respect that made others do what she asked. And one who could set you alight if it came to that. "A river," she said.

"How so?" Joel was exhibiting more curiosity than usual. Then again, one got the sense that Audra was the type with rare answers to big questions nobody bothered to ask because they didn't expect anyone to be able to shed any light on them.

"It's more like Mark Twain's mighty Mississippi. He was a river pilot early in his life, you know. Lost a brother to an exploding boiler. He laughed at those who tried to shape the river and tell it where to go. Such efforts usually made things worse rather than better, and in the end, the river would do what the river wanted. So when it cut a new channel through what had been a curve, it felt no need to provide a reason to the town that suddenly found itself with useless docks far from the water. Essence is like that. It seeks permission for nothing and provides no justification for where it goes."

Po signed, and Joel spoke for him. "What about here in Demeter?"

"Well, keep in mind that Demeter's not really supposed to exist. By far, the lion's share of it is made up of those who, having passed on, would have had their Essence captured by our opponents were it not for The Margins spoiling their plans and causing it to flow here. That's why we gather all the ambient Essence we can in The Margins. When things are set to right, the Essence of Demeter should, in theory, continue on its way to The Commons. In theory."

Po and Joel, waiting for Audra to continue, marveled at the spectacle of the fireflies. The insects' display was akin to watching a living aurora.

"Demeter is as sentient as any Essence in The Commons," Audra said. "Look up the concept of panpsychism and the theory of a conscious universe if you want to get further into it." She watched the fireflies and was lost in thought for a moment. "But sentience isn't the same as being communicative. Just ask any wife. I used to think I could hear Demeter murmuring sometimes, but as The Margins has grown, it rarely attempts to speak. Or, I should say, it rarely attempts to speak to me."

"So it is its own quiet entity?" Joel said for Po, interpreting again.

"It's many, many quiet entities joined through a common

experience, which is its own formidable adjacency. It's also just as strongly made up of the individual experiences—happy, sad, cruel, and kind—of those who make it up. Just like us. We are what we have enjoyed—and even more what we have survived."

Po signed again. "So those aligned against us"—and he knew that Audra either couldn't or wouldn't name their foe because to do so could put whatever plan she was involved in at risk—"must see the Essence stored here as a waste or a missed opportunity because it's power that is unavailable to them."

"Somewhat," Audra said carefully. "They don't intend for it to be unavailable to them for much longer. We're counting on them to come after it." She turned from the light show to Po. "And you may well end up playing an important part in that."

## 25

## THE INSOMNIAC LIMBO

Rain didn't believe the Railwaymen and whoever was directing them when they said Annie was safe. Not that they'd lie. But they didn't know what they were up against—and Rain did.

By all rights, she should have drowned in the fight against Brill. Despite the Humboldt squid and the strength they lent her so she could deliver Zach's marble to Paul, she'd been under for way too long.

Under any other circumstances, she would have died. She didn't, and that wasn't due to any power of hers—or even of those who had her back. It was because nobody had given Brill a good fight in a long, long time.

That was the reason. That, and the fury of The Commons and the need of that realm, its charges, and the Essence locked up within it to be free.

Paul, too, had protected her. Paul and the fact that Brill had been rusty. Rain couldn't prove any of that, but she knew. And she worried that whoever they were facing now had learned from Brill's mistakes. They wouldn't go down so easy.

Not that it had been easy.

Whenever Rain tried to sleep, she found herself between slumber and wakefulness, which was probably why she was able to process her returning memories and the in-between state they inhabited so easily. It wasn't any scarier than it had been for a long time.

Everybody's footing was precarious. Everybody living and otherwise. It was only a matter of recognizing it.

Now she lay on her borrowed bunk in the dark, shotgun by her side. She didn't want it out of her reach.

The nether-region. Like dreaming but not. Was she asleep? Was she seeing visions of something real?

It didn't matter how she defined it. She just needed to be ready to help however she could.

Rain clung to what was real. And what was real was Emmett's snoring.

She'd come to care for the man, but who could get any rest with what sounded like a drunken chainsaw for a roommate?

And Nematode. She'd begun to see him, too. She hadn't told anyone, but she suspected that if she did, they'd say the little man she saw was her interpretation of Annie's description.

Rain knew different. She saw him the exact same way Annie did.

A flash outside the window. The train, still slow-rolling, was passing over a storm. Neither she nor Emmett had bothered to shut the shade, and she wasn't going to do it now. Not while Nematode sat on one of the empty bunks, staring at something or someone who wasn't there.

Another flash reflected in his glasses. Not staring at nothing. Staring at Annie. In the compartment next door, where they'd put her and Zach so they'd have privacy and relative security and would be within easy reach should anything happen.

Nematode. The bocanna.

Rain knew what having one of those was like. Some days she still caught herself rubbing the place where the spider tattoo had occupied her—and occupation was the only way to look at it. Some days she couldn't believe it was really gone. And hers had only been on her.

Annie's was a true invader. It was *in* her.

The creep factor got ever stronger. With the next flash and glint of the spectral Nematode's lenses, it appeared to Rain that he was looking at her.

Rain looked away. She wanted to think that he might not be aware of her. But he was. Adjacency. The same strength that fed him was tied to the strength that had held her in thrall for so long—the strength that had led her to betray Paul even when she'd so badly wanted to leave him and save him.

Nematode was aware.

The next flash told her he was indeed watching her. He knew she was there. He knew they were trying to help Annie.

No, that was just her mind messing with her, the way it always did in the darkness of post-midnight, which was the insomniac's limbo. A limbo that could swallow you, your hope, and anything you ever might see as a source for love in the world.

The bocanna.

The interloper.

Looking at Rain.

With the next flash, the reflection of the glow on his lenses became a gleam in his eye. The victory of uncovering a secret.

No.

She wouldn't let herself believe that was the case. That was just the darkness having its way.

Darkness.

Between bursts of the lightning's fury at all below it, she couldn't see the bocanna.

It should've been a relief.

It was anything but.

Rain feared Nematode would take advantage, that a subsequent glow would reveal him standing above her.

The next flash showed her something worse. Nematode was indeed looking at Rain, and before the light subsided, she'd seen what she wished she had not.

The loathsome little man gave her a small smile. A small, knowing smile.

He knew.

He *knew*.

With the smile, the train did something it hadn't done the whole trip. It sounded its whistle, piercing the night and prompting a response from the lightning-lit clouds.

Then darkness again, the whistle continuing to sound.

With the next flash, the bocanna was gone.

And it wasn't the train whistle at all.

It was Annie screaming.

## 26

## THE RAVAGED DON'T BETRAY

Audra drove Po in the Ohm for at least an hour, illustrating just how much Demeter had grown. It was, as she'd said, an ever-changing landscape.

While she was based in it and had a stronger connection to Demeter than anyone else able to get there, Audra admitted that she knew very little about it. "I understand what it allows me to understand," she said. "My job is to make sure that's enough."

The first half-hour took them through gray plains covered in light snow, and the Ohm's heating system kicked on. Po was concerned for Lars, who pedaled behind them. But Audra assured him such conditions wouldn't bother the Dodger, and since Lars was able to keep pace with the car quite easily, Po figured that fending off the cold wasn't much more of a burden for him.

"Audra?" said Joel, speaking for himself as they passed a scarecrow in the distance that turned its head to follow their progress.

Po felt the scarecrow's eyes on him. This was no place to stop.

"Yes, Joel?" Audra respected Joel as an independent entity with his own agency, which was yet another thing to like about her. Most of the people Po and Joel encountered looked at the Tamagotchi as just a translation device or a toy of no consequence.

"I'm sorry to make you break it down even more simply for the likes of me, but what's the plan again?"

"In terms of?"

"Overall. What more can you tell us about what's going to happen? The boss here may be steady enough to deal with whatever comes along, however surprising or just plain scary-as-hell it is, but I like an idea of what to expect."

"Not here, Joel. Not out on the road, where things remain in flux. Let's wait until we get where we're going."

"In flux?"

"Demeter is a big place. It's safe in our area, for the most part. But remember that barriers are decaying and realms are merging. We can't be certain who or what may be roaming around out here."

Po assumed it was best they'd left the scarecrow well behind them. He was further convinced when Lars appeared alongside them, pacing the speeding car with ease, and signaled for Audra to stop.

"Somebody's back there," the Dodger told her when she'd pulled over and rolled down the window.

"Trying to catch us?"

"Trying to give us enough of a lead that we don't notice them." The Petrel pulled binoculars from his jacket and peered down the road behind them. "They've stopped. They're closer, though. Probably took them a second to realize we weren't moving anymore."

"What do you propose?" Audra said.

"We can't have whoever it is follow you to where you're going. Allow me to create a diversion."

"I don't want you taking any foolish risks, Lars."

The Dodger grinned. "Whoever said my risks are foolish?" Before Audra could argue or give him any kind of order, he stood on the pedals and headed off down the stretch of road they'd just covered.

Po couldn't see who the Dodger was charging, but he didn't envy them facing down one of the best messengers in existence hell-bent on making a nuisance of himself.

After another half-hour of driving, the snow began to fade as the cold plains gave way to scrubby hills under a bright sun. Now it looked like brown summer outside.

"California," said Audra.

"Southern?" said Joel.

"This part. Demeter's chosen to model itself after it. Or its idea of what it's like based on the memories of others."

The temperature outside rose as they drove. Audra hit a button in front of her several times, cycling the dashboard display through different configurations until a little thermometer readout popped up to tell them it was now topping 100 degrees outside.

After a long while, Po saw a blur of tall buildings in the distance, but they faded in and out every time he blinked. Finally, they disappeared altogether.

They exited at a sign for a place called Griffith Park and continued down a winding access road until they passed through a gate with a large welcome sign. Audra parked in a lot by a trailhead.

Po got out. It was hot, and the sun overhead seemed dedicated to baking them into powder.

Audra pulled a parasol out of the Ohm's little trunk. "My burns are sensitive to the sun, and my encounter with the fire entity made them more so," she said. "If you like, we can squeeze under here together."

Po waved her off as Joel explained that Po was a glutton for punishment who would never allow a lady to suffer in his stead. He also noted that Po was one of those heroes he'd mentioned earlier, his tone indicating once again precisely what he thought of such people.

The dusty trail was wide. Audra explained that it was a fire road, assuming that Demeter was modeling itself after the real Griffith Park.

Po kept thinking he'd need to slow his pace for her, but she had no problem leading the way at a brisk pace. Once again, he had to admit there was always a lesson to learn about not underestimating the aged, whether it be Audra, Porter, or any other white-hair with power to spare despite their advanced years.

"Damn, it's hot," said Joel.

Po signed for him to lay off that line of conversation. He didn't want Audra to feel bad about not sharing the parasol with him, even though he'd refused it.

"It's not far," she said.

"Not fair at all," said Joel, and Po signed for him to lay off that one, too. The Tamagotchi had heard her correctly and was just being difficult.

The trail curved around and through the scrubby hills it was cut into. Where the fire roads split, Audra chose a steeper path heading up into the thick old-growth trees above. It was the only hill with such trees atop it.

The path led into a stand, and within it they found several picnic tables and a few benches. A two-plank wooden sign with white letters carved into it read, "Amir's Garden. Since 1971."

"Who was Amir?" said Joel.

Sometimes Po didn't know if Joel sensed what he was going to sign or if the Tamagotchi had just gotten to the point where they thought alike. He tabled any more consideration of what it might mean if his mind worked like Joel's.

"The man who started planting and creating this after a fire," Audra said. "And fire has visited it since. That's what I have in common with it, and it's why I'm a little more confident we can talk here. The ravaged don't betray one another."

Po signed.

"These trees have been here far longer than mere decades," Joel said for him.

"This is Amir's dream of his garden, not the one in The Living World. Though that's certainly a nice place to rest, too."

Po let his impatience get the best of him. Ken would not have approved of that lapse, but Ken was not here. He pushed that thought away. "Why have you brought us here, Audra?" Joel said for him after he signed, and Po was glad that the Tamagotchi relayed the question in the Po tone intended rather than his usual irascible way of speaking.

Po was asking an honest question; he didn't want Audra to think he was unhappy about coming here. For one thing, he could sense that she was right; he could tell she was more formidable here, and it came from her but also from the very trees and terrain.

"I can talk to you here. I can tell you the plan, and I need to because you're a part of it. As is this place."

Joel said nothing, and Po remained as he was, waiting for her to continue.

"I need to take great care in what I say to you so that you know only what's necessary." Audra rubbed under one of her sleeves slowly; Po suspected she might not have realized she was doing so. "We need to seal the gaps and stop the powers of The Commons from leaking through so that those we're matched against are deprived of that advantage. We have to reverse the formation of The Margins."

Joel laughed. "Where could you possibly get the juice to do that?"

Audra didn't react the way Po feared, and he hoped she'd noticed that Po hadn't signed before Joel had spoken. "You're standing on it," she said. "You just drove across it."

Po fought to keep the surprise off his face. He partly succeeded.

Audra didn't seem to notice or care. "Those we're pitted against plan to use the nukes to ignite the Essence of the charges they're keeping bottled up in The Living World. I think they believe they can also use those who have ended up in The Margins. They plan to seal up all of the gaps except for what they control."

"And what can we do about that?" said Joel before Po could sign the same question. "We're just going to let them grab the hippies' missiles? Are the *hippies* going to let them grab the hippies' missiles?"

"We're going to let them start the process so that the missiles' Essence is put to our use, and then we'll seal all of the gaps. Every single one."

"How?"

"I can't tell you that."

"You can't tell us much, can you?"

Audra shot Joel a look. It wasn't nearly as withering as the Tamagotchi deserved, in Po's opinion. "I can tell you that I need you two to stay here, that I'm going to look for Lars before he gets himself killed, and one other thing besides."

Joel held his digital tongue.

Once again, Po thought Joel might have noticed Audra's displeasure—and that maybe, just maybe, he was able to learn some manners after all.

"Okay, what?" Joel said.

"Look behind you."

Po and Joel turned. The picnic tables, benches, and thick trees remained. "I don't see anything special," said Joel.

"You wouldn't. Po would."

Po didn't know what he was supposed to see, either. Then he spotted it.

"Do you understand?" Audra said quietly.

Po signed.

"Perhaps," Joel said for him. "What am I asking it for?"

"It already knows what it needs to give you."

Po signed again.

"What am I offering?"

Audra was quiet for a moment. Even when Po turned back to her, she was too lost in thought to meet his eye. "You'll know when it's time for you to know. Just as I'll know what I'm giving up to help pay your way."

"You haven't been told, either?" Joel said for Po.

"If I had, I couldn't say."

"Then why are you scared?" said Joel, his tone as sympathetic now as anything Po might have mustered.

"Because I know the cost of such things. True good is bought with true sacrifice. That's the coin of it. And that's all I can tell you."

Neither Po nor Joel had anything to add.

"I'll signal you with the Speaky Shrieky when it's time." Audra started back down the path.

"Time for what?" Joel said.

"You'll see." Then she was gone through the trees.

## 27

## A VAGUE BAT AND NOTHING MORE

Zach didn't realize he'd wrapped himself around Zach's mother until Rain and two of the Railwaymen pulled him off. Then Choo-Choo Charlie was half-carrying him to the other side of the sleeper-car room.

Choo-Choo Charlie—Emmett—was strong, and Zach could tell he was only using as much strength as he needed to get Zach out of the way. That allowed the Railwayman called Doctor Lenny, who wasn't really a doctor but was just as good or even better, according to Emmett, to get to Zach's mother.

From there, Zach, squinting into the overhead lights they'd turned on when they came in, missed a lot of the detail. Mostly, he missed it because once the panic of hearing Zach's mother's screaming subsided, he shifted into a moment of true seeing.

He couldn't recall who'd called it that or if they'd even said it to him, but that's what it was. The thing started, they'd said. And you were in it. You moved.

"No," said Rain as Emmett and Doctor Lenny tried to hold Zach's mother still long enough to give her a shot. She said it firmly enough to stop the two men, which was impressive, given all that was going on. "Not under. Local. You can't put her down too far."

"Why not?" said Doctor Lenny.

Zach's mother screamed again. Lost in her own nightmare, she didn't appear to know anyone was in the room with her. She probably hadn't felt Zach's hug.

Zach almost never hugged Zach's mother. It saddened him that it hadn't been enough to help—and that she'd never know he'd tried.

With the scream, Doctor Lenny moved to give Zach's mother the shot.

"The bocanna knows we put the rider in there," Rain said. "It knows the rider's there to kill it, so it's trying to get the rider first. Then it's going to take control."

"That could kill her," said Emmett. "They won't do that. They need her."

"They need her alive." Rain looked over at Zach and hesitated, choosing her words carefully. "That's all they need. They'll hurt her as much as they have to rather than let us screw things up for them." She studied Zach for a moment longer. "It has to go." She turned her attention to Emmett. "Now."

"Not yet. We can't." Emmett looked away first. Again, notable. Zach suspected that Emmett and the other Railwaymen did not give in easily, but Rain's influence had grown to the point where it looked like they did.

"We have to get her to the gallery." Doctor Lenny gathered the syringes and implements he'd brought with him. "If I can't put her under, we can't do this here. I can't have her moving around."

Emmett nodded his assent.

Zach's mother tensed up. Then she began to thrash.

Doctor Lenny pulled something from his pocket and

jammed it into Zach's mother's mouth. She bit down and shook it like a dog. Whatever it was helped to muffle the next scream.

When Lydia, a young Railwayman whose arms were sleeves of ink, arrived with a gurney, Rain turned to Zach. She was going to take him out of the room.

You were in it. You moved. Apalala-Aidan and his conversation were part of the memory of this now. It was delivered in the voices of the young bespectacled man and the dragon in the closet.

Zach moved. He stepped into the tiny bathroom of the sleeper car and shut the door behind him, locking it quietly so they wouldn't hear. Not that they were likely to anyway, but small things make big things go wrong.

With the door closed, he was plunged into complete darkness. He knew where the light switch was but didn't reach for it.

Through the door, the voices were muffled but understandable.

"Up and over," said Lydia. "On three." She counted.

Zach's mother cried out yet again.

His eyes began to adjust to the blackness. The dark had shapes in it, though he couldn't identify them yet. His hand in front of his face was a vague bat and nothing more. Still, he could see its flight.

His hand. Waving. Again. This time she wouldn't know. That was a good thing.

The reason behind it was not. It wouldn't be for nearly so long this time—if everything worked. That, too, was good. But the reason behind it was not.

In the thing.

Those in the thing often had no say over the shape of it, and Zach had none now.

On the other side of the door, Zach's mother began to cry. It was equal parts pain and grief. Zach couldn't let that into the room with him. If he did, he might not be able to do what was needed.

That was part of the movement, to turn her pain from something that upset him into something that motivated him to take the steps. Steps for him alone.

Again.

The bat flew, clearer in the easing darkness as his eyes continued to adjust.

Flying away. Waving.

Again.

The gurney thumped against the doorframe as they rolled Zach's mother out into the train's hallway.

"Left, left, left," said Lydia, which wasn't her real name but was only a nickname since real names were too filled with power to leave flying around freely, according to those who didn't give them out. "No, left." Silence. "Got it," she said.

More silence.

Now Zach could make out the toilet and the little sink. He still couldn't see the shower.

"Zach?" Rain said through the door. "I have to go with them in case I can see something they can't. But I'll be back, okay?"

Zach didn't answer. He suspected Rain hadn't expected him to.

Rain tried the door. That was why Zach had locked it. One of the Railwaymen would be able to open it with a key, but Zach knew Rain wouldn't bother with that now.

He thought he heard Zach's mother cry out again, but she had to have been too far away for that.

More silence.

Zach assumed Rain had left because she had to, but there

was no reason to open the door to check. Not when it might mess up the moment of true seeing.

Behind Zach, in the cramped shower stall of the sleeper-car bathroom, a massive presence occupied the darkness where there'd been nothing a moment before. Something too big to fit in the shower, the bathroom, the room.

You moved.

The darkness lightened further. He didn't look behind him.

When he saw what he needed to see in front of him, he concentrated only on that.

A mirror hung from the back of the door.

Zach raised his hand.

So did Mirror Zach.

## 28

## REFLECTION OF ANY SORT

"One cannot be too careful about these things." Truitt used a black thermos he'd liberated from the kitchen to pour the martinis he'd mixed in the museum's bar into three plastic mugs. They'd relocated to a room in the island's communicable-diseases hospital, which was a long-neglected relic of a complex with an abandoned feel to it that did nothing to soothe Jeremy's foundation-level desire to get the hell out as soon as possible. This was one of the buildings he'd studiously avoided when he'd thought he was alone for the night.

Given the choice, he'd have stuck with that approach.

Truitt hadn't explained what they needed to be careful about. Jeremy assumed it had something to do with ambient light since the windows of the place were covered in heavy fabric, ensuring none could get in. There wasn't much light out there to begin with, but whatever was there was denied entry.

It might have been to block reflections. There was no glass anywhere in the room, which they'd walked to through dark corridors as fast as they could while avoiding chairs and tables discarded decades before and left in the middle of the hallway. Truitt had even ordered Stacey to take her watch off and put it in her purse.

Big business hated reflection of any sort. They never wanted to consider the consequences of their actions.

Jeremy stifled a laugh. Now was not the time to have Truitt wondering what the hell he thought was so funny. It was an even worse time to answer that question truthfully.

"What was this place, Mr. Truitt?" Stacey wandered about the room like a cat let out of its carrier in a brand-new space.

It was a strange space: in the rear, three concrete tiers with cement steps on either side and a deep cast-iron sink at the front. That it was lit only by Truitt's floating screens—miraculously waiting for them, blank and glowing, when they came in—lent the loneliness of the old facility an even eerier air, particularly since the three folding chairs at the front of the room served notice that nobody else would be joining them.

"An autopsy theater." Truitt cupped his hand over his phone while he reviewed something on it as if trying to hide it from spies floating above. His tone wasn't quite one of annoyance, but he wasn't welcoming conversation, either. The big thing he'd planned—the one they'd been waiting for—was afoot, and he had the look of someone who knew that no matter how careful his preparation, he didn't have much control over how it went from here on out.

Truitt set the briefcase he'd brought with him on a small table with rusty legs and punched a combination into its lock. He popped the latches delicately, like it was something he didn't want to provoke. When he lifted the lid, he was bathed in a soft, golden glow. He smiled at whatever was giving off that light.

It didn't return the favor. The light from it looked like it was trying to go around him as much as it could, silhouetting him on the grime of the wall behind him.

"Go ahead," Truitt said. "Have a look if you like—if it will reveal itself to you. But be quick about it."

It took Jeremy and Stacey a moment to understand that he meant them. And it took a moment longer to realize he wasn't going to turn the case so its open side faced them. They got up and came around behind him to see.

At first, the case looked like it was filled with the golden light. But after a couple of seconds, either the light adjusted itself for them or Jeremy's perception was dialed back. He could make out the source of the glow—a gold plaque of some sort. When he bent closer to read it, the light brightened a bit, as if whatever was engraved there was not for his eyes. He could see only that there were letters on it before he had to look away or risk his eyesight.

It had the same effect on Stacey, who rubbed her eyes. "Ow. I think I'll be seeing that when I blink for the next five years."

"We're not meant to read it." Truitt was able to gaze at the plaque longer than Stacey or Jeremy, but he had to squint. "It doesn't matter whether we can see the name or not. I already know whose it is." He closed the lid partway. Whatever the name on the plaque was, he wasn't going to share it.

"Why an autopsy theater, sir?" Jeremy watched the glow on the front wall of the room. The peeling paint of the cinder blocks seemed to feed off the yellow light.

"It's not the function." Truitt scanned the blank screens around them, frowning slightly at the inactivity. "It's the location. Because this place was built to address contagion, it was also designed to be separated should there be an outbreak. If anything goes wrong, the problem can be compartmentalized."

"Like the Titanic," Jeremy said before he'd mustered the good sense to keep that observation to himself.

Both Stacey's and Truitt's expressions communicated their disapproval quite clearly.

"I mean, the way they had compartments to seal off any breach."

Stacey tried to give him a comforting smile. It came off as more of a grimace.

Truitt ignored Jeremy and went back to checking his phone. He scrolled a few times and then began thumbing rapidly.

One of the floating screens came to life—black and white, with a single string of digits and numbers. Then several more lines. Then multitudes. As they filled the screen, the size of the font shrunk to accommodate them all.

"Launch codes," Truitt said before they could ask.

Stacey nodded as if she understood perfectly. She shot a look at Jeremy to see if he had anything to add once it became clear Truitt didn't expect a reply from them.

Jeremy had nothing. He was distracted by the image that floated out from the center of his brain and onto the insides of his eyelids each time he blinked. The name that led off the wording on the plaque, which had been unreadable when he'd tried to look directly at it.

Something foreign.

Possibly Arabic.

Egyptian, maybe.

It began with a "K."

## 29

## GONE DOESN'T MEAN WHAT IT USED TO

Neither Charlene nor Nicolette noticed the pile of rocks shaping themselves into Quarry's head again until D.W. and Reinhard came into the room. D.W. nearly dropped the tray of coffee he was carrying, but Reinhard saved it.

"Quarry?" said Charlene.

"Liam?" said Nicolette.

The answer that came back was a question of its own. "Did you get that?" The head spoke in Liam's flat voice, which was even more difficult to hear than it had been before. Not only did it lack volume, it also carried an obvious exhaustion that managed to translate across the distance despite the face's lack of expression.

"Ten-nine, Liam," said Charlene. "Quarry's barely able to make us hear you."

"No target." Liam raised his voice in an attempt to make up for the weak connection. "There's no target at all."

D.W. put the tray down and handed out coffee as they all exchanged confused looks.

"Do you understand?" said Liam.

"We copy," said Nicolette.

But they didn't. The fact that there were no targets wasn't news. The situation was the same as it had been during the preliminary countdown and the early countdown to launch.

"I'm afraid you don't understand," said Quarry in his own voice, though that, too, was weak and difficult to decipher. "It's why you can't hear me. I'm unable to leave the base now that I'm there. And there is no target."

The room exchanged looks again, all of them thinking hard, trying to figure out what they were missing.

"T minus ten minutes." Liam's voice seemed fainter still.

"Oh, my God," Nicolette said to D.W. It was as if they were the only two in the room. "There's no target. But he's still counting down."

"Exactly," said Quarry.

"Nobody's going anywhere in ten minutes," said Reinhard.

"There's no stopping the countdown?" Charlene already knew the answer.

"Quarry, do you have any influence over Foundry? Any leverage?" Reinhard knew that answer as well, but Charlene couldn't blame him for trying.

"Foundry's whereabouts are unknown. He left once he locked the countdown in. He is thorough. If he was confident enough to leave, he's confident there's no stopping the process. There is no target. The missiles will detonate in place."

Silence reigned.

"Well, I can't accept that," said Nicolette, her voice almost painful to hear. "There's always something to be done." She looked to D.W. for affirmation.

D.W. had none to give.

"I'm with Nicolette," said Reinhard. "There's always an option to try."

Nicolette stared D.W. down as he thought the situation

through. Finally, D.W. shook his head. Yet it was clear he didn't want to believe it, either.

"Liam," Nicolette said to Quarry's face on the floor. The effect might have been comical had the situation not been so awful. She continued to stare at the stone visage when there was no answer from Liam or Quarry. "That's thousands of our people."

Charlene knew exactly how Nicolette felt, given those she herself had just lost. Then again, Nicolette was looking at everyone in her entire command, so maybe Charlene didn't know at all.

"Liam?" said D.W.

Silence.

D.W. and Nicolette had eyes only for each other.

Nicolette got up to face D.W. She flexed her fingers, as if needing something to fight, and began pacing.

Reinhard and Charlene watched Quarry's head, as if they might compel it to speak and give them something useful.

For too long a moment, there was no sound in the room.

"I ask for your trust," said Audra Farrelly.

Everyone in the room looked at Quarry.

"You have no choice, I suppose, and you have no say in what's going to happen regardless. But if you want your friends and loved ones to make it through this, I do need you to trust me. Otherwise, there's no chance for anyone or anything."

The View-Master. It sat on the table, forgotten, and Audra's voice came from it.

"Oh, right. You're supposed to be Audra," said Reinhard. His tone was more combative than Charlene's would have been, but her feelings were the same.

"I'm supposed to be and am. And I need your help. But you can't help me if you don't believe me."

*The Catalyst*

∿

"How do we know to believe you?" said one of the women.

Audra thought it was Charlene, but since she, Nicolette, and the others were more concept than person to her, thanks to all of the information passed to her in textual form, Audra was still getting used to which voice was which. "You don't." Audra looked from the Speaky Shrieky to the Dodger, who was the only other person in the Octagon conference room with her. She appreciated Lars's presence but found herself missing Po more than she'd thought she might. The monk's quiet, assured way of being in the moment was much needed. "But again, you don't have any choice. If we're to get through this—and I mean all of us getting through this—your belief and trust will help the outcome because the Essence of the missiles is so adjacent to all of you."

"I remember you, Audra."

The man's voice again. It was familiar. It came to her. "Hello, Reinhard." Audra didn't ask how the old Vigil was. Despite the years passed, it was no time for pleasantries or reunions. And though their work had caused them to cross paths more than once ages ago, Audra didn't expect any warmth from the man. She wouldn't have had any to spare, in his shoes.

"How do I know it's you?"

Audra nodded to no one in particular. Like Charlene, Reinhard was justified in his suspicion. "You don't."

"Last I heard, you were gone." What Reinhard said was more statement of fact than accusation. And again, she didn't blame him.

"Gone doesn't mean what it used to."

Silence.

Audra hoped the Vigil-turned-Envoy conceded her point.

She'd have to proceed as if that were the case. "Anyway, there's no time for alternatives."

"Why are you doing this?" The other male voice. That had to be D.W., the second Dharma Ranger.

"Because none of us have any choice in the matter. Not even our foes. These developments are unexpected, and this is our only way out."

More silence.

Then the other female voice. Nicolette. "Convince us."

So Audra explained, revealing as much detail as she thought was needed to win them over without placing the entire plan in jeopardy by saying too much. When she finished, she waited.

Luckily, it didn't take long. Everyone in the conversation understood that time was at a premium.

"We'll go along with it," said D.W. "But only because we have no choice."

"I understand. And thank you." Audra knew it was ridiculous to express gratitude to those forced into assent. But she sincerely meant it. She looked to Lars again; he merely watched her and listened. "And you, Charlene?"

"Porter has my trust. You say you have his. I don't have any choice but to believe that, too."

Audra nodded, knowing full well they couldn't see the gesture. It was for herself. The agreement was a tenuous link in the chain. But all the links were.

"You should know," said Nicolette. She let the phrase hang there.

"Yes?" But Audra already knew. What was coming was what she would have said in the woman's place.

"You should know that even if this isn't your doing, we'll hold you accountable. I will. If you're lying to us and our people are harmed."

*The Catalyst*

"Understood. But I'll add this before I go. If I'm lying to you, we'll all be the least of one another's problems."

The Dodger watched the Speaky Shrieky, waiting for an answer. Then he watched Audra as the silence stretched on.

No response was coming. That would have been Audra's answer, too. The lives of all their people were on the line.

Of course, they had no idea what else was at stake.

After Lars left, and there was no one there to see, Audra allowed the shaking to overtake her.

## 30

# INCOMING

"Incoming," said Joel.

Audra's message was one word: "Now." Then a follow-up: "Please."

The Tamagotchi chuckled. "I like her, boss. She won't let her manners lapse, even in the middle of all this. You could learn a thing or two about that."

Po's answer was only for Audra when he signed, "Thank you." It occurred to him that none of the weight of the current situation was Joel's fault, but he did not have it in him to jest with the Tamagotchi at the moment. Joel was correct. He could indeed learn a thing or two about that.

The Dinuhos Tree was not anything like it had been when Po, Ken, and the others saw it in The Commons. Then it had been thick and squat, with widespread branches that lent it a subdued strength despite its lack of majesty. This incarnation of the *ficus religiosa* was fighting the other trees and assorted flora for its share of Amir's Garden. It was spindly, and the trees surrounding it looked as if they were poised to shove it out of the way to claim the next rainfall. It lacked the walkway and sign that graced it the last time Po had laid eyes on it.

But its purpose and bearing remained the same. The door was there, small and slightly off-kilter, and the Dinuhos would forever radiate quiet strength no matter its outer appearance. The door was hardly large enough to accommodate a man's hand, while the Tree itself looked to be a tight fit for an entire human form. Still, Po had no doubt as to why it was there. To question it, in fact, might well doom his chances of having the Tree help him. He bowed to the Dinuhos, subtly and quickly, to pay it respect without being ostentatious.

"What's it doing here?" said Joel.

Po signed that the Dinuhos was there to give them what they needed so they could help Audra.

"What do we need, and what are we doing?"

The other trees seemed to part as Po looked the Dinuhos up and down. At first, he thought it was an illusion. Then he understood that what his senses told him was both true and not true.

There was no communication needed. The Dinuhos existed between planes, between worlds—a higher power. Perhaps it had spent all these years granting small wishes to those waiting in line for its own amusement. More likely it had done so for its own reasons. Only it knew what it expected of the bargain Po needed to strike.

Audra didn't. If she had, her message would have said so.

Po approached the Tree without hesitation. It wasn't that he thought he could fool the Dinuhos. It knew he had no idea what this exchange would be. But he needed it to understand his level of commitment.

"Boss?" Joel was a little undone by Po's lack of a reply to his question.

Po focused on the process and didn't respond. He reached for the door and pulled it open. The space within would have been too large for the tiny opening. But the door, its pull-ring still in his grasp, had grown without Po noticing.

"Boss."

To answer Joel now, with the Dinuhos door open, would have been disrespectful. Po drew his offering from his robe and put all of his effort into hiding what it cost him to offer this most precious of his few belongings.

He placed the sunglasses inside the Tree and gently pushed the door shut.

The door disappeared into the trunk of the Dinuhos, its outline healed into featureless bark. The pull-ring was gone in an instant, as if its presence had been a trick.

"Boss," said Joel, concerned. "Seriously."

Po watched the Dinuhos. To lose faith now would mean he was unworthy of the duties with which he'd been entrusted. He bowed once more—deeper but still brief.

In the same way the door disappeared, it returned—back in a blink, as if its former absence were now the trick.

Even Joel was unable to come up with anything to say.

Both of them knew that whatever waited behind the door would send them down the path determined for them. And there was no way for them to know—if there was a way for anyone to know—what it would mean for their success, failure, or ultimate fate.

Po reached for the door. It opened easily. And in doing so, it welcomed him fully, drawing him in whole. He'd been wrong about the door being small, about the tree being hardly able to accommodate a man.

The ground beneath them, the very air around them, handed Po and Joel over to the Dinuhos.

"Boss," said the Tamagotchi one more time.

Po stepped into bright, warm light.

*The Catalyst*

∼

IT WAS as if the sun rose only within the golden box canyon in which Paul and Porter waited. The sunbeam that called the canyon home widened until it laid claim to the reflecting pool, the two of them, and all of the gold plaques on the high walls surrounding them. The bright metal plates blazed like newborn stars, each unable to contain the unexpected life within. When the beam regained its focus over the little reflecting pool, a thin ray remained separate, aimed at a spot on the wall.

Paul had no attention to spare for the beam's target at the moment. Not once he recognized the figure left sitting on the bench as the main beam fell back to its former position. "Po?"

The monk, in his familiar saffron robe, looked up from the sunglasses he seemed shocked to find in his hands. His eyes lit up as he realized who stood in front of him. He leapt to his feet, his smile giving the sunbeam a run for its money, and grabbed Paul in a grip tight enough to numb both Paul's arms. His squeezing would have made a python proud.

"It's good to see you, too," Paul said once the monk eased up enough to allow him to breathe and speak again. "It's good to see you, too." He felt stupid repeating himself. He wanted Po to know that he'd grown since last they'd parted, that he was someone who didn't need so much help and protection. But there was no denying his joy, and the monk didn't make any effort to hide his own.

It was only after Po gave him a shake hard enough to knock his teeth together that the monk released him. Po looked around him and realized where they stood, his glee becoming awe.

Po took a step back to greet Porter, but the Envoy gave him the gentle smile of a friend who'd seen him just days before and had expected to see him again. The monk collected himself and regained his usual serenity. Was there a slight undercurrent of wariness for his friend and colleague?

Perhaps that was what made the gray man hold back. He was never one to try to hide the stakes from those he worked with, fought alongside, and respected. "I'm glad you're here—and that we're facing this together," the Envoy said. "Welcome back to the Shrine of the Lost."

Po's eyes found the spot on the wall highlighted by the small, separate sunbeam. His expression changed yet again.

Paul followed his gaze and understood. The plaque that was supposed to be there was absent, and that absence felt like a physical void in the Shrine itself.

Porter said nothing.

Paul followed suit.

Po continued to stare at the bare spot on the wall, his expression unreadable now, which was worrisome.

"Boss?" said Joel.

# PART II
## CORDON SANITAIRE

## 31

# A DECISION ALL OUR OWN

The hand she held said what the voice exhausted by pain could not. It had no strength in it. Annie had been through too much to remain awake, but Rain didn't need a squeeze to relay the woman's toughness. Annie's inner presence was self-evident.

They wheeled her into the room after the tortuous procedure. The cause of her ordeal, clamped inside a mason jar, sat across from them on a corner shelf, almost completely obscured by shadows. The bocanna, Nematode, was sealed away there after being extracted from its station inside Annie's knee.

Rain was relieved the jar was a solid color—black, or maybe a dark navy— and not transparent, which prevented her from discerning any movement within. That meant no trigger for her own memories. The things that had taken up residence on Paul and on her—the peeper slug, the spider tattoo—remained distant.

Out in the open, Nematode had looked nothing like a man with glasses, of course. It was more like some sort of long-fingered polliwog covered in veins and jelly. That network of blood vessels, which had rooted inside Annie and linked to her own veins and arteries, was the initial challenge. Cutting it had been like defusing a bomb—delicate work, where a mistake would have killed its host just as surely as severing the wrong wire on an explosive device.

Even after they'd done that, the only way to expel it from her joint was to make the environment too unbearable to remain. Hence all that screaming. And the howl of a Railwayman who assisted and was unlucky enough to discover that Nematode had a mouth loaded with nasty teeth only added to the mayhem.

Now it was over, and Annie had survived. There'd been no guarantee of that.

Annie remained on the gurney she'd ridden to her current resting spot. She'd suffered several coughing fits, but she accepted water from Rain after the fourth or fifth attempt. When she stirred and tried to speak, her effort was like the protest hack of a child with a chest full of flu.

Rain put the water bottle to Annie's lips and helped her take a small sip.

"What—" Annie stopped as the word came out in full croak, surprised by the sound of her own abused voice. She accepted more water and tried again. "What did I do that was so bad?" Still ragged but better.

"How do you mean?"

"It must've been"—Annie hacked again—"something horrible if you guys thought I deserved that." Another cough. No, an attempted laugh.

"Riders are no joke. I had one once but nothing like that. It was even odds at best to get it out without crippling you or worse. But there wasn't a choice."

Annie closed her eyes and was still. "Oh, please," she said, trying to keep the raggedness to a minimum, "it was easier than living with my ex." She coughed again, and it really did sound like it hurt. "For getting us out of that, you may rip my knee out daily, if you like."

"You got yourselves out. To where we were. We just reached down and pulled you up onto the horse as we rode past."

Annie laughed again, softly, and Rain was comforted by it. In that sound was gratitude and skepticism. Both of them knew it hadn't been easy for the Railwaymen to grab Annie and Zach without losing all involved.

Rain hadn't expected to like this woman. She didn't know why she'd taken that attitude, but she was pleased to be surprised.

"It's still here, isn't it?"

The jar seemed to move in response.

"Yeah." Rain shifted uncomfortably. "We thought we killed it, but I don't think so. Nobody's going to peek in to find out, either. I wanted to toss it off the train, but they said we need to keep it close until you finish withdrawal."

Another laugh like a cough—with real amusement underneath. "Hooked again. First pills, then Bobby. Now this. They must have marked me for a junkie."

"No," Rain said after a few long moments. "That you are not. Trust me."

Now it was Annie's turn to hesitate before speaking. "I apologize."

"Don't." Rain offered the water again, and Annie took a larger swallow than she had before. When Annie squeezed her hand in lieu of saying she was sorry again, Rain squeezed back.

No, she hadn't expected to like this woman. And she still wasn't sure if it was such a good idea, much as she was fond of the kid.

"My ex and a knee goblin. Any guesses as to why they did that?"

"The going theory is that it was redundancy. If one layer failed, the other one would've done the job."

"What was the job?"

"I don't know." Rain reached over to the nearby bed to check that her shotgun was still there in its holster. It was at least the fifth time she'd done it in the last hour. Who was the junkie here? "No one else knows, either. That or they don't tell me."

Annie nudged herself sideways and grunted. No painkiller could make up for what had been done to her to force Nematode to let go. "Which one was the backup monster—the one in my knee or the one in my bed?"

"Unknown."

"Or they didn't tell you."

Rain nodded.

"But they had no problem telling you to ride the train to hell to see if you could pull the gimp lady and her son away from the heavily armed goons."

The train. Rain noted the clacking of wheels on tracks. As far as she knew, they remained in the sky with no tracks to make that sound. "Right."

Annie shifted once more, and her resulting cough turned to another laugh. It wasn't easy to pinpoint the transition. "Well, I'll make a deal with you, sis."

Sis. Surprised again. Rain wouldn't have thought she'd like being called that by anyone. It was dangerous to have too many friends—and even more of a flirtation with peril to believe those who said they wanted to be yours. "What's that?"

"Can I have some more water?"

Rain moved to put the bottle to Annie's lips, but Annie

gently took it and pulled from it all on her own. She handed it back without a word of thanks. It wasn't necessary.

"When you and I are in charge? We'll make them tell us everything." Annie coughed again, but this one was taken in stride. "Except what to do. That's a decision all our own."

## 32

## AN EARTH-SHATTERING KABOOM

"Layer upon layer, contingency upon contingency." Truitt conducted his floating screens like a maestro. Though Jeremy knew the human brain wasn't capable of true multitasking, no matter what colleagues at various jobs insisted, the hatchet-faced, white-haired man was fully capable of it.

Assuming Truitt was fully human—or had been at one time.

Next to him, Stacey watched the old man's bone-tendril fingers draw rows of numbers to him and stream them back to their places, changed in ways only he could comprehend. Her expression was unreadable.

Jeremy figured she'd had a good deal of experience watching the powerful flaunt that power and thus had a lot of practice masking her opinion of it. She'd dropped into cypher mode.

He wanted to do the same but was afraid he'd look like he didn't understand what was going on.

And he didn't.

All he could grasp thus far was that Truitt's plan was to use the potential Essence of an entire arsenal of nuclear weapons to seal all of the gaps between worlds except for the one or ones that Manitou controlled. That part he got.

He also understood that the three of them were sitting in the middle of one such gap, and that Truitt somehow depended on Jeremy and Stacey to keep the door from slamming on their heads.

"I'm a couple of steps behind, sir," Stacey said.

Jeremy had to hand it to her. She had a way of laying the honorific up there without sounding like she really meant it. At the same time, it wasn't clear that she didn't. Again—practice. And it was a reminder to Jeremy that he was flying above his recommended altitude and needed to mind his wax and feathers.

Truitt continued working for a while. If Stacey was a promising talent, he was a master. "How so?"

"We can use the Dharmas' missiles because of Foundry, who has them under control and has adjacency to us."

"Friendly adjacency. Adjacency that is amenable, which makes all the difference." Truitt pushed a tier of spreadsheets with the flat of his hand. They fell away from him in formation as another host of them rotated around to the front. "That is the catalyst for what follows."

Stacey studied the new screens as they presented themselves—but only, it seemed, for as long as it took her to determine they wouldn't clarify things.

Jeremy didn't need to look to know that. He was flying blind.

"It's what follows that's not clear to me, sir," Stacey said. "Are the nukes enough to close down all of the portals?"

Truitt let his hands fall to his legs with a double-slap, pushed back from where he sat—which was almost funny since there was no desk in front of him—and turned to face

Stacey. He, too, could shade his expression with no effort. "You understand that I brought you here to witness and internalize. Both of you. So what I reveal is what I think you need to know."

"Yes, sir," Stacey said.

"And only what I think you need to know."

"Yes, sir."

Jeremy nodded—and felt like an idiot for doing so. But it would have been worse to do or say nothing.

"You're familiar with how a hydrogen bomb works, in that, simply speaking, it uses an atomic bomb as a trigger?"

"Yes, sir," Stacey said.

Jeremy believed her. He nodded once again—for the same reason as before.

"Think of our missiles as the atomic bomb. It will take all of their Essence to trigger the additional massive payload of the Essence required to do the job. They are the small bombs we use to set off the big one."

Stacey leaned forward. Not only did she understand, not only was she unafraid to ask for more, she believed she was entitled to the answers.

Jeremy was indeed well above his ceiling. The sun was hot, the air was thin, his wings had way too much flex to them, and feathers were beginning to loosen.

"What's the big bomb?" said Stacey.

Truitt gave her an accommodating smirk—nice try, kid—and turned back to his screens. "You'll have your answer when there's an earth-shattering kaboom."

"Can you tell me how you've gained access to the big one, at least?" Stacey watched him hard enough that he had to feel her gaze boring into his back. She really did have brass ones. "Sir?"

When Truitt answered, Jeremy guessed that he was

impressed with her line of questioning. "Adjacency." Another host of spreadsheets and graphs fell away from him, their places immediately assumed by others of their kind. "Command and control." He beckoned with one hand, and the new sheets cycled forward to show themselves off, one by one. "A woman whose employ we engineered whether she wanted it or not and her strange child—her very strange child. They're both key to the plan, but she is the key to the key. No her, no him. Which is why we had her under our domain at home and at work. Between the two of them, we have access to the creatures we require. Adjacency."

Stacey nodded.

Jeremy nodded along with her. "What sort of creatures, sir?"

"I won't specify right now since there's risk in that, but would you believe me if I told you they were the nastiest buggers you ever saw?" Truitt turned fully toward the two of them again. "Vicious, revolting things." He didn't want to reveal his hand, but he was definitely enjoying the tease.

Again with the nodding. Jeremy wondered if it might not be more efficient to never stop.

The nodding was interrupted by the sound of breaking glass. It came from all around them. Two full sets of spreadsheets collapsed into shards of glowing pixels, one after the other, the pieces bouncing off of one another and showering the space below, spark-like, before fading into cinders and vanishing.

Truitt whirled back to face the remaining screens and the last of the falling numbers and sparks, his hands flying about. He was too surprised to make a sound or say anything, but for the first time in the exchange, Jeremy knew one thing for certain without asking.

The man would smirk no more.

## 33

## THE INVADING EYES FROM THE JAR

It was a very, very not-good place. Zach wanted to turn around and find the way back to the train but kept walking down the hallway anyway.

The place stank of blood, and every wall ran with pain. It was a home for cruelty and the joy of hurting, and Zach needed to get through it as fast as he could.

It had been a prison, but keeping prisoners was just an excuse for its real purpose. Harm. Change of the worst sort. The tearing of a person who would never be put back the way they'd been, and the pleasure of watching those who'd been hurt come to that realization.

Not good.

Even the mosasaurs had been better than this. The monstrous dragon fish, terrifying as they were, had no choice about their nature.

Those who'd served this place had sought it out. They'd liked those things.

Zach had to leave. But he had to leave the right way to get where he needed to go. If he got it wrong, he would never leave at all.

Door after open door passed, each beckoning to him. Some wanted to trick Zach into entering, while others merely wanted to see if they could frighten or upset him.

No to one, yes to the other.

He kept walking, though he didn't know where he was going or how he would know when he'd arrived.

As he walked, he listened to the sound of his feet on the floor. The floors were tile, but what the tiles were made of was another question. They sounded like bone. He never wanted to know what kind of bone. And he shouldn't have been thinking about that anyway. He needed to listen to his footsteps.

They mixed with the sounds of the footsteps of others who'd been there. At least one or two sets were familiar—nearly as familiar as his own—but those were the ones he needed to watch out for. If he allowed himself to be distracted and follow those instead of his, he might take the wrong path.

And in this place, the wrong path was very, very wrong.

Zach listened so intently to his own steps that he nearly passed the open door before spotting the man sitting in the room with the jar. The door was more than open. There was no door at all, just a doorway.

The man, looking down at an angle rather than at Zach, offered the ghost of a smile. "Hello," the man said.

Zach said nothing to the man. He knew he was supposed to meet him, but he entered the room slowly.

The man sat next to a large jar of what looked like dark soup. And eyeballs. Moving eyeballs.

There was something wrong with the jar.

There was something wrong with the man.

In the man's case, it wasn't his fault.

Zach crossed the threshold slowly to judge the effect, as if pushing against a bubble to breach it gradually instead of with one fast pop. This was not right. That was only fitting, given where he was. But the sense of not-good wasn't as strong in the man. It was there, but it was not supposed to be.

In the jar, several of the eyeballs turned toward Zach, sighting prey. Their irises were all the same shade of black—ink-stained and ebony where other people's were brown, or blue, or green.

Zach did not venture any closer to the jar of eyes.

"I can't look at you," said the man. "I can't give you away. It's the same reason I can't call you by your name." He stared intently at the floor. "They're fighting me."

The man's eyes were of the same darkness as those in the jar. They were not his. That was the wrongness coming from him.

Zach took a step back when the man reached into the pocket of his suit jacket, but all he pulled out was a card with his face and name on it.

"Take it," the man said. "Don't read it out loud. Don't say my name here, either. You only want to be as connected to me as much as you need to be. No more."

It took a long moment for Zach to decide to take the card from the man. Even when he did, he was relieved when the man simply handed it to him and didn't try to grab him or touch him in any way.

Zach had to remind himself that whatever the man was, it had been done to him.

"You'll take that with you," the man said. "And you'll know where to go when you arrive. But isn't that always the case? It's blind luck if anyone figures it out before they get there. Luck. That's all." He struggled to keep the eyes—not his eyes, the invading eyes from the jar—off of Zach.

Zach knew he needed to hurry away from the man. The man didn't know how long he'd be able to avoid looking at

Zach, and Zach had an idea that he absolutely should not be there when the man gave in. And he certainly shouldn't look back at him or meet his gaze in any way.

Not good.

"Tell my friend," the man said just as Zach crossed back over the threshold and into the hallway. "Tell my friend I'm sorry I can't be with him, but it's for the best. Tell him it was good to see him. Please. If you can. If not, he'll know just the same. All of them will."

Zach continued down the hall before the man could look at him. The man couldn't deny the eyes any longer.

The hallways stretched on. Now it was Zach who struggled to keep from looking at things. The rooms called to him as they had before, but the calls were more urgent now, as if the rooms knew he was moving beyond their reach.

Zach recalled another place where he'd walked past doors calling to him. All travel was like that. You needed to know which doors to open and which to pass by. Because when you found yourself where you were not supposed to be, you could try to blame the room—but the fault was yours.

Around a corner and then another.

Now a doorway beckoned with the proper way of wanting. This was the door.

The man had been correct. Zach knew where he'd been going once he arrived.

The door wasn't open wide enough for Zach to see into the room. He considered pushing it open without going inside but knew that would be a mistake, an insult. So he stepped in and shut the door behind him. That, too, was what was needed.

The room wasn't a room, no matter how much it looked like one. It was no different than the color-changing mosasaur that had swallowed him whole so long before. If he waited long enough, he'd hear the walls breathing, just as he'd heard the other walls crying out with the pain in them.

He wouldn't remain long enough for that.

The room was just light enough for Zach to see, though he couldn't figure out where the light came from. It was just there, like a separate entity that had taken up residence in the space or was visiting only to show him what he needed to see.

Not that there was anything to see beyond the small chair in the center of the floor and the layer of dust on it.

Zach hoped it was dust. Its surface had a fluff or layer to it that was not supposed to be part of it. So much of this place was not supposed to be.

When Zach turned to his left, he was disoriented. At first he thought he'd misjudged the size of the room, but he was looking into a large mirror that took up the entire wall. The disturbingly fluffy chair was reflected there. That, however, was not the most unsettling thing.

The most unsettling thing was that the room was reflected in the mirror.

But not Zach.

## 34

## THE RIVER OF EXPLETIVES

In the short time since being promoted to the Manitou headquarters and gaining direct access to Truitt, Jeremy'd had plenty of opportunity to confirm the wisdom of keeping his mouth shut when the wheels were coming off.

Now was one of those times.

Not all four wheels, perhaps, but given the river of expletives flowing from the old man and the heat of his anger, they'd lost the ability to steer or brake, at least. Thus, Jeremy's silence reigned over all as the king of choices.

Jeremy and Stacey had maneuvered themselves behind Truitt in order to study the remaining screens from his vantage point and, should the opportunity arise, offer something that might resemble a helpful observation or suggestion.

Such situations were tricky: one needed to avoid becoming a convenient target for wrath, but maintaining silence for too long might achieve the same result if it translated as apathy. So the two of them hovered at what they hoped was the right distance while exchanging glances intended to inform each other—glances doomed to fail.

For all his cunning—and Jeremy did not doubt that Truitt

possessed plenty—he did the same as anyone faced with a setback. He kept trying to raise the screen that had collapsed, as if one final attempt might mean success where all previous tries had confirmed the disaster.

"It's gone," said the old man. "Gone." His fingers wove tapestries in the air as he ignored the screens floating in front of him and tried yet again to resurrect the fallen one. Somehow, his repetition in the same tight voice was worse than if he'd been screaming because it meant his pent-up fury had yet to settle on a form of expression. And Jeremy, who had plenty of experience with the practice, didn't want to see Truitt aim all that anger at Stacey. Or him.

While Truitt stared at his hands as if they might volunteer a solution, Jeremy and Stacey risked another glance at each other. Maybe Stacey was wordlessly trying to signal something. More likely, she was waiting for something worthwhile from Jeremy.

Jeremy's phone vibrated in his pocket. Before he could think better of it, he pulled it out.

A text from Abel.

How was that possible? Was the message pre-scheduled, or was it something weirder? A pinpoint of light blinded him for an instant—the gold glint of the little plaque in Mr. Truitt's case reflected in the phone screen.

Reflected.

There weren't supposed to be any reflections in the room, right?

Stacey slowly moved closer to him. Her hand casually stretched out to block the phone from the boss's view. She aimed a withering glance Jeremy's way. How stupid was he?

A movement in the glass.

The glint passed out of frame as the phone suddenly grew heavy—not too heavy for Jeremy to support but certainly heavier than it should've been. As Jeremy regained control of his phone, the gold arc of the reflected plaque made its way around the far wall of the room, comet-like.

Truitt saw it and whipped around to glare at Jeremy and Stacey. "What was that?"

Jeremy didn't answer. He was distracted by Stacey's hand, clamped over his and more aggressively blocking the phone from Truitt's vantage point. Jeremy struggled to avoid wilting with gratitude. She'd put herself at risk to rescue him.

"Getting friendly, are we?" Truitt eyed their joined hands. He turned his chair to face them and reached out to grab Stacey's wrist. He was faster than Jeremy would've predicted. "Please," he said, and his tone left no room for doubt. If she didn't remove her hand from Jeremy's, there would be squeezing—or worse. "What are you two up to, especially at such a time as this?" The lack of anger made it scarier.

Neither Jeremy nor Stacey could come up with anything to say. But Stacey was savvy enough to know when to cooperate, particularly because Truitt didn't appear to be full-on mad at them—so they still had something to lose. She let go of Jeremy's hand and the phone in it.

Truitt's face was complete impassivity as he took in the phone and the glow of the plaque that was once again reflected in the glass. Now it was his turn to reach out to cover the screen. Clearly, blocking the reflection was the priority now. It also prevented the old man from seeing who'd supposedly texted Jeremy. He turned the glass toward Jeremy and Stacey but kept a hand over it, raising an eyebrow to ask Jeremy if the phone was his.

Jeremy nodded.

Truitt nodded in return and let the phone fall to the concrete. It landed screen-side down, the telltale flat smack of aggrieved glass broadcasting the result of the impact. He stood and stomped a heel into the back of the case, grinding it. Then he picked the phone up, gave Jeremy and Stacey a meaningful look, and flung it into the darkness, where the two-hit clattering announced its arrival at the wall and its return to the floor. A sound like that of scattering pebbles followed. Without so much as a glance in the direction of the phone's banishment, Truitt looked from Stacey to Jeremy and held Jeremy in a gaze that was calmly worrisome.

Before anyone had a chance to say anything, a tiny whoosh of air followed by the softened wooden clack of something shutting upstaged him. The meager light in the room lost its gold.

The case with the plaque in it had closed itself.

## 35

## RICH GIRL AND LOST BOY

It was happening again. Zach stood, exposed, in plain view of danger, because someone or something larger and stronger than he was told him to do so for a greater cause.

But now he was a little older. Old enough to wonder if he should listen. Old enough to recall that the last time he did, it had worked out badly for the world and its surrounding worlds, leading to the current moment: Zach in the middle of the room with the people he thought of as Rich Girl and Lost Boy and the white-haired man named Truitt.

So far, all was as Apalala-Aidan had said it would be. The young man who was no man at all had told Zach he wouldn't be able to travel with him because his presence would not go unnoticed by Truitt, who Zach called by his real name because to deny the true name of such a person was to give him even more power.

Truitt could not be allowed to notice Apalala-Aidan or Zach. So it required just enough presence and influence on Apalala-Aidan's part to hide Zach from the eyes of the three in the room. He wasn't a ghost, and he wasn't invisible. He just wasn't there as far as they were concerned.

As far as the room and its objects went, Zach was present.

While Truitt reached for Lost Boy's phone, Zach went to the gold plaque. He had to move quickly because Truitt was distracted, and Apalala-Aidan was forced to use so little of his strength in order to go undetected that the advantage he gave Zach could be cut off at any time.

The plaque did not burn Zach's hand, which had been his first fear. But he wasn't able to remove it from the box. He couldn't even get his fingers around it to pull.

The panic was familiar. It was the same one that had struck when he was surrounded by mosasaurs—when he was in pain, wet, and bleeding. At any moment, he expected the little farmer to arrive and speak up, exposing Zach to the others in the room.

His fingers would not close around the plaque. He had no relationship to it, no adjacency.

And he didn't know how much longer Apalala-Aidan would be able to keep him hidden.

Khentimentiu. Another true name. A very powerful one.

Zach knew it. From his time in the water and when he was one with the last mosasaur, he knew it.

It was all the connection he needed. The name wasn't of someone who was there anymore, of someone he could feel. But it was enough.

Meanwhile, Zach heard something being destroyed, but he had no attention to spare for what was happening with those who didn't currently recognize that he was there. It wasn't a good idea for him to pay attention to them and risk having them do the same to him.

Zach didn't pull the plaque out of the box. It came to him.

But it did so with enough energy—with enough will—that the lid fell closed.

Truitt, Rich Girl, and Lost Boy turned his way.

∽

A LITTLE KID stood by the now-closed case with the plaque in his hand. A pint-sized thief who planned to make off with the prize, which was glowing brighter than ever, as if it were happy to be held by him.

Where the hell had he come from? Jeremy was distracted, sure, but that little boy had not been there until just now.

Jeremy's experience with the Rubbish Gladiator and not letting the people around him know what he was seeing came in handy. He didn't know if Truitt or Stacey could see the kid, but he'd pretend he didn't until they let him know one way or the other.

The kid's eyes met his.

Jeremy concentrated on not letting him know he saw him.

No good. The kid knew. And he looked only at Jeremy.

Jeremy risked a glance at Stacey, who broke off from watching Truitt to meet Jeremy's eye before returning her attention to the old man. She wasn't looking at the kid.

Neither was Truitt, who had eyes only for the case. He stood and walked over to it, placing his hand on the lid. He was right next to the kid but didn't show any sign of seeing him, and the kid returned the favor. "What say you, Mr. Johns? I'm going to open this. Will I find my plaque waiting for me?"

No. Because the kid was hanging on to it with both hands as he stepped aside, putting a small distance between him and Truitt.

"I would hope so, sir." Even Jeremy was surprised by how much it sounded like he meant it. "Why wouldn't you?"

Truitt really didn't see the kid. That, or he was playing Jeremy and didn't think Jeremy saw. Or he was playing him and knew he did.

Too many possibilities. And all of them felt fatal for someone.

Jeremy made up his mind. When Truitt opened the case to discover the plaque was missing, he'd do whatever he needed to do to stop the old man from harming the kid or Stacey.

Assuming Truitt could see the kid.

"Miss Galena?"

"I'm with Jeremy."

Truitt opened the case and was bathed in the glow of the plaque within. Or, if not the plaque, something golden and hot. The weight and presence of something very big and very scary made itself known to Jeremy. Not on purpose, maybe, but known just the same.

Apalala.

Jeremy was certain of it.

The dragon of the program that meant so much to Manitou. Its presence was such that it was nearly impossible to hide. But did Truitt feel it?

Heat. With the light came the heat.

Truitt winced the way you do when you've opened an oven, only to discover it's too hot, and you're too close. It was a close approximation of the light that had come from the plaque. And if one weren't aware of everything going on—and Truitt may not have been—it could be explained as heat and weight from the suddenly more present plaque.

It wasn't.

Jeremy knew.

The kid walked away from Truitt and the case, his eyes still on Jeremy, surprised. Somehow, he could tell Jeremy had no problem seeing him. And that wasn't supposed to be the case.

Or perhaps he was even more surprised that Jeremy wasn't calling him out or letting the others know about him.

There was an eerie calm to the kid. Like he knew he was in danger but was used to it. Or knew what he had to do to get away and was simply setting about it.

The little pieces of glass from Jeremy's smashed phone glinted in the golden light from the case and from the plaque the kid held. The plaque seemed brighter still. It really liked being with the kid.

The kid moved toward one of the shards of glass—in no hurry, as if he had all the time in the world.

Jeremy looked to Truitt, who stared into the open case as the light and heat of whatever was in there began to subside. Satisfied, he shut it again.

The kid vanished. Just blinked out, along with the plaque he held and the intense heat and heavy presence of whatever he'd brought with him.

The shard of glass the kid had gone into came at Jeremy, growing as it did so, opening wide like a mouth.

Jeremy, in turn, approached it through no effort of his own.

Then he left the building, too.

## 36

# THEIR PART AND PURPOSE

Audra felt the first ripple in the reality around them while sitting on Effie's now-empty deathbed, the Speaky Shrieky within easy reach. It was fitting for her to do so, and it was a good place to pay penance for her role in what was about to happen.

Sacrifice was a fire that, once lit, did not stop burning. Never satiated, it needed only new fuel to continue. She knew that. She knew burning. Better than anyone, perhaps. Better, even, than a true fire entity itself, since they were of the flame while Audra was only acquainted with it.

Eventually, the flame consumed its host.

It had happened to her.

It would happen to others now.

Audra hadn't set the wrong in motion. The transgressors did that. But she would direct the fire, together with Porter and the others included in the effort, several of them doing so without knowing their part and purpose.

She ran her hand over the sheets, which hadn't been changed after Effie's passing. Her scars meant she had a much different relationship with the fabric and other things she touched than did those who'd never encountered the flame. She was forced to ask just about anything she came in contact with for mercy. Her sense of touch was fried—lessened in one sense but amped up in another. Maybe that was why she intuited the disturbance in the air around her when no one else appeared to.

Yet.

Maybe it was something she deserved, given what she'd done over her many Journeys. Sins committed in service, yes, because of duty—but sins she had to carry with her all the same.

The sensitivity and scars. Debts paid for forgiveness sought.

Whether Audra was ever forgiven was an answer never provided to her. And for what she was about to do, the scales would go violently against her—most likely permanently.

*Sorry, Effie. You paid for trying to do what was right.*

In Audra's long years of attendance to her calling, she'd learned one lesson over and over—nobody and nothing ever went easy on you for daring to attempt that.

"Ma'am?" Lars stood in the doorway.

Audra had forgotten she'd asked him to check on her because as things got going—and they were definitely getting going—she shouldn't be alone. She had no idea how the changes might affect her, and they would need her to give direction and answer questions.

The Dodger respected the threshold. He wouldn't cross it without asking first. "Are you all right?"

Audra ran her hand over the sheet. *Sorry, Effie.* She gave the Dodger what she hoped was an encouraging smile. "Yes, assuming they believed me. Do you think they did? Do they trust me enough to go with us on this?"

The Dodger leaned against the doorframe. "I'm not sure I

would if I were them. But does it matter? The missiles go bang —or they don't."

"It matters. Their trust is what will give us the edge over our adversary. Without it, we're at risk. That's the fragility of this chain of ours. One bad link breaks the entire process."

"We'll find out," the Dodger said.

Another ripple in the fabric of the space around them washed over Audra. "Did you feel that, Lars?"

Worry darkened the Dodger's features as he tried to figure out what she might mean. "Feel what, ma'am?"

Audra didn't want to scare him. That would come soon enough. She tried the encouraging smile again but knew it wasn't working. "That's all right." She considered the bed where Effie had been taught what came to those who aspired to heroism. "You will."

∼

AT T MINUS TWO, the faint sound of a man screaming something unintelligible emerged from Quarry's mouth. A woman trying to calm him followed. Then both were overwhelmed by someone trying to scold them into silence before another woman managed to talk them all down.

"My apologies," said Quarry. "I'd meant to filter out such outbursts."

D.W. didn't try to mask his distress, but one glance from Nicolette settled him.

"How much have you had to filter?" Nicolette said. Good as she was at maintaining her game face, her own concern leaked through.

Charlene had to admire the woman's control. All of her people were facing imminent vaporization, and she wasn't with them. She also had no idea if the troops were maintaining discipline or if utter chaos had broken out among the Dharmas.

"That's the first." Quarry's voice was as difficult to make out as ever. The elemental had already proven himself to be an excellent liar, so Charlene had no guesses as to the truth of his claim. But she knew that she wanted it to be true, so she told herself it was. Mainly because it helped keep her mind off the fact that if Audra Farrelly was lying to them—or even if the woman who said she was the legendary former Envoy was telling the truth but couldn't live up to her promises—Charlene and everyone in Envoy HQ were lined up to be turned to mist not long after the Dharmas.

Nobody seemed to know the total megatonnage of the ICBMs nor what kind of damage they'd do over the distance between the silos and the room in which they sat, but there was no doubt that none of them had a hope of survival if the birds went off.

"I don't do this," said Reinhard after the room's silence stretched on for what felt like a good deal longer than the countdown had left.

"What's that?" Charlene spoke without looking at him.

"Nothing. I don't do nothing."

D.W. nodded knowingly.

The odds were pretty good that nobody in the room at the moment—the two Dharmas, Charlene, and Reinhard—could say they were any better at just sitting around, waiting for doom to arrive.

"T minus five," said an unknown voice, one as faint as the others issuing from Quarry's mouth.

"Oh," said Nicolette. She offered nothing after that because there was nothing else to say.

"Four," said the stone-pile head. "Three. Two."
"Oh."
"One."
"Oh," said Nicolette.

## 37

## THE FUNNY THING ABOUT CRAZY

The street outside Billy Clyde's was packed with fast-moving commuters who, in true New York style, either cut around Jeremy without so much as looking at him or made a big show of having to do so. Despite being borderline nauseated by the disconnect of suddenly finding himself out on the sidewalk and miles from the room he'd just been in, he was comforted by that one aspect of life being as it should.

The golden glow gave the kid away.

Jeremy spotted him through the living stream of business-wear mannequins, staring at himself in the Billy Clyde's window. He was a near-perfect reverse copy in the dirty glass below the bar's ancient neon sign, which had half its *B* out while most of the rest labored to sustain its sickly luminescence.

The kid held a light of his own—the gold plaque he'd swiped. But he wasn't focused on it. He had the plaque loosely grasped in one hand, hanging from a slack arm. Instead, he stared deeply at his own reflection.

"Hey." Jeremy kept his tone flat, his volume low, so that he didn't scare the kid or convince any passersby to save the threatened child from the creepy man outside the bar.

No response. From what Jeremy could see between the passing heads turning the child and the glow into a staccato silent film, the boy's energy was committed to returning his own gaze. It was a wonder he managed to hang onto the plaque, which was a distant second, interest-wise, to his own countenance in the glass.

Jeremy cut a path through the commuter current. It was something every New Yorker did from time to time but only when the moment was important enough to call for it. The point was to avoid having to brave the indignation to begin with. That was one of the rules. If you didn't know it, you shouldn't be permitted over a bridge or through a tunnel to access the island.

Jeremy had no plan for when he got to the kid. That's how far things had moved beyond any space he understood.

Not long ago, he'd never have considered grabbing a strange child on a crowded street. But he didn't used to have any concept of rooms filled with venous Jell-O molds or tiny tattletale monsters that screamed at you from the wall, either.

The funny thing about crazy? You invited it in. You steered it to the couch and grabbed it a beer a lot faster than you'd ever have predicted.

Almost there.

There was a private-equity lady to dodge. Maybe two. And a guy hustling phone cards. Then Jeremy would have to decide what to say to the kid.

The kid. He continued to stare at himself in the glass, the glow spurned like a Tinkerbell who'd never be forgiven for trying to kill Wendy.

Jeremy had a hunch the kid knew exactly how close he was to him despite the unblinking self-absorption. In a moment or two, there'd be no question of his being aware; it would just come down to what Jeremy intended to do about it.

That decision never needed to be made.

As Jeremy cleared the flow of executives and office drones and approached the kid, it registered that he couldn't see his own reflection in the window. He should've been there in reverse, about to break the boy's concentration.

Something scraped along the sidewalk between Jeremy's ankles and disrupted his next steps with an expert twist. He was able to get his forearms out in front of him in time to avoid face-planting on the concrete, but he smacked one of his elbows hard enough to send a jolt of pain up his arm to his shoulder.

He allowed himself a brief moment to celebrate not breaking his nose or his wrists. Then he would get up, ready to meet his assailant with words or fists—okay, one fist until his arm recovered—whichever it came to.

"You suckers. You patsies. You victims. You fools."

There was almost no point in rolling over to see who'd tripped him.

The Rubbish Gladiator stabbed a plastic bottle with a bit of neon-yellow something-or-other in it and sentenced it to the purgatory of his can as he moved past. If he felt any remorse for making Jeremy hit the deck—or even knew he'd done it—it didn't show. "Battle meat," the Gladiator said, letting the flow of people carry him along. It almost sounded like his heart wasn't in it now that he'd completed his real mission. Or perhaps that was Jeremy's wounded pride coloring his interpretation.

By the time Jeremy got to his feet, he knew what he'd see.

The kid was gone.

However, the glow from the kid's hand, the light of the

stolen plaque, remained in the window glass, like a memory burned into it.

Weirder still, the golden mirage included the faint impression of something massive and fiery accompanying the equally illusory image of the boy fading, growing smaller and more insubstantial as the reflections of passersby wiped them away. There was still no reflection of Jeremy.

It occurred to Jeremy that such a thing usually indicated something very wrong—as in, maybe he was undead. But he was too preoccupied with another mystery to bother entertaining such nonsense.

The light of the dissipating pair did nothing to answer what seemed to be a rather important question.

Was the kid riding the dragon, or was the dragon riding the kid?

∽

THE QUESTION FADED. Jeremy was back in the room with Mr. Truitt and Stacey. He prepared himself to explain where he'd been, how he'd gotten there, and why, though he didn't know any of those things.

No questions were forthcoming.

Truitt studied two of his floating matrices, frowning to himself.

Stacey watched Mr. Truitt, glancing over at Jeremy to see if he had anything to add.

Jeremy didn't. He was just so damned glad that they hadn't noticed his absence. Which might've been what his missing reflection was about.

Maybe he hadn't left at all.

His elbow throbbed in protest; the trip to the dirty concrete had been real.

Madness.

All of it.

Yet Jeremy knew one thing.

Truitt behaved as if that plaque he valued was still safely tucked away in the nearby case.

Jeremy wasn't about to tell him that whatever was in there now, the real golden glow had left with the kid. And the kid, along with something Jeremy understood to be at least partly Apalala, was now miles into the window of Billy Clyde's.

## 38

## A FELLOW TRAVELER AND FUGITIVE

They went fast. Very, very fast. Fast enough for the blood oozing from Zach's many tiny cuts to dry in the wind. They had to go fast if they wanted to catch the train.

No plan was perfect. Apalala-Aidan said that more than once while telling Zach what was going to happen, but he needn't have bothered. Few understood that better than Zach.

Quite often, a circumspect approach proved just as effective as a direct attack. A basketball that rolled around the rim before going in scored the same number of points as it did passing through without any contact. But a boy running through closing doors could also find that the smallest difference in the space between them meant everything.

You thought it through ahead of time, and you did your best. Then you tried not to crash.

That was all.

In the stories Mrs. Good Morning Class read to the class at Ambit, there would have been a picture of a dragon with Zach on its back or with him being cradled in a cage made by its giant curled fingers and talons. It would've been drawn to make the dragon look friendly. Both Apalala-Aidan and Zach would've been smiling, and Mrs. Good Morning Class would have made sure everyone got a look at the drawing so that they'd see they shouldn't be scared; they should be happy.

This kind of flying was not for that drawing. For one, it wasn't a clear physical situation that could be illustrated so neatly. Apalala-Aidan might have been a dragon, but he also might not have been. A dragon could have been the only thing Zach was able to understand. A representation, as Apalala-Aidan told him.

Which was fine. Zach didn't need to see Apalala-Aidan's true face or form to know how to relate to him.

The two of them weren't necessarily flying through the sky in physical form, either, though Zach's senses, with the air whipping around him and the clouds passing below, made it seem as if they were.

But they were moving very fast. The cuts and the blood said so.

Zach wouldn't have been able to travel through the shard of glass without Apalala-Aidan's help. Even with it, he got cut. Nothing deep. Nothing that would leave a mark or, as Mrs. Good Morning Class would've said, affect his permanent grade. But damage was done because broken glass meant the plan wasn't perfect.

Zach was beginning to understand that for one reason or another, all meaningful acts spilled blood. It was only a matter of whose, how, and how much. Heroes bled.

Was Zach a hero? He couldn't say. Maybe nobody could. If Apalala-Aidan thought so, he wasn't saying, either.

Apalala-Aidan wasn't carrying Zach across the real-world sky in the truest sense of it. Traveling through the glass wasn't flying. But hallways and soaring were how Zach's mind made sense of it. Because if it couldn't do that, Zach might have more than little cuts to worry about. He might do damage that wouldn't ever heal.

Zach couldn't see the train up ahead, but they were getting closer to it. He also couldn't grasp why going through glasswork that was intact meant he'd been able to travel to the white-haired man to steal the glow back with Apalala-Aidan's help, yet stepping into a shard meant he had to be carried—or the next closest thing to carried.

It was much harder. But if anyone could get him back to the train, it was Apalala-Aidan.

The glow. The gold plaque. Zach still held it in his hand—or did so in his mind's understanding of where they were and how they were moving. He could do so without any trouble because the plaque was an in-between thing, just like Zach. They fit together.

The glow did not fit Apalala-Aidan. He was of one place and was in pain when in-between. And being so close to something like the glow, even something so small, made it hurt more.

But Apalala-Aidan could endure a lot more pain than he was laboring under now. A lot more. That was why Zach was glad to have Apalala-Aidan on his side. Or something that was as close to being on his side as he was able to understand.

Maybe an alliance was nothing more than wanting the same things. Maybe a friendship was, too. Zach didn't want that to be true. Otherwise, what hope was there?

The train was somewhere under them now. Zach couldn't see it, but he felt it. If, that is, the relationship between where they were and where the train was resembled real-world location at all.

Apalala-Aidan needed to move at the same speed as the train. Or whatever that was a substitute for. And he needed to do many other things Zach couldn't comprehend and didn't want to know about.

Zach would leave Apalala-Aidan with the glow, and he would take it from here. That was how it had to work for many reasons.

No plan was perfect.

Apalala-Aidan banked and dove.

Zach closed his eyes for no reason whatsoever.

◈

THE KID COULDN'T STILL BE in the bathroom.

Yet he had to be.

Rain had searched for Zach all over the train except for the place she'd left him. Why she saved that for last, she didn't know. Maybe she needed that hope to kindle while looking elsewhere. Maybe she was too much of a coward to entertain the thought of telling the mother in the other room—who'd just endured an ordeal painful enough to level an entire defensive line, never mind a petite mom—that they'd managed to lose her son on a moving train. Scratch that— Rain had managed. She'd search the train ten more times before facing that.

Something moved behind the bathroom door.

Something much, much bigger than a little boy.

Something much, much bigger than the bathroom.

Something was burning. And when that faded, something crazier took its place: the faint struggles of far-off conflict, random shots, and the cries of men embattled.

"Zach?" Rain rapped on the door softly and kept her voice low so that others on the train wouldn't hear a budding crisis and show up to help. "I'm coming in."

Before she could, the latch clicked, the door opened, and there was Zach.

His return was a cause for celebration, to be sure—but not a large one, given the state of him. Dried blood from myriad cuts formed hard little beads on his face and hands. His clothes retained the burning smell she'd picked up a moment before. And he looked like he'd been up for a week or two.

The questions fought each other on the way out of her brain. So much so that none of them made it.

The boy looked up at her. Despite what appeared to be a bit of light emanating from his closed hand that quickly faded to nothing, despite the blood, despite his obviously having been through something big, all Rain saw was a fellow traveler and fugitive. Another transient placed among those with more solid foundations, even when they were on the move. Another refugee of circumstance. As was the case with other junkies, members of this tribe recognized one another without a word being uttered.

Which was why, though Rain's first thought was to clean the kid up, she instead offered him a deal that shocked even her, though it shouldn't have. "I won't tell if you won't," she said.

## 39

## WE CANNOT DO THIS ALONE

"If you don't want to help us, I understand," Porter told Po.

Paul tried to read what passed silently between the monk and the gray man. Words alone were unequal to the task of communicating the situation. But he wasn't able to follow. Both men were older and more experienced than Paul; it was as if they were going back and forth on a frequency he couldn't receive.

It was no sure thing that Po fully understood what Porter was asking. But he didn't need to in order to be uneasy. Even Joel the Tamagotchi didn't seem comfortable with what had been revealed thus far—and from what Paul could discern, those were only the basics of the plan.

As Paul understood it, the hippie soldiers were now called the Dharma Rangers. Their missiles had been hijacked by Gerald Truitt, the older man whom Paul recalled working as Brill's assistant. Truitt and whoever he was allied with now were going to use them to set off an even greater store of Essence in order to seal up the gaps between The Commons and The Living World. That would stop the realms from crossing over and eventually collapsing into each other, which was what created The Margins.

Paul tried not to think about how all of this was his fault.

Truitt wanted to seal the openings except for those he controlled so that he could continue his Essence pillaging, which he and those he was working with had planned for since long before Paul and the others defeated Brill.

Porter and Audra, who Paul remembered only from dreams—or something close to dreams—intended to seal all of them.

Got it.

So why did Po, a master of hiding his emotions when he wasn't angry, look like he wasn't buying it? And why, despite having come all this way out of love and trust for Porter, did Paul feel that at some point, he'd have to admit feeling the same way?

Furthermore, as happy as Paul was to see Po, why put him in this position at all? Porter had as much adjacency to Audra and the Essence under her control as Po did—more, maybe.

Porter hadn't told Po everything. Which was a problem because he'd let Po in on everything he'd told Paul. And maybe the details that weren't yet revealed would only provide more clarity to a picture Paul didn't want to admit he was seeing.

The gray man was keeping something under wraps. And from the look of him, strained and seemingly growing more tired by the moment, it was something big—something not easy to control or hold back.

"I can see you're not on board," Porter told the monk. "And I know you're not alone in that." He might have meant Joel the Tamagotchi, Paul, or both. "I've brought us to the only place with enough power and access to make this work. And I'll ask all of you to trust me."

## The Catalyst

Po gave a nod. It wasn't one that said anything about full trust, but at least he was willing to let Porter say what he needed to.

The light in the Shrine changed. Porter was now fully supporting himself on his staff.

Paul was torn between concern for the gray man and wanting to know what burden could do this to him here, in a place of light and grace. The space grew darker somehow, and Po's expression turned to one of wariness.

Even before the monk adopted a defensive position, Paul had an inkling of what he'd see when he turned around.

Behind him, the sunlight had retreated from a corner of the Shrine. The narrow but deep indentation in the stone wall now contained shadows. Those shadows, in turn, contained still more.

The shadows were hungry.

Another feeling Paul had forgotten crept up his back and settled into his head, where it began to sow fear. *Run. Run or fight. But do something.*

"We cannot do this alone," said Porter. "And so I've invited that which will either convince you to work with me—or convince you to do everything you can to defeat me. I hope it's the former. Because we cannot do this without him."

Paul looked into the shadows.

The shadows looked back.

## 40

## BULLIES, COYOTES, AND CATS

There was a one-panel comic Charlene had nearly forgotten all about. It was front and center on a refrigerator on some base in an altogether different life, one lived before she rode in the wrong vehicle on the wrong road. In it, a hulking bully, face bursting with cruel intent, beamed pure menace at his usual target, who was protected for the time being by a tiny whistle-bearing gym teacher inserting herself between the two of them. "I can't decide who has it worse," the target tells his temporary guardian angel, "him for having to wait to punch me, or me for having to wait to be punched."

Char had no idea who put it there, but the yellow of the paper and the grease dried on the magnet holding it said it had been sitting there for quite some time because everyone using the fridge could relate.

It wasn't that the comic was funny. It was that it was true.

The air in the room was heavy with doom, the atmosphere pressurized and ready to crumple all of them. And the memories of cartoons watched and images taken in continued.

The coyote broke the fourth wall to stare helplessly at the viewer as the shadow of the falling boulder grew around him.

The nervous dog looked into the camera as a cat, bug-eyed with fury, crept up on him from behind.

Quarry's head, which was nothing more than a basic radio receiver at this point in the game, issued the faint sound of somebody among the Dharmas whistling "My Bonnie Lies Over the Ocean." For whatever reason, they were stuck on the "bring back" part. And for some other reason, nobody told them to stop.

"You feel the heat, too, right?" D.W. said to no one in particular. "It's not just me."

The Dharma Ranger already knew the answer, but Charlene nodded her affirmative. It was something to do. And the motion didn't feel vigorous enough to break whatever filmy barrier kept the killer breath of the nukes from turning them all to vapor. She didn't know who'd woken them up and set them off, just as she couldn't say whether it was Audra who was somehow keeping their wild Essence at bay.

Audra had to have been involved. That was where the trust she'd asked for came in. Whether or not she had help was unclear. Most likely. And whoever or whatever it was, they had to accept the safety of that trust, or it wouldn't be able to save them.

Yes, she felt the heat. D.W. had to check? What did it mean to live in a world where the unreal and the real were so interchangeable you had to ask someone else which was which?

The heat.

Her brain was boiling in its own fluid. Cooking through.

What was that process called? Sous vide. No, that wasn't a fit. That involved lower temperatures. The Essence restrained by the veil, dying to get at them, was anything but low. Yet here she was, thinking of bullies, coyotes, and cats, so wasn't it likely that her mind was being microwaved despite the promise of safety?

Char looked to Reinhard. Their eyes met. The Vigil-turned-Envoy was in his element, as if he spent all of his days in a pressure cooker. What was it like to be that man? Char never wanted to find out.

"How long ago did we hit zero?" she said, for the countdown felt like it had ended an hour before.

"A minute." Reinhard's voice was as steady as his presence. "Two, maybe." He was rock solid. Char promised herself that if the two of them made it out of this, she'd be sure to give him work that made the most of his talents.

The faraway whistle continued to loop the same part of the song as something kept the sun from rising, which was just fine by Charlene since that same sun would turn them all to cinders.

The whistler's bonnie would never be brought back.

Not when the boulder was poised to flatten the coyote.

Not when the shadow slowly grew whenever it thought nobody was looking.

Charlene envied Quarry's head and Reinhard in equal measure.

With the heat ticking up a degree or two, pushing ever harder against whatever held it back, she couldn't help but wonder what it must be like to be made of stone.

∽

She was asleep, but Zach's mother knew Zach was watching her. Maybe Zach's mother felt Zach with her in her dream, which Zach was almost certain she was having, given the way she seemed to be trying to talk to someone who wasn't with her in the bunk the Railwaymen had put her in. Her lips moved. Her eyes shifted under her eyelids, and her head twitched now and then, her expressions shifting from concern to outright fear.

Zach's mother knew Zach was there because Zach wanted her to know.

Zach watched her sleep and heal with a presence he never shared with her when Zach's mother was awake. He didn't know why. Most likely because the thing in the jar—the rider, the bocanna—remained in the room with them.

Because to take it away too soon could send Zach's mother into withdrawal, Rain said. Because part of Zach's mother still needed it close, though she wanted to be far away.

Zach's mother would be far away from it soon, though not soon enough for her. It was all part of the coming together Apalala-Aidan had warned him about—the coming together that would lead to the proper separation.

Zach, Zach's mother, and the others had come together to end the time of Mr. Brill. Only it hadn't done what they'd all hoped. It had done something else. So now another coming together was necessary.

Apalala-Aidan tried to prepare Zach. Zach knew there was no preparation for such a thing. Not when nobody could know how it would truly end up. Maybe the big pieces. Maybe. But not the small ones. And without knowing about the small pieces, one didn't know at all.

Apalala-Aidan told Zach that Zach and Zach's mother were big, but Zach knew that wasn't true. None of them were so big—not even Apalala-Aidan, who was much, much bigger than Zach and had a much, much bigger part to play.

They all had parts to play. When they were done playing them, nothing would come together again for a very long time, if ever it did. Not so tightly. Not so fast.

Zach's mother shifted. Zach thought she might wake up,

but she didn't. She was healing much faster than the train people had predicted, Rain said. It was because the rider was out. Out, but not gone, and that was why they had to keep her close to it. But she was healing quickly anyway.

Zach's mother tried to say something in her dream. She was trying to talk to Zach, it seemed.

Zach didn't answer, but that took almost everything he had. Everything he had that wasn't about struggling not to worry over the heat trying to reach him—the heat from his friends and the heat from things that were not his friends.

For a traveler like Zach, those things were many indeed.

## 41

## WELL DOWN A BAD ROAD

"You're around the bend," Joel told Porter. "Way around it and well down a bad road." The Tamagotchi wasn't speaking for Po in the strictest sense—he hadn't signed anything—but Po didn't disapprove, either. He just might have worded it differently.

Porter's mouth was a grim line. "Don't you think I knew you'd say that?" He looked Po in the eye as if Po had said the words himself. "Yet I brought you here. What does that tell you?"

Paul, standing next to Porter, wore an expression of unvarnished worry. Po suspected Paul thought he was hiding his concern, but he was unsuccessful because it was too strong.

Once Po got over his initial shock at where he'd ended up and who'd been waiting for him, he saw why Paul felt the way he did.

The Envoy was under a great deal of strain. It wasn't the past-tense exhaustion of someone who'd tried to do too much for too long; it was the weariness of a man maintaining an effort despite his doubts about how long he could keep it up. Porter radiated gray, his skin an unlikely combination of ash and flop sweat. He leaned heavily on his staff as Paul watched, ready to grab him should he falter.

Po signed.

"Are you all right, Porter?" Joel said for him.

Porter's lopsided grin was all shaded amusement at the idea of someone inquiring as to his welfare. His forehead shone, his jaw set. "I am a man in cross-allegiance—in a place between places." He took a moment to rest, his eyes widening at something that wasn't there. "I ask you to join me."

Paul looked from Porter to Po. It was impossible to tell if he was more worried about Po refusing to go along or his mentor's obvious distress.

"What the hell does that mean?" said Joel.

"Hear him out," Paul said. "Hear us out. Please."

The Envoy nodded in acknowledgement of Paul's support, and his hands nearly slipped off his staff.

That was when Po felt the weight in the air, the movement of something large and heavy borne by the Shrine itself—and, to look at him, by Porter as well. Something pressed upon the very space they occupied, either trying to gain entry or attempting to destroy it.

"What it means, my friend, is that now is a time of in-between." Porter shifted position, trying to bear the pressure with a different part of himself. He looked like he had no options left. "The Margins is a place between places. So is the Shrine. But because of The Margins, the Shrine is in danger of being a way station for travelers and things unforeseen by its creators." He shifted again. It didn't appear to help. "We allow some in and keep some out. We deviate from our promises because we've found that the only way to get to the agreed-upon destination is a route we cannot reveal. We betray an alliance because it's the only way to honor it." Another shift. "Am I making any sense?"

"No," said Joel. Now he didn't speak for Po, who understood what Porter was driving at and was still willing to give him a chance to explain.

With the sensation of the Shrine being compromised came the brief presence of another, one who couldn't enter entirely and whose whole being was not welcome. The light of the Shrine behind Po grew, illuminating the space in which they stood except for the shadows, which, if anything, deepened. Po didn't need to look in order to understand what had happened.

One of Porter's knees briefly buckled, but the Envoy found himself and straightened as best he could. Po could sense a great strength—more than one, perhaps—combining to drag the gray man down without succeeding. Porter was stronger than Po had realized.

Paul lightly touched a hand to Porter's shoulder.

The Envoy closed his eyes in gratitude. And he endured. "You know what is behind you, don't you?" he said, eyes still shut. He winced and shook off some new weight—or, perhaps, the recognition that the current burden would not ease. "Look."

Po turned. The plaque—Ken's plaque—occupied its rightful place again. The weight in the air and upon the space of the Shrine dissipated. The glow of the plaque subsided, its aura drawn into the shadows and crevices of the Shrine.

The gray man watched Po for a response.

Paul stared openly at Po, his silence asking for understanding.

"Everyone seeks trust," said Porter. "I've sought it from someone who doesn't know she shouldn't give it to me, though my intent is true. Now I seek yours."

The shadows behind Porter and Paul shifted.

"Boss," Joel warned.

Po had already readied himself. He didn't know how many opponents he faced, but there was no question about one of them.

Moving without sound. Warping the light of the Shrine. Lending the powerful place a more forbidding air. The familiar dark being Po had hoped never to see again emerged from the shadows.

Mr. Brill's Shade joined them.

## 42

## FINGER CHURCH

"Something's gone awry." Truitt cycled through his floating metrics and graphs so quickly that Jeremy and Stacey had to look away. For Jeremy, it was a matter of not vomiting in front of his boss and colleague. He was prone to motion sickness, even when it was something else moving and not him. And the stress of wondering whether he'd be caught for not saying anything about the plaque didn't help.

In any job that included exposure to the higher-ups—and exposure was the most appropriate term—it was always a harbinger of disaster for the underlings when the big guns found something amiss in the key performance metrics. In this case, however, Jeremy was grateful for something to distract Truitt from Jeremy's brief disappearing act—assuming he'd noticed.

Jeremy figured the old man didn't know the plaque was gone. But he would eventually, and having mysteriously vanished for a spell wouldn't be a good look.

"Whither the Bruckers, Mr. Johns?" Truitt flipped backward through his screens and once again reviewed the indicators, which hadn't budged.

"I'm sorry, sir?"

"I know you're familiar with Annie Brucker and her son." Truitt's tone never strayed beyond the realm of rational discussion. "You know of them from the deeply concerned Mr. Dowd, correct?"

"Yes, sir."

"Well, then. For the benefit of Miss Galena and myself, might you tell me where they've gone?"

The kid.

Was the little kid who'd absconded with the plaque Annie Brucker's son, Zach?

Jeremy stalled long enough to ensure his voice betrayed nothing of his worries. "I'm sorry, sir. I don't know."

"I'm aware. Nor do I. The question is, does that matter?"

Jeremy risked a glance at Stacey, who didn't try to hide any of her concern for him. She was a decent sort. Most anyone else at Manitou would delight in seeing a potential rival wriggling on a pin. "I'm sorry, sir. I don't know."

"I'm aware of that as well, but do try to vary your phrasing. The question, again, is does *that* matter?" Truitt paused, and Jeremy wondered if stress sweat really did stink worse than regular sweat. Could Stacey smell it? "At ease, Mr. Johns. You're not on trial here. I don't do those—just judgment and sentencing. Miss Galena, you're newer to all this than Mr. Johns. Would you benefit from some explanation?"

"Yes, sir." Stacey, too, was uncertain about her status and what might happen to it if she didn't produce the right answers.

"I worked for a man, if a man you could call him, who had one leadership tool in his entire kit." Truitt swept all of the screens into a stack that faded back across the room, dismissed. "Fear." He turned to face Jeremy and Stacey. "Have I ever told either of you what I used to do in my past life?"

Jeremy and Stacey both shook their heads. Jeremy spared a glance at the distant screens. He assumed they remained unchanged and that Truitt knew it.

"I was a professor. I taught business strategy. I got my doctorate in military history and discovered that I could make far more money with that knowledge in the corporate world. Then I found I could make even more moonlighting as a consultant for large multinationals whose day-to-day existence was so unspeakably dull that they characterized everything they did in terms of heroism and battle to jazz it up. That's what corporate titans do. They can't live with an image of caring only about wealth, so they dress up their passion in layers of war talk. It was easy money. I threw Sun Tzu quotes at them for a few hours, backed it up with case studies, and deposited the checks. This was back in the days when you had to physically deposit them, Miss Galena. Barbarism, I say."

Stacey didn't give in to the temptation to look at Jeremy.

Jeremy returned the favor.

"Two Sun Tzu quotes do come into play here, actually." Truitt steepled his fingers and peered at the two of them over the tips. "The first is to let your plans be dark and impenetrable as night, and the other is that all warfare is based on deception. My last job was toiling under one of the most monolithic thinkers I've ever met—also one of the most vicious and violent. He understood one approach, as I've said: threaten and punish; confront and eviscerate; dominate and victimize. All very unpleasant and certainly not the most motivating—particularly if you were unfortunate enough to be female."

Once again, Stacey continued to sit attentively. Jeremy

assumed, as he figured she did, that Truitt wouldn't have characterized it that way if he agreed with it.

"Where the hell am I going with all this?" Truitt collapsed his finger church and slapped his hands on his knees. "Apart from the tripe I fed clients long ago, I learned from my most recent manager—if we may call what he did management, which we may not—that the head-down rush into battle on top of a policy of cruelty has its shortcomings over the long run. In fact, it can leave you with your ass in ashes after it's been handed to you by a teenage boy." He chuckled ruefully. "It pays to have more than one plan."

Jeremy and Stacey waited for him to continue. Some offering from their side was expected. "Mr. Brill?" Jeremy said.

"Mr. Brill. A one-plan man. And again, that's not a term I really believe should be applied." He gestured to the screens, which seemed to be more distant than they should have been, given the size of the room. They swooped down into their former positions.

As far as Jeremy could see, they still hadn't changed. The readouts were all frozen.

Truitt didn't pay the paralysis much mind. "Three levels of planning," he said. "Three. You can do some follow-up reading with what I'll make available to you should we all emerge from this victorious, but here is the simple breakdown. The first wave was to put Annie Brucker and her son in the care—and again, that's not really a word to be used in their situation—of her ex-husband, who is a decidedly not-nice person. Mr. Brucker was given his marching orders to ride herd on the two of them. The point was to keep tabs on the little boy and encourage the former missus, who was made to forget that she was a former, to work as hard as possible to hand her knowledge and abilities over to us via rote tasks. Mr. Brucker was aided by a sentient and rather icky rider placed inside her person that was in turn aided by a regimen of injections to make her open to suggestion."

The screens rotated through a quick review of their metrics, seemingly of their own accord.

Jeremy fought once again to prevent the resulting queasiness from having its way with him.

"Now," said Truitt. "It appears that my main route of choice, to hijack the mother and ex-wife's access to the central nervous system of several realms—which she sees mainly as a reef of sorts—has been denied me. She and her son are beyond my reach, it would seem. And my rider no longer answers my queries or entreaties, so I can only assume it's been discovered and dealt with. Yet I am not distressed. Why do you suppose that is, Mr. Johns?"

Jeremy still had nothing to offer. It was well past becoming a trend.

Stacey started to say something, thought better of it, and stopped.

"Miss Galena?" Truitt was enjoying himself.

"Another dark plan," said Stacey.

"Another dark plan! I like that." Yes, the man really was having a jolly time. He gestured toward the screens again, and a new one came forward. On it was a dense, hideously complicated schematic of a network of some kind.

Now Stacey joined Jeremy in looking away. To gaze upon the blueprint for more than a second or two was to risk falling into it.

"This is what Annie Brucker built for me," said Mr. Truitt. "Not only couldn't we have done it without her, we couldn't even have conceived of such a thing. All day, she made connections without understanding what she was handing us, yet hand it to us she did. In fact, it's rather laughable to call it a backup. Now why would that be, Miss Galena?"

Stacey offered a blink or two and a minor squint.

"Because the living arrangement and the implant were the deceptions," said Jeremy. "This was the real plan all along."

Truitt clapped his hands and pointed at Jeremy in approval, unable to contain his glee or the smile of satisfaction that accompanied it. "And so." He pointed toward the schematic with equal enthusiasm.

The flash from the massive network on the screen made all three of them avert their eyes. Jeremy had to blink several times before he realized the lights would dance on the insides of his lids for the next week or more.

"And so." Mr. Truitt crossed his arms in gratification. "And so."

## 43

# HERE WE GO

There was only one way to the top of the Backbreaker, and that was the corkscrew stairway. There was no way to carry Audra up, even if she would have accepted the Dodger's help. "I'm not fast. I'm tenacious," she told him. And that's how she eventually ended up on the platform perched on a high hill overlooking the plains below.

The Backbreaker was the nickname of a hillside ride that had officially been designated the Looper when the owner of a theme park known for its injured—and, occasionally, dead—customers dreamt it up. And dreamt was all it was, for to say it had been designed was to be overly generous.

It was a simple idea—an enclosed waterslide tube with a loop in it—but no engineer was ever consulted. And certainly not anyone who knew anything about safety or the human form. So when it was tested, too many bloody noses and wrenched spines came out the other end for the attraction to open to the public.

Audra's climb was difficult, for the wooden steps were perpetually wet with the drippings of repeat customers imagined by the attraction's owner. And even though the Breaker—

as it was called by those who loved shortening names—sat alone without its slippery tube attached, and though there was no water anywhere around it, its steps remained drenched and perilous.

Still, Audra made it to the top in order to watch what was coming to Demeter. She had no control over the process once she'd done her part to kick it off, and she wanted to bear witness as it unfolded.

Below, as far as her aged-but-still-sharp eyes could see, an ocean of bison covered the ground in an endless blanket of horns, beards, and brawn. This was yet another way that Demeter and its gathered Essence displayed the range of life and playfulness within.

"A sea of microbuses," said Lars, looking over Audra's shoulder.

"Yes, but microbuses that will hook and trample you if you're foolish enough to get too close."

"What's going to happen to them?"

"When the detonation gets the process going fully, you'll see a reaction from them, and they'll start to move. From there, I honestly don't know. Judging by what's been communicated to me, they'll be among the first to be pulled in, along with the plant life and other expressions of Demeter Essence."

Lars looked down at the platform beneath their feet. "But not this thing we're standing on, right?"

Audra laughed. "No. The nature of the process precludes it from doing harm to any being that's retained its living form."

Shadows of clouds passed over the vast stretches of bison like dark hands stroking their backs, comforting them for the ordeal to come. The gentle breeze caressing the platform came from behind them, and though Audra knew the bison weren't true-to-life, she was nevertheless glad the wind was at their backs. She'd been made no promises that the beasts wouldn't smell.

With the next slight increase in the air current, the animals began to mill around. Something was happening, and the bison could feel it now.

"Here we go," said Audra.

∼

Po's instincts picked up on what didn't fit before his conscious mind managed to. He should have attacked by now in order to gain whatever edge he could. Instead, he wanted to joyfully tackle his foe, which made no sense.

"Boss?" Joel had sensed Po's feelings.

Paul watched the walking shadow and Po, as if he hoped to understand what was happening but saw no way to get there.

The form.

The form and the build.

This was not the toad-like bulk of the Brill-spawned monster they'd all battled, the enemy defeated by the sacrifice of a beloved friend. A good part of that bulk was there, but the creature stood upright, like a man. There was the suggestion of something else in place of its horns and it's knotted form. Draped shadow, like fabric. Something to the shape of the head.

A hat and coat.

"Boss," Joel said again—a caution this time, as if the Tamagotchi intuited what Po wanted to do.

Porter reached out with his staff to pull Po back. "It's not what you thought. But it's not what you think."

If Po had any doubt about his feelings as the living darkness made its way out of the shadows, they were banished by Paul's reaction. The young man, no longer the boy Po recalled, was wrestling with the same emotions Po was. Part of him looked like he was going to call on his formidable abilities to defend them, and the other looked to be greeting a long-lost comrade.

"Hello, friend," Porter said once it was clear Po wouldn't make any sort of move toward the Shade. "Am I speaking to a friend?" The Envoy's fatigue was palpable. As was that of the Shrine around them. Its very walls glistened with something akin to perspiration. The structure itself was stressed, almost as if it were empathizing with Porter. He'd held Po back. But he was also restraining something far, far larger and more powerful—he and the Shrine both.

The shadow man-beast stopped at the word *friend*. It sniffed the air, sampling the scent of the sound. Then it folded its arms in a way so familiar to Po that it was a blow to the heart.

Po was never more grateful for his pursuit of silence, for he hadn't the words to give expression to what was in him—and wanted out.

"We need your help," Porter said. "We need you to complete the chain that will greet the Essence our foes are sending and convince it to follow our path, to go where we wish, not where others wish. That will require the combined strength of those of us who unknowingly helped perpetrate the deception and wrong to begin with. Do you understand?"

The altered Shade made no move, which was the best they could hope for at the moment. Its normal mode, after all, would have been to try and kill them.

Porter extended his staff out vertically and held it above the floor of the Shrine. The staff shook with the effort, and Po wondered again what struggle would require so much energy and effort from the Envoy and the Shrine he'd helped to build. He struck the Shrine floor with the staff, and the force radiating from the impact was vast. It weakened Porter further, but he held on. He was strong beyond the look of his years. After a moment, he placed his other hand atop the staff and looked to Paul.

Paul hesitated, refusing to meet Porter's gaze. Whatever came next, it wasn't easy for him. Then he looked Porter in the eye and placed his hand atop the Envoy's.

The walls of the Shrine shimmered then, as if they were hiding behind a desert heat. The ground trembled.

Porter looked to Po. "I asked you for trust. You should understand that while I can't tell you precisely what you'll take part in should you join this effort, you are choosing a side —even if you're not certain whose it is." He blinked sweat from his eyes. "Do I have your trust, Po?"

Po looked from Porter, to Paul, to the Shade, and then to the staff.

"Boss," said Joel, but there was no conviction in it, no indication of what choice he wanted Po to make.

Po knew. He'd always known. He reached out to place his hand on top of Paul's.

The walls of the Shrine shimmered again.

Porter's knees nearly buckled.

Now the Shade. They were trusting the dark monster, too, making themselves completely vulnerable to its hunger. The beast drew close, and it occurred to Po that none of them had the strength to defend themselves against it. There was no reason it wouldn't all end here.

"Boss," Joel said again.

With the Shade's approach, Po could feel everything inside him pushing against the confines of his skin—of the thin shell of his consciousness. Life. Memory. Love. If the creature wanted to take all of that from him and leave him vacant and adrift, he'd be utterly unable to prevent it.

Paul's face hid nothing of what he was feeling. Nistar, he'd been called—and despite the way the worlds had shifted, he remained one. Yet he was offering himself up to the dark forces of his former enemy, too.

The Shade became a part of their group.

Po was acutely aware that the only thing keeping him and his friends from being stripped of their very Essence was the monster's unwillingness to do so.

But how long might that last?

## 44

## NAUSEA FROM THE TEEN YEARS

There was a reason Charlene had stopped trying to make herself enjoy weed while still a teen. Whenever she smoked, it ended up making her focus on whatever negative sensation she was feeling, ballooning it to the point where it was the whole of existence. If she felt a little sick, as she often did after a couple of drinks that preceded a quick session with friends, then the weed made her think only of that. When she suffered from cotton mouth, and water wasn't handy, her mind couldn't set that parched feeling aside. It was never the case that she thought there'd be permanent damage from any of it, but in the moment, it was almost impossible to convince herself entirely.

That was the heat assailing everyone in the room with her.

Heat but not heat.

Light but not light.

One moment, they felt that something was being held back—a huge force wanting to overwhelm them. The next, it was upon them without warning.

Hot.

Oven hot.

Light and whiteness to the point where she couldn't see anyone else in the room.

Couldn't hear.

The sensation of being roasted alive was all.

She'd never felt heat like this, and she'd never survive it.

Until, that is, she understood that she would.

Part of her did.

Not consciously, perhaps.

More like a small someone in the back of the room stood up and waved frantically until Char received the message. *This hurts like it's real, but it isn't. You'll make it through this, even if you don't accept that idea until it's over.*

Burning hair. There was no smell like that, and once it made its way into her nose, it would never leave.

Until the voice told her that, too, was illusion. Or partial illusion.

There was no burning; only the signals telling her there was.

Char suspected the small voice knew it was exaggerating the silver lining of the situation. There was no indication that it appreciated what it was to have the moisture in you boil your skin away, even if that wasn't actually happening—to feel it occur, whether it occurred or not.

So familiar. Nausea from the teen years. With a few hundred degrees thrown in just for laughs.

A hand grabbed her leg. The touch focused her pain, and Char tried to pull away. Another gripped her shoulder. Someone familiar said her name.

Reinhard.

The former Vigil said something else, and she heard it, but its meaning slid away and into the boiling.

A cry of pain from somewhere else in the room. Such sounds hadn't made it to her before.

Now they did.

And just as Charlene was beginning to wonder if that meant the situation was getting better or worse, the heat began to subside.

But only just.

How long did it take to fade to the point where the pain of it—the perceived pain, she had to remind herself—was unbearable as opposed to world-ending?

Hours?

Minutes that felt like hours.

Did time factor into this?

The exhalation of breath somewhere near. A man. Someone who'd held his breath and had only just let it out.

What did that mean? Had he given up, or was he relieved to know things were getting better?

They were getting better.

"Charlene," Reinhard said again.

Now Char heard him more clearly. She laid her hand on top of his where it rested on her shoulder. She wasn't alone in this ordeal. He was suffering through it, too—and yet he still tried to look after her.

Hadn't she recently promised herself she'd give him work to match his talents? Why hadn't she realized he had it now?

Another drop-off in the terribleness. There was no other way to put it. It had been awful only a moment before. Now it was really bad.

Quite the improvement.

"Wow," said a woman. Nicolette, wherever she was in the room. "Wow."

"Hang in there," someone else said. D.W.

It occurred to Charlene that she could go either way on that sentiment—blast him for being too much of a Pollyanna or thank him later for trying to see everyone through this thing.

She'd forgotten just what this thing was. How had it started? Why were they on fire?

Another drop.

"Good God," said a voice from far away, and now things must have gotten better because Charlene had the mental capacity to understand it was a voice from Quarry's head that was not Quarry's.

Someone in the silo facility, which meant the silos were still there. That had to be good, right? If they'd survived being the source of all this, then there had to be hope for those in Envoy HQ.

Further improvement. Then the rebound pain, like a doctor pushing on the sore spot and asking which was worse, pressing in or letting it out again.

Letting it out again wasn't great, but it was much better than the initial push.

More of a drop now.

Another voice from Quarry's head asked D.W. if he was still there.

"We're here," said Nicolette.

Charlene was impressed with the woman's faith. She herself was still trying to blink some moisture back into her eyes and wasn't completely sure she'd survived.

"Well, that was fun," said D.W. "But here's the question. We know where it came from. We do, right?"

"Yes," said Nicolette.

"But I know the next question," Charlene said.

"Me, too," said Reinhard. "Where the hell is it going?"

Truitt's screen displayed crude late-twentieth-century graphics—a video game or a movie from that time showing what nuclear annihilation looked like through the lens of an old-school tube monitor. In such a film, military types and those trying to stop them from destroying the world usually stared helplessly as dotted lines representing ICBMs in flight arced and descended on various spots around a world map. Then the screens would flash brightly with expanding circles of white as the world died amid squealing telephones, radio static, and television snow.

What was on Truitt's screen at the moment was not a map Jeremy recognized. Rather, it was a white-on-black graphic representation of what Jeremy first took to be a weird pomegranate of some sort.

"A pine cone?" said Stacey.

Truitt rewarded her with a slow nod.

A pine cone, then. Whatever it was, a storm of missile-like dotted lines entered from all over the screen and began a slow rain onto it.

Stacey glanced at Jeremy for a quick visual check. Both of them took comfort in not understanding what was happening.

"Just watch," said Truitt. "Each individual chamber up there is a realm. A world. Now look at what separates them. Do you see?" With a wave of his hand, two of the chambers—Jeremy preferred to think of them as cells—turned a pale green. The screen zoomed in enough for them to make out gaps of various sizes in the line separating the two. "Those are the targets. All except the one we're going to keep open, which is one of ours."

"Are there enough?"

"Enough what, Mr. Johns?"

"Missiles, sir." The screen zoomed in further as the ICBMs descended. The gapped line between The Living World and

The Commons split into two while the realms bled into one another—the gaps remaining, the division an overlap now. With the increased focus, those gaps were too numerous to count. Some were so small, Jeremy had to squint to make them out. And there was no question that there were more gaps than ICBMs.

"Don't get literal on me, Mr. Johns. It's not a true representation of what's occurring. There's no physical occurrence at all. It's a visualization. That's why the system opts for this retro tech. It helps reinforce the notion that what you're seeing is not in any sense real."

Stacey looked to Jeremy again, and he gave her a subtle shrug. Neither of them were keeping up.

"I saw that." Truitt was almost playful. Things were going his way, and he was clearly feeling uncharacteristically generous. As the missiles continued their descent, he sat up to watch more intently. "Now it gets interesting."

Jeremy couldn't be sure if he was addressing them or himself.

A blue layer began to materialize above the center overlap of the realms, a uniform cloud forming over the entirety of it.

"Watch now," said Truitt quietly. "Watch." No wonder he'd been a teacher of strategy. He was like a little kid watching one of his play out.

The missiles began to converge, all of them headed for the floating layer.

"Watch."

Jeremy and Stacey shifted in their seats, unable to contain their own anticipation, though neither of them knew what they were anticipating.

"Watch."

The missiles all met at the new layer.

DOWN BELOW, the bison grew ever more restless. It was difficult to determine whether any one of them led the others; the disturbance appeared to be evenly distributed. Audra had only heard of such things happening, mostly in old files describing events that may have been real or could have been theoretical models used to prepare the Envoys and Vigils for such an eventuality.

There was nothing to do but watch.

"Which direction will they go when they start running?" said the Dodger.

"They won't. They'll scatter. But we won't know until it's over if they've dispersed as much as we need them to." Then Audra crossed her fingers. Because she wasn't sure they'd know even then.

## 45

## THE MOMENT OF SUCH A REUNION

With all that he and Porter had been through together, it was an odd time for Paul to question how well he really knew the Envoy. Nevertheless, as they stood together—the staff as their fulcrum, with Porter's, Paul's, and Po's hands stacked atop the center spindle of the crafted head—that thought arose.

Paul's memory told him to believe Porter—the process they'd begun was necessary to carry the day. But Po was clearly unsure, as was the Tamagotchi he wore around his neck.

The way the Shade regarded them—and it was definitely looking them over despite lacking discernible eyes—was purely a dynamic of predator and prey. It brought to mind a moment from Paul's childhood at one of the numerous shelters he'd lived in, when one of the nastier kids caught a daddy longlegs and tossed it into a spider's web just to see what would happen. What horrified Paul most was the moment the spider spotted the free meal just as the daddy longlegs seemed to realize where it was. Both tensed up, and the prey's fear left it paralyzed as the spider pounced and killed it.

Paul was the daddy longlegs being scoped out by the Shade. It had taken all of them to fight it to a standstill before Ken sacrificed himself. Now here it was, and Porter expected them to do nothing to defend themselves.

Just having the dark creature so close drew Paul's energy from him. The effect was muted, however, as if part of the Shade wanted to kill them all but was held back somehow.

Where had the monster been? How had it changed, and why was it here now?

"Porter," Paul said. But he couldn't think of anything more to add.

The Envoy didn't respond as the Shade approached. His silence held when it joined their group and reached out to cover their hands with its much larger shadow appendage, which was somewhere between hand and paw.

There was something familiar about the Shade's presence, both good and terrible. When it made contact with Po's hand, the monk started slightly and stared at the black beast in combined wonder and horror.

The walls of the Shrine glitched in sympathy. That was the only word for it. It was like an image on a monitor with a bad cord, blinking out momentarily and returning in full.

Porter let out a sigh of relief as whatever burden he and the Shrine had borne was lifted.

No.

Not lifted.

Focused.

Completed.

Whether friend or foe, those you've been in battle with form an intimate bond with you. Their group, now joined, had thrown down for keeps more than once. They were missing Rain and Ken, but those now present made for a potent combination.

As grim as a struggle for one's survival could be, there was a nostalgia for the violence that was discernible only at the moment of such a reunion.

Paul sensed the Shade's hunger. Along with that, he felt another will controlling it, ensuring the monster would not do the damage it had been created to do.

The paradox of that was central in Paul's consciousness for but a second. A wind arose from nowhere, and the world went negative—its lights darks; its darks lights. Paul worried he might pass out, but that wasn't an option. The only choice now was to become one with the surge washing over all of them, over and through the Shrine.

Appease.

Outlast.

Survive.

"Boss," warned Joel the Tamagotchi.

A moment later, the Shrine and Porter relaxed, releasing something fundamental and crucial that had been dammed but was held back no longer. And though he had no detailed understanding of what was happening, Paul could feel himself helping them, his innate abilities joining in whatever process Porter had set in motion.

The reunion had been needed—the recall of the struggle for the restoration of The Commons before Paul's defeat of Brill did the division of the realms such grievous harm. Now was their opportunity to get it right.

It was all they could do to hold on. And Paul began to understand that it was not just them.

They received help from something else. Something far larger than all of them—and infinitely more powerful. They couldn't do what was necessary without that greater force.

Paul glanced around the group and knew: this was Porter's doing. The Envoy had cut a deal. And with that knowledge

*The Catalyst*

came the certainty that the gray man had kept the arrangement to himself.

Still, he'd asked for their trust.

Paul, Po, and even the Shade had no choice but to give it to him now that the process had begun.

After that, there was nothing else to think about.

After that, they were on fire.

## 46

# A PEBBLE IN A PUDDLE

Audra didn't want to see the massive herd broken up. From a distance, it occupied her vision as a single entity, albeit one consisting of tightly interconnected pieces. A community. The huge beasts, slow at rest but quick and powerful when roused, were beautiful in their amalgamation. She didn't want to watch the bison provoked into chaos.

But what it would take to carry out the grand strategy to set things aright had nothing to do with what Audra wanted.

Ripples from the center of the herd spread slowly outward at first but soon picked up frequency and urgency. Shortly thereafter, what started as a pebble in a puddle was a bomb in an ocean. None of the bison were grazing anymore. They mulled about it in an increasing state of distress.

It hurt Audra to witness it. But it was what had to happen.

Her nerves caught fire. All of her recent burns ignited at once.

"Ma'am?" The Dodger reached out to support her.

"Don't touch me," Audra said as she moved away from

him, her tone sharper than Lars deserved. He was only trying to help.

She was just about to apologize when the curtain of flame erupted across the prairie. It cut along the herd's eastern flank in a wall that started at the north end and advanced to the south in the blink of an eye.

Audra's pain jumped the fence right along with that flame. She heard herself shriek.

The Dodger grabbed her shoulders despite what she'd said.

Audra went to the ground just to get away from him. That was worse.

The thunder of hooves.

Audra looked up to see the bison moving away from the flames in a wave. "No," she managed. It needed to be a dispersal. Anything else was a misdirection of the Demeter Essence and the ICBM Essence underlying it—a ship listing too far to one side, the shift in its cargo sealing its doom. "No."

"What's happening?" The Dodger was lost, and Audra felt for him despite her own suffering. Lars knew the importance of what they were doing, even if he didn't understand it all. But he grasped enough of it to know he was helpless in the face of this new development.

If only Audra could've enjoyed the luxury of such ignorance. "Help me up," she said, knowing full well what inviting his touch would mean.

His hands on her, pulling her to her feet, were worse than she'd expected. But Audra channeled the pain into the effort she sent out over the prairie. She wanted to start her own fire in front of the moving bison in an attempt to head them off.

It was absurd. A fantasy. But she had to try.

The great beasts trampled her best attempt before she'd managed to raise so much as a spark, and she crumpled into the Dodger's arms. Without him, she'd have been laid out flat, but what followed pushed all of that out of her mind.

The pain didn't matter. Not compared to the awareness that flowed into her as the hooves of the now-stampeding animals ground her inadequate attempt into the nothingness it deserved.

The in-between state of Demeter and The Margins, the numerous gaps and the crossing-over collapse of the realms meant adjacency carried far more power than it should have. And with that power, knowledge came to those who were touched.

Touched by awareness.

And betrayal.

Audra could divine the source and destination of all before her—all that she was a part of via her planning, involvement, and relationships. The breach of trust nearly robbed her of her breath, and when she was able to give voice to the faithlessness, it took a supreme effort to utter his name. "Jonas."

The moving wall of flame rose to tree height as it drove the ocean of horns and hooves before it in one dreaded direction. Audra's nerves lit up anew. She had an intimate acquaintance with that fire. It had touched her before, using her own tendency toward combustion to burn her severely despite its claim of wanting to cause no harm.

She knew the source of that flame. It was far stronger than she could ever dream of being, its only failing the lack of understanding as to how little it would take to do her in.

It made no such mistake now. It came out in full force to herd the bison in the direction it wanted.

"Lars, let me go, please."

The Dodger hesitated. He didn't want her to fall.

She sank to her knees with his help, her eyes on the awful spectacle before them.

The flames drove the bison west in a single wave. It was as if the entire prairie had begun a panicked migration. Under duress, the huge current of Demeter Essence went where it was compelled to go.

Adjacency, through all of the pain, told Audra what that destination was.

Friendship.

Loyalty.

Faith.

What did they mean at any other time if they meant nothing now?

"Lars." With the Dodger's help, she was able to get her hands around the Speaky Shrieky for one feeble attempt at changing the tide of what was probably past the point of being altered.

And it was. Audra studied the device as if it were new to her—just long enough to accept that it had nothing to offer. She couldn't reach Porter in any way that mattered. Even if she figured out some way to make him hear her, she'd never be able to convince him to listen.

"Jonas." Audra couldn't be certain she'd said it aloud.

"Ma'am?"

"Jonas, no."

Now she was sure she hadn't been heard.

Certainly not by Porter.

Maybe not even by the Dodger.

And maybe not by anyone at all.

## 47

# THE SAME THINGS FOR DIFFERENT REASONS

"I am not your friend," Apalala-Aidan told Paul, who looked like he was feeling far too ill to consider calling anyone at the table such a thing.

Zach felt bad for Paul, who'd been very kind to Zach and Zach's mother on the bus, when none of them had known what kind of future awaited. Zach felt bad for anyone who wasn't used to the things he was used to.

Zach had only ever known a state of being in-between—of traveling and wandering. In his world, nothing was ever what it was supposed to be because there wasn't any correct state for it. There was no getting used to it, liking it, or hating it. There was only living with it.

They were at the same table Zach had sat at with Apalala-Aidan when it had been just the two of them. Now Paul, Porter, and Po joined them.

Paul, Porter, and Po.

Zach couldn't say why he thought of the three by their proper names. It was wrong to think of them in any other way, given their shared experiences. Perhaps something in Zach's manner of moving through the world was changing.

That didn't surprise him. Things were always changing in the way Zach moved through the world.

It was another aspect of things moving fast.

A purple crayon lay on the piece of paper in front of Zach. It was like a dream, where it had always been there, and he hadn't noticed it. Or it hadn't, but once it appeared, it was like it always had. He picked the crayon up and began making lines and marks without giving any thought as to what he was drawing.

Paul looked feverish, confused. He studied the palms of his hands, which were shiny with sweat. His face was reddish, with patches of glistening beneath his eyes, as if he'd eaten something spicy.

Again, Zach felt for him. Zach made his way through the same spaces others did but not via the same coordinates. He traveled a few steps to the side, at a different angle. Which wasn't good or bad. It just was. It was all he'd ever done.

It all seemed new to Paul, and Paul looked like it was. He eyed Apalala-Aidan with the same unease Zach had felt when he'd met the young man. Somehow, it was less unsettling to see him in his dragon form than in his current guise of a skinny human with glasses. Your instincts told you your eyes were lying, that there was something very dangerous you were missing, that you couldn't trust what you saw.

You couldn't.

People milled around their cafe table, surveying the wares at the booths but never buying anything. Many of the people looked as uncomfortable as Paul, as if they'd attempted to accept that they were where they were but couldn't shake the feeling of wrongness.

Po betrayed nothing of his feelings. He sat without expression, watching the others, focusing on Apalala-Aidan in particular.

The face on the tiny screen of the toy that wasn't a toy hung from the monk's neck, mulling things over. Zach could tell because its dot-eyes rolled back and forth, watching its own thought bubbles as they rose from its head and popped. The toy that wasn't a toy was silent, though Zach suspected quiet was not its favored state. He wondered what the toy that wasn't a toy's name was. Once he discovered it, he would use that proper name, too.

Apalala-Aidan picked up the cup in front of him. It was the same one that had held the dark liquid he'd shared with Zach. Now, however, he upended it and put it back on the table upside-down.

Nothing spilled out. Either it was empty, or the foul drink inside had decided to stay put.

"Who is this?" Paul asked Porter, keeping his eyes on Apalala-Aidan.

"Someone who's telling the truth—he is not our friend." Porter had no time for softness or comfort. "He's friend to no one. But he's here to help us do what we'd never be able to do alone."

"Where are we?" Paul still didn't take his eyes off Apalala-Aidan.

Nor did Po.

"We are in a place of meeting." Apalala-Aidan slid his upside-down cup around in a few lazy circles. It appeared as if he were disturbing something trapped beneath it, against the table's surface, with each slow and deliberate cycle. "We are only able to meet because of what you did. And that's what we are here to address—what you did."

Paul's eyes darkened. Everyone at the table knew what Apalala-Aidan meant.

It was what they all had done. But Paul was the one to win

the final battle—so he carried most of the resulting burden. That was his choice. At the same time, it wasn't.

"Aidan is from The Pines, Paul," said Porter. "Because of what we saw as our victory, the barriers between realms have been breached, and more will be in the near future. Those in The Pines must never be able to access the other realms. Aidan was only able to do this by accident, when he ended up inextricably linked to software residing on the network of an old friend of ours—who, as you might imagine, is also no friend at all. Aidan's presence serves to further erode the barriers, so that the collapse of The Commons and The Living World into one another will be followed by the joining of all realms. That cannot be allowed to happen."

"Apalala," said Apalala-Aidan. "That was the software that pulled part of me into it and allowed me to be exorcised by someone at our adversary's company who didn't know what she was doing. She did, however, do me an inadvertent favor, as the module they were building for the next phase of the software was pure atrocity. As dark as those confined to The Pines may be, there are yet darker hearts to be found in the realm of man."

Zach studied the lines he made on the paper as if they'd been drawn by someone else. He was as eager to see how it would turn out as he would've been had another person created it. Because it was very much as if someone had.

No one noticed his handiwork.

"Adjacency drew me to Zach," said Apalala-Aidan. "I was weak and frightened, neither of which I've ever been before." He looked at Zach. "Zach gave me shelter when I needed it. That kindness, too, was unfamiliar." He moved his mug around in another circle. Zach couldn't decide if he was waiting for something to finish underneath the mug or if he wasn't particularly conscious of the movement. "So the part of me that remained in The Pines was able to bring Porter to me in order to deliver me here, where I made my proposal to him."

Porter watched Paul, who didn't appear to be any more at ease than he had been before.

"And?" said Paul. "I'm waiting for the big *and*, Porter."

"And," said Porter, "there are two plans—Audra's and the one Aidan and I have come up with. She doesn't know about ours."

Paul looked to Aidan, perhaps coming to a decision about him. "Does she know you're working together?"

"She does not." Porter spoke as if he needed to get it out before he wasn't able to anymore. "She must not." He glanced at Po, his expression more than a little guilty.

Po did not betray what he thought of that, either.

Reaching over to lay a hand on Aidan's mug, Paul pulled it toward him without lifting it at all. He, too, handled it like there was something underneath that might escape.

Aidan watched Paul without expression.

"What's her plan? And what's yours?" Paul said.

"Chemotherapy," said Porter.

"What?" Paul took his hand off the mug and let it hover over the vessel.

"A sloppy analogy and not a pleasant one," said Porter. "Chemo is the process of poisoning the entire body in the hopes that you'll kill the patient's cancer before you kill the patient. If the cancer returns, you do it again. And despite all the suffering, it still may not work."

Paul's hand dropped to the upside-down mug again.

"The real secret to curing and healing is to somehow make the body recognize the cancer so that the immune system targets the bad cells on its own. You need to make the host—the body—aware. And you need it to act on that awareness."

Gripping the inverted mug loosely, Paul rotated it in his own circle. Once. Twice. "I'm still waiting for the *and*."

"And Audra's plan is chemo. Chemo that won't work. Ours is aimed at teaching the body—the realms—to fix the problem for good."

Paul lifted the mug. There was nothing underneath. He looked surprised.

Apalala-Aidan still said nothing.

Paul held the mug over the empty surface. "So why not bring Audra in on it?"

Porter nodded, as if acknowledging the question's validity. "We've known each other a long time. We've had disagreements over similar decisions in the past. We are both stubborn and prone to absolute faith in our own wisdom."

"But—"

"If she had any notion of what we're planning, she would do everything she could to stop us." Again, Porter's tone was matter-of-fact. He'd already accepted the betrayal of his long-time friend and colleague. He glanced at Po again, but looked away when the monk remained stoic as ever.

"If I agree to help, what does that mean?" said Paul.

"We are going to start a process that will take a very long time to complete," Porter said. "From the time it starts to the time it finishes, The Living World will be open and vulnerable to outside forces."

Paul dropped the mug to the table with a bang loud enough to make several of the shoppers around them take notice.

A look from Apalala-Aidan made the observers lose interest.

"That doesn't sound safe to me," said Paul.

"It's not," Porter said. "It's absurdly dangerous. It will almost certainly lead to war."

"Between?"

"Us and our adversaries, which right now are an entity called Manitou and those it thinks of as its allies." Porter's words came out heavily, weighted with the understanding of what such a war would entail.

"War is not good." Paul stared at Apalala-Aidan as he said it, but the words were meant for Porter.

"No. It is not. So we must be good at it."

Paul tapped the mug against the table's surface without the reverence he'd had for it just moments before. He looked to Po for guidance, but the monk maintained his distance. "And my part in this?"

"As vital a part as you had in creating this situation with me," said Porter. "Our abilities are needed to cause what's necessary to happen. Po's participation is critical because of his adjacency. And Aidan's strength is indispensable. Neither of us would withstand the forces at play without him. I move the Essence. You alter it as only a Nistar can."

Paul watched Apalala-Aidan, his eyes hardening. Without any warning, he shoved the upside-down mug across the table at the young man, who caught it easily.

When Apalala-Aidan began making slow circles with it again, Zach thought he saw him smile.

"There is no black and white here," Porter told Paul. "No good and bad. There are only those working toward the same things for different reasons. An in-between time calls for in-between answers."

"I'm not saying no."

Porter studied Paul for a moment or two and nodded. "In an in-between time, that will do."

Zach watched Po until he'd decided the monk and the toy that wasn't a toy weren't going to commit to anything out loud. Then he looked down at his drawing, which he'd finished without realizing he had. He stared and let his sight and mind relax in order to see what it was. Once he recognized it, there was no other way to interpret what otherwise might have been an abstract blur.

It was a pine cone, seen from the bottom.

And it was in flames.

## 48

## APALALA AND ZACH SAY HELLO

The flash this time was shockingly bright. It didn't hurt. But maybe the optic nerve wasn't capable of communicating pain. And people should know better than to subject themselves to the white-out he, Stacey, and Truitt had just endured.

"Watch now," said Truitt.

When Jeremy was able to semi-clearly make out the old man—who scanned the displays as if nothing notable had just happened—he saw an intense joy that was utterly novel. The old Truitt was like a man who'd given up on anything good ever happening for him. In his place now was someone who looked decades younger.

"Watch," Truitt said again.

Jeremy and Stacey watched as well as they could.

Stacey alternated between extended blinks and opening her eyes wide.

Jeremy took no joy in her discomfort, but it made him feel a little better that she, too, had been hit hard by the flash.

On the largest display, the layer over the inverted pine cone pulsed with the Essence it had absorbed from the multitude of ICBM detonations. All of the missiles were gone. Only their energy remained, settled in like snakes working to engulf and digest all of the represented worlds.

"Remember now—don't interpret any of this literally," said Truitt. "No missiles were launched. Nothing has been physically impacted or attacked. This is all a model."

"A simulacrum," Stacey said.

If Jeremy were more suspicious or, frankly, cared more about competing with her, he might have mentally dinged Stacey for trying to impress the boss. That didn't matter now.

Truitt gave Stacey a token glance of approval. The display was all that mattered.

And the display earned the honor. The Essence layer broke up into a network of lines that coalesced along the barriers separating the inner and outer borders of the pine cone. Each line glowed, the divisions and boundaries of the individual cells receiving a thorough going-over from the Essence. It joined those partitions, merging with them until the entire representation was once again what it had been. Only now, brighter streams of Essence flowed through the lines of demarcation like veins carrying a fast-moving blood they could scarcely contain.

"Now," Truitt said. "Now."

As the effect of the flash diminished, Jeremy was able to make out more subtle distinctions in the array of lines and shapes that made up the upside-down pine cone. The boundaries were not uniform; they were as uneven and rough as the lines on a real tree or cone—thicker here, thinner there. And the Essence inhabiting them followed those flaws like a living force, taking up complete residence, exploring all of the facets, shapes, and borders.

After a time, the Essence began to coalesce around the borders of two of the pine cone's segments, both of which were adjacent to the large central segment with the thick ring encircling it.

"Can either of you tell me what the Essence is seeking out?"

Stacey waited a moment to give Jeremy the opportunity to answer.

By the time Jeremy picked up on that, he'd waited too long.

"The Commons and The Living World," she said.

Truitt gave a satisfied nod.

Stacey was laying claim to the star-pupil spot, even if it wasn't intentional.

Jeremy didn't mind a bit. In fact, this development convinced him more than ever that it wasn't a position he was interested in.

The display zoomed in on the center of the pine cone until the double-walled ring around it and the surrounding regions filled the screen. The Essence now attached itself solely to the pieces representing The Commons and The Living World. The dividing line between the two realms had bifurcated, the dual lines intersecting each other, leaving the area known as The Margins in between.

The intersection was neither and both. Minute spaces and gaps in the double-barrier were plainly visible, and they were rendered even more obviously by the bright Essence that flowed to those gaps, concentrating on and bridging them.

"Now," Truitt said.

The three of them watched in what would have been silence were it not for Truitt's breathing. In Jeremy's experience, the old man had always been a cool customer. He remained one now, for the most part, but his inhalations and exhalations were audible. He was wholly invested in this process and its outcome.

Truitt began to speak again, but the effort trailed off in a grunt.

Something was off.

What had been a smooth process was going awry.

"Come on now." Truitt's tone remained commanding, but there was no denying the touch of doubt.

The Essence focused on all of the gaps in the crossed-over barriers between The Commons and The L.W.

"Come on," said Truitt.

Jeremy waited for what was supposed to occur: the Essence was meant to leave one gap in the barriers open while closing the others.

Instead, it was working on all of the visible gaps, repairing each and every one of them.

Truitt's breathing quickened.

The double-walled ring around the center nugget, which represented The Pines, began to glow even brighter than the Essence working on the lines of The Margins, L.W., and Commons. That brightness grew and came forward.

What made its way to the center of the screen was almost funny. But Jeremy had no urge to laugh—and he doubted Stacey did, either.

A pixelated cartoon dragon with big googly eyes and exaggerated Groucho-like brows floated to the forefront, digitized wings flapping clumsily. On its back was a little boy who was blank-faced, even by the standards of the '80s-era graphics on display.

"What?" Truitt hissed.

Neither Jeremy nor Stacey were foolish enough to hazard a guess.

They didn't have to.

The explanation, if one could call it that, came with the blocky words that chunked their way across the screen under the hovering dragon and boy. "Apalala and Zach say hello," read the cartoonish line of text, which grew until it filled the screen.

With that, the dragon took a deep breath and blew out a thick cloud of smoke and flame that started as bad digitization but grew into a real-world conflagration.

Truitt's breathing stopped.

The pine cone and the floating screen caught fire.

## 49

## THE RULES OF REALITY

"Boss." Joel's voice was far away. "Boss, this really hurts."

Po agreed but couldn't do anything to indicate that to Joel.

They were on fire. And Po could focus only on keeping them from being swept away by the heat coursing around and through him—the force doing its best to devour them.

"This hurts, boss."

Po had nothing more than hope to offer the Tamagotchi. And he couldn't even tell him.

Nor could he say where they were now. They'd been in the Shrine, and then they'd been in the market in the former train station. But Po hadn't been fooled. When asked to believe they were in the latter, they'd remained in the former. That was part of the in-between state, as Porter called it—a state Po knew was far more comfortable for Porter, the being called Aidan, the child Zach, and even Paul than it was for him.

It was likely they remained in the Shrine. But the massive flow of Essence through that conduit distorted any sense of place.

Through the Shrine.

Through each of them.

And all of them.

As Porter indicated, they were all needed for the transfer to work. Whether because of their adjacency to the fight that ultimately brought the gaps into existence or because of their role in the struggle that set all of this in motion, each of them was necessary.

That was why they were all burning.

Physical location had no meaning in the middle of a firestorm.

You were alight. That was all you needed to know. That was all there was.

"Boss."

The train-station market. The Shrine. The fire.

In-between.

They were in each place—and all places at once.

In flames.

"Boss."

∽

"I'm sorry, Charlene," Quarry's head said from its spot on the table.

Charlene was exhausted enough from being cooked to pity the disembodied rock man. He'd been on the wrong side. Then he'd jumped to theirs. She wasn't prepared to say that theirs was the right one just yet because she couldn't be sure which side was which. "For what?" she replied.

"Need you ask?" said Reinhard.

Charlene ignored the former Vigil.

"For the part I've played in this."

Charlene wanted to suss out what Quarry meant by that,

but her mind wouldn't work. "In what? This thing we've all played a part in?"

Static issued from the stony opening that served as Quarry's mouth. Somewhere between radio hiss and a sigh of disagreement. "I helped access the missiles. Now look."

"At what?" Reinhard said. "We don't even know what's happening."

The rock man was silent for a long moment. "But I do."

Now nobody in the room had anything to say.

"Guys?" Another voice from Quarry's head. Liam. Faint, but definitely Liam. "We have a target after all."

"What?" said Reinhard.

"What's the target, Liam?" Charlene didn't want Reinhard stepping in, and he would if she didn't shake off her fatigue. She had nothing but respect for him, but he would bring his own combustive touch to the situation, and they'd already had more than enough fire.

"Good question." Liam's transmission was clipped—nearly inaudible at the beginning and end when he spoke. It would've been something to complain about but for the fact that they shouldn't have been able to talk to him at all, given the distance and circumstance.

When did Charlene stop marveling at talking to a hippie warrior about a massive nuclear detonation via a talking stone head? Well, that's what happened when you didn't have time to worry about the things that otherwise might make you doubt your sanity.

Liam continued. "We don't know. It's not anything that shows up on any coordinates we can grasp."

"That makes no sense," said Nicolette. "It has to show up on something in order for you to have it."

"You'd think. But whoever chose these numbers doesn't see it that way. Our systems have adapted to the overlap of

The Living World with The Commons. Not well enough for us to know exactly where things are in The L.W., of course—and definitely not in The Margins. But we'd know, roughly speaking, if they were headed for any of the three places we can touch. They're not."

"Then where?" said Charlene.

"Unknown."

"Not true." Quarry's voice was louder than Liam's. "Not in any way, unfortunately."

∽

All of the worlds collided for Annie, but that was okay because it was just a dream.

Wasn't it?

She was asleep. That was all she wanted to do. Sleep and heal.

So if she was sleeping, it was a dream. The rules of reality dictated that had to be the case.

Only here Annie sat, in front of the switchboard—and she wasn't wearing the VR rig. It felt like she really was there.

In the room, two noises competed with each other—one that made sense and one that didn't even come close.

The first was the sound of the train. That was an anchor. She was on the train. If that wasn't true, then nothing was.

But below the sound of the train was the low hum of insects that had once been angry with her but now tolerated her presence because they understood she needed to be there.

Fine. No more stings.

The switchboard. How could she be back in front of it when she was also on the train? Why was it covered in dandelions that had taken root in whatever sockets weren't claimed by plugged-in cords? Why did the cords blur in the poor light, distorting themselves to the point where when she blinked, they almost looked like tentacles?

Tentacles.

Oh, lord.

That little detail made everything else fade. It contributed to the little twist in her stomach that confirmed something well beyond her was happening, even though she was a critical part of it. Annie and the work she'd done under Bobby's influence.

The tentacles and dandelions weren't even the worst of it. The worst was that the cords were plugged in to form a completely unfamiliar pattern, one nothing like those she'd seen when working this board. It wasn't anyone else's board; it was hers.

Somebody had taken her work to another level. For no reason she could name, the pattern laid out between the dandelion growth made her queasy in its wrongness. Nothing she could explain but wrong all the same. Whatever they were connecting, whatever messages or information flow they permitted, it definitely went against the rules.

Maybe that was why she was here. Because there was something she could do about that.

Annie had to stare at the cables for a long while in order to build up the courage to act and then decide what that action would be. She reached out to pull two of the plugs she thought might disrupt the entire scheme.

The buzzing grew louder.

When she laid hands on the first plug, it jumped beneath her like a living thing surprised.

Wet. Slime.

It looked like a cable. But it felt like a tentacle.

Before Annie could pull it as planned, she awoke in the dark of a bunk on the moving train.

There was only the train noise now.

The buzzing was gone.

∽

THE DISPLAY and the pine-cone map of the realms burned longer than they should have. They didn't follow the rule of bonfires or even the smaller, more controlled sort Jeremy grew up with—when his father used only those prepackaged fuel logs that promised a uniform burn time. With any other fire, you could watch the thing being burned change shape, diminish, and, ultimately, give itself over to the force satisfying its hunger.

Not here. Not when you were talking about the everything of all, the entire set of worlds upon worlds upon worlds.

Jeremy didn't know what was happening on the screen or what was represented by the realistic flames started by the cheesy dragon and the kid, both of whom were now gone. He glanced from Truitt to Stacey.

There was no sign that he'd given away anything of how the dragon and the little boy weren't new to him.

When it all subsided into a small circle of heat and flame around the pine cone's center, it looked like nothing had burned. The realms were untouched, and the screen itself bore no signs of damage. No melting. No stench from whatever the housing was made of. If it even had a housing.

But you wouldn't know that to watch Truitt. He'd clearly thought he understood what was supposed to happen much better than Jeremy or Stacey did.

They caught each other's eye again to confirm that neither of them knew what was going on. Then they focused on the white-haired man staring at the screen.

Truitt rubbed his legs with his hands. Then he found his

chin and massaged his jaw as he struggled to figure out what they were seeing.

The missiles were gone.

So was the inferno.

There was only an intense glow, as if the ring around the center of the pine cone were a hot coal.

Truitt exhaled a little. "Madness," he said to himself. "Madness." He was a little louder the second time, like he wanted to be sure Jeremy and Stacey heard him. "What we're seeing cannot be what is occurring—and certainly not what anyone would plan."

Jeremy's impression of Truitt shifted. He'd initially taken him to be a garden-variety authoritarian whose expression of frustration or rage was due to someone defying his wishes, knowingly or unknowingly. And there probably was some of that in him. But it looked like what bothered him most now was the lack of coherence. He couldn't make sense of the situation, and that, to Jeremy, made him more interesting—and much scarier.

Jeremy and Stacey exchanged looks again to determine which of them should speak up. There was no question that someone should.

"What is it, sir?" said Stacey.

Truitt's hands moved from his jawline to the back of his neck. It didn't appear he'd ever be able to massage the stiffness out of it. "It's utterly unhinged," he said. "The Pines." He leaned forward, elbows on knees, head in hands. "They're attacking The Pines."

## 50

## AN EXQUISITE CORPSE

"This hurts, Boss," Joel the Tamagotchi said again, but Po didn't answer him.

Paul felt sorry for the little living toy, who, more than anyone else at the market table, probably had the least say over his current circumstance. Paul was fairly sure, however, that any expression of sympathy would not be greeted warmly. Anyway, all this thinking was just a way to distract himself from the question Porter was putting before him.

"I understand your hesitation," Porter told him from across the table. "I'm asking you to have blind faith in me. You've seen me working for the good of all in my past travels with you, but those efforts got us here, didn't they? So why listen to me at all?"

The others at the table showed varying levels of interest. The young man who was either Apalala, Aidan, or both watched him with as much intensity as Porter did. The kid, Zach, watched him, too. But Paul suspected Zach's awareness was both in the current setting and off somewhere else at the same time.

Po was experiencing something completely different from the rest of them. Joel, too.

"What happens if I don't do this?" Paul said.

"Everything I'm attempting hits the wall," the Envoy replied. "All of the pieces must align for this to have a prayer of working. All of the adjacency, all of our abilities in one combined push. I can direct the Essence where it needs to go. But only you can alter its very nature in order for it to achieve what we need."

Around them, shoppers congregated around various merchant booths and food counters. A bar of sorts offered "beer from around the world and beyond." A group of businessmen laughed progressively louder with every unintelligible comment they added to what sounded like an exquisite corpse told in an alien tongue.

Paul and the others were surrounded by people living their normal daily lives. And he and his group were planning to do something that might end every one of them.

Joel said something about burning.

Paul tried to ignore it. But if Joel was complaining, then he could only imagine what Po was silently enduring. "How would I do it even if I wanted to?" he said. Most of the memories of what he'd done to get them to this state of collapsing realms had returned, but he was not at all confident in his ability to call upon and master his powers. And he couldn't understand why Porter was.

"We'll help you with that," Porter said.

Paul looked to Apalala-Aidan, but the young man's expression was inscrutable. "How?" Paul asked Porter.

Porter said nothing.

Nor did Zach.

Nor did Po, though Joel said something about burning again.

When Paul looked to Apalala-Aidan again, there was an old, slightly dirty portable reel-to-reel tape recorder on the table in front of him. It hadn't been there before. Apalala-Aidan plugged an earpiece into it and gently pushed it across the table toward Paul.

Paul hesitated.

"Blind faith," Porter said. "It's not an easy decision."

Paul picked up the recorder and studied it. "How do I use this?"

The gray man had been out of normal life for so long. It hadn't occurred to him that a younger person might be mystified as to how this device of the ancients worked.

Apalala-Aidan actually cracked a smile.

Paul might have figured it out himself, given the time, but he was hung up on the unfamiliar details of the thing. It said "solid state" on it. What could that mean?

Zach reached across the table to grab the ear plug and mimed putting it into his ear. He handed it to Paul. Then he pulled the machine to him and slid the main switch from "stop" to "play."

The reels began turning as Paul pushed the plug into his ear. There was nothing at first. Then a medley of sounds reached him, as if they'd had to travel a long way.

They started off very faint. Ice in glasses and drinks poured at someone's party. Children singing "Happy Birthday" with a man and woman, both flat, trying to lead them. Laughter from adults. A far-off crowd cheering, and an announcer excited about something Paul couldn't quite make out. More cheers, then groans as whatever it was went wrong. An old, scratchy record of a woman singing "Bye Bye Blackbird," her voice like a bell.

The singing went on, and the conversations continued. The clinking of glasses as someone toasted. A girl laughing, shrieking, "No! No!" The splash of her being tossed into water, screaming and giggling.

Paul had forgotten his eyes were open.

Apalala-Aidan watched him. All of the sounds, singing, and voices were messages meant only for Paul.

Paul knew what he needed to do.

Before the light and heat overtook him, he saw Apalala-Aidan say something to Zach.

And with that, Zach knew what he needed to do, too.

Though why Paul understood that only now was a puzzlement. For in a way, Zach had always known what he needed to do.

Now, however, it was understood—so had Paul.

∽

"I'm stretched rather thin," Quarry said. "But being in many places at once means I can see narrow views from numerous perspectives."

Charlene looked to Reinhard, who had eyes only for Quarry's disembodied head. The former Vigil was taking the rock man seriously in a way he'd refused to thus far.

"Are our people all right?" Nicolette barely succeeded in giving voice to her question. If she didn't ask, she wouldn't have to hear the answer.

"The state of being all right isn't what it was only a few long moments ago," Quarry replied. "None of us are all right."

"What's happening, Quarry?" said Charlene.

"They're trying to blow down the wall around The Pines," the rock head stated after a moment. Quarry's tone was flat, as if he, too, were trying to get an emotional handle on what he was saying.

"The Pines is a myth," said D.W., and Reinhard gave a

slight nod of agreement. But it looked more like he was backing a claim he wanted to be true, not one he really believed.

"Many of us are myths," Quarry replied. "Right now, I'm a pile of talking rocks who's switched sides."

"Who's trying to blow down the wall?" Part of Charlene didn't want to ask any more questions. Like Nicolette, she probably didn't want to know the answers.

"One of yours, I think," the rock man said. "One of yours and a few other people. One's a kid. Another might be a dragon. Yes, I'm serious."

Charlene looked to Reinhard again, but the former Vigil continued to study Quarry as if doing so might reveal a direction for him to go in or a target for him to destroy.

Quarry made a sound like a breath. "It's all bouncing around and fuzzy. I'm getting names, but I can't be sure who they're tied to."

"What names?" said Reinhard.

"One is Zach. One is Paul." He paused. "And I believe you know a Porter?"

## 51

## A DREAM FOR US

Annie had always been a light sleeper. The slightest thing—or nothing at all—would jolt her awake, sentencing her to an hour or more of staring at the ceiling, dreaming of being better rested.

At some point, Annie realized what she didn't have in common with other sufferers. They were left to lie, fully awake, exiled from the land of slumber. That wasn't the problem for her.

Hers was not being able to tell whether she was asleep, awake, or somewhere between the two. When she was lucky, the state of confusion didn't leave her feeling tired after a bad night.

What it did leave her feeling, however, was a strong sense of doubt about her mental health. What was a dream? What was real? And which one posed a larger threat?

That wasn't the kind of question easily solved on a flying train in an in-between world. Not after she realized there was someone in the room with her, despite the locked door.

Annie knew who'd come in, though he wasn't much of a night visitor anymore. She tried to roll over to face him but found herself in that neither-nor state where she saw the room without being able to open her eyes or move.

"Evening, Ms. Brucker," said a tinny little voice behind her, sounding as if it came from a speaker.

∼

Zach's mother jumped when Joel, the toy that wasn't a toy, spoke.

"Sorry," Joel told her. "Did I get the title wrong? I'm a translator, so you'd think I'd keep up. But no. Would you rather be called by your first name?"

Zach's mother turned away from the switchboard to face Zach and Joel. "No, it's fine. I just didn't expect to be here." She raised her hands to her head and looked surprised when she was able to touch her face and hair. "I'm not in my rig?"

"No," Joel said. "The way things have crossed over, and with the power of the guy helping us, you don't need it."

"Am I at work?" Zach's mother looked at Zach as if he were the one answering.

Zach lifted the necklace holding Joel over his head and handed the Tamagotchi to her.

"Easy there," said Joel, and he wasn't kidding. "I go back with you, kid. But only if you're wearing me."

Zach's mother stared at the device and the little face it rendered.

"I come in peace," said Joel.

"Hello." Zach's mother's tone made it clear she was only able to respond because good manners dictated it. "Who are you?" She looked to Zach for an answer, but he deferred to Joel.

Apalala-Aidan had been right to insist Po let Joel come along with him rather than have Zach bring the Dynamite 8 or the reel-to-reel to Zach's mother's workplace. Joel would be better at putting what Zach's mother needed to do into words because Zach's understanding was native. That was the word Apalala-Aidan had used, and Zach didn't get what he meant by it. He was never comfortable going by thoughts or guidance he didn't fully comprehend, but this looked like it was the right decision.

"It's a long story," Joel said. "We can use the time a lot better if we get to work sooner rather than later. But I'll answer your question with a question. Do you trust your son?"

Zach's mother looked hard at him. Zach already knew what her reply would be. She only hesitated because she needed a second to make sure he was indeed who he wanted her to think he was. One look was all it took. After all, she was Zach's mother. And he was Zach.

"Good," said Joel. "Let's do this."

Zach's mother handed Joel back to Zach, and Zach put Joel around his neck again. The Tamagotchi was right. Everyone needed to be in their place, and failing to return Joel to Po would throw everything off.

Zach's mother turned back to her switchboard. If she was surprised that its sockets had multiplied exponentially since she'd turned away or was startled by the large piles of different-colored patch cords that hadn't been there a moment ago, she hid it well. She turned to Zach again. "This is a dream, right?"

"If it makes it easier for you to do this, it's whatever you like," said Joel. It was indeed good that he'd come with Zach.

"Do what?" This time, Zach's mother spared a glance for Joel, but she continued looking at Zach as if he were the one calling the shots.

Before Joel could tell him to do so, Zach pulled the folded-up piece of paper from his back pocket, carefully unfolded it, and handed it to Zach's mother. It wasn't quite his drawing any longer, though he hadn't made the changes. It was the same fiery pine cone he'd drawn in the station market, but now it was more like a diagram of which patch cords to put into which sockets in order to recreate the drawing, with orange and yellow cords placed to represent the flames. It required many, many cords and colors to properly depict the details of the cone and the fire, but the switchboard's vastly increased array of sockets and the impressive supply of cords would be sufficient. The question was whether or not Zach's mother would be, too.

"It would be a dream for us if you were able to put that together," said Joel. "Fast. Without any mistakes."

Zach's mother studied the diagram. She chewed the inside of her lip gently. Then she looked at Zach again.

Zach nodded at her and smiled.

Zach's mother smiled back.

He recalled the time of the dragonfish and the giant clock. And he knew it would work if she had anything to say about it.

"I'm on the job," she said.

## 52

# THOUGHTS WHILE BURNING ALIVE

A state of neither-nor.
Neithernor. One word.
It was why Po and Joel could be in the burning Shrine and in the station market at the same time.

The Margins was the natural result of everything collapsing, a growing intersection and a slow-motion death march. What had been separate no longer was. What had been one was now many.

Po wouldn't have believed he'd be able to understand it, but he did. Because it wasn't he alone who grasped what was happening; it was all involved, and it involved all.

The hive mind. The hive mind would perish together, as one.

Melted. Fused.

The fire. The heat. The melding.

Once Po allowed it to wash over and through him—and he had no choice in that—it reached a point where his senses were no longer reporting back.

Point taken. Understood.

The heat would end him and all of them. Just as Joel kept saying.

It hurt.

Joel. Joel was silent.

Po knew without looking—because he wasn't able to look—that Joel was no longer with him. The Tamagotchi couldn't be in more than one place at once for whatever part he was needed to play. So he'd gone off. And with the join and flow of all of that heat and Essence moving through the Shrine—through all of them via their presence and adjacency—Po understood that Joel was gone for a specific reason.

The join and flow could allow him to understand what Joel had been called to do whenever it chose to. But it might not.

Thoughts while burning alive. Po had never considered what his would be, but now he knew. No matter that he'd never asked.

The join. The flow. The experience.

If Po let it have its way without trying to understand any of it, he might survive. Give it nothing to grab hold of, nothing to use to pull him into the river. Cling to the bank and let it move through, over, and around.

It was more than a thought. It was his only hope.

*Hold on. The only hope.*

The words were not Po's. Nor were the thoughts, but he felt them as keenly as if they had been. They weren't even his language.

They weren't him or anyone he knew. Yet he felt them. His hands on rough, living wood, climbing against the cold flow to branches above, where he'd be safe from the rising, moving waters as long as he held on.

The join. The flow. The Essence through the burning Shrine.

It was, of course, made up of those who'd lived and were, as far as they knew, living now. A name didn't come with the pointed need to hang on. It was beyond names. A boy who had nothing left but staying out of the waters, saving himself from being taken away.

The join.

A child in the dark watched a closet door, terrified of whatever had arrived behind it.

Boy. Girl.

Po got the sense he might have been tied to that fear a little more closely than he'd first thought. But he wasn't able to know anything more before the fear was bumped aside by that of another unidentified child.

This one hid in the closet and knew the threats that lay outside of the tiny safe space—which wasn't safe at all—by name and by face. Those threats were joined by others the child hadn't encountered yet but was aware of just the same.

The flow.

A man looked up the number of the woman he was going to offer the job to, excited for once that he was going to give someone good news, help someone. The man's name swept past too fast. So did the woman's. But Po knew she was going to tell him she'd accepted another position, even though it wasn't true.

Would tell him.

Had told him.

An older lady focused everything she could muster into walking down a street in Boston under her own power. Turning down an offer of help from passersby yet again, she burst into laughter and almost fell. She recovered and continued on, and two men who weren't with each other both assumed she was touched in the head. Only Po understood that she'd thought of something from long before that was worth the laugh. But he didn't know what it was.

On and on it went.

A little girl looked for her dog at the same time the dog looked for her. Both knew something bad was going to happen to the other if they weren't reunited soon. Only the dog was right, but neither it nor Po would ever find out what the bad thing was.

On and on.

On and on.

Po stopped listening, lest he care too much and be pulled away until he was no more.

Removed. Banished. Burned.

Po's hand was on the hands of others in the Shrine. He was but one among many whose plaques and honorifics gave them a lasting presence there, in a place where sunlight had never left but where so much heat had never before visited.

The plaques.

Ken's plaque had returned, Po knew.

Or was told.

Zach had returned it somehow.

And in a way he couldn't understand, Ken remained.

Or had returned.

Or had never left.

Because such was the way with The Commons and all of the realms it would collapse into. No one really left. Even when they weren't themselves anymore and hadn't been since forever began.

They remained.

Everything did.

Burned.

The heat came from the one in the closet. In The Pines. In

the network. From the adjacency and the Essence of all of them now that they were all one.

Burned.

Audra had been burned. She'd burned herself.

The dragon had burned her a second time.

Was burning her now. Burning all of them.

Audra knew that. So did Porter.

Audra didn't know about Porter.

Not what Po knew.

And Paul.

And Zach.

And the man-who-was-the-dragon-who-was-the-man from The Pines.

All of this joined and flowed because of what Paul had done in his victory over Brill.

Because the worlds were falling into one another.

Slowly, perhaps. Slowly enough that so many wouldn't know of their looming end until they'd ended. And if it were somehow to reverse itself—if Porter, Audra, and the living Essence succeeded in whatever was to be done—this shared information and ability would once again separate.

Not entirely, perhaps, for Po and the others were likely to remember all who had passed through the Shrine and through them.

But slowly.

Too slowly for any measurement.

That would not stop its movement. The rules were one way until they were no longer that way. And even when they returned to that earlier state, they would not be that way ever again.

One understood, even if one didn't accept it. Or one let go and was pulled away.

Into the flow. Into the join.

So Po held on.
And Audra burned.
Po burned.
Porter burned.
Paul burned.
Zach burned.
Porter had a secret. Porter and the man-dragon-man.
Po knew what it was.
And now?
So did Audra.

## 53

# BETWEEN A LONG BLINK AND A NAP

Sweets Don't Fail Me Now, the candy store where Audra had met Porter the last time around, was now a nautically themed coffee joint called Fedallahs. Its logo was an oddly cheery whale encircled by a harpoon and its trailing line.

Porter sat brooding at a table in the rear, no cup in front of him. If the current setting had sprung from his mind, he still didn't appear to feel at home in it.

"If you don't order anything, they'll ask you to leave," Audra told him as she grabbed a seat.

The gray man forced the corners of his mouth upward, but his heart wasn't up to supporting the failed smile. He looked drawn—and grayer then usual.

"How do you do it, Jonas?"

"Do what?"

He was going to make Audra say it. She leaned back in her chair to adopt a casual stance she didn't feel, looked Porter in the eye, and didn't waver. "Put the entire universe and all of its realms in jeopardy while also conjuring up this place and visiting it with part of yourself."

"You're here, too. How do you do it?"

Good lord. Audra watched him, trying to figure out if he was playing dumb to stall for time. "How's the coffee?"

Porter looked to be outside of himself for a moment, then shrugged. "I haven't tried it."

Audra studied the fixtures around them, which were probably picked up for a song when the local Crab Trap or some other seafood eatery had shut down—lots of netting and cork, lobster hotels, and a buoy or two. "Did the Pequod supplement its income with shellfish?"

Porter didn't answer.

"Jonas. It's a chain. That's not even your style. You hate chains."

The gray man shrugged again. "They're the only ones who can afford the rents these days."

Audra wanted to laugh but didn't have it in her. She stood, went to the counter, and waited long enough to realize there wasn't anyone there to serve her. So she went around the counter, helped herself to two of the smallest cups they had and left a few bucks by the register. She dumped a healthy helping of creamer into hers—she seemed to recall that Porter preferred his black when he drank it, though maybe that was one of the other Envoys—and went back to set them down on the table.

Porter made no move to touch his.

Audra hadn't expected him to.

"I thought you'd be angrier." Porter's voice was like a weak echo of itself. He really was burning the candle at both ends.

"I didn't even have to send a message for you to know I wanted to meet—you just knew. That should tell you something about how quickly the collapse of the realms is progressing." Audra blew on her coffee and took a sip. Charred. Just like the other chains. Would she ever be free of burning? "It can't work, Jonas. That's why I'm not angry. You don't have the adjacency to the Demeter Essence to make it do whatever you have in mind. You need me, and I'm not about to go along with your cockamamie scheme—which I don't believe, by the way."

"What don't you believe?"

"That you're really making a run at The Pines, though maybe you think you are. If so, that's troubling enough."

The gray man closed his eyes for something between a long blink and a nap. Whatever he was up to, it was costing him. His complexion was ashier than it had been when she first sat down.

Ashes. Again with the burning.

"I have all the adjacency I need," Porter said. "Or, rather, we do."

"With the collapsing realms and the breaching of the barriers, maybe you think you do. You and the dragon." Audra watched him to see if he'd be surprised she knew who he was working with, but he betrayed nothing. "Again, you can't be the one to handle all of the Essence you'd need in order to even dent the border around The Pines. Apalala—or Aidan, or whatever he calls himself—has to do it. He and I only ever came into contact that once. That was more than enough for me but not enough for the adjacency your plan calls for."

Porter struggled to keep his eyes open, but his gaze was as alert as ever once he focused on her. "If I tell you why it actually is enough, do you promise not to boil me in my own blood?"

As soon as he said it, she could tell he regretted it. That was nothing to laugh about. No Envoy joked about a colleague's abilities being used in such a way.

"I'm sorry," he said.

"No need. Besides, after what your friend did to me, it'll be some time before I'm able to make a proper s'more, never mind cook you the way you deserve if you actually intend to go through with this."

Porter nodded. "I am sorry," he said, and she knew he wanted the apology to cover more than just his ill-advised jest. "But you wouldn't be pleased knowing that the last time we sat across from one another, it wasn't me you were sitting with."

Audra sat up straight. That her old friend would allow her to sit with a creature of The Pines without knowing it and establish a greater degree of adjacency was a crime for which words were not adequate. She took a long sip of her execrable coffee. "I suppose this world isn't what I believe it to be, then."

"This world isn't what anyone believes it to be. It never has been."

"Maybe not. But its people are. At least the ones with whom I'm well acquainted. And I know you better than you know yourself."

Porter raised his eyebrows. Audra suspected that was all he had the energy for.

"You know you can't breach The Pines," Audra said. "That would be like popping open the world's biggest appendix and flooding the body with the most unthinkable infections in all of existence. It simply cannot happen."

"Then what do you think I'm doing?"

"I don't know." Audra sat back again and took another appalling sip. "But you've either come under the sway of the dragon, or you want me and the others to think you have. If it's the former, tell me now. Wink, maybe. Or send a signal as soon as you're able. I'll do whatever I can to help you, and I'll pull Charlene and the Envoys in along with everyone else I can reach."

Porter leaned back and closed his eyes again. When he opened them once more, there was a quiet strength she hadn't thought he'd be able to muster. "With the increased adjacency, his presence is a danger to you," the gray man said, and Audra knew the concern in his voice was real. "Even he can't control the damage he might do to you. You cannot afford to be close enough to try and stop us."

Audra stopped herself halfway to another sip. "I can't do that to myself anymore." She watched Porter as she set her cup back down and chose her words carefully. "I'm sure you have reasons for whatever it is you're doing, Jonas. And I harbor the same concern for you that you harbor for me. Please don't make me find another way to accomplish what we need. It's not easy for me to say that because it sounds like I'm worried you won't do the right thing. And I'm really not."

Porter said nothing at first, and Audra knew her words had struck deep. "Throughout the history of the realms—of all the realms—momentous events have hinged on how the players defined what is right," he said.

Audra got up to throw her coffee away. When she'd binned it and turned back to Porter, he was gone.

Before she left, she asked herself if she'd been entirely honest in saying she wasn't worried about his choices. She decided she had.

But only because she'd had no choice.

## 54

## MEMENTO MORI

Paul and Porter stood downstream from the spillway at the base of a massive dam. It was so high that Paul had to crane his neck to the extreme just to make out the top of it despite being quite a distance away.

The riverbed on which they stood was parched; no water had made it past the dam in some time.

"This is the barrier?" Paul still felt like he might drop from the heat, even though they were no longer in the Shrine. Their location didn't seem to matter; he remained hot as hell.

"This is *a* barrier." Porter squinted as he studied the dam.

"Between realms?"

Porter gave a half-chuckle.

It occurred to Paul that the kid he used to be would've been offended by that, but the Paul who'd grown since last seeing the Envoy was not.

"No," the gray man said. "We'd never be able to see those barriers. Their size and power puts them beyond our minds' ability to process. This is a visual representation of the barrier holding back the Demeter Essence we need. The real thing is far larger than this."

Paul didn't understand completely. But as his consciousness worked its way through what lay before him, he was able to make out more detail. Dotted across the near-vertical wall of the giant dam were—something that made no sense. "Are those goats?"

"Ibex, I believe."

Paul tried to keep Porter from seeing that he didn't know what an ibex was. Nor did he feel comfortable asking the Envoy the larger and more obvious question, which was what he, Porter, and the ibex were doing here. And what did Porter expect from Paul when Paul didn't understand any of what he'd experienced so far?

"You've come up against them before."

Clearly, Paul's memory hadn't completely returned, then. "I have?"

"Your friends more so than you—but you as well."

Paul tried to recall that particular experience. It wasn't there. "Why don't I remember it, then?"

"The better question is why you remember anything."

"You don't know, either?"

"Of course I do. Memento mori."

"Which is?"

"You really want to talk about that now? I said it was the better question. I didn't say this was the best time to ask it."

After a long moment, Porter acknowledged Paul's glare. "Memento mori. A reminder of your mortality—that you must die. With the crossing of the realms, you encountered one or more from your time in The Commons. Though in the case of you and Rain, they served to remind you that you did die. Now don't get sidetracked."

The gray man was right. Paul needed to focus. And whether he recalled his experiences with these creatures or not, the feelings he picked up on despite the distance made their take on things clear enough. The most pressing emotion to emanate from the horned beasts was a dead-calm guardedness.

Paul might not have known them, but they knew him and Porter and were wary of their presence. And beneath that, something stronger, more familiar. "They feel it, too."

"Feel what?"

Paul suspected Porter already knew the answer to that. "What put me on that bench, wanting to get back to The Commons to fix what I did."

Porter nodded. Of course he'd already known. "What you all did. You could not have done such damage alone."

Such damage.

There it was.

Even Porter blamed Paul for what they now faced.

"And, for the record, it's 'we all,' " Porter said. "They were there, and so was I. I can't have you robbing me of the credit for my contribution to this debacle. When the trophy is awarded for crushing the universe into a ball and destroying all life both known and unknown, my name is engraved on the cup alongside yours and theirs."

Paul had no response at first; sharing the blame didn't make him feel any better. Then he remembered what Porter had told him. "I'm resulting."

"You are."

That helped. A little.

After a while, Paul was forced to look down for a few moments to spare himself some serious neck strain.

When he looked up again, one of the ibex stood in front of them—close enough for Paul to take in the remarkably black and endless void in its eyes but far enough for it to prepare a defense should he and Porter have violence in mind.

Porter had said they knew him. Did they? If so, what were

they afraid of? What had he done to them that he didn't recall? Or was it something he did recall?

With that came the question, unstated as it was. There were no words spoken aloud, none broadcast into Paul's skull like some afternoon sci-fi flick. It was more like a dream that didn't need images interpreted. It was pure message.

There hadn't been a question.

Then there was.

And it was simple.

Did Paul and Porter intend to walk the path Porter had set them upon? If so, they were not welcome.

Audra and these beings had an understanding—a plan of attack. Porter and Paul had a place in it. Should they choose to abrogate the responsibility assigned to them, then they could not stay.

Porter's reply was equally clear without word, sound, or image. He understood their position. He would adopt it, too, were he in their place. But that only made him feel worse about what was going to happen should they choose not to go along with what must occur.

The heat returned.

Paul had forgotten it, but now sweat broke out on his forehead, under his arms.

Bad sweat.

Flop sweat.

Not the kind from a good run.

The kind that comes when things are wrong and likely to get worse.

The ibex offered no answer. Which was its answer.

In the beast's endless eyes, in the ridged sweep of its horns, Paul saw where he'd encountered the animal and its brethren before—the form they'd taken. And he understood the forces he and Porter were up against, though not why the gray man chose to oppose them. The two of them didn't have a chance against these creatures.

Porter spoke without speaking, the chosen verbiage Paul's understanding of it. *Do not force us to go this way.*

The ibex answered in the same manner. *Do not mark me and mine with the stain of your own mind and choice.*

Then came the silence.

Silence outside of time. Paul didn't know how long it lasted because it didn't last at all. Not in that sense.

It was.

It was not.

But it most definitely was.

Porter and the ibex faced each other, unblinking.

Paul went from watching to gazing into the animal's eyes with equal intensity. He was a part of it now as well.

The heat.

Paul and Porter were in the Shrine and, at the same time, here below the huge dam.

Everything fell into everything else, a little at a time.

They weren't in two places at once. They were in one place expressed in two ways.

That was the problem.

If it continued, it would be the end of all.

A rivulet of sweat ran down into Paul's eye, burning when it got there. It continued down his cheek as a tear.

The ibex.

The dark in its eyes.

Bottomless.

Multiple.

They weren't facing one animal but every animal scattered across the wall of the dam and all of those beasts' brothers and sisters backing them unseen. If this came down to a fight, it wouldn't even be one.

Which was why it couldn't.

Right?

Porter's answer was so subtle Paul almost missed it. He shifted his staff in the dirt ever so slightly, planting it a tiny bit more firmly. Before, it had been resting. Now it was placed.

"Paul," said the Envoy.

"Yeah?"

"Do you understand why what we saw as your victory has come to the brink of defeat for everything and all?"

Paul was supposed to answer that but couldn't.

Porter didn't wait for him. "We all played our role, as I've stated." The gray man never wavered in his stare-down with the ibex. Plural. With all of them. "I played mine. Po played his. So did Ken, Annie, and Zach. Audra. And Truitt. Especially Truitt."

With the mention of that last name, the ibex scratched the dusty earth of the dry riverbed with a hoof. It, too, never let up in the intensity of its gaze.

"You were a Nistar," Porter told Paul. "You are still. As was Brill. And that changed the calculus of everything. We should have understood it then."

The ibex gave a snort.

The heat. Had it increased?

Sweat ran into Paul's eye again. He didn't wipe it away.

"Your abilities aren't meant so much for war or destruction as they are for directing, guiding, and changing, Paul," Porter said. "You're an artisan more than you are a fighter." He rocked the staff back and forth, digging a little deeper into the soil. "Rain is a warrior."

Why did Porter call out Rain?

"You are critical to this," Porter said before Paul could ask, rocking the staff again. "But we need a fighter to help you." With that, he gave his staff a turn.

Nothing happened.

Not at first.

Then it was only the outrage of the ibex that told Paul something had changed.

Something big.

Something terrible.

The shadow that pushed past Paul was all too familiar, given how much he'd fought it. But it was different from when he'd seen it last.

Pushed was the wrong word. It made no contact with him. Yet it was close enough in passing that he felt it just as keenly as if it had.

Almost a friend.

Almost what he'd seen and felt in its presence at the Shrine.

But then it was past him, moving impossibly fast.

A split-second before the ibex braced itself for combat, Paul knew.

The Shade.

All of its corruption and harm. The mix of bull, toad, and something far, far worse nearly clipping him as it built up momentum.

Before Paul had a chance to say anything, before Porter was able to straighten up from resting on his staff, the fight was joined.

Mr. Brill, in Shade form, charged the ibex.

The ibex leapt forward, too.

Their horned heads met with such force that it sounded as if the air itself cracked.

They remained that way, straining against one another, forever.

Each shifted position again and again, trying to gain an advantage. But never did they part.

Then the dark monster changed tactics. It gave a little ground, grabbed both of the ibex's horns in its clawed mitts, and pulled the magnificent creature to it.

The ibex thrashed wildly and nearly broke free from the Shade's grip.

That alone was impressive since, as Paul and those with him knew from hard experience, to touch the creature was to lose your life's potency.

More thrashing as the animal forced its head down and forward in an effort to muscle the Shade off balance.

It was no use. The Shade merely hunkered down and stayed low, maintaining its hold.

The ibex gave all it had. But it was unable to make any progress against its foe.

Then it was the Shade's turn. It remained low to the ground, and its shadow form seemed to thicken with effort, marshaling its formidable strength.

Both creatures pushed themselves to the limit.

It had already been clear there'd be only one victor.

Now it was obvious there would be only one survivor.

A tearing.

A breaking.

A rending.

It wasn't apparent which combatant was doing damage to the other.

Or maybe they were trading harm.

Then the ibex screamed.

## 55

## BEHIND THE WALL OF SLEEP

With the last of the patch cords plugged in, Annie fought to keep her head from smacking against the switchboard counter in a declaration of exhaustion. She leaned on the counter instead, head in hands, long enough to begin wandering into the sleep zone. Was sleeping even possible when she was already in a dream world? Probably not. But nothing else made sense, so why would that?

It was warm—hot, even—behind the wall of sleep. Yet when she raised her head to scan the huge array of cords she'd labored to arrange, there was no obvious source of warmth. Still, it was coming from them. Maybe the board was overheating.

"You can't," the little toy around Zach's neck said when Annie reached for one of the cords to pull it out. The Tamagotchi. Joel. She'd almost forgotten its name. "You can't take it apart once you put it together. Not yet. Anyway, if the heat's freaking you out, that just means you did it right. It's working. Stand up and take a look from the side."

Annie hesitated. But then, she'd listened to the little

machine when he'd told her to put in all that work, so why defy him now? She wheeled her chair to the right in order to view the board and its patch-cord pattern edgewise. Nothing changed.

"You need to get up."

She pushed her chair back to stand. Her whole perception of the cords sidestepped. Heat emanated from the red, yellow, and orange pattern of the array in waves. For a moment, the wires glowed like embers, but then they were just wires again. The heat didn't go away, however. Whatever it was she'd built, it ran hot. Very hot.

"You can still touch them," Joel explained. "They won't burn you. But you can't pull them out again."

"That's all right." Annie sat and wheeled her chair back to her usual spot in the center of the switchboard but kept her hands on its surface.

"I'll rephrase. We need you to touch them again. You don't have to like what you get from it. You might even hate it. I would. But a quick touch is all the buy-in we have to have for what the process needs from you."

"From me?"

"From you. Everybody who was critical last time around is critical now, too."

Annie got it. The switchboard. The reef. All different facets of the same prism, maybe. She reached out to wave a hand over a section of the cables, and the sensation was that of being where she was supposed to be. It was more than welcoming; it was coming home. She patted a cable, testing to see if it would burn her.

It was warm.

Home washed over her then. Before she knew she was going to do so, she grabbed fistfuls of the cables in a gentle but insistent grip.

There was no halfway here. If she was going to make contact, it would be contact that counted.

Old friends.

None she could name, but the familiarity was beyond naming.

It was simply there to greet her.

"Wow," Annie said. "Goats? Something like goats? Last time I hung out with these guys, they had tentacles."

The fear struck her then. Waves of it.

Along with flashes of very real, intense pain.

Not hers, but that didn't matter. It was shared by all who plugged in, all who left themselves open to it. Not that Annie felt like she'd had a choice.

She hadn't.

She never had.

"Oh, no," she said.

Then the grief silenced her.

∾

Zach's mother began to let out a sob but swallowed it.

Zach understood that. He'd done it himself in the rare times he was driven to cry—or, sometimes, laugh—but didn't want to let it out.

There were the feelings with which you greeted the world. They were like the puppies on the leashes he saw on the streets near I'm-Bobby's house. Not Zach's or Zach's mother's house. I'm-Bobby's house. It hadn't been a home for them.

The puppies always tried to pick up things they shouldn't, and their owners always told them to "leave it" before they could chew or eat whatever it was.

That was what those feelings were. They wanted to jump

out at the world. Devour it. Leap up on strangers who didn't want them to. So they had to be pulled back. Put down.

Zach knew.

Zach also understood the strength and pattern of Zach's mother's breathing as she mounted a fight to keep those feelings from getting away from her. Something tried to break through her breath again, but she was able to stop it.

This was bad.

Zach's mother had been tricked. If not tricked, then led without anyone telling her where they were taking her, what she would see—and what she would help make happen.

Bad.

Zach's mother didn't understand what Zach understood. Something good had been used to make something bad when Paul and Rain and Zach and Zach's mother defeated the angry man. The white-haired man and those he worked with had been waiting for that.

Now something bad would be used to make something good. A lie and a betrayal of the universe itself was the only thing that could stop the damage and bring back the good.

Good to bad. Bad to good. It had to be that way.

Everything was about balance.

Zach's mother didn't know.

Zach walked over to where Zach's mother hung on to the cables just as she let go of them. Her hands slid down to the shelf at the bottom of the wall with all the holes and cords, the warmth from its pattern flowing off of it in waves.

She hid her face in her hands again.

Standing behind her, Zach gave her a hug. Touched her. Tried to relate his own feelings without allowing them to frighten her. He wasn't used to letting his feelings out, and he was afraid she wouldn't be accustomed to receiving them.

Zach's mother's fingers drifted down from her face to cover

Zach's hands. She swallowed another kind of crying and took another deep breath.

Zach hoped that Zach's mother would understand why he'd played a part in this, hoped she'd someday see that the suffering he helped to cause would have been there anyway. And much worse.

That was what they were trying to avoid. And he hoped she'd still be able to look at him once she understood. Still be able to love him.

He hugged her, and Zach's mother squeezed his hands.

Zach was glad Joel didn't try to speak for Zach, though Joel wanted to.

But it was for Zach to let Zach's mother know what he needed so badly to say without saying it.

He was sorry.

## 56

## ST. ELMO'S FIRE

Being up on the Breaker made it easier to see the wall of slate-colored fog rise up from the prairie's horizon. It rolled in to confront the bison in their massive headlong stampede.

Something was going wrong.

Audra was forced to watch it, helpless to affect what unfolded before her and the Dodger and their excellent view. "Lars," she said. And then she said nothing more.

The fog wasn't like any Audra had ever seen. As it advanced on the bison, it darkened into inky smoke—a weather-created mist no longer. It was a black, forbidding barrier that came up from the ground to join the overhead storm clouds. Or did it hang from them like a curtain? Maybe it stood on its own, awesome and malevolent.

For once it reached a midnight-ebon blackness, it stopped like a living thing contemplating the onrushing horned beasts, as if it knew it didn't need to approach them. They were driven to come to it.

And come to it they did. Until it was too late for them to do anything but.

The ones in front seemed to grasp their dreadful mistake all at once, as if they hadn't been able to see the fog only moments before. The smoke lit up with bursts of St. Elmo's Fire, bolts and lines of which jumped forth from the darkness and danced across the horns of the approaching animals, concentrating chiefly on the closest ranks of charging beasts.

The lead bison tried to stop and failed, collapsing into the turf and erupting into screams of pain and fear as those behind them smashed headlong into the fallen or ran them over before joining them in their ruin.

Heartbreaking.

Soul sickening.

Nearby, the Dodger gaped at the spectacle, as devastated as Audra.

How could Audra avoid being incapacitated by what was happening in front of them?

The bison were the Demeter Essence, living beings no longer but still vital and precious in their potential to move on to the next step in their Journeys, wherever those might take them. Now they were being destroyed in the unfolding pageant of violence.

The third wave tumbled in turn, those behind pushing the fallen forward before tumbling down themselves. The beasts crested in a great wash that vanished into the black fog.

The crackle and glow of the St. Elmo's Fire rejoiced in the sacrifice, the smoke devouring the riven animals. The bison couldn't throw themselves into the slaughter fast enough. Fear of something behind them pushed them forward.

"Jonas," Audra hissed into the Speaky Shrieky, for Porter was the only one involved in this abomination who she could hope to reach. "Jonas, for the love of God."

The heat and flames did more than drive the bison forward. As Audra and the Dodger watched the great herd's destruction, more bison joined the stampede just as quickly as the ones ahead of them met their end.

At the rear, something equally horrifying. The flames, rather than scorching the prairie grass, caused the earth to cough up more of the terrified animals—generating them, becoming them itself.

This was the very fabric of Demeter, the treasured Essence that had been diverted from its rightful path. Now it was being mined—coerced or terrorized into changing form so that it could throw itself into the smoke and electricity.

It hurt. The screaming from the herd as it perished in blackness left no doubt of that.

"Jonas!" Audra cried into the Speaky Shrieky.

The Dodger watched her, mute. In his eyes, Audra read her own understanding of what was occurring.

Porter was not going to answer. He was either beyond her or had chosen to go so far to the other side that her efforts would perish in a fog all their own.

The flames grew higher, hotter. With the heat came greater waves of bison hurling themselves into the mist. They crushed those before them beneath sharp hooves before themselves meeting a ghastly end.

Audra said Porter's name one more time.

The Dodger didn't even look at her when she did.

The bison died in surges, and Audra could only watch her stewardship throw itself onto the pyre as she mourned.

## 57

## KILL SWITCH

Jeremy had lost all track of time. The line between day and night meant nothing because the demarcation between fantasy and reality had taken a powder, so why would any other rules apply?

Sometimes Jeremy suspected he'd lost his mind, too. But then something such as the odor of his old friend stress sweat and the realization that he was the source of it restored faith in his own senses and state of mind.

No hallucination stunk like that. And crazy people didn't worry about the woman in the room picking up the scent.

They were in a former autopsy theater. Jeremy found himself wondering for a moment if he was the first person in its history to worry about bad smells.

Truitt's screens hung in the air, most of them filled with pixel snow, fast-moving clouds, or full-on storms. Jeremy figured they weren't screen savers because magic screens wouldn't need those. So maybe they were bored because Truitt was ignoring them.

That was the kind of thing that went through your mind

when you might well be witnessing the end of all existence. Or worse—you might be helping it along.

"I don't accept failure." Truitt stared at his phone. Earlier, he'd flipped it around a few times while considering his setback, and on its tiny screen, Jeremy spotted the same pine cone representation with the glowing circle in the middle.

Jeremy and Stacey locked eyes long enough to assure one another that he wasn't talking about them. So maybe they'd make it out of this.

Another flip of the phone. Yes, it was indeed the pine cone with the illuminated Pines in the center. "I don't accept it because Brill didn't accept it, and that might be one of the few things I agreed with him on," Truitt said—once again, mostly to himself. "To accept failure is to begin the process of dying. I've done that once already, and I don't like to repeat myself. The whole idea is to arrest the process, to avoid moving on to our judgment—whatever that may be—thus determining our own destiny. Isn't it?"

Jeremy and Stacey knew a rhetorical question when they heard one.

The old man continued to gaze into his phone. Then he looked at the floating screens with the clouds and the storms. One held his attention. On it, a wolverine was scaring two full-grown wolves away from their own kill. A nature show at the universe's grand finale. Fitting. "Are either of you familiar with the concept of a kill switch?"

"Yes," said Jeremy.

"It's for stopping a process or a machine when something's gone wrong," said Stacey. "Is that what you mean?"

"That's precisely what I mean." Truitt still didn't look at either of them. "And precisely what our last remaining option is." He scrolled through a screen or two on his phone before looking up at Stacey and Jeremy. "I'm not only willing to take my ball and go home, I'm willing to slash it open and set its flattened corpse on fire if it means stopping whoever's on the other side of this fight." He waited for a response.

Jeremy nodded as if he understood.

Stacey did the same, and Jeremy wondered if maybe she really did.

"The only distasteful part of doing that? We'll be inadvertent heroes and stop the lunacy of breaching The Pines, which is something so profoundly stupid that even my former employer wouldn't have tried it." Truitt allowed himself a ghost of a smile. "Though I'll admit I underestimated the depth of that man's brainlessness more than a few times." He flipped the phone around again but didn't look at the screen.

Jeremy was able to see it hadn't changed. It was still the pine cone.

Another flip. "But I suppose I can stomach such gallantry if it means we're also saving our own skins. Sparing all existence from being set upon by whatever hungry horrors will be freed if we do nothing preserves us, too."

Jeremy felt pressured to say something. Anything. "If you can handle being a hero, I think Stacey and I can, too, sir." He was mystified as to where that had come from.

By the look Stacey gave him, she was, too.

"Be careful what you think you can handle, Triple J." Truitt looked to see if the use of the unloved nickname left a mark. He'd never used it before; Jeremy hadn't even known he was aware of it. "You and Miss Galena have a part to play in this, too—and it will mean being much more deeply involved than you are already."

Jeremy and Stacey both decided silence was the wisest choice. Now Jeremy was convinced Stacey didn't get any of this, either.

Truitt waved his hand, and all of the floating screens

retreated. "You are the only ones here—and I, for once, seek counsel on a decision. So let's vote, shall we? The kill switch. Assuming it works, do we use it?"

"If it does, what then?" said Stacey.

Truitt shrugged. He seemed amused by the conversation, and Jeremy didn't think that was a good thing at all. "Other than not being at the mercy of things so awful they've been imprisoned since creation? Just about anything's preferable to that. Don't you think?"

Stacey nodded.

So did Jeremy.

"Are those votes in the affirmative, then?" Truitt waited for a response but none came. "You must speak aloud."

"Yes," said Stacey, less sure than she'd been only a moment before.

"Yes," Jeremy echoed, his confidence no stronger than hers.

"Well." Truitt regarded them long enough for Jeremy to worry that maybe their votes committed them to something they hadn't understood. Then he began thumbing his phone screen with such focused intensity that Jeremy and Stacey might as well have been elsewhere.

And maybe they were.

## 58

## ANYTHING BUT NUTS

"I don't buy it," said Reinhard when someone floated the idea that maybe Porter had lost his mind.

Charlene, between having her brain boiled in its own juices and the stress of all of existence being in jeopardy, had already forgotten who. But the former Vigil, who didn't have more than a passing professional relationship with Porter as far as Charlene knew, rose to his defense with a seriousness of duty that only soldiers achieve when standing up for other soldiers.

What made it even more surprising was that Vigils and Envoys traditionally harbored mistrust for each other because of the nature of their work. And while Reinhard had made the jump over to the Envoy side, he'd often maintained that guilty-until-proven-innocent bias against his new colleagues.

Charlene hushed D.W. and Nicolette, who were talking over each other to the point where she couldn't tell whose side they were on. "What don't you buy, Reinhard?"

"There's nothing to indicate Porter's jettisoned his faculties."

"How is trying to breach The Pines anything but nuts?"

"Under almost all circumstances, it is. But clearly, Porter's acting on information we don't have."

"That being the case, and if he is of sound mind, we might assume he's simply gone rogue." Charlene looked around the room. She didn't want to believe it herself, and nobody else appeared to be particularly enthusiastic about adopting that position, either.

"I'm with Reinhard," said Nicolette. "I don't buy it."

"Regardless," said Reinhard, "we don't have to know why he's doing it to stop him."

"I'm not seeing an obvious way to do that," said D.W. "Not when all of our guidance and oversight has been overridden."

"There's no fail-safe?" Charlene wanted to kick herself for not having thought of that before. "Every Cold-War book I ever read mentioned them. Were those not real?"

"Nic and Liam and I used to psyche each other out about that when we were kids," said D.W. "We'd tell each other this lever or that button would shut the whole facility down if we hit it. When Nic was little, we had her near tears, begging us not to push the stop button on an elevator."

"So you've heard of one there?"

"Heard," said Nicolette. "But that doesn't mean it exists."

The group pondered the ramifications.

"Actually," said Liam via Quarry's head. His voice was half-hiss and barely audible.

"Actually, what?" Nicolette said.

No answer. If they'd lost the connection, they'd have to wait.

"I'll jump in," said Quarry. "In this case, the reality matches the myth."

"Meaning what?" said Reinhard.

"The Journeyman responsible for the missile complex's existence based it on movies he'd seen. As has been stated already, those stories often included fail-safes. It's been rumored for a long time, but Foundry, having tapped deeply into the silo systems, found that very function. And he's received the direction from his side to use it. But it would be easier and faster if he were to gain the approval of those in command of the complex."

"Who's directing him?" Charlene said.

"His current employer and my former one."

"Why would we go along with something the bad guys want to do?" said Reinhard. "Doesn't that tell us to want the opposite?"

Good question.

D.W. looked to Nicolette. Charlene could see the wordless discussion between them. In addition to the risk of playing into the other side's hands, it would mean shutting down the Dharmas' whole complex. And there wasn't any time to talk about what it might take to bring it back online afterward, assuming such a thing was even possible.

"What's the downside of approving a shutdown?" Charlene asked them.

"Our entire home is bricked, and we might never get it restarted," said Nicolette.

"But at the same time, we stop Porter and Company from bringing about the end of the world as we know it, and we can ask him what he was thinking after we breathe a giant sigh of relief," said Charlene.

"And then there's plenty of time to get you people up and running again," added Reinhard.

"Home versus the world," D.W. said to Nicolette.

"Liam?" Nicolette said quietly.

"Still here."

"What do you think?"

A burst of static was his answer for a few long seconds. "I don't see what we have to lose," he said. "Beats doing nothing."

"Agreed," said D.W.

Nicolette nodded. "Approved."

"From here, too," said Liam, still barely audible.

"Acknowledged," said Quarry. The stone head collapsed into a heap of lifeless rocks.

Only after Quarry left did Charlene realize that they'd only hear from him again—if ever they did—once the universe was saved.

## 59

# THE WORST THAT THE WORLD HAD TO OFFER

After it was over, Paul fell into an old habit—one hammered into him by experience and misfortune ever since he'd understood he'd be battling his way through life on his own. It had gotten him through every rough home, shelter, or school he'd ever had to endure, and it served him well now.

There was no point in dwelling on the pain of the thing; you figured out how to move past it. Maybe later you could consider how to keep it from happening next time.

In the aftermath of the Shade's destruction of the ibex, Paul's main task, as he saw it, was to forget what he'd just seen and heard. That was the necessity.

There was no way he could handle having what he'd witnessed take up residence in his head over the long-term, popping up on occasion to remind him of the worst that the world had to offer. Seeing it for himself, he was faced with the truth: there was no way to understand such a thing.

The monster had utterly destroyed the ibex, and in that destruction had violated it in a way that was as vicious and personal as could be. Taking its Essence didn't begin to describe what the dark beast had done to the graceful animal or how it had done it.

It had devoured it. Torn it apart physically and even spiritually.

Nothing could have prepared Paul for seeing such violence so cruelly visited by one being upon another. The Shade had slaughtered the ibex with insatiable hunger and indescribable glee.

Paul hadn't been able to look away for a time. When he finally had, hearing it in isolation was worse.

Left behind after the animal's Essence had been ripped out and ingested—and it was a far greater quantity than any one being could have offered up—was a burnt husk of what had been. Even the spilled blood—and there was plenty of that—was blackened like oil.

The smell was death.

What made it harder was looking away and settling his attention on Porter, who he'd initially thought might stop the horror or, at minimum, be as riven by the crime as Paul was.

Porter had just watched, impassive. He may have flinched at the worst of it, but Paul couldn't even be sure of that. If so, he possessed a capacity Paul never would. And it certainly wasn't something Paul envied.

Now the gray man continued to observe as the predatory character of the Shade seemed to melt away and the shadow beast appeared to deflate slightly. It could have been exhaustion, but Paul couldn't shake the impression that the monster was grief-stricken by its own actions.

"How?" Paul said.

Porter stared at the Shade. "How what?"

"How could you allow that to happen?" Anger rose up

within Paul, and he waited for it to subside. He might never be able to force it down again if he gave it voice. "How could you just watch that?"

Porter studied the Shade, which heaved with what Paul would have sworn was human-like mourning had he not just witnessed the awful thing it had done. "To witness is to take responsibility," the Envoy said. "I will not endeavor to avoid the ugliness of the path I've chosen. We live with our decisions. To run away from the results? There's no lower act of cowardice." He continued to watch the Shade. The gray man was looking for something, but Paul didn't care what it might be.

"Why, Porter?"

The Envoy turned to Paul, silent for a time. "If I could spare you or any of us what must be done and still achieve our end, I would. But that's not an option. Some sacrifices are made by heroes who do so willingly. Others are suffered by those with no say in the matter." He looked down at the remains of the ibex before focusing on Paul once more. "I didn't set this in motion. Nor did you. Yet we caused it to happen—and here we are."

"What's your sacrifice?"

"Being forced to make so many others pay the price." Porter watched the Shade again. "It cannot compare to what's being taken from others, and I won't ask you to forgive me. I wouldn't, in your shoes. Again and nevertheless, here we are."

"What happens now?"

The Envoy watched the Shade more intently.

The monster remained in place, no longer shaken by emotion—if emotion was what it had displayed. Now it resembled an idle machine, paused to await further instruction.

"Our friends and enemies have cut the cord in order to

bring a halt to this process." Porter gave his staff a turn. Paul couldn't tell if it was a deliberate move or an absentminded tic. "That, too, is what we needed to happen."

"Who's we?"

"Those who do what must be done. The next move is Po's."

## 60

## EVERYTHING TASTED LIKE DREAD

The burning subsided. It remained—and would look for an opportunity to return to its full strength—but it was tolerable.

Po faced an open phone booth, surrounded by people and their noises, while someone tapped him on the shoulder. The sounds of the crowded marketplace enveloped him—paper wrapping, haggling, an ancient cash register and its bell. He hadn't been roasted alive after all; the rhythm on his shoulder would have been too much to bear. The logic of that deduction felt like an accomplishment.

"Excuse me." The woman behind him stopped drumming on him for a moment. "Are you using the phone?"

Po turned and found himself in an entirely different setting.

D-cubed. The tunnels beneath the silos.

An old lady hummed to herself in a familiar voice. Liquid poured. A spoon slid around the inside of a mug.

"Plum." Mrs. Blesmol set two cups of tea down on her table and accompanied them with a tray of cakes. "They're impossible to find out of season, don't you know, but when worlds collide, rules don't matter a whole lot, do they?"

The burning. Po rubbed the spot where he'd been tapped.

"Come sit," said Mrs. Blesmol. "There's not much time, and you've an important decision to make."

Po made his way to the table, sat in the chair Mrs. Blesmol indicated, and spread his napkin on his lap. He waited for the aged, delicate mole rat to put a cake on his saucer. There was a choreography to it, and a misstep would not be desirable.

Mrs. Blesmol chuckled to herself and dunked her cake into her tea before sampling a soggy bite.

Po could hardly conceal his surprise. Dunking violated a half dozen of Mrs. Blesmol's points of protocol. Yet here she'd done it without hesitation, as if that had been her way all along.

Custom crumbled in ways large and small. One could only hope the new order would be kinder than its predecessor.

"I don't suppose there's anything wrong with having everything backward," Mrs. Blesmol said after washing the cake down. Speaking with her mouth full would have been a truly worrying shift. "That being the case, I should forgive myself for being wrong about only the most important parts of the situation." She set the rest of the cake down on the saucer and leaned forward to beam at Po. "I don't know what you did, dear, but I've found them again. Or, rather, they've returned to me."

Po managed a small smile. He had no idea what Mrs. Blesmol was getting at. He wondered if all the time spent alone had finally caught up with her. But given that he'd recently been set alight, endured the accompanying pain of it, and only just found relief because she'd somehow summoned him, he didn't want to be rude.

Mrs. Blesmol gave him an amused grin and sipped her tea. "Nice try, dear, but I didn't expect you to understand. Not my actual little ones. They will come back to me when they're ready, if they're still able." Sadness made its way across her face until she was able to shoo it away, and she brightened once more. "My adopted children have awakened, though I suppose they'd insist it was they who adopted me." She chuckled to herself again, dipped another piece of tea cake into her tea, and popped it into her mouth. She was very pleased.

Something shifted in the tunnel walls around them. Many, many somethings. In the walls, in the ceiling. The scratching of uncountable beings scuttling unseen.

Mrs. Blesmol watched Po. "Mmm-hmm," she said and took another sip of tea. "They're here for you. They've let bygones be bygones, and they hope you can as well. I'd believed them all gone, but I should've known there are far too many for that. They were dormant until needed."

Po's skin itched and burned in spots as he struggled mightily to tamp down his surprise and horror.

"No, dear," said Mrs. Blesmol. "No grudges. We can't have those. Not if we're going to save the world. You want that, don't you? They do."

The muridines. Or, as Po and the others had called them when trying to avoid being eaten alive, the beetle-rats. They hadn't known the proper name then. In confirmation, the sites of his numerous long-since-healed bites stung anew.

"Drink your tea, dear." Mrs. Blesmol picked up a second cake and placed it beside Po's first, which remained untouched on his saucer. "And please have a few of these. I'm an old lady who lives underground. Fabric's not easy to come by if my waistline goes."

Hoisting a cake, Po tried to ignore the scratching all around them. It was louder and faster now—and possibly more enthusiastic. He took a bite and sipped the tea. Everything tasted like dread.

"Po." Mrs. Blesmol focused on him. "I'm a strange one for living in a tunnel with weapons that could wipe out millions as neighbors, I'll grant you. Those I love aren't beloved by others, especially those they're trying to devour. I'm eccentric, and that's being kind. But have you ever thought me crazy?"

Po shook his head. Compared to others in The Commons, Mrs. Blesmol was the definition of reason.

Mrs. Blesmol smiled tenderly. "And do you worry I've lost my little rodent mind now?"

Po dunked one of the cakes, put all of it in his mouth, and took his time chewing. The idea of cozying up to the muridines was unhinged, but Mrs. Blesmol was not. He shook his head again.

Despite what she'd just said about watching her weight, Mrs. Blesmol was pleased enough with his answer to grab another cake in celebration. "Well, thank you for that. Because it's really rather simple. Audra and the living Essence of The Commons have their own adjacency to the Demeter and missile Essence. As do Truitt—Brill's former assistant—and Manitou, via the mechanisms they've put in place and what they've set in motion. And we've scared them enough to put the brakes on, which gives us our chance."

Po signed the obvious question: who?

"Myself and the children. The many, many, many children —far more than anyone knows about, in the oldest and deepest lairs. More than I'd ever known about, even. Their brethren have gone beyond reach and knowledge. They've long been said to be able to cross into other realms—though I've never figured out if that's true, and they're certainly not going to tell me—but there are legions of the little darlings left behind. And they chose to reveal themselves because they know they are needed."

Po drank some more tea and waited for her to continue. The list had to be longer.

"Jonas Porter, of course, but you knew that. A woman named Annie Brucker and her son Zach, who are key to this. And our friend the man-dragon, who, as I'm also sure you understand, is much, much more than that."

Po tried to decide whether his next question might be insulting. But he needed her answer. "Do you trust him?" he signed.

"Yes," Mrs. Blesmol said, and Po believed her. "He is of his realm. But to condemn every being there under all circumstances is to misunderstand the way of things."

Po didn't know what to make of such a claim.

Before he could sign again, she guessed his next question. "What do I want of you? Why wouldn't you ask that?"

Po was relieved at not having to. To do so would implicate him somehow, but he needed to know, of course.

"Adjacency has always been critical, but with the realms coming together, it means power unlike any it's meant before. If we succeed, that will fade again. But for now, your adjacency will suffice. You, Po, are the link between me, my children, the ICBMs, and Demeter. With Mrs. Brucker's assistance, guided by her son and our friend from the place I'm not particularly comfortable naming when the barriers are crossing over, we have the influence we need. Again, because of the boundaries failing. The Brucker boy will always be able to cross over. You are able to as well, given your ability to step back from separation and see the entire picture. So we can turn the tide and do what we need to do."

Po finished his tea and his second cake and watched her watch him.

"They're willing to hurt anyone," Mrs. Blesmol said. "The old who've earned better treatment by virtue of surviving this long. Babies who deserve love because they've been dragged into being without anyone asking their permission. So we need to teach Truitt and his lot a lesson they should already have known—never piss off an old mom." She sipped her tea again. Then she began to explain.

Before she'd finished, Po knew what his answer would be.

## 61

## CRASH JIBE

He'd gone elsewhere. Now Po was back.

It was the in-between state of things. The crossing over. A representation of Po had remained all the while, but because Paul's own Nistar abilities sensed the monk's conscious Essence crossing over to another place, Paul hadn't seen him as being present at all.

Now he was.

Whether he'd left or not, Po wasn't having a good time. He grimaced, bearing the millstone of something endured.

The burning.

For Paul, the heat wasn't as acute on the parched landscape beneath the dam as it had been in the Shrine. It looked to him as if it remained real for Po.

Which was strange because beneath the twist of pain on the monk's face, Paul could've sworn there was—no, that was hardly possible. But maybe.

A deeper sense of peace that even the burning couldn't dislodge. Why?

Another mystery: Joel was absent from around Po's neck.

And he wasn't the only one missing.

## The Catalyst

It wasn't until Paul stepped back that he noticed Porter peering into the distance at something headed toward the dam at an alarming speed. Something so dark, small, and far away that Paul wouldn't have been able to identify it had he not realized the Shade was gone.

Distance didn't seem to be a factor for sound in this place —a place both real and not. It was as if someone had hastily programmed a simulation without bothering to get the acoustics and the physical laws right.

The Shade was an example of that—the Shade and whoever else was a part of it.

What came next was because of the Shade. Or because of whoever else inhabited the creature's form along with Brill's original Essence.

It hardly mattered, really.

Because what came next was the act of something committed only to the worship and perpetration of destruction as devotion.

A distant sound of impact. Something stone-like against stone.

The response from the dam was understated at first—a resonant acknowledgement of deep harm and a subsequent rumble.

The shift of something with mass and Essence almost beyond measure.

Something moving within its confines with palpable fear —panic at being liberated when no liberation had been sought.

Freedom. Terrible freedom.

The Essence's imposed slipping of its bonds announced itself with a crack that pierced the peace of the parched riverbed like the report of artillery. Then came the true rumble—one worthy of what the Shade, Porter, and, really, all of them had wrought.

The distant dam broke open, its captive Essence crashing forth like a liquid wall.

They would never get out of the way in time.

Not Po.

Not Paul.

Porter didn't look like he'd even try to escape what was certain to be a ferocious removal from the board. There was no fleeing in the Envoy.

Instead, the gray man slowly but purposefully made his way over to Po and Paul and wrapped an arm around each of them, drawing them toward him. The rush of the wall of Essence grew in volume to the point of rendering all other senses useless.

Porter didn't pay it any mind.

Paul and Po followed suit. They had eyes only for the staff, which Porter planted firmly into a crack in the riverbed before taking their hands and placing them over the top of it, gripping their fingers firmly to make sure they held on tight.

Paul understood.

There was no riverbed.

No approaching wall of water-like Essence.

No dam rent asunder.

Not really.

For all Paul knew, the others saw what was coming as a different representation entirely. The only thing he was certain they all experienced as one was the heat that found them again.

They'd never left the Shrine, despite all that had occurred.

And what Paul, Porter, and Po had to do next would be the end of them and the end of all if they faltered for only an instant.

A new sound now. A sound of three.

It came from Paul.

From Porter.

And even from the silent Po.

It was the cry of the mortal threat arrived and met. The shouted challenge from those who find clarity at last on the border between triumph and loss.

That which the demolished dam had released slammed into the trio and washed over them.

And the battle was joined.

∞

It was as simple and vicious as a sailboat boom sweeping across its deck without any warning to the crew. A crash jibe, if Audra recalled youth sailing correctly.

She and the Dodger went from safe but horrified to being in real danger in no time flat. The Breaker would never withstand the rushing tide.

Strangely, another analogy came to mind as her brain struggled to process the death they faced under countless approaching hooves. The L in Chicago. That time in her living years when she'd visited the city and exited a station, headed for the lake on a day too cloudy to tell where the sun was.

She'd walked and walked, and it was only after far too long a time passed without an appearance from Lake Michigan that she was forced to admit she'd gone the wrong way. Yet so certain was she of her trajectory that it felt like physically twisting her surroundings around in order to make it to the shore.

It was both revolution and shift. Demeter had more to do with a dream state than it did with The Living World.

The deadly mist. The monstrous fire opposite it.

The landscape-wide, endless stream of bison running from one to the other.

One moment, Audra and Lars were witnesses to a slaughter. The next, they were in the middle of it, mortally threatened. The mist was behind them, the fire a long way ahead of them. And the infinite ocean of onrushing bison was now headed straight for them. When it got to them, their perch would collapse into the rolling current.

Another memory.

A teaching job Audra accepted just a few years out of school, when budgets were slashed to a draconian degree. So many veteran teachers quit in frustration that Audra was an instant old-timer.

She'd gone to a bar with her principal and an English-teacher-cum-science-teacher who'd been there as long as she had. The principal bought them both bourbon and observed that they'd seen how everyone hung tough or bailed out under harsh conditions. But now they were about to see how people reacted when things were markedly worse.

"Now we'll see who runs, who screams, and who cries. And we'll know who we can count on," the principal, whose name escaped her now that she was about to be pulped, had said with a tight smile.

Now was then. Her last moments would be spent seeing how valiantly the Dodger perished, his demise no one's fault but hers because she was the one who'd put him in this position.

Audra turned to the young man to either apologize or try to comfort him in the path of the charging wall of beards, breath, and horns. And he showed her his character without knowing she was looking for it.

The Dodger laughed.

Audra decided that if she had to perish for real beside

anyone—assuming her Essence would be smashed into the general, limitless mass that was Demeter—then there weren't many other people she'd rather have standing with her.

Near the end, Audra considered using her heat to convince the bison to veer to either side of their tower. But given the damage done to her, her best efforts would generate only a drop in the comparable typhoon compelling the great beasts to hurtle as fast as they could to their doom.

So Audra joined the Dodger in his mirth and laughed with him.

It seemed a valorous enough way to go.

## 62

## WHAT MANNER OF MOTHER

When was a dream no longer a dream?
What if it never was?
When was a child no longer a child—and when was a child no longer your child?

What if he never was?

No.

That was not a mother's thinking. Annie had never had to police herself about questions like that, not even when nothing else in her life felt like it was real or had any weight to it. Not questions about her son.

Zach was her little boy, though she had to admit it was getting more and more difficult to call him little. He'd been a huge presence in her life since day one. The biggest. But increasingly, his place in the world looked to be of a scope she'd never imagined.

There was so much she didn't know about her boy. She couldn't help but wonder what kind of a mother she was, given that. What manner of mother raised a child capable of what Zach was doing?

The Humboldt had helped them—helped all of The

Commons. Yet her son, Porter, the dragon in the closet, and other forces uncounted were manipulating them as if they were some unfeeling resource to be exploited. They were laying claim to the Essence of countless beings who would never have the hope of a Journey if their effort succeeded. Never mind threatening all of existence by aiming those massive amounts of Essence at the gates of hell.

That was the only way Annie could get her head around such a place as The Pines, even if the analogy wasn't perfect. Hell, at least, was for those who'd been given the choice between good and evil and had chosen the latter. As she understood it, those in danger of being freed from The Pines were so bad that Creation itself quarantined them before they'd even had the opportunity to prove themselves deserving of imprisonment.

Thinking. She was doing too much of that.

They all had their part to play, knowingly or not. Annie's was to redirect adjacency, the strength and influence of which was multiplied exponentially in the crossing-over state of the realms. She learned by doing it, which was something else requiring an adjustment.

She performed an act, and that act informed her of its origin and, potentially, its effect. It didn't predict the future, but it revealed likelihood.

Adjacency and Essence. To a large degree, the realms ran on those two phenomena.

"We're killing them," Annie said.

"Not us. Not technically."

Annie knew Joel was speaking for himself, shaping information gleaned from Zach and giving it his own voice. It was yet another thing not to trust, she reminded herself. There were no guarantees that Joel's words were what her son intended her to hear, though he didn't seem too upset about anything said thus far.

"We're aiming the gun." Annie studied the array of patch cords, and as she did so, the patterns and their effects became more and more clear to her. She wasn't sure that was anything to take comfort in.

"The bullet hasn't arrived yet." Again, there was no telling what was coming from Joel and what Zach had wanted him to say—if anything at all.

Annie examined the patch cords again. They were tea leaves. Augury. Bones cast and lines on a palm. Or, more accurately, the reef, seen first in pixels and then real as life. Violence had occurred. Innocents were suffering. And the sin committed and damage done would soon be immutable.

"What do you want?" said Joel.

Annie turned to regard the two of them. If they didn't know what she wanted, there was no point in saying it aloud.

"The guidance—the spirit of the message—has already been sent and heard," Joel said. "The conduits can be released."

Annie considered the cords anew. Fresh patterns now presented themselves. "Can they be saved?"

"No. But they can save themselves. If you tell them how."

New patterns. How could that be? Nothing in the layout of the cords had changed, so how had she missed what was there all along?

"Only you can tell them," said Joel.

With that, Annie saw that the Tamagotchi's phrasing expressed yet another aspect of their current reality she'd missed until he'd said it.

Only she could tell them.

Annie reached for the cords with one hand, hesitated, and

switched to the other. Then she used both to make the necessary changes, praying she was doing the right thing.

When it was done Zach rested his hands on her shoulders and laid his head against hers. Joel didn't have to speak for her son. She understood that he was saying he was sorry.

She just didn't know what for.

~

Horns. Hooves. And fire behind them.

Audra closed her eyes as the bus-sized beasts approached.

According to one school of thought, the bison couldn't kill her because she'd already been taken out of The Commons by the Ravagers who'd attacked her. As far as she knew, she remained conscious and active only because of the in-between state of things, which didn't allow for her to be committed to anything so sensible as following the rules and perishing permanently.

The Dodger, on the other hand, was among those blocked from his rightful Journey by the Brill-induced stoppage of The Commons and its normal processes, which remained a long way from regular operation. The boy had something to lose, and thanks to Audra and Porter, who'd betrayed her misplaced trust, he would now forfeit it. For that, she was truly sorry, deeply saddened, and outraged on his behalf.

That guilt was probably what delayed Audra's realization that no more thunder was approaching. It had been washing past their tower for a stretch of moments. Past it. On either side.

And while Audra should've had her nose and lungs filled with the soil kicked up by the river of bison sweeping past within inches of the stairway she'd worked so hard to climb, she didn't. She made herself open her eyes and discovered that she wasn't immediately blinded by dust, either.

Within a moment or two, all was silent, the leviathan flow blowing past soundlessly, like a projection. Either the bison had been removed from the reality they'd shared with Audra and the Dodger, or the converse was true.

"Lars."

The Dodger didn't respond immediately. He blinked once or twice and looked around at the benign-but-terrifying rush of galloping mass as it passed them by below.

On and on it went. Time had no meaning in these moments, when it was possible to say both that the elapsed minutes were few and that the passing was nearly eternal.

The approaching fire pushing the wild-eyed bison before it was the sole element of urgency now. A wall of flame almost too bright to look at, too vast to contemplate, it drew ever closer in its herding of the animals.

With that closeness, the unreality of the fire revealed itself, too. Audra's pain, the sensitivity to heat she'd endured since her encounter with the frighteningly powerful fire creature, stopped signaling the coming destruction. The light of the fire remained, and the prairie grass was incinerated, but there was no heat.

After an eon of the silent hoofed flood, the last of the bison passed, and the fire was upon them.

Audra was forced to close her eyes as it obliterated the safe space between the two of them and vaporization. The insides of her lids were aglow.

The Dodger's hand grasped Audra's. She hadn't realized how close he was. And she squeezed back, unconvinced that the lack of heat guaranteed they'd be spared.

So it went for another stretch of timeless time. But when

the impossible light had faded from her lids, Audra cautiously opened her eyes again.

The Dodger clung to her hand hard enough to grind her knuckles together until he, too, opened his eyes. "Sorry," he said, sheepish as he let go.

Audra rubbed her hand slowly and thoroughly, surveying the aftermath.

They stood alone on the tower, above endless fields of ash, under a bright and sunny sky.

The Dodger, who could navigate fast-moving streams of cars, trucks, and other assorted traffic without so much as breathing hard, remained incapable of speech for a long moment, wide-eyed as he looked around before finally settling on Audra. "Can we go home now?"

Audra didn't know for certain what had just occurred. But she had her theories, fueled by the freakishly amped-up adjacency.

The challenge for her at the moment was to sort through those guesses and focus on the one that mattered. One bit of Essence was easily identified among all the others, and that one entity told her what she needed—and more than she wanted—to know.

Porter remained in the middle of this. Along with the others. What any of it meant beyond that was beyond her. But the other obvious identity couldn't be explained in any way that was excusable or even comprehensible.

Brill.

Jonas Porter was working with Brill.

She pulled out the Speaky Shrieky and spoke into it before she could second-guess herself into being coy. The only approach was the direct one. "Jonas," she said. "I know."

The Dodger backed away, staring at her with mixed concern and—was that fear?

Waves of heat were coming off her, and she couldn't tell if she truly felt no pain from the use of her abilities or was incapable of registering it in her fury. Did it matter?

Audra smelled burning plastic. The sides of the Speaky Shrieky, where her fingers and thumb grasped it, softened and gave way a bit. "I know," she said into it again. "And now you and I face each other across the line. That's your doing." She held the Speaky Shrieky out to Lars. "Is this too hot for you to hold?"

The Dodger carefully took it from her and tossed it from hand to hand, letting it cool.

Could they go home, he'd asked. A reasonable question.

Maybe they could. But home might not be there when they arrived.

Porter and the others were making a run at The Pines.

"Lars," Audra said. "Despite everything you've just been subjected to, do you think you could see your way to giving me a lift?"

## 63

## EGRESS

You've been in a fight, Porter had told Paul the last time Porter was in this place. Worse than a fight.

Now they were both in one. And neither of them needed to be told.

Porter sat alone in an ancient wooden Adirondack high on a dune in the desert. This was where he'd said goodbye to Paul a lifetime ago, when he saw the victorious boy off on his voyage back to The Living World.

Or so they'd thought.

It was no victory.

The L.W. now found itself compromised by at least one other realm because a win was a loss was a win, depending on who did the tallying.

It was appropriate that the distinction between victory and defeat, between one world and another, was not clear here in the hot sand. This place had never been in just one location, in Porter's experience. And his first time here was certainly not an instance of victory.

Porter shifted his weight in the Adirondack, which was also known as a Muskoka, a Cape Cod, or a Westernport. All names for the same piece of furniture, which had found its way here to wait for him by means unknown. It shared its name with the couch recliners used for patients in sanitariums. The cure chair, that one was called. But Porter didn't expect to be healed of anything.

Judging by the few remaining flecks of paint on its battered wood, the chair was a traveler and a survivor, like him. It carried its scars and its sins alone, with no one to give them voice, just as he himself seldom spoke of his own. If one carried on long enough, one collected such a record. The truth of that record and to whom it was revealed was decided only by the one bearing it.

Ultimately.

For everyone decides his own truth and lives with it. Whether or not it jibes with the version others would tell is immaterial if the tale is never exposed or challenged.

Light.

The light changed subtly.

In a more solid or defined place, there would be a shadow thrown by the boy standing behind him. Such was not the case here.

"Hello," said Porter without looking back.

The answering silence confirmed the visitor's identity.

"Your name is Zach."

Again, nothing. There'd been no question, so for Zach Brucker, there was no need to answer.

When Porter blinked, the boy stood in front of him.

"It's a pleasure to meet you, Zach," said Porter. "My preference would have been to make your acquaintance under better circumstances—and in a situation where the two of us hadn't contributed so meaningfully to a quite awful result."

The boy watched Porter as if he were waiting to get past the pleasantries and exchange something meaningful, but everything that passed between them carried equal weight. Such was the way of their predicament. The trivial had no place here or in any of the crossed-over realms.

"I'm currently in the Shrine of the Lost," Porter told the boy. He almost asked Zach where he was.

However, the boy wouldn't have told him because there might not be one clear answer to that question—and there was most likely no good reason for Porter to be told. Maybe the boy knew that. Or maybe he was just careful.

The latter being true, it was most welcome. When all of the other forces at play were putting existence itself at risk based on preference and hunch, somebody had to act with common-sense caution.

"I'm sorry there's no seat for you." Porter knew Zach didn't much care about that—and that neither of them would remain long enough for their legs to tire. Assuming anything tired in this place.

Again, naught but silence from the boy.

"I can tell you a thing or two that you should know, for we are fellow travelers in a way those who move with us are not." When Zach still did not reply—and Porter hadn't expected him to—Porter weighed whether to explain what differentiated the two of them from the others.

The best way to illustrate was a chess analogy. If Porter was a rook, able to move only up and down or side to side, Zach was more of a combination bishop and knight, able to slip across the board diagonally or up and over. However, there were exceptions to those rules for both of them, depending on circumstance, and the boy's abilities transcended Porter's in key ways, allowing him to move in a manner that squares and boards could not define.

Zach's silence convinced Porter to try another tack. "Does anyone else know what you can do? Do you?"

As if in answer, Zach bent down to scoop up a handful of sand.

Joel the Tamagotchi swung from his neck. Porter couldn't be sure without grabbing Joel to have a look, which might have scared the boy away, but it appeared as if the Tamagotchi was sleeping. Or maybe he wasn't able to be fully resident here.

Zach held the sand out to Porter and let it run slowly through his fingers until it was gone.

"I understand," Porter said. "In our current situation, there's no solid answer to that question, and it wouldn't stay in that state even if there were."

Zach's hand dropped to his side.

"Well, I'll tell you why I'm here, Zach." Porter sat up in the Adirondack, which was an awkward maneuver, and leaned forward to look the boy in the eye. "This is a place of exit. An egress, issue, outlet, point of departure. Like many things, it has many names."

The boy blinked. Porter assumed that was as close as he might come to acknowledging what was being said to him.

"I found myself here for the first time a very long time ago —if time has meaning now, which it may not—in one of the darkest moments of my work as an Envoy. The details aren't something to be told here and now, but I'd been guiding a Journeyman named John who'd decided not to go on. No matter what I said, he wouldn't. The more he refused to continue, the more it upset me, and the more at peace he was. Finally, I understood that my job was to see him off to wherever it is that those who quit the game go. Once I accepted that, I was alone here, left to figure out where I'd gone wrong and why I'd failed. He was gone."

Zach's gaze dropped to the sand. Porter assumed he was going to scoop up more of it, but the boy considered it for a moment before looking back up at Porter again. Was that sympathy in his eyes?

Porter knew better than to read emotions into the situation simply because it was what he wanted and not what the boy was feeling or trying to convey. "Audra came and got me. I wasn't planning to leave. But she talked to me and made me understand that the choices of others were ultimately theirs to carry, not mine." He shifted his foot in the sand, and Zach looked down again to study the movement. "That lesson has served me well, and it's a gift I don't think I've ever repaid."

Zach looked up at Porter once more, and this time Porter couldn't miss the understanding there.

"All of which is to say that I feel bad, Zach. Awful. I know I'm doing what's right—or what's as right as I can determine at the moment—but it doesn't feel like it. I'm betraying the friend who's done more for me than just about any other, and it's lousy. So here I am at a place of leaving while I'm also back in the Shrine, hard at work on my betrayal. The crossing of the realms allows me to both act and feel like a terrible, terrible person in two places at once for that action. Do you understand?"

Zach watched Porter intently.

Neither of them spoke for a stretch.

"Do you?" Porter repeated. "Because it could be that I'm ascribing feelings to you in order to make myself feel just a little better. But I'm hoping you're here because you know what I mean. Do you feel bad?"

The merest suggestion of a smile crossed the boy's face, and Porter understood that from Zach, that was probably the most vigorous response one could hope for.

Porter felt no need to continue. Not to tell him who the Journeyman who'd doomed himself had been or how Porter carried that loss with him now. All that needed to be clear between them was that Audra had saved Porter—and Porter was going against her anyway. "We betray only when we must, Zach." He sat back in the Adirondack again. "We move forward with the plan, and we convince the realms and their Essence of our intent. If we believe, they believe. Enough for them to do what we need. Then we move on and learn to live with the result."

The boy said nothing, but the wraith's smile remained.

Porter understood why he'd come and what he'd been looking for. Maybe shared guilt and understanding was the closest thing to absolution the two of them could offer each other.

They would move on from here.

They would do what was necessary.

On top of what they'd already done.

And it would have to be good enough.

## 64

## THE UNIVERSE THROUGH A STRAW

Paul thought his eyes were closed. But he wasn't certain.

It was like trying to prove he was dreaming in the middle of the dream. He couldn't do it.

Other sensations were easily identified, however.

The heat was no easier to endure than it had been before.

The burning.

Here in the Shrine of the Lost, where Paul had been all along.

It was different now. Or maybe it was what it had always been, and Paul was just now able to understand it.

An alias. A shortcut. That's what the Shrine was.

The amount of Essence that needed to pass through the Shrine—and through Porter, Paul, and the others—would have obliterated all involved. It would have been like trying to suck the universe through a straw. To even attempt such a thing would have been absurd.

But that was the roundhouse model, like a railroad facility that served to redirect trains passing through to other tracks.

In this case, the combination of their group and the Shrine

was more like an air-traffic-control tower. It gave Porter a facility for telling the Essence where to go. Then the Essence made its way through the gaps Paul and Brill had opened up, via the crossing-over state of The Margins, and went straight at The Pines.

They all needed to be there for it to work, as Paul understood it. Porter provided access to the Shrine. That was pure adjacency, since Porter was one of the ones who'd created the place. Porter and his ability to jump things told the Essence it was possible to travel from point A to point B and gave it guidance.

Paul's Nistar ability, which centered around changing Essence from one form to another, allowed the Essence to know that it could adopt the form needed.

And Apalala-Aidan, with his own vast abilities and place of origin, provided access to The Pines, completing the chain. The nukes were the catalyst, setting off the Demeter Essence, which Porter and the Shrine guided through the gaps and Margins.

Paul told it what form it should take when it got there.

Then Apalala-Aidan aimed it at his prison home.

If all worked out as it was supposed to—and it was at the moment—the barrier between The Pines and everything else was at risk. Paul was both a part of this and not. It was like standing by the Mississippi after weeks of rain and sticking a finger in, pretending you could tell the water where to go and what to do when it got there.

Yet that's what they were doing. And Paul could barely manage not to get sucked into the flow and drowned in it.

Trust.

Porter had asked for his trust.

Paul didn't know enough to give him that. The best he

could do was to play along and do his part to shape how the game ended.

That and pray the gray man knew what he was doing. And had told the truth about it.

Because nothing had been said about the plan for after they finished putting the universe in mortal peril. Paul just assumed Porter had one.

Man, was it hot.

～

BELIEF. Belief was all.

Porter saw the totality where he'd seen only components, like hearing each instrument's part played individually before finally understanding the entire symphony.

The ICBMs, to Demeter, to Apalala-Aidan, who was the only one powerful enough to serve as the spearhead for all of the Essence aimed at the barrier around The Pines. Everyone who had to touch it or be aware of it—Paul, Porter, the Shrine, and all other necessary parties—working together toward one purpose, even if not all parties knew what they were doing. Especially if not all parties knew, for that would lead to sure failure.

The heat. To know of it was to perish from it, even if one survived the ordeal.

That was the point.

Cauterization. A burning away of the corruption, a sealing of what had been broken open.

The hands on the staff were one.

The effort was one, though the awareness was not.

What came afterward would be its own struggle, but that was a concern for days to come.

For now, Porter and Paul fed Apalala-Aidan, who burned

bright and would soon storm the gates from outside his place of confinement, and all of the realms and all of existence itself would take notice.

Tear down the wall. Free The Pines. Unleash the leashed. Unbind the bound.

It couldn't be done without belief because the fear he needed to come afterward required a whole-minded commitment.

The only thing we have to fear is fear itself. One could only hope.

The heat in the Shrine grew ever more oppressive.

Now Porter's struggle was to limit his understanding of what was happening, to quiet one voice in his head while allowing the other to make itself heard.

The dragon was coming—in all its fury, with all its desire to disrupt and transgress.

Underneath the others' hands, Porter tightened his grip on the staff. They would all allow it, all help the Essence make its way to freedom.

In doing so, they would free a realm that had been in chains since the birth of everything.

Belief.

Porter had always known of its importance. Now it was more crucial than ever. To believe was to be afraid. To be afraid was to be free.

Porter tightened his grip further.

The others did the same.

~

THERE WAS no sound of anything approaching. It was more a feeling.

Rain, Zach, Annie, and Emmett were in the dining car

when no meals were being served because meals never really needed to be served. Eating was what happened when someone wanted to remember what it was like to be normal.

Of course, nothing was normal, which was why the four of them had made their way to the table to sit and stare at one another.

When Rain was a child—it was difficult to remember she'd ever been one—she'd had a tough cat, a former stray that adopted her. A big gray mess of a bruiser with one permanently flopped ear and a droopy eyelid, he had no name because he didn't appear likely to accept one.

That independence suffused his being. He came and went when he wanted, with the emphasis on the went part, except for when storms blew in.

When thunder and lightning ruled the air, the big stray materialized. Wherever Rain was, he was, without announcement or warning. She never understood how he got into the house half the time. Maybe he'd been there all along but hadn't wanted her to know. But in the time of storms, he needed to be with her. That was all the explanation she'd ever get from him.

The current gathering in the dining car was much the same. None of them knew why they'd been apart and then assembled; they just knew they didn't want to be alone.

Her guard down for a moment, Rain thought of Lexi and those she'd left behind. Did Lexi feel alone? She pushed the question away. It wouldn't serve her now. Nor would it do to worry about how she might feel when matters like that refused to be put off. Such considerations were fine for those without Rain's responsibilities—but not for her.

A presence above the train journeyed across the sky.

The temperature in the dining car rose, the air shifting around the train. Light from outside, like the sun rising.

No. Setting.

A meteor coming to take them out. Bright, bright orange. Fast. Fast and big.

The heat grew. The light intensified.

When it passed, it was close enough to send a pulse through the train and through them. The entire car bumped sideways, and the little people inside were rattled to the core.

Rain felt it in her teeth. She closed her eyes. When she opened them again, Zach was the only other one looking around at the faces. The kid probably hadn't closed his at all.

Emmett opened his eyes.

Annie did the same.

Rain wanted to ask them what the hell had just happened. There was no need.

They all knew. It wasn't their first encounter.

Zach knew best of all. The kid knew a lot of things he didn't let on about.

They all understood that the very big thing blew past them on its way to doing God-knows-what to God-knows-who God-knows-where. And it was gathering speed as it did so.

Whatever was on the receiving end would not be able to stand against it. No way. And of the four of them, only the kid might have known what was going to get hit.

Rain didn't ask. Rain didn't want to know.

Neither did anyone else.

∽

"No." Truitt hadn't looked away from his phone for a couple of hours. He hadn't dismissed Jeremy or Stacey or talked about getting them off the island, either, so they assumed he still wanted them there.

They sat in the former autopsy theater, saying nothing but

exchanging meaningful glances to reassure each other that they weren't supposed to leave. That's how Jeremy saw it. Or maybe Stacey was trying to tell him she thought he was an invertebrate because he hadn't stepped up into hero mode and gotten any additional information out of Truitt the whole time they'd been sitting there.

Truitt grunted.

Jeremy tried to work himself up to asking for the latest.

Truitt chuckled appreciatively, shook his head, then laughed again. "Lady and gentleman, we have been played."

Stacey looked at Jeremy, who shrugged. "How so, sir?" she said.

Once again, Jeremy wished he'd spoken up first—not to impress the old man, but to maintain his standing with her. Or improve it, even. He didn't know why he wanted that. But he did.

"It's quite devious. They did to us what we did to them." Truitt thumbed his phone again and then looked at Jeremy before settling on Stacey, as if he wasn't sure which one of them had spoken. "How so? Well, we waited for them to behave according to our plan and inspired them to do the same to us." His jaw tightened, and he worked it briefly, a dark anger rising to the level of his eyes before he let it go and returned to his admiration and black amusement. "The kill switch. They wanted us to use it." He chuckled again and shook his head slowly. "Well played, you mush-brains. I underestimated you."

"I'm not sure I follow." Jeremy nearly said *we*, but he wasn't sure it was also true of Stacey.

Still focused on his phone, Truitt waved his hand in the air.

His screens emerged from the shadows. All were black—no graphs, no pine cones, no nothing.

Truitt tapped his phone again and checked the floating screens. Bright pinpoints appeared in the center of all five of them. He let out a soft, puzzled grunt as the pinpoints grew into small flares in each of them, accompanied by a rumble so deep it felt as if their building were shaking, rousing itself from sleep after realizing it had dozed off.

Stacey started to say something but Truitt waved her off.

The flares grew exponentially larger on all screens—fast, big. The rumbling grew, coming toward them.

Truitt frantically waved his hand to dismiss the screens, but they struggled to close themselves against the occupying flares, the brightness so extreme that all three people in the room had to look away.

It was an explosive impact of god-like proportions.

The largest bomb—no, bombs—anyone had set off, ever.

Larger.

Even the walls of the theater were too bright to look at.

"Down!" Truitt dove for the floor with a surprising quickness for a man his age.

Stacey and Jeremy hit the deck, too—just as the world blew up around them.

Jeremy heard the fractured *ting* of a small window breaking.

Truitt's phone.

Just before the air of the theater slammed into him, and breathing became his only concern, Jeremy heard Truitt say something to himself. He couldn't make it out clearly, and a moment later, it was forgotten among the larger concern of survival.

But it sounded like "Much to do. Much to rue."

## 65

## THE PANIC ROOM

G-man could handle the heat. He was a damned demon, after all. Yeah, it felt like it was melting him from the inside out, starting with his lungs and moving on from there. And it made his wounds ache worse than they had when the Ravagers first shot him. But J.P. was with them here in the panic room, and the old fire-breather was mourning the loss of his daughter in addition to being cooked along with the rest of them, so if he could hang in there, G-man could, too.

The panic room. It was more of a bomb shelter, truth be told. But since nobody wanted to admit their office was merely a renovated building from the '50s, which was where the shelter came in, they'd updated the name in order to make the space feel more contemporary. Nobody had bomb shelters anymore. They hadn't since forever. But panic rooms were all the rage.

Rage. That's what the heat felt like. It was really the adjacency that was the problem. Adjacency and the demons' ability to chase it down was why they were so good at what they did—and why they were so damned vulnerable to whatever the apocalypse being played out at the moment was called.

None of them were able to come up with a name for it. G-man just thought of it as the Big One since that's what it felt like somebody had set off. And it was as long-lasting as it was big.

There was a dirty joke in there somewhere. But when it felt like his scales were peeling off, he didn't feel much like laughing.

Of course they'd come back to the office. Where else were they going to go? After the Ravagers slaughtered so many of them and word came back that Effie was gone—not just gone to get help but gone for real—the attack abruptly ended. As fast as it began, someone called the Ravs off.

So, given the grief that had eaten its way into all of them, given all of the work waiting to be done to deal with their dead and wounded, and given the mourning that had already begun and would continue forever, they'd stayed put.

J.P. had decided.

G-man had to hand it to him. That's why J.P. was the leader. His little girl left him behind after saving their butts, but J.P. was still the big thinker who knew more than any of them when something good or bad was coming—and how they should deal with it.

"The PR," J.P. had said, snapping out of the long and silent grief that had shrouded him since the report of Effie's death arrived. "Now."

Nobody asked any questions. They knew he meant the large shelter they'd been unable to reach before the Ravagers launched their attack, and they knew they had to get themselves and their wounded into it but fast.

G-man didn't know how long ago that had been. He did know that this blast or wave or whatever you might call it was related to the scary-powerful fire being they'd accidentally messed with. Though it was way, way bigger than even that guy. He was just a part of it. And if something as huge as the fire being was only a fraction of this assault and was dwarfed by the larger heat of it, then G-man couldn't be sure they were going to survive.

Singing. J.P. was singing now, and the rest of them joined in.

It was an old song, one they'd all been taught as babies. If pressed, G-man couldn't have recited the words, and he was willing to bet nobody else in the dark shelter could, either. But they came to him—came to all of them—with ease and, surprisingly, went a long way toward distracting him from the ache of his bullet wounds and the damned heat and its relentlessness. He'd never thought about the words before. Something involving the devil beating his wife, which was a weird song for demons to sing, when you thought about it.

But G-man didn't think. It was too hot to think. And thinking wasn't going to get them through this. The singing wouldn't, either. Not by itself. But it would help.

Man, it was hot. So damned hot.

Cooking hot. Oven-up-too-high hot. When-do-the-alarms-go-off hot.

But there weren't any alarms. And nobody who'd come on the run to hose them down. They were on their own to make it through this. So they sang.

G-man hung tough. Because J.P. was hanging tough. And if they ever came out the other side of this, J.P. was going to need him. He was going to need all of them.

They'd bounce back, whoever was left. And they'd find an angle.

That's what they did.

That's what they always did.

So G-man sang his heart out. The heart he thought had been burned or shot out of him by this point.

And he hung in there for J.P. and for poor, poor Effie, who'd deserved better than she'd gotten.

But, man, was it hot.

## 66

## I DREAMT THE WORLD BLINKED

Lexi would later describe the sensation as a combination of body-wide static shock and gut punch. She was sleeping in the little tent Grease lent her when the weird head-to-toe energy pop zapped her spiritually as well as physically, snapping her awake.

If that hadn't done it, George Wickham biting her ear and the dual impacts of a large dog and a puppy would have more than sufficed.

"Ow!" Lexi rubbed the site of the bird's attack.

George Wickham, who was allowed to come and go via one of the flaps, sidestepped across the floor of the tent, eyeing her. He didn't appear to be even the littlest bit sorry.

Angus licked her afflicted cartilage while the puppy yapped at her. Whatever that snap of energy had been, it was no dream—the critters had felt it, too. She told herself the parrot had been trying to wake her for her own good. She even thought it might have been true.

Who could say what the pooches were doing? Their eyes darted wildly from Lexi, to George Wickham, to each other, and back to Lexi faster than she could track.

Angus wanted to stay put with her. The puppy wanted out.

She went with the pup's choice and unzipped the flap, stepping out into the early morning of the park.

Outside, the others were gathered around one of the picnic tables that served as both meal-prep line and dining area for the little community, which had steadily grown since Rain left Lexi, Angus, and George Wickham with Grease and her crew.

Rain.

Lexi found it painful to consider her, so she did it as little as possible. To think about Rain meant chewing over her abandonment of Lexi and the critters—and the fact that she might not ever come back, either because she didn't want to or because someone else didn't want her to.

Which wasn't to say that nobody whose absence was keenly felt ever returned. Broward, for instance, who'd been the source of a lot of Grease's anxiety, showed up early one morning.

Grease nearly lost her mind when she emerged from her tent to find him making coffee, but the bearded young man just shrugged. He'd been gone; now he was back. And he wouldn't tell anyone where he'd traveled to or what had happened to him. Nor would he explain the refusal. Lexi wasn't sure he knew. Not that it seemed to bother him at all.

Still, Grease had been right about Broward being mostly dependable, despite his trademark spaciness. He never seemed to be quite all there, but you could count on him to help if he said he would. The problem was getting him to say that.

The dogs came out of the tent behind Lexi—the puppy noisily and Angus in complete silence, which the big guy was able to pull off when he wanted to despite his usual galumphing ways.

George Wickham landed on Lexi's shoulder and perched there, once again impressing her with his ability to find a purchase without scratching her. Their agreement held: he didn't break skin; she didn't grab him for a nail-cutting. She'd just have to see if the ear-biting would become a thing.

If so, it would be a bad thing. Just as coffee was good, while other things were somewhere in between. Like how she'd left the place Jabari had found for her, even after she'd promised him she wouldn't, because she needed to move on.

Freedom was good. Breaking a promise wasn't. But Lexi wouldn't be tied down by anyone, no matter how well-meaning they might be.

"Morning, Long John." Broward was once again on coffee duty. He'd been calling Lexi that since George Wickham started using her as a mount. "High-test? You can have fresh, if you're willing to wait, or you can enjoy the battle-hardened stuff that's left over from yesterday right now."

Lexi grabbed a mug, one of many purloined from area diners by the denizens of Grease's camp, and nodded in appreciation as he poured the latter.

"No cream," Broward said. "Sorry."

Lexi nodded her understanding and thanks, as she did every morning. There was never any cream. And Broward wouldn't stop apologizing for it, though he never seemed to want to obtain any, either.

Around them, Grease and the others who'd preceded Lexi in coming out of their tents murmured to one another, many with eyes still swollen from sleep and camp living. Mostly, though, they remained with their own thoughts.

"Had a hell of a dream. And I wasn't alone," Broward said, watching the little stove's propane flame as it worked the coffee pot over. That was his way. Those he addressed knew who he was talking to without him having to make it clear. He waited for Lexi to speak, but she waited for him to continue. "I dreamt the world blinked." He looked at Lexi for a reaction. She waited, wanting more specifics. "Everybody did, in their own way, though I'm not sure they'd put it the same way." He gazed into the flame for a while more before understanding that she wasn't going to volunteer anything.

Lexi didn't want to put whatever it was she'd felt into words. She wasn't sure which would've scared her more, failing to convey what she'd experienced—or succeeding.

"You, too?" Broward turned to her now.

So did all the others, even those who pretended not to. They'd all stopped speaking.

Lexi said nothing for a moment. She didn't trust herself to speak because to say it was the world blinking was more pleasant than anything she might've come up with. Anyway, it was too big a thing to talk about. "I dreamed this guy talked and kept me up all night." She gave the parrot on her shoulder some side-eye, but George Wickham offered no hint of an apology.

"He talks?"

Lexi shrugged, and George Wickham bobbed his head with the gesture like an avian shock absorber. "In dreams he does. As of last night."

Broward studied the bird. "What'd he have to say?"

"I don't remember," Lexi said, though she did.

With a brief half-smile, Broward returned his attention to the coffee. "Far out," he said.

Boy, was it.

Lexi watched Broward watch the coffee and avoided eye contact with anyone else. She looked to Angus and George Wickham, both of whom were polite enough to look away. That was the reason she loved animals more than humans.

Standing still was impossible; she knew now she was meant to leave.

She needed to go home.

But she also needed to know where that was.

## 67

## THE BIG JERK

Sometimes Jabari thought the kids were ghosts. Other times, he was sure that he was, too—that somehow he'd died, and nobody told him, so God sent all these lost children to clue him in. But not by saying anything directly because that would make too much damned sense.

Well, that wasn't quite it.

The kids didn't know much more than he did. The difference was, he couldn't get past his own ignorance. He insisted on trying to figure it all out, while none of them cared about solving the mystery.

The kids were truly in the moment. Along for the ride until they weren't.

From there, he couldn't say where they went. They were just gone.

Jabari wanted to think Paul was crazy. That the wild tale he'd told him about the land of the dead and universes colliding and fictional characters being real because everything had been broken until Paul and Porter fixed it was just the product of a mind that had taken the big tumble. That Paul's guilt over his huge win leaving everything more broken than ever—broken the way someone else wanted it to be broken—was the result of shame, or too many drugs, or too much shame about doing too many drugs.

But Jabari believed. Because being turned to stone will do that to you.

He didn't recall anything of it beyond looking into eyes that were holes, kicking off the whole process. But he was brought back by bad dreams.

Only he knew they weren't dreams. He could tell the difference.

The werewolf was real. So was Porter and Paul's fight with her.

And everything after.

Anyway, it wasn't like he was living in a normal world now. Not even close.

Not with the ghost kids. Or ghost him. Or both.

He was in a weird in-between time that felt like an eclipse. But the heavens would realign, and the shadow hanging over everything would be pushed away again by the light. Though maybe that was just misplaced optimism.

For now, Jabari tried to stick with what felt real. With what worked, to a degree. That was his routine.

He received texts from nobody, or maybe it was a bunch of nobodies. Not even a blank-face icon and an unknown *from* number. Nothing. And the text was always the same kind of thing—an address and a first name. That was it.

Those were the lost boys and girls. To be picked up and rescued, wherever they were.

Alone in empty houses out in the burbs. Standing outside dark, abandoned schools. Waiting in the middle of nowhere in farm country. Hanging out by the shoulder of some winding rural road.

Jabari learned the hard way that he couldn't ignore the

texts. The first time he tried, it just kept repeating. And the girl he picked up by a deserted playground, Marci, screamed and cried once he made it there—wanting to know where he'd been, and didn't he realize what it meant to stand there all alone when she'd already been waiting so long?

So Jabari went.

The Midnight Angels RV never needed gas, despite sitting on empty. And the lost children never made it to New Beginnings, even though his job was to try to take them there.

It made no sense. And while none of the texts told him specifically to do that, they didn't need to. It was like breathing.

That was what he was supposed to do—complete the assignment that couldn't be completed. Somehow, that was what the universe wanted. Or God. Or whatever greater force was behind all this.

He knew enough not to ask questions. From everything he'd seen, nobody would be around to provide any answers.

All of that started to change, though, when the big jerk hit. That's what Jabari called it. Reality slipped sideways and nearly knocked him out of the bed he'd borrowed in New Beginnings because that, too, was what the universe wanted. He was supposed to stay there, wait for his texts, pick up the kids one by one—they were always alone when he found them—and then try to take them to where he slept.

Try.

Because without fail, he'd pull up to the building, or make it to a light a few blocks away, or whatever. And there'd be a moment when he'd look away to pay attention to the road, or get out of the van and come around, only to have, say, the windshield support come between him and the kid. And in that blink of an eye?

Gone.

No words. No sound.

Gone.

The first time it happened, Jabari searched for an hour, convinced the girl had gotten out of the van and slipped into New Beginnings without him, even though he knew damned well she hadn't.

Denny. That was his name. Denny was the first.

And after Denny had come Chris, Lisa, Sandi, Danny, Donnie, Luke, and a steady stream of ghost kids taking ghost rides.

Until the big jerk, that is, when reality stepping to the side pulled him out of a sound sleep. Right away, he knew something had changed. Something fundamental and important.

Shortly after that, the first real text came in. A teenage boy this time, the first older pickup after the endless string of ghost kids. The boy had a first and last name, a phone number, and a profile pic that showed up normally and everything.

Jabari went to pick him up in Deerfield, only to get another text about another teen—a girl this time—in a deserted house in Unincorporated Glenview. That was important—that he understand her home was unincorporated. He had no idea why.

Nor did Jabari understand why he knew the two of them would make it back to New Beginnings, which was way more satisfying than he'd have thought just a week or two earlier.

Now he felt like he was making a difference. It was confirmed when he stepped around to the side of the van and opened the sliding door for the two teens, who actually went into the building with him. They'd made it.

And it was definitely different when, as Jabari was explaining to the two of them that he didn't technically work for New Beginnings and would have to figure out their situation along with them, they were interrupted by the sound of the front door opening.

Nails scrabbled on the floor as that big dog came running in the way dogs do, like he'd never been in this space before, and it was going to be the coolest ever. But he pulled up short when he spotted Jabari and the two new teens.

Lexi came in behind the dog with a parrot on her shoulder. Given the weirdness of this in-between world, which suddenly felt less in-between, that didn't even rate a question.

"I couldn't stay in the park anymore," she told him as she threw her stuff on the front desk with a note of finality. "We've got a lot of work to do."

"We do?" Jabari knew it sounded dumb as soon as he said it.

The two new teens studied Lexi and Jabari as if picking a side were a requirement, and they didn't want to choose the wrong one.

"Yeah." Lexi frowned at Jabari as though he were a grade-A cement-head. "You didn't think I was going to leave this place to you, did you?"

Jabari hadn't thought that far ahead. He hadn't expected anyone to make it into New Beginnings without disappearing first. His phone buzzed with a text. He checked the screen.

"Go." Lexi logged into one of the desktop computers. "And get used to it. There are a lot more of those coming."

Jabari went. And he hoped this pickup, and the one after that, and the one after that would all make it through the door with him when he got back.

It made him feel alive.

~

*The Catalyst*

MAISIE DOUGLAS DIDN'T like Foster Beach. She thought Kathy Osterman Beach was way better. But her brother Jamie, who insisted on being called James now that he had a girlfriend, dragged her there because it was where the girlfriend wanted to go.

At nine years old, Maisie remembered when Jamie used to like taking her to the beach with him on summer days, when both their parents were working. That was ancient history now—even though it had only been the year before.

Now there was Olivia. Olivia made Maisie's brother change his name and change their beach. Maisie suspected Olivia liked Foster Beach because it had more boys to look at —boys who weren't Jamie.

Maisie didn't worry much about Olivia because she was pretty sure Olivia wouldn't be around long. While she was, though, Maisie planned to annoy her as much as she could to punish her for breaking the heart of Maisie's big brother, which hadn't happened yet but was totally going to.

So Maisie said she had to go to the bathroom again just to make Olivia take her, which Olivia did not want to do. The first time Maisie'd done it, she'd really had to. Not this time. And probably not the next time, either. It was worth it just to see Olivia's face squinch up.

What Olivia didn't understand—and Maisie did—was that having more boys to look at meant having more people on the beach. And a nasty bathroom. It couldn't be helped. Chicago's beach season was short. So at the first opportunity, families swarmed the lakefront until they outnumbered the grains of sand. That last part was what Jamie said, anyway, though Maisie didn't believe it.

Either way, the Park District people tried to keep up with the cleaning. They really did. But if you timed the hour wrong, you'd get to the bathroom just before the next scheduled cleanup, and that meant you just had to deal with it.

"Gross," Olivia said as they entered the open-air ladies' room. She wasn't wrong. Used paper towels spilled from the garbage can because the hand dryers were weak or broken, and nobody bothered with them. The paper towels collected in wet clumps on the floor, and the floor was wet because the paper got washed into the floor drain and clogged it.

Thus, the bathroom floor was a slick of cement-and-sand disgustingness. Maisie's beach shoes could handle that. Olivia's could, too, but that didn't help much when she'd left them on the towel with Jamie, even though he'd advised her to put them on.

Now Olivia was stuck. She had to walk across the wet, sandy floor barefoot—skin on public muck and goo, because going back to get her shoes would be an admission that she was weak. And, worse, that Jamie had been right.

Olivia and Jamie weren't that far along for Olivia to comfortably admit to "James" that she'd been wrong. And they never would, if Maisie's prayers amounted to anything.

"All right," said Olivia—which meant it wasn't—as she tried to stare a dry path into materializing on the floor. That wasn't going to happen. Both of them knew that. "While I'm here." She took a breath, held it, and headed for one of the stalls.

Maisie wanted to stay where she was, making it obvious to Olivia that she'd tricked her into a trip to the bathroom for no reason. But Maisie figured she might as well pretend to go so that Olivia didn't rat her out to Jamie. She wanted Olivia mad at her, not her brother.

The clogged drain gurgled and the sickening paper plug covering it shifted just as Maisie chose the stall a few doors down from Olivia's. That was weird. Weirder still was the puddle that began to grow around the drain. Why would water come up instead of going down?

Maisie heard Olivia peeing.

Maisie didn't want to hear Olivia pee.

The bathroom plot definitely had its downsides.

She stepped carefully into the stall, closing the door behind her and latching it. Then she waited for Olivia to finish. Maisie wanted to be sure Olivia would hear her flush the toilet, even though Maisie hadn't gone.

Movement by the drain, which Maisie could see through the crack between the stall door and frame, caught Maisie's eye. What had been weird was really weird now. The puddle was making its way across the floor toward Olivia.

Maisie wanted Olivia to have a bad time—but not that bad a time. As much as she didn't like Jamie's girlfriend, she couldn't help imagining how she'd have felt if the horrible drain water were to target her feet instead of Olivia's.

A moment later, no imagining was necessary. Maisie wanted to believe it was just her imagination, but she knew it wasn't when the puddle hesitated on its way toward Olivia's door, as if sensing something, and then changed course.

Now it was coming Maisie's way.

Maisie was in bad-dream territory, but it was not a dream. Beach shoes or no, she climbed up onto the toilet seat, steadying herself on the top of the metal toilet-paper dispenser with one hand so that she wouldn't slip and fall in.

The puddle began to come under the stall door, flowing around the support pillars as Maisie heard Olivia pulling paper from the roll. Her throat tightened up to the point where she was afraid she wouldn't be able to say anything. "Olivia," she managed.

Practically a whisper. Not loud enough.

"Olivia." Better that time.

"What?" said Olivia from her stall. She must've heard something in Maisie's voice because there was no annoyance in her tone. "Maisie?"

The puddle continued to collect under the door and around the base of the toilet, coalescing. It had sand in it, which made it thick. No, not sand. Something else. Something that formed on the surface of the nasty water and began to go solid, rising up like a tube.

Fear gave Maisie her voice, and she began to scream in a high-pitched panic siren that surprised even her with its volume. It wasn't a pay-attention-to-me or a get-Jamie-in-trouble-because-I'm-mad effort. It was screaming all its own—and it sent the sound of her terror far and wide.

Later, after the lifeguard who'd been in the men's room had come running to find Maisie hanging from the stall wall, balanced on one bare foot atop the broken toilet-paper dispenser with a beach shoe lying where there was no longer a thick puddle, Maisie couldn't remember making the leap. She would never have thought she could.

And when the lifeguard walked Maisie back to Jamie on the beach, Olivia thanking him more than she needed to, Olivia tried to tell Jamie that Maisie had been scared by a centipede or a spider or something. And that Maisie might have said it was a squid, but that was impossible. She tried to tell him while maintaining eyes only for the lifeguard, who agreed with Olivia—and who was older and more tanned than Jamie.

All of which Jamie noticed.

The bathroom trick had succeeded beyond anything Maisie could've hoped for. Jamie looked at Olivia while Olivia looked at the lifeguard, and something in his eyes told Maisie that Olivia wouldn't be coming to the beach with them anymore.

Not that Maisie cared much—or cared at all. Maisie was never, ever coming to Foster Beach again, no matter who tried to take her. Maisie wasn't coming to the lake again, and if she could get anyone to listen, neither would her family or friends.

The world was no longer what it had been before she and Olivia had gone into the bathroom.

Maisie had been worried about perverts. Or kids dirtying up the place. Yet neither of those things had borne fruit.

There'd been a squid in that puddle. With tentacles. Or maybe it was a bunch of giant worms, which was even worse. Whatever it was had risen up out of the water to look at her. To kill her, even.

And whatever it was had teeth.

Lots and lots of teeth.

## 68

## THE MYSTERIOUS TUBE OF STUPIDITY

The B.C. Guardian couldn't hunker down into the steam sauna deeply enough. It didn't matter how hard he tried to compact himself. He'd had the sense to stop attempting it when the unit was on and steamy, at least. But it had taken becoming disoriented, unable to figure out which way was up, and panicking to the point where he was certain his heart was on the verge of detonation before he'd gained that wisdom.

Something was coming.

There were no specific warnings about what it was or when it might be expected, because there never were. His terror was nameless, his anxiety a phantasm that managed to be all too real despite its penchant for remaining behind him no matter how quickly he turned to surprise it.

It was just there. It was something to be anticipated, dreaded—without any hope of preparing for it.

It was the monk's fault. The monk and that cranky toy around his neck. Nothing had been the same since their intrusion.

Well, to be fair, it wasn't really them. The Guardian's sense of dread had been well established long before their arrival. If anything, their visit was a confirmation of the thing to come, not its catalyst.

"Oh, me," said the Guardian before he could remind himself that anything waiting for him out in the room would be able to hear him. It or they might have assumed the castle to be empty, but not if they'd just heard his muttering. "Oh, me," he said at the thought of how foolish he'd been. Then he cringed at how he'd compounded the error.

Even without the steam, the air inside the sauna grew increasingly hot and stale. The Guardian began to wonder how long it would take him to breathe up all the suitable atmosphere in the enclosed space before poisoning himself with his own exhalations. Could that happen to a mythical if no one imagined he'd be vulnerable to asphyxiation? The head hole at the top allowed some air to come in. Would that be enough to save him, even if he were able to die from a lack of oxygen? What if it wasn't oxygen? "Oh, me." He sighed to himself for failing yet again.

The questions stopped when the sauna and the room jumped sideways.

The worry stopped, too. And the fear.

It wasn't just the room. It was the whole castle. Maybe the park and the city beyond.

Something big had just gone sideways, up, and down in the world outside the sauna, and this time the Guardian didn't think it was just his own paranoia.

Something had side-shuffled. Backed up. Reset.

That was it. Reset.

Moved.

The Guardian poked his head out of the sauna and, with hardly a pause, unzipped it and stepped out, testing the stone floor with his paw to ensure it was still solid enough to support him.

It was.

All of it was, as far as the Guardian could tell.

Something fundamental had changed in the world, as if he'd closed his eyes at night and, opening them but an instant later, found himself surrounded by bright morning. Or when the lightning went unseen, but the following thunderclap sent dogs scurrying for the closet or the safe haven under the bed.

There was no music playing. But there might as well have been—a song he thought he recognized before further listening revealed it was another piece of music entirely and had been the whole time.

"Oh, me." There was no fear in the Guardian's voice. Not anymore.

That fear had been a talisman against imagined threats. He had no time for that now.

Now was the time to see what had changed in his world, for something had—to the point where it might not be his world at all.

No need for anything rash, though. For the time being, the Guardian would consider his options for how to get out of the castle because he doubted his assigned duty remained valid in such a drastically altered reality.

Everything felt new, and with that newness, the Guardian thought he might actually have a chance.

That, too, was new. And he wasn't about to let it go to waste.

～

Whizbang went looking, though he'd been told not to.

He didn't apologize for losing his friends. He knew doing

so wasn't good enough and wouldn't bring them back. Only looking would. So that's what he did.

Now Whizbang was lost in the darkness of the Lincoln Tunnel. Hopelessly, thoroughly lost.

He'd known full well that heading into it was dangerous and dumb, particularly since he'd already admitted to the Dodger and Audra that it was irresponsible to the point of dereliction for him not to tell them about the others who'd preceded him into the mysterious tube of stupidity.

Now here he was. In the dark.

He'd stood outside the tunnel on the New York side, waiting for any sign that Biscuit, Lottie, Poppy, or Roadkill might be on their way out. He'd known all that time that it wasn't going to happen. So in he went, telling himself he had to at some point—that he might even find a new source of Essence, and wouldn't that make everyone happy?

In the dark.

It didn't take long for the tunnel to eat all the daylight or for him to realize he'd made a big mistake—the same one made by the others. If he hadn't picked up on it when he turned on his light, only to find it didn't work, he for sure did once he turned around to go back to Manhattan and saw that it was just as dark behind him—and there was no way out.

So Whizbang doubled down on the error and kept going in.

He walked his bike in the black, unable to see his hand in front of his face. It occurred to him that he could easily walk himself and his bike right into an open shaft if one were there. A surprise hole in the floor wouldn't make sense, of course, but neither did the tunnel closing behind him.

Yet he walked. And he didn't let himself worry about never making it out. Nor did he allow himself to consider that his friends might not, either—assuming they'd ever been there.

Until the world rolled over.

That was the only way he could have put it.

Like a sleeping giant deciding it was sick of lying on one side, the tunnel rolled onto the other. For no reason he knew.

Whizbang wasn't one to express complex dynamics in word or thought. Not that he was stupid. He just understood in his gut what was and what wasn't and didn't feel the need to talk about it.

That reluctance was put to the test when they all rode past him in the blackness.

It was pure luck they didn't slam into him since they, too, had no lights. And as far as Whizbang knew, they weren't any better at seeing in the dark than he was.

But there wasn't any time to mull it over. Whizbang turned his bike around, mounted up, and pursued them at a full-out sprint.

Suicide. Riding this fast was dumb, dumb, dumb, when you couldn't see a thing in front of you. But in this new world, one where his friends had somehow returned to him, it was a risk he was happily willing to take.

The gambit paid off when a pinpoint of light bloomed way up ahead.

It delivered further when Whizbang understood without seeing them that he'd caught his friends—all four of them—and was riding beside them in the blind air of the tunnel.

None of them spoke. But Whizbang never doubted that they were aware of him. He knew.

So did they.

The dot of light up ahead grew.

Soon, Whizbang could make out the vague shapes of the others flanking him, though he wasn't brave enough to look at them directly. He was afraid they might disappear.

The others didn't look at him, either. But as the light

increased, Whizbang knew it was Lottie who was closest to him. And when she picked up on who was next to her, she laughed and kept pedaling.

They raced out into the daylight and kept riding to put the tunnel well behind them.

Whizbang, Biscuit, Lottie, Poppy, and Roadkill—granted a second chance, handed a reprieve.

A chance at what? None could say.

A reprieve from what? No idea.

Something had changed in their world. Something abrupt. Something as profound as everything that had come before.

That was the way worlds were shaped and reshaped, Whizbang supposed. And maybe he wasn't so bad at thinking the big thoughts after all.

He chanced a glance at Biscuit as they rode, and Biscuit returned it. That was as far as it went, but that was all you needed from Biscuit.

On they sped, headed for home.

Or whatever home this rolled-over world might have waiting for them.

~

On his nighttime rounds at Stella Grace, Edsel made sure no residents tried to flout the in-bed deadline. There wasn't anyone in the game room. Everything was stowed away except for that chess board with the ark and animals, though the ark was gone, and there were only two animals in sight.

Edsel hadn't seen the set in a while and hoped that what was there wasn't all that was left of it, though it was a relief that any of it had survived after disappearing for so long he'd almost forgotten it existed. Someone must've spirited it away to their room, which was another violation of the house rules.

Down the hall, everyone was either in bed or washing up, which was a good sign of a nice, uneventful evening to come. Things had been jumpy earlier in the day in a way he couldn't put his finger on, with minor staff mistakes and one or two major resident episodes coming out of nowhere.

But they'd made it through. Now Edsel had his fingers crossed that they'd burned through all their hairy karma, and the rest of the shift would be copacetic.

On the return trip, he discovered that he probably hadn't crossed enough fingers.

The game room door was almost closed. He hadn't left it that way, and no other staff members should've been down this hall before Edsel cleared it.

That was another rule. Edsel didn't know the why of it, but it didn't matter. A rule was a rule. They didn't all make sense, but breaking the senseless ones would trigger just as much hassle from up top as a breach of the legit ones, so they had to be enforced equally.

To make matters worse, whoever was in there was whistling. That would let the other residents know a rule was being broken, prompting them to consider doing the same.

Edsel pushed the door open. The whistling stopped.

A boy Edsel hadn't seen before sat studying the two pieces on the board, running his fingers through his hair, which made it stand up in pickets.

Edsel drew closer. The two pieces—the squid and the peacock—were in diagonally opposed corners, both facing outward. They'd been turned toward each other when he'd left the room, so the boy must have moved them.

It shouldn't have annoyed Edsel, but it did—probably because nobody'd told him about the new resident. That had been a problem before, and he thought he'd taken care of it.

"Hello." Edsel's tone was one of practiced moderation. Not

knowing who this boy was or what had brought him to Stella Grace, he needed to keep the situation nice and leveled out. "You're new here? I guess nobody told you, but you're supposed to be getting ready for bed—and getting in it."

The boy stopped fiddling with his hair. He leaned back in the chair and continued to study the board, hands folded across his stomach.

"Hello?" Edsel worked to maintain a tone of understanding.

"They did it," the boy said. "Didn't see that coming."

"Who did what?"

The boy ignored him.

Edsel took a step closer, but only one. He didn't want to spook the kid. "I don't think we've met. I'm Edsel. What's your name?"

The kid picked up the squid and the peacock, considering each in turn. "Huey will do." He placed the pieces on the two black center squares, facing one another. He leaned right, then left, checking them out from different angles. Then, satisfied, he leaned back in the chair again.

"Nice to meet you, Huey. I'm glad you're here. But I'll be even happier if you let me walk you to your room before we both get in trouble."

" 'Who did what,' you asked." Huey's attention lingered on the pieces and the board before he turned to direct it at Edsel.

Edsel wished he hadn't. The eyes on him were like a physical touch—not a malevolent one, by any means, but it felt like they were looking into him, that they could see whatever they wanted to see.

"Don't you want to know?" said Huey.

Edsel's mouth felt like it was filled with dust. No, he didn't want to know. He didn't even want to get this boy back to his room. Nor was he confident that there was one assigned to him. He just wanted to back out of the game room and close the door. And tomorrow, he'd return to find the kid, the game, and the remaining pieces gone. That was what he wanted—as bad as he'd ever wanted anything.

"Now I've gone and scared you," Huey said. "I'm sorry. I forget how easy it is to do that to people. Don't be afraid."

It rapidly became apparent that simply telling someone not to be frightened fell well short of convincing them.

"I'll tell you what happened. Will that help?"

Edsel nodded, even though it wouldn't. But he wasn't about to defy this boy.

Huey pointed to one of the sprinkler heads on the ceiling. "What would happen if I lit a piece of paper on fire and held it up to that?"

The question shook Edsel out of his state of fear somewhat. "If you have matches, you need to hand them over." He remembered who he was talking to. "Please don't do that, Huey."

"It would drench the room, right? Or if I ran around holding the burning paper up to a bunch of them, it would be an indoor storm throughout this whole place. If that went on long enough, if you convinced the sprinklers that everything was on fire, and they soaked the place for a really long time, you'd have to redo the whole interior. Wouldn't you? You'd have to reset."

"Please," Edsel said.

"They burned the sprinklers." Huey looked to the board again. "That's really the only way to put it." He turned his gaze back to Edsel. Back into him. "Who would have predicted that? Not me, I'll tell you. Or anyone. Nobody would've thought that would work. It's so crazy and idiotic that it's brilliant, right?" Huey smiled, and that was the worst thing he'd done so far. It wasn't evil. It had no harm in it. It was just too much, like flipping on the light in the bathroom after feeling your way to the switch in the dark.

Edsel backed out of the room and shut the door behind him.

Marlys, headed Edsel's way, stopped when she saw him in the hall. "Hey. Everything all right?" When he didn't answer, she took a few cautious steps toward him. "Edsel?"

Edsel didn't know where to start, so he pushed the gameroom door open without looking inside. He locked eyes with Marlys until she understood that he wanted her to go in with him.

Once she joined him, he looked into the room with her. But only once she joined him.

Huey was gone. So was the board and its two remaining animals.

Edsel felt Marlys's eyes on him, but he offered no explanation. The tension left him. And that would have to do for now, no matter what came next.

For Edsel had no doubt something would come next.

And he prayed it would steer clear of Stella Grace and everyone in it.

## 69

## BELIEF AND PATIENCE

"We killed our home." Liam said it out loud to himself. That way, he wouldn't be able to deny his part in what they'd done to the complex by initiating the shutdown.

The Dharma Rangers had put out an announcement to the entire populace to alert them that their whole world would be going black but would be back real soon. Then Liam retreated to his quarters to figure out how, exactly, he was going to deal with himself if what they feared came to pass and if they really did brick everything they'd worked so hard for.

The first time he spoke the words aloud were right after the combination bedroom and living room in which he slept was plunged into complete darkness. He repeated it while waiting in that dark—bereft of a flashlight because he forgot where he put his, ignoring all knocks at his door because he desperately needed to be alone.

That was when the pinging of something tiny knocking on glass began from across the room. Liam promptly ignored that, too.

But when the emergency power kicked in, he got up to investigate the repeated pinging, only to find a tiny pink-and-purple man in the fishbowl containing the mechanical goldfish whose batteries never died. Formed from the gravel lining the bottom of the bowl, the little man tried to say something. But his little voice couldn't form anything intelligible thanks to his being underwater, so he pointed to Liam and then indicated the room beyond the bowl.

Liam stared at the little man in disbelief. The Commons specialized in people, beings, and happenings way weirder than what he was seeing, but having one visit his personal space was just a bit more than his brain was ready to handle.

The mechanical fish didn't seem to mind, though. It navigated the confines of its watery kingdom, as it always did, and the little gravel man ducked whenever it threatened to ram him.

Curiosity got the best of him. Liam pulled the bowl forward on its wooden shelf.

The little man promptly collapsed into a mound of gravel at the bottom of the bowl.

Liam went and sat back down, ignoring another knock at his door and someone calling for him through the heavy steel of it. He needed to see if the complex would continue waking itself up before presenting himself to the people who depended on him.

His curiosity unabated, he returned to the shelf and gently pushed the bowl back up against the wall, where it had been.

Immediately, the little gravel man reformed, but now he put his little gravel hands on little gravel hips and stared at Liam impatiently with the holes that appeared to be his best approximation of eyes. Apparently, the little man needed the bowl to be in contact with the wall in order to exist.

Liam stared as the man pulled a little foot up out of the

gravel and made a show of tapping it to communicate his continuing lack of patience.

Now Liam had a decision to make. He could pull the bowl away from the wall again and continue to wait for the complex to make its comeback, or he could be a leader and see what the tiny gravel man wanted.

Was there ever really a question? He reached into the bowl and scooped up the gravel man, who promptly collapsed into a pile of wet rocks in his palm. But when Liam put the gravel on the shelf and pushed it up against the wall, the gravel promptly formed into a head.

"Could you make me bigger?" the head squeaked.

Liam obliged, scooping up most of the gravel from the bowl and dumping it on the head, giving it a good wet fistful to work with.

The mechanical fish didn't seem to mind having its real estate devalued.

"Thank you," said the head, its voice lower on the range now. Not a bass by any means, but low enough to restore some dignity to whatever this thing was. "You don't know it, but you've already been working with me. Your communications are going to power up again shortly. When they do, I can reestablish your connection with your friends at Envoy HQ."

"Who the hell are you? *What* the hell are you? And how do you know what's going to power back up and when?"

"I'll let your friends explain when you talk to them. Otherwise, you've no reason to take my word for it. Also, that's not the most important part right now. Your nukes are dead."

"I know that. We know that." Liam still couldn't believe he was talking to the little gravel man, never mind taking him seriously. "It's not the worst thing, you know. They were all potential downside with no upside."

"They're not going to stay dead. In time, they're probably going to rearm and once again be viable."

"And?"

"And you'll want to make sure they don't launch themselves when they do that."

Liam thought that over. He decided to believe the little man-head. Moreover, he decided to like him.

"How soon will comms be restored?"

∽

THE VIEW-MASTER HAD nothing to say. It hadn't been especially helpful of late, but Charlene nevertheless sat alone in her office, trying to will it back to life, refusing to believe that it might really be defunct. For if she'd come to any conclusion about herself, her job, The Commons, and the linked realms—given what little she knew of them—it was that the land of the departed and everything in it was somehow alive.

Maybe more alive than anything in The Living World.

But not the View-Master. Not now.

For the umpteenth time, she tried to coax the device into talking to her. It maintained its silence.

So now it was a question of belief and patience—sustaining her belief that the situation could improve and remaining patient enough to wait for an indication that it had. There was no way of knowing about any of that when all sources of communication from the outside had gone dark.

"A watched toy never speaks," said Reinhard from the doorway.

"This is the fourth time you've stopped by." Charlene placed the View-Master on her desk more gently than usual, fearing she might break or offend it. "You're no better at the waiting game than I am."

"I'd hoped I was better at pretending, though." The former Vigil settled into one of the chairs across from Charlene's desk. Of all those who felt comfortable enough to enter and sit without asking, Reinhard made her the happiest. He was an old-school hard-ass, so any familiarity from him made her feel as if she'd made some sort of progress.

"The Dharmas are stone-cold stoics compared to you." Charlene sat back in her chair, relieved at the opportunity to distract herself by needling Reinhard. "They haven't been in here once, and it's their home we're talking about. Hell, even June hasn't been by, and she's the biggest busybody in existence. She'd tell you that herself."

The former Vigil gave her a knowing smirk. "D.W., Nicolette, and I battled it out."

"Battled what out?"

"Who'd be the one to bug you for updates so that you wouldn't be driven nuts by all of us."

"And you won."

Reinhard chuckled.

"June agreed to that?"

"I put her on rock-watching duty. She's in the conference room with orders not to budge unless Stony Curtis manages to get in touch."

Charlene watched the View-Master, trying to will it to obey her. "What's your take on wishful thinking, Reinhard?"

"Why?"

"Because you've never struck me as the most hopeful guy. And I've never been the most hopeful gal. Yet here I am, convincing myself that something important has happened. Can I convince you, too? If not, aren't I just using wishful thinking as a crutch?"

Reinhard considered that. "Something has happened." He picked up the View-Master and turned it over in his hands. "We all feel it at a gut level, though we don't want to trust that feeling—even when we should. It could have been confined to our part of the realms, but I don't think so. I don't think you do, either. That's why you're sitting in here, babysitting a gadget. Because you know it, too, but your biggest fear is that you're wrong."

"What's your biggest fear?"

"That you're wrong."

Charlene watched Reinhard continue to roll the View-Master over and over until he noticed her eyes on him.

"Sorry." He started to put the device back on her desk.

"Not at all. Maybe you can talk it into giving us something."

Reinhard peered into the View-Master's eye pieces. He grunted, which would have been a minor display of emotion for anyone else but was soul-baring for him.

"What?"

The former Vigil offered the View-Master to her, and Charlene took it, grateful that she felt no need to admit she hadn't even thought of looking into it. She'd grown too used to it speaking. Raising it to her own eyes revealed green text on a green background so dark it was nearly black: *Reboot initiated*. "Great. No wonder it hasn't said anything. I wonder how long it's been rebooting."

"Maybe it's not. Maybe that's the message."

"What is?"

"It's not the View-Master rebooting. Something else is."

"Such as?"

"Something bigger. A lot bigger."

Down the hall, June Medilll cried out in surprise. That was followed by a heavy crunch against the wall out in the hall and then the sound of stone rolling down the tiles, getting closer. Footsteps—June's, presumably—followed.

A rock rolled into the doorway, bounced off the frame, and entered. It stopped in front of Charlene's desk, next to Reinhard.

June appeared in the doorway. She started to apologize but thought better of it. "He's back."

Given the rock's arrival, neither Reinhard nor Charlene felt the need to ask who June meant.

The fast approach of other footsteps out in the hall, followed by the rumble of more rocks headed for Charlene's office.

Reinhard had been right.

D.W. and Nicolette weren't very good at the patience game, either.

## 70

## A HOME BETWEEN TWO PRONUNCIATIONS

Only cats used the outdoor stairways in Franklin Hills. So Zach's mother said, and so she believed. That was because she couldn't see the others who passed them when Zach and Zach's mother were out for a walk.

But Zach could.

Zach's mother didn't own a car, so they did a lot of walking, both to get where they were going and for what Zach's mother called just-plain fun. It made Zach's mother proud to live in Los Angeles without relying on a car to get around.

They were able to do that because they lived in Los Feliz, a place Zach saw as an in-between neighborhood because the right way to pronounce it was the wrong way in its native Spanish. But locals would correct you if you tried to say "Feliz" the way it should have been said.

A home between two pronunciations. Zach liked that.

Zach also liked that their apartment building was a place that had gone through transitions. The garage, which they had no need of, had been a barn at one point. The parking lot outside its gate had a tiny Mexican place in the middle of it, and it was so small—about the size of four phone booths put together, Zach's mother said—that everyone who cooked in it had to stand. The customers ate on folding chairs out on the asphalt, and nobody complained because the tortas were so good.

When they first moved in, Zach's mother was hesitant to try the torta booth. She never said she was scared. She was hesitant. Because it "didn't look like much."

Then Zach's mother heard they'd won a James Beard Award. And she tasted the food. Now they ate there all the time. It was another of their in-between places. It looked like one thing but was actually another.

They never visited the train that brought them to LA. It had flown over Venice Beach and Santa Monica, circling out above the Pacific before heading back east, then going to ground to take advantage of existing Metro tracks and the Red Line tunnel before stopping in its current hiding spot somewhere in the abandoned Pacific Electric Railway tunnels.

They'd disembarked and said their goodbyes to the Railwaymen and to Emmett, who told Zach about how they'd gone through the La Brea Tar Pits and would've seen dinosaur skeletons if the lighting had been better.

Zach's mother told him later that Emmett had been pulling his leg.

Zach couldn't understand why Zach's mother and Emmett would try to impress Zach with dead dinosaurs when he'd been swallowed by a real one. But it was a neat trick that Emmett was able to pull his leg without him ever once feeling it.

Anyway.

Because the tunnels were either Living World ones that weren't used anymore or imagined ones that had never been excavated and built to begin with, there was no telling if Zach's mother and Zach would've been able to visit even if they'd been allowed to. When Rain came to see them—though she'd only done that a few times—she mentioned leaving with the Railwaymen for a while, so Zach assumed the train was no longer there.

That was the way of the Railwaymen. They couldn't stay put—and didn't.

Which was something that might have been said of Zach and Zach's mother, too, but they couldn't compete with Emmett and the others. They couldn't even compete with Rain, who seemed to be on her motorcycle more than she was on her feet whenever Zach and Zach's mother saw her.

They didn't know where Rain was or when she'd come see them again.

In the hot weather, Zach would float in the pool, which was in the middle of their apartment building's rectangle-missing-a-side. He'd float on the pool noodles the way Zach's mother showed him, watching planes headed for LAX cross the parallel rows of big palms on either side, hearing the wild parrots rumble with one another and listening for the high-pitched hum of Rain's cycle.

Rain wasn't coming, but Zach listened for her all the same. And Joel the Tamagotchi was gone, back where he should be.

Zach and Zach's mother were where they needed to be, too. That's what they were told. For the time being.

The planes crossed, and the parrots quarreled. The many cats who called the apartment building home battled one another. They hunted squirrels that were way too savvy to be caught. They tried to avoid being themselves preyed on by the coyotes that snuck into the courtyard at night, and they periodically got sprayed by the skunks that helped themselves to the food put out for the cats.

It was all a big drama. And only Zach saw it because Zach's mother was too worried about what came next.

Zach didn't worry about what came next, even though he couldn't divine whether any of them would make it through it. It was going to happen how it happened no matter who fretted over it. Why worry when it was enough to be afraid?

And oh, how Zach was afraid.

Given the little he did know about what was on its way, why wouldn't he be?

"Time to choose, my friend," Zach's mother said from her chaise lounge, watching the two neighbor guys argue over whatever they had in the dented, rusty smoker that always turned out perfect meats of all sorts no matter what they looked like when they went in. Her instincts told her they should keep to themselves for the safety of everyone, even though they both liked it when the neighbor guys invited them over for pulled pork, brisket, ham, chicken, or other things she called "the deliciouses."

Zach knew what she was going to say next. Either he had to let her put more sunscreen on him, or he had to get out of the pool and sit under the umbrella to avoid being cooked. The wrinkled pads of his fingers told him to choose the latter.

Life was more normal than ever for Zach and Zach's mother, though that was just an illusion. I'm-Bobby and those he worked with might come for them at any time despite the precautions taken to hide them. Rain might show up in a hurry, telling them they had a few minutes to pack—or maybe that they had no time to pack at all. Zach hoped he'd be dry and dressed if it came to that.

In the meantime, it was calm, and he could float.

In LA, you told yourself and others that you were whoever you wanted to be, and nobody questioned that because they were doing it, too.

Zach and Zach's mother wouldn't talk about how they'd helped reset the universe and all its realms by betraying those who meant them well. She'd managed to tell the beings she'd initially met as Humboldt how to avoid destruction. But there was no question that she and Zach had sided with Porter and deceived Audra's side in order to carry out the gray man's plan. Zach's mother hadn't understood what that would ultimately lead to, though she did now. Sometimes there was no choice but to do such a thing—both to those who deserved it and those who didn't—even when you weren't as clued in as you wanted to be. But it wasn't a good idea to dwell on it.

Zach would float and float. He'd watch the squirrels tease the cats and listen to the parrots lecture one another, and he'd try to find a way to come to terms with what they'd all done this time.

But he wouldn't get there. Because more was on its way.

Friends were still friends, except for those who weren't. Allies questioned whether they'd known them at all. So did enemies. It didn't have to make sense. Nothing had to.

Zach pulled himself up out of the pool and stood on the concrete apron, dripping. He never used the steps. And he let Zach's mother help towel him off because it made her feel better to fuss over him while they waited.

For wait they would, there in Los Feliz.

Things were nice, and slow, and quiet. They would remain so. Until it was time for them to move fast again.

And that time was coming.

## 71

## WHAT WE HAVE ENJOYED

When Audra arrived, the Shrine was still hot, and Porter and Po were out cold. Asleep, unconscious—the distinction mattered little. She should have gone to them there on the ground to see if either might need help, but she was in no mood to provide comfort. Not to those who'd done what they'd done.

So Audra sat on the bench. She tried to take some relief from the sunbeam's warmth, and she did her best to ignore the presence of the thing nearby.

After a time, a bout of coughing announced to Audra and the dark presence hiding in the shadows that Porter had survived. She wasn't sure how to feel about that. And she couldn't help but wonder what the thing in the shadows thought of it—if it thought anything at all.

Audra couldn't bring herself to look at Porter. At least the man knew enough to sit on the other end of the bench after he picked himself up, putting as much distance as possible between them. He shrank from the sunbeam holding her in its embrace, the heat a reminder of what he'd just endured. Good.

"The Dinuhos brought you?" Porter said.

"It was waiting for me. I think it feels guilty about its role in helping you. I hope it does. I'm not sure it has feelings." Audra scratched at a fleck of something on her sleeve. "And I might say the same of you, old friend."

Porter had no answer for the way Audra loaded the last word. He looked across the pool and into the shadows. Was he able to communicate with the darkness waiting there? If so, that was another worrisome thing.

"It occurs to me, Jonas, that I'm able to sit and enjoy the warmth of this sunbeam, which I invited in here. Ever since I was attacked and nearly killed by your new ally, I haven't been able to get near any source of heat. That I can do so now is something I'd like to celebrate. But I can't entertain the thought of happiness for myself in the wake of what you've done."

"I knew you might be able to find a way to come here—"

"To this place I helped create? To this place you've desecrated with your faithlessness?" Audra stopped there. She didn't want to give Porter an excuse to abandon his attempt to explain himself.

"To this place that had to be brought into play for us to have any hope," Porter said. "To this place I prayed you wouldn't try to enter because I knew you might be able to stop us."

"Us." Audra spat the word out like an obscenity. "Jonas, when you say that, do you understand that you've aligned yourself with both the most recent scourge we've faced *and* the latest one to arrive?"

Porter slowly rotated the heel of his staff against the Shrine floor. "The threat outweighed the risk."

"I couldn't come here to try to stop you. Do you know why?

Because the force you chose to work with nearly killed me, and I wasn't able to get anywhere near it."

Porter's chin dropped almost to his chest. In another time, that might have told Audra she'd said enough. Now she couldn't imagine it.

"You knew." It came out like a hiss. Not that she cared. "You knew we thought that the orders and communications we were receiving were from the collective consciousness of The Commons when they were actually coming from the dragon."

Porter might have winced.

"You didn't know what he was? How did he appear to you, Jonas? As a friendly advisor? Something formidable but tame? I never had that luxury. I wasn't presented with anything at all before he lit me up."

Porter started to speak but gave up. He'd probably been about to plead the dragon's case and argue that it hadn't injured her on purpose. And that was probably true. But it was beside the point. Even Porter understood that.

They sat on the same bench in the same silence—together but apart, each waiting for the other to give.

It wasn't a contest Audra cared about winning. "You worked with a creature of The Pines. The Pines, Jonas. And a representation of Brill—a force so dark in his own right that we weren't able to move him, never mind unseat him, for a long time."

"We had no choice."

"What?"

"That was the only way it could work. It had to be enough Essence. From the right sources. To shock the barriers into resetting. The combined Essence and presence of the last of Brill combined with a denizen of The Pines aimed squarely at The Pines barrier so that The Margins and the overall collapse could be recognized and reversed. We alerted the immune system."

Audra turned to look at the man she'd thought to be a friend. Did he really believe what he was saying? "You had to destroy the universe in order to save it. Listen to yourself." Audra stood and began walking in a small circle. "We had a plan. You agreed to it."

Porter shook his head, but his chin remained low. And he still couldn't look her in the eye. "I did. But I knew it wouldn't work."

"You knew, or the dragon told you?"

"Does it matter?"

Audra had a strong urge to launch herself at Porter and bounce his skull off the Shrine floor until he saw that it did indeed matter. Of course it mattered.

Po stopped her.

Before Audra had even thought to check on him, the monk had awoken and recovered as silently as he did everything. And just as soundlessly, he'd made his way over to the shadowy part of the Shrine to face the darkness waiting within.

"The threat outweighed everything," Porter said almost entirely to himself.

Audra didn't reply. Now that it was done, Jonas could settle all of that on his own.

She wanted to call Po back for his own safety, afraid he might not understand what he was dealing with. Then again, he'd just helped Porter and that same darkness carry out the monumental betrayal the old Envoy had planned. She wasn't happy with Po, either. But since she hadn't shared her scheme with him the way she had with Porter, she couldn't blame him as much.

Watching him, it slowly came to her.

Po understood perfectly what he was facing there in the shadows.

And until this very moment, Audra hadn't.

## 72

## WHAT WE HAVE SURVIVED

"The process needed all of you."

Paul came to in stages, each a separate segment of information making itself clear to him. He was looking out at the lake, which was a beautiful blue.

Sediment. That's what made it look like that. Wind had pulled sediment up to the water's surface, though it wasn't windy now.

Sitting on the bench, he had something small and pointy, like a stone, trapped under his leg. It hurt.

"That's why they sent the lamprey after you," the voice continued—a familiar voice. "And why the mythicals and Ravagers mounted diversionary attacks. Because they wanted to do whatever they could to break up the team and pick off at least one, just in case. They weren't sure if they'd be able to. But they didn't really think they'd need to, either. You surprised them. And congratulations are in order, but only if you understand what happened."

"Huey?" This was a dream. Paul had been at the Shrine with Porter and the others. They'd all combined their strength to do—what? He couldn't recall what it was or whether they'd done it.

Maybe that had been the dream, not this.

Huey Dusek sat at the other end of the bench. It was the same bench where Paul had tried to end his life in order to get back to The Commons and fix whatever he'd done wrong, even though he hadn't known what it was.

The thing under Paul's leg. He pulled it out and held it up. The squid figurine from the Noah's Ark set. At Stella Grace, hundreds of years before. Yes, this was Huey.

Huey didn't acknowledge that it was him. "Seeing you is a nice surprise, Paul," he said. "When I told you goodbye, I meant it. Then again, what you all did has thrown a monkey wrench into everyone's expectations. Except Porter's. I'll give him that. When he breaks the rules, he makes it count."

The squid felt like it was trying to wriggle out of Paul's grasp, but that wasn't possible. It was just a figurine made out of—well, he didn't know what it was made out of.

"Throw it," said Huey.

"What?"

"The Humboldt. Throw it into the water. It needs to go find the others."

"The other squid?"

The question surprised Huey. "Sure. If that works for you. Or the peacock. Same thing."

"Really?"

Huey considered that. "No."

Paul didn't want to do anything Huey might later regret asking him to do. "Won't it ruin your set?"

Huey smiled in genuine amusement. "That was never mine." He shook his head at Paul's ignorance and clucked softly to himself. "Throw it."

Paul obliged before his doubt could get in the way. He was

struck by a strong sense of déjà vu, but it was someone else throwing something out over a body of water and changing everything, not him. He didn't know if that was what he did now or not.

The squid never hit the water. It was just not there anymore.

"Thank you," said Huey.

There were more questions than Paul could ask in what he suspected was a limited amount of time, so he started with whatever came out of his mouth. "Who are you, Huey?"

Once again, Huey was mildly amused. "Who are you?"

"That would take a while. Mostly because I'm not sure I have an answer."

"Why do you assume I do?"

Paul definitely had no answer for that. He'd just figured everyone knew more about themselves than he did.

"Sometimes the world needs a face," said Huey.

"Which world?"

Another amused smile, this time with a nod, as if Paul had surprised him.

Paul looked out over the lake. The water was no longer blue. It was brown. He worried that he'd harmed it by throwing the Humboldt in. He'd been told to, but a lot of hurt came from the things he'd been told to do. "What did you mean by all of us being needed, Huey?"

"All of you who punched the holes to begin with. The major players and, in small ways, the minor ones. The Dharmas. The nukes. The muridines."

"Muridines?"

"The beetle-rats. That's their true name. They may not like it, but it is."

Everything Huey said led to more questions. "Was Porter right, then? Did we reset the—?" It sounded too stupid to say out loud. A small group of people could really reboot the universe?

Huey was still having a good time with Paul's confusion. "No. You can't move a whale with a thumbtack. And we're talking about infinite whales."

"What, then?"

"You send up a flare, set off an alarm—and let it know it needs to move."

"To get its attention."

"Sort of. I mean, you already had that when you defeated Brill. And that assumes you're talking about an external entity when we're all part of it."

"Porter made it sound like we were threatening existence itself by going after the barrier protecting everything from The Pines."

"It had to look like you were." Huey sat up on the bench, and his eyes took on an intensity that hadn't been there before. "You had to make it believable."

"And did we?"

"Hell, yes. Scared the bejesus out of me."

"Sorry."

Huey shrugged. "It was time for a wake-up call." He settled back again, and all amusement left him. "But here we are. Now it's a crapshoot. And it'll be war, one way or the other."

That didn't make Paul feel any better. "Is that because of us? Because of me?"

Huey thought about it. "No," he said quietly. "We were always going to have that. We always do." The hint of another smile, but it was a sad one. "We always will."

Paul and Huey looked out over the lake for a while. The water darkened further still.

# EPILOGUE: TO LIVE SUCH A THING

"You knew about this, too?" The woman, Audra, remained angry at the man, Porter.

The two of them were separate entities with their own names and experiences.

What was it to live such a thing?

"No." Sitting on the bench, Porter was but a short distance away from Audra. It may as well have been miles. "We had an inkling. Nothing more. Until it was time."

"Until it was time." Audra's words dripped with disdain.

The Darkness heard the words of the two and let them in because it understood that they were important. And yet again, it didn't know why.

What the Darkness did know was that it hungered. It always hungered. But what it had just been through with the others, with the staff, left a void like no other in its experience.

Sustenance was within reach. Within reach by the prey's own volition, the prey having stepped to the edge of the shadows that protected the weakened Darkness from the sunbeam.

The sunbeam appeared to feed the woman, Audra.

What was it to live such a thing?

So much the Darkness could not imagine—though it used to know, used to remember. A single mind. Honor that stood on its own and knew no hunger, no absence.

A friend. A brother.

Love for a friend and brother.

"It's traveled as much as the rest of us have," said Audra. "Do I have that right?"

"More," said Porter. "It's been watching. All along."

"But not just watching."

"No."

Audra gazed into the Darkness, and the Darkness gazed into her. "Those powdered Ravagers we found."

Porter nodded. "I suspect so. And an uncounted number of beetle-rats. Muridines. That's what they're properly called. Did you know? I hadn't wanted to. I'd hoped to put those miserable creatures behind me—but that wasn't to be, either." The man called Porter gazed into the Darkness, too, where it stood both protected and laid bare by the shadows it attempted to hide within.

There was no hiding. Not for long. Not anymore.

The prey. The prey stood within reach, eyes averted, as if gazing into the shadows with the others might end him. His was a lost presence among lost presences, unable or unwilling to face the Darkness.

"Does it know what it is?"

Porter considered the Darkness before answering. "Hard to say. On some level or levels? Maybe. Or not. But I suspect he will now."

"Two Nistarim we know of, Jonas. And more we don't, most likely. A sacred power made unclean to serve your needs."

Porter didn't reply. He had the look of a man who didn't question a decision once he'd made it. The Darkness understood, though it didn't know the why of that, either.

"A thing such as that should not be," said Audra.

"Nothing that's happened since the barriers were breached should be. And here we sit."

"It'll come at a price."

"Doesn't everything? Ask our friend here."

The Darkness understood that Porter meant him.

Friend. The Darkness considered that word, there in the shadows.

The prey lifted its attention from its robe, a saffron that hurt the Darkness to look at yet also comforted it. The prey's gaze was one of sorrow.

Of caring. Of anger. Both at once.

The Darkness felt itself drawn to the caring. To the love.

Friend.

To the love of a friend.

"It's Brill's monster," said Audra.

"Yes," said Porter.

"It's Brill."

"Yes."

Audra's gaze narrowed. "That shouldn't be."

"And yet it is." Now Porter focused, too. "And not only Brill. Not nearly."

The prey was not prey. The prey was a friend. But only if the Darkness focused on one of its unknown names. Which it was able to do. More so, perhaps, because it had exhausted itself helping the others.

He. He had exhausted himself.

Friend. The friend stepped into the shadows, unafraid of the Darkness. Or maybe he was afraid but risked himself anyway.

The Darkness hungered but did not feed.

"Po?" Audra's tone was one of love, too. A different love—but love.

The friend. Po.

The Darkness had known that. And hadn't.

But he knew it now—and always would.

Po stepped into the shadows, seeking the Darkness, and reached out to place his hand on the Darkness's head. Then he leaned forward and placed his own head against the back of his hand.

Prey. Hunger. Feed.

The Darkness wanted to warn his friend Po of the danger but saw that he needn't. Because Po would not have heeded him. And there was no danger.

"Joel," said Porter. "This is the first time you've met them?"

"I'm just meeting one," said a voice from Po's throat. It, too, was not prey. It was something else. "I'm only recognizing the one I want."

"As Audra said, they were never supposed to be more than one, but they are," said Porter. "So if you choose to see only one, who'll say you can't?"

The entity called Joel didn't answer. He didn't need Porter's affirmation because he, too, had decided for himself that his understanding was as correct as anyone else's.

The Darkness knew then that Joel's understanding was Po's. It came from him. And Po understood like no one else.

Po's hand pressed harder against the Darkness's head.

The Darkness, in turn, held hunger in check when he had never felt the need to do such a thing. Not for the Ravagers. Not for the muridines. Not for anyone or anything.

But he did for Po. Because Po showed him that he was a he and not an it.

"Hello, friend." Joel's tone was softer than it had been only moments before.

The Darkness knew that what Joel said next would change everything.

"Hello, Ken."

**ALSO BY MICHAEL ALAN PECK**

The Journeyman (The Commons, Book 1)
The Margins (The Commons, Book 2)

# ACKNOWLEDGMENTS

I wrote this book alone, but I polished it and put it out into the world with a team of indispensable helpers: Dan Fernandez (cover and graphic design); Irit Printz (feedback); Marti McKenna (editing); and Megan Christy (proofreading).

Buckets o' gratitude to all of you good people.

Thank you.

Copyright © 2021 Michael Alan Peck

All rights reserved. No part of this book may be reproduced in any form or by any electronic or mechanical means, including information storage and retrieval systems, without written permission from the author, except for the use of brief quotations in a book review.

Dinuhos Arts, LLC
5315 N. Clark St., #230
Chicago, IL 60640

ISBN: 986082384
ISBN-13: 978-0-9860823-6-8

This is a work of fiction. Names, characters, businesses, places, events, and incidents are either the products of the author's imagination or used in a fictitious manner. Any resemblance to actual persons, living or dead, or actual events is purely coincidental.

Printed in Great Britain
by Amazon